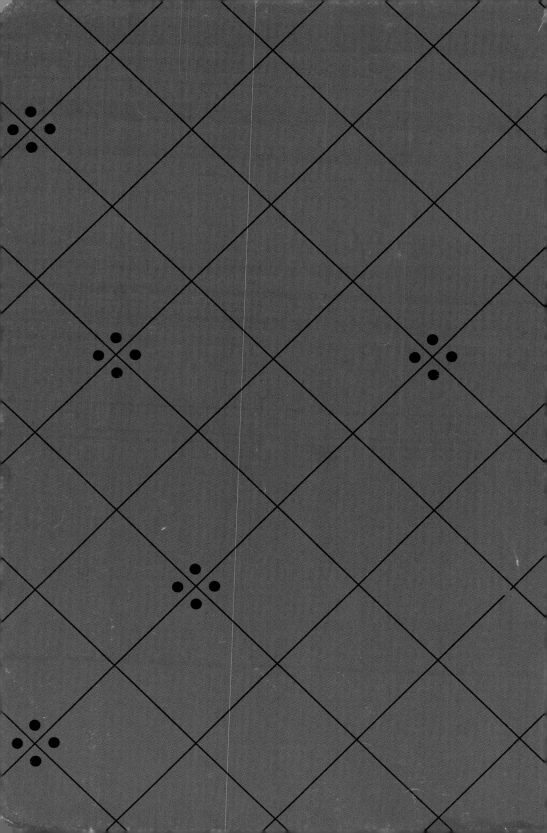

DRAGON KINGDOM
of Wrenly
SHADOW HILLS

By Jordan Quinn

Illustrated by Ornella Greco at Glass House Graphics

LITTLE SIMON

New York   London   Toronto   Sydney   New Delhi

LITTLE SIMON
An imprint of Simon & Schuster Children's Publishing Division
1230 Avenue of the Americas, New York, New York 10020
First Little Simon edition February 2021
Copyright © 2021 by Simon & Schuster, Inc.
All rights reserved, including the right of reproduction in whole or in part in any form.
LITTLE SIMON is a registered trademark of Simon & Schuster, Inc., and associated colophon is a trademark of Simon & Schuster, Inc. For information about special discounts for bulk purchases, please contact Simon & Schuster Special Sales at 1-866-506-1949 or business@simonandschuster.com. The Simon & Schuster Speakers Bureau can bring authors to your live event. For more information or to book an event, contact the Simon & Schuster Speakers Bureau at 1-866-248-3049 or visit our website at www.simonspeakers.com.
Designed by Kayla Wasil
Text by Matthew J. Gilbert
GLASS HOUSE GRAPHICS Creative Services
Art and cover by ORNELLA GRECO
Colors by ORNELLA GRECO and GABRIELE CRACOLICI
Lettering by GIOVANNI SPATARO/Grafimated Cartoon
Supervision by SALVATORE DI MARCO/Grafimated Cartoon
Manufactured in China 1120 SCP
2 4 6 8 10 9 7 5 3 1
Library of Congress Cataloging-in-Publication Data
Names: Quinn, Jordan, author. | Glass House Graphics, illustrator.
Title: Shadow hills / by Jordan Quinn ; illustrated by Glass House Graphics.
Description: First Little Simon edition. | New York : Little Simon, 2021. | Series: Dragon kingdom of Wrenly; book 2 |
Summary: Ruskin the dragon and his friend Cinder are sent to Shadow Hills, the most mysterious place in all of Wrenly, under false pretenses by sinister forces.
Identifiers: LCCN 2020024870 (print) | LCCN 2020024871 (eBook) | ISBN 9781534475038 (paperback) | ISBN 9781534475045 (hardcover) | ISBN 9781534475052 (eBook)
Subjects: LCSH: Graphic novels. | CYAC: Graphic novels. | Dragons–Fiction. | Fantasy.
Classification: LCC PZ7.7.Q55 Sh 2021 (print) | LCC PZ7.7.Q55 (eBook) | DDC 741.5/973–dc23
LC record available at https://lccn.loc.gov/2020024870

Contents

Chapter 1
We Now Return to Flatfrost 6

Chapter 2
After the Sun Rose 22

Chapter 3
No Quest Would Be Complete 39

Chapter 4
Later 53

Chapter 5
Who Are These Statues Of? 67

Chapter 6
See You on the Other Side 81

Chapter 7
Meanwhile 95

Chapter 8
I Tracked You 105

Chapter 9
Word Had Spread 118

Chapter 10
One Enchantress Alone 128

Chapter 1

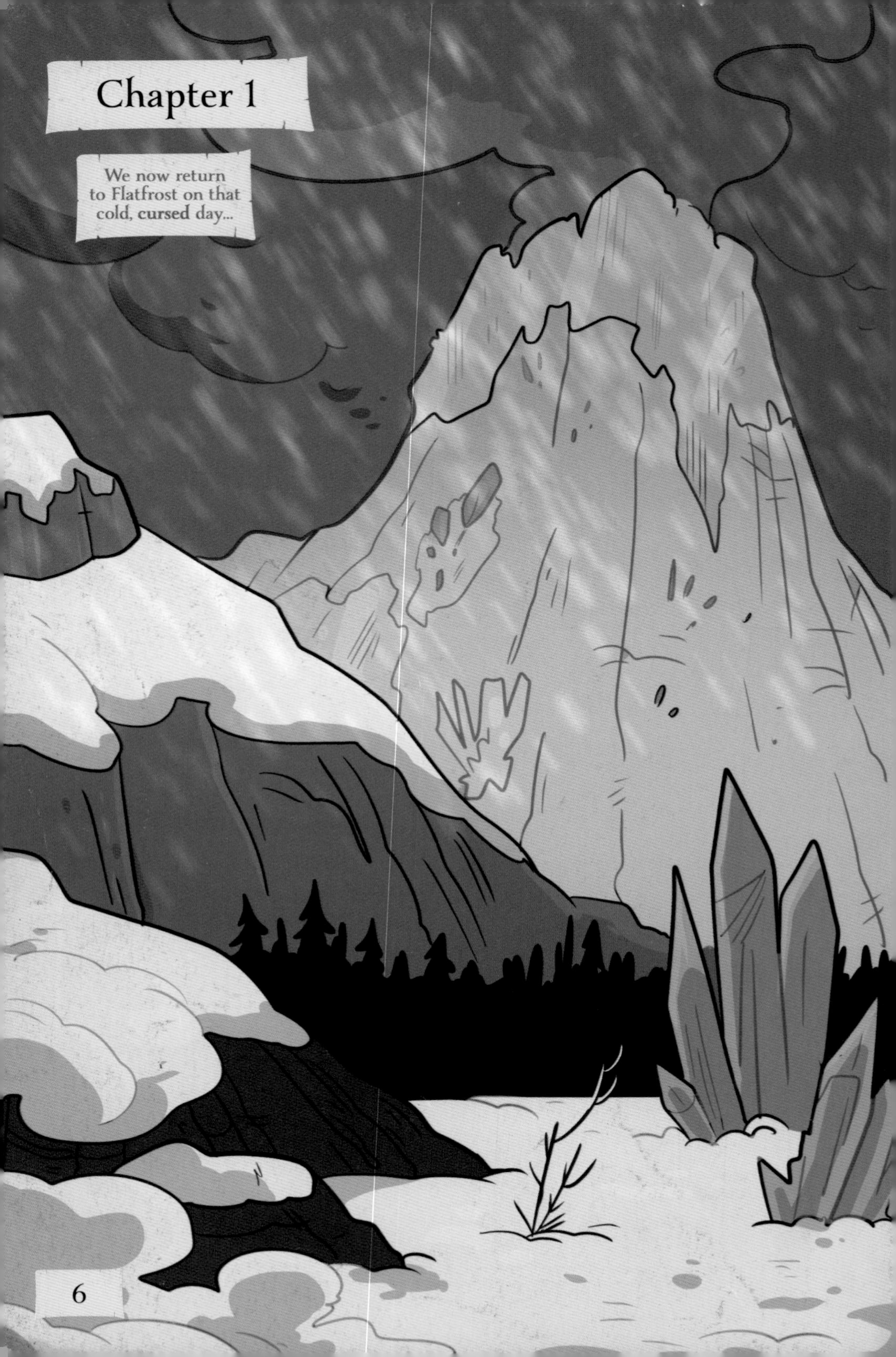
We now return
to Flatfrost on that
cold, cursed day...

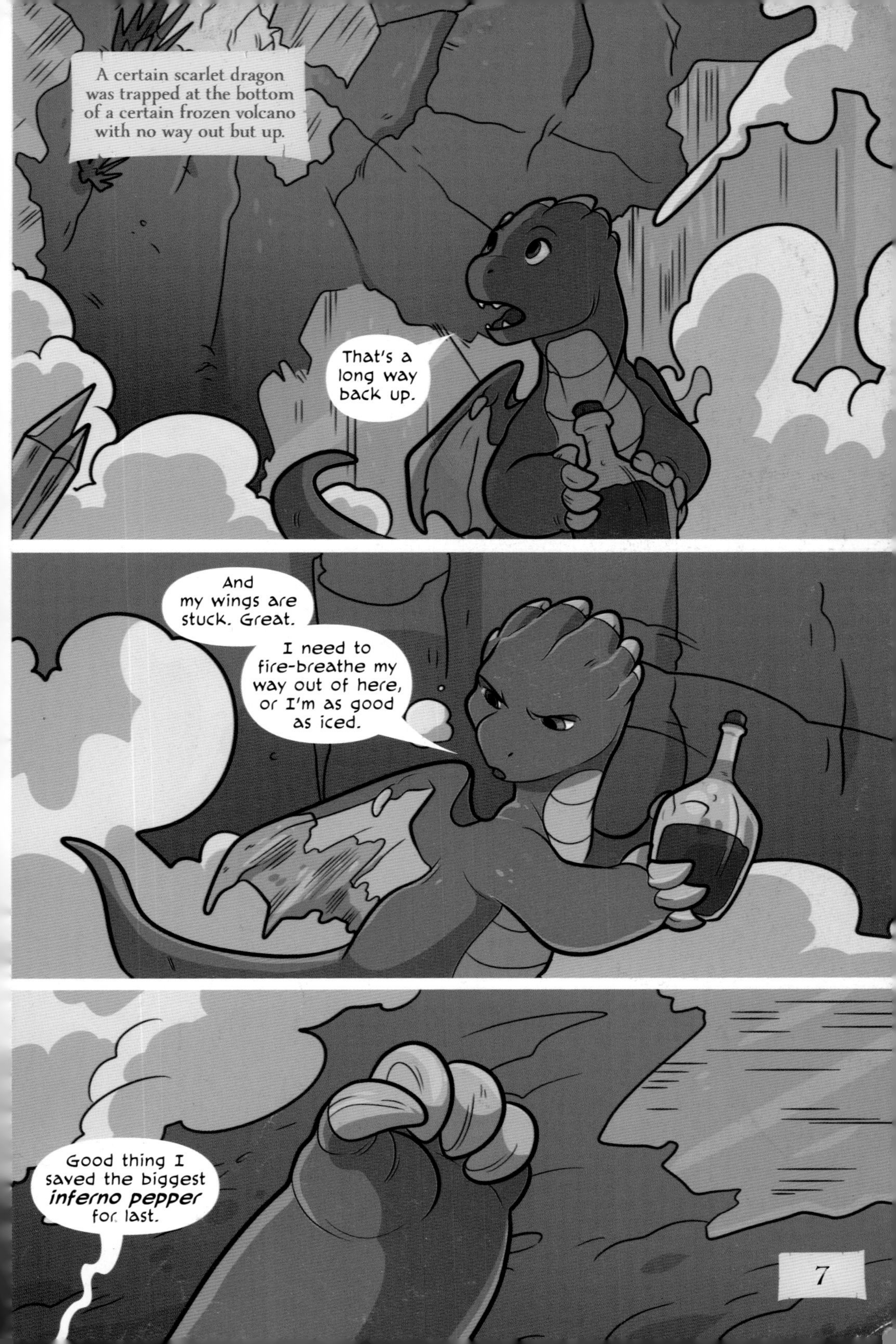
A certain scarlet dragon was trapped at the bottom of a certain frozen volcano with no way out but up.
That's a long way back up.
And my wings are stuck. Great.
I need to fire-breathe my way out of here, or I'm as good as iced.
Good thing I saved the biggest *inferno pepper* for last.

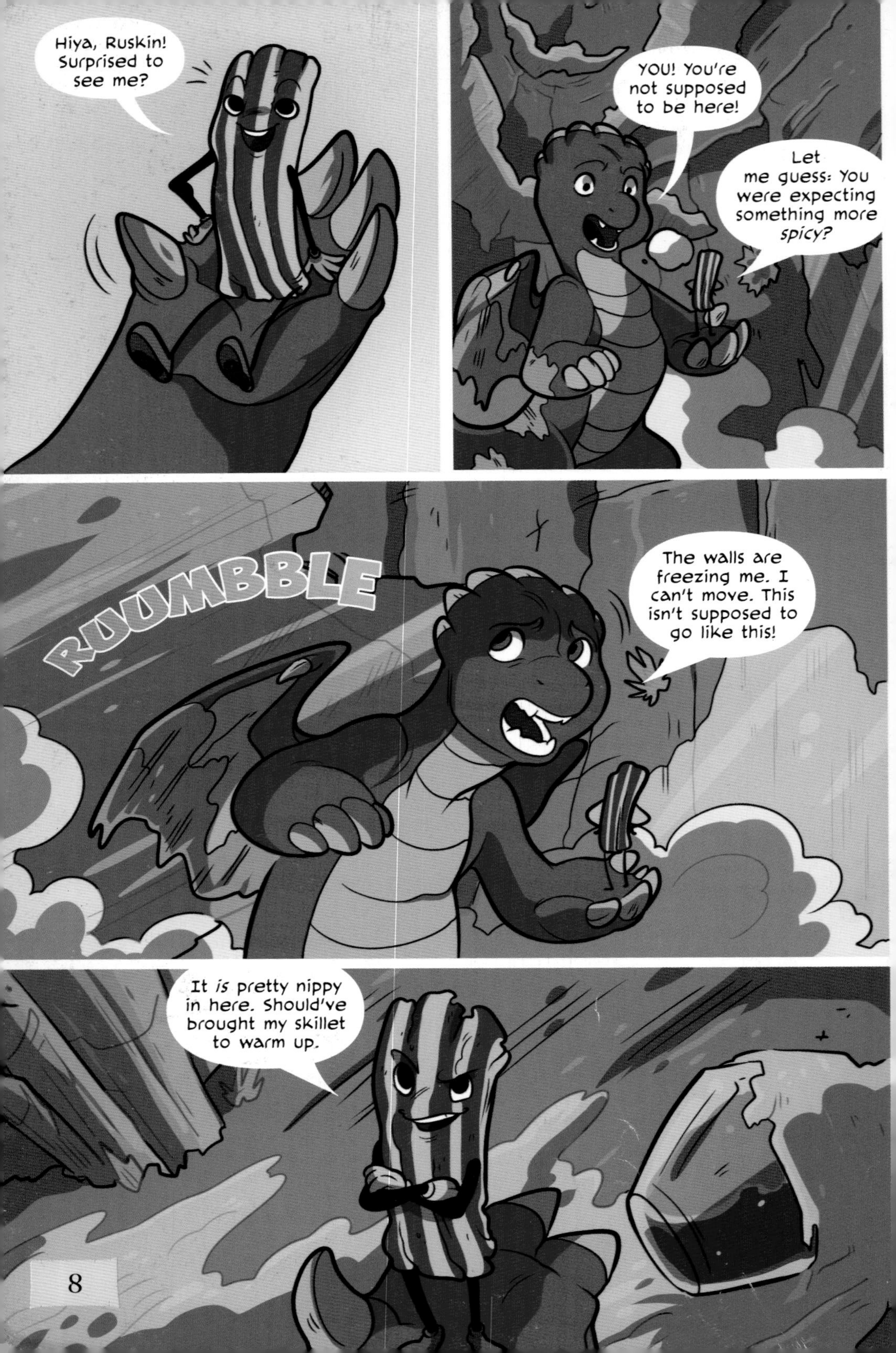
Hiya, Ruskin! Surprised to see me?
YOU! You're not supposed to be here!
Let me guess: You were expecting something more *spicy*?
RUUMBBLE
The walls are freezing me. I can't move. This isn't supposed to go like this!
It *is* pretty nippy in here. Should've brought my skillet to warm up.

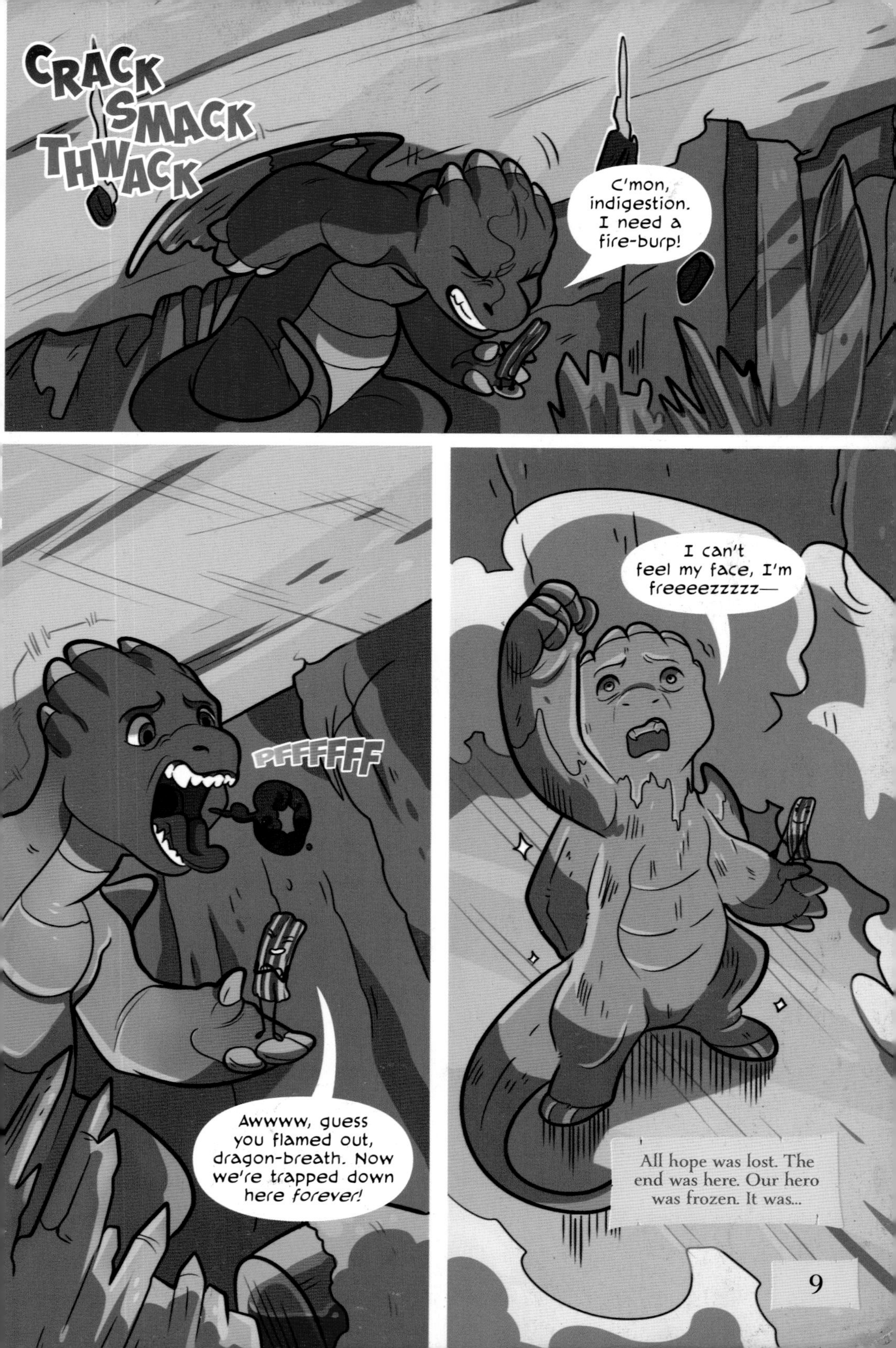
CRACK
SMACK
THWACK
C'mon, indigestion. I need a fire-burp!
PFFFFFF
Awwww, guess you flamed out, dragon-breath. Now we're trapped down here *forever!*
I can't feel my face, I'm freeeezzzzz—
All hope was lost. The end was here. Our hero was frozen. It was...

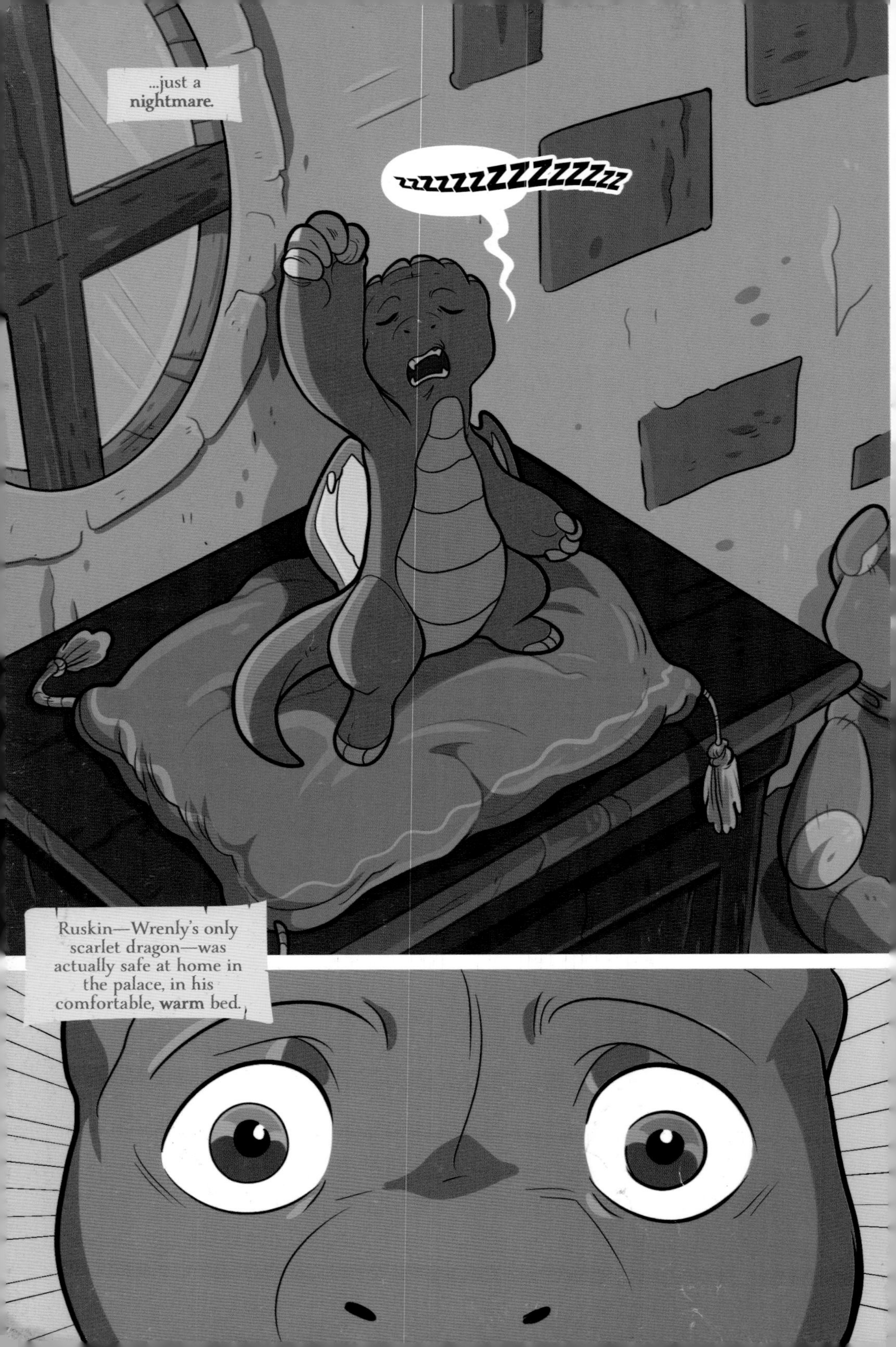
...just a nightmare.
zzzzzzZZZZzzzzz
Ruskin—Wrenly's only scarlet dragon—was actually safe at home in the palace, in his comfortable, warm bed.

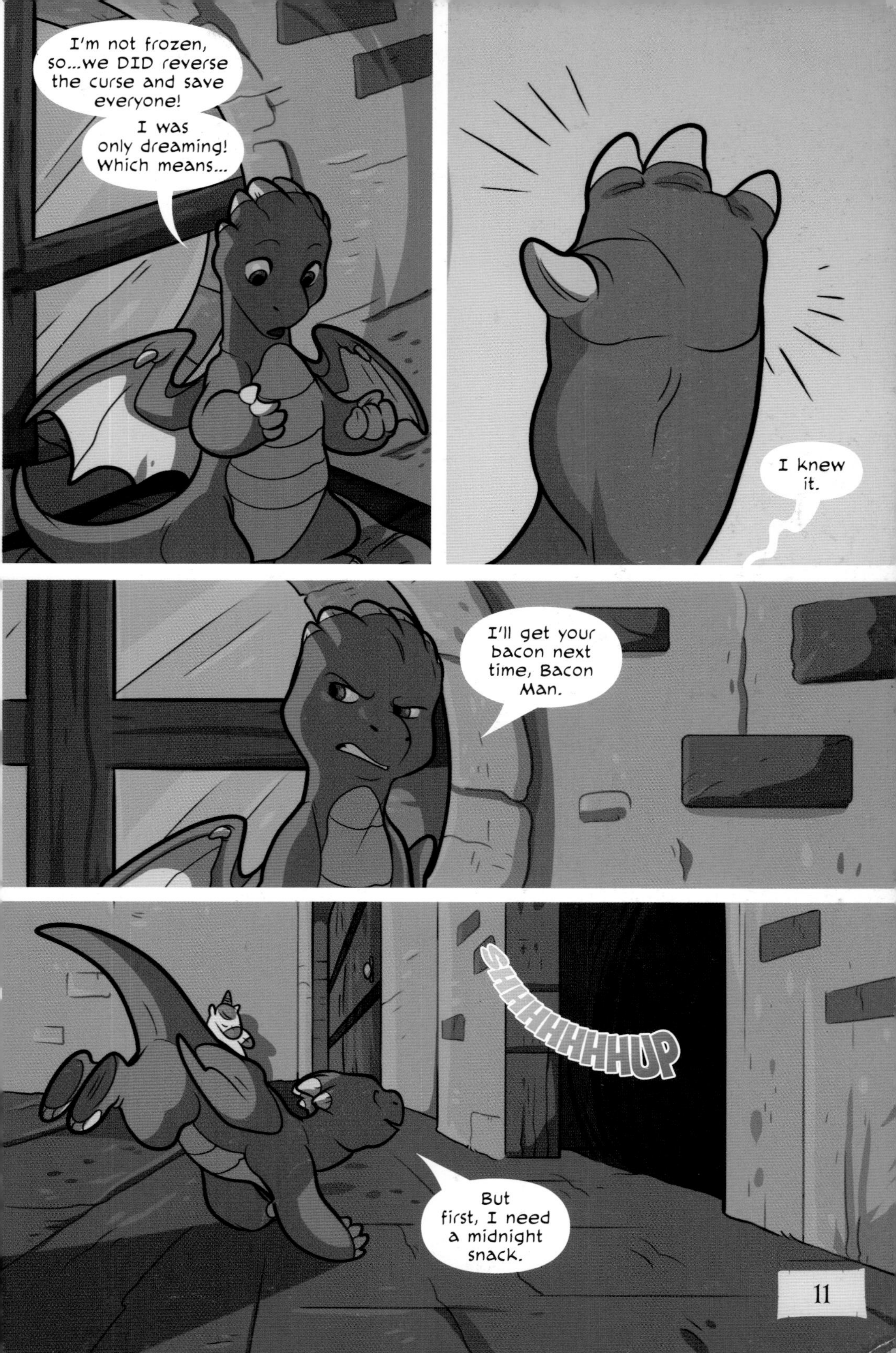
I'm not frozen, so...we DID reverse the curse and save everyone!
I was only dreaming! Which means...
I knew it.
I'll get your bacon next time, Bacon Man.
SHHHHHHUP
But first, I need a midnight snack.

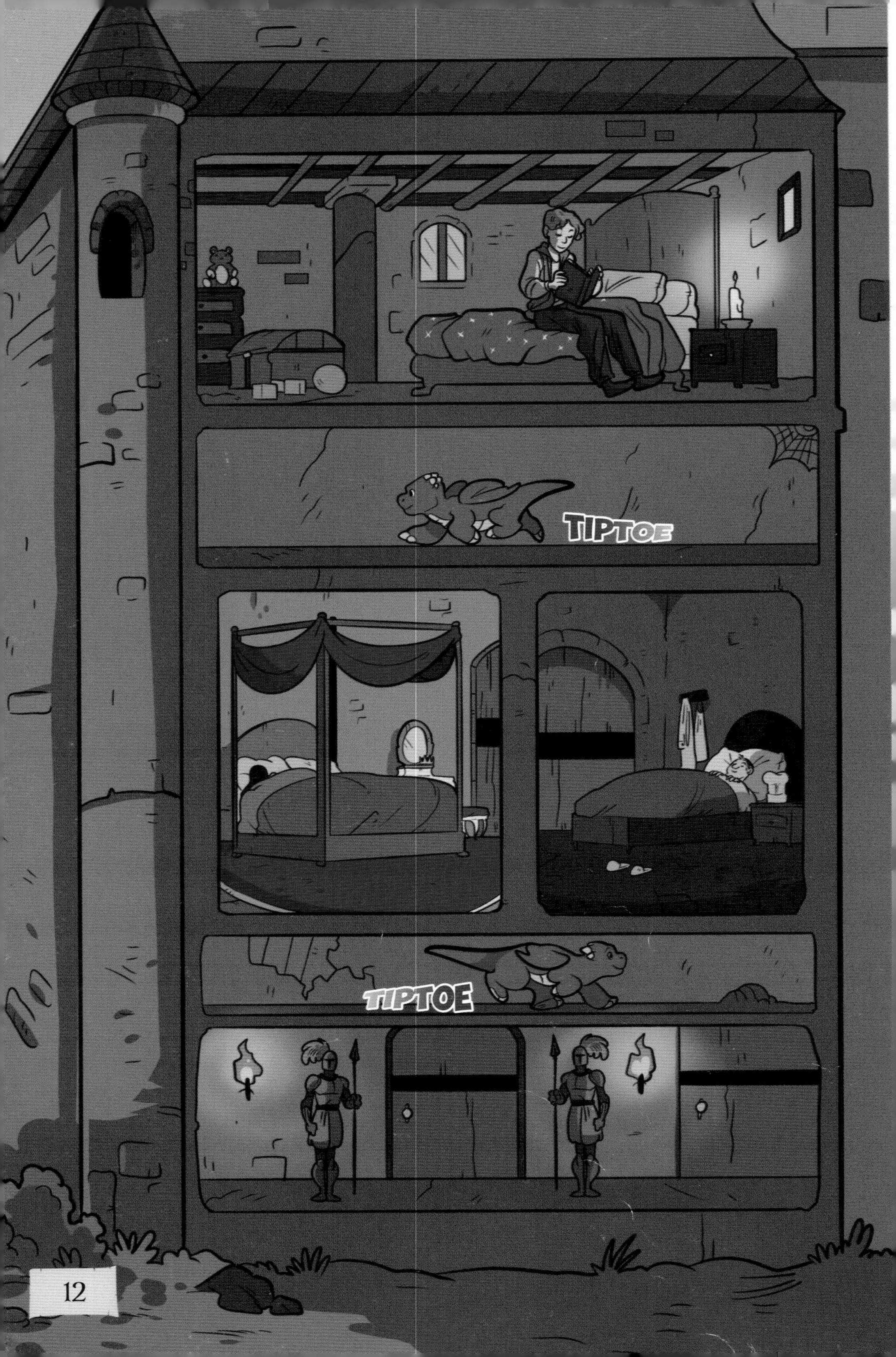
TIPTOE
TIPTOE

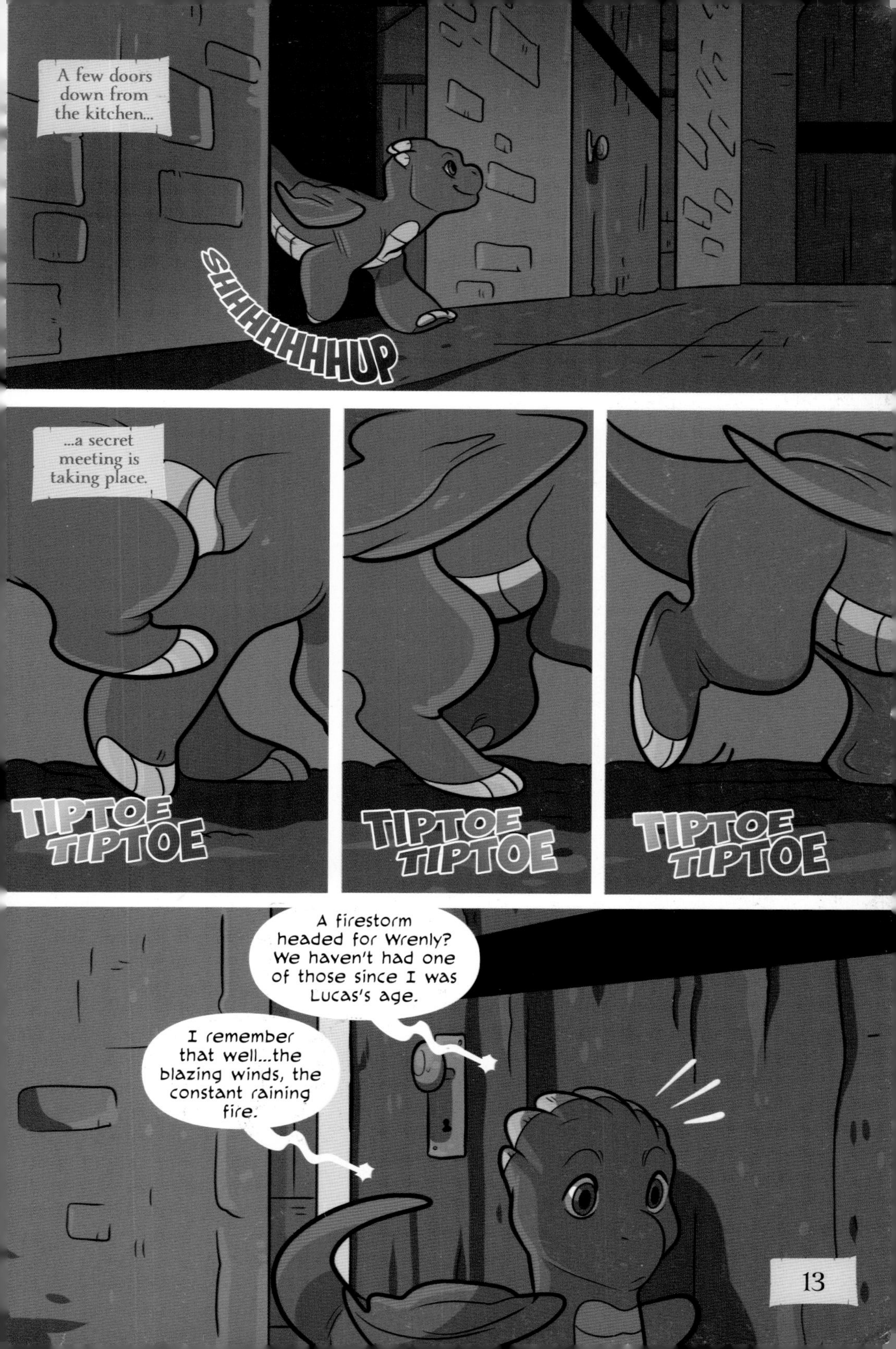
A few doors down from the kitchen...
SHHHHHHHUP
...a secret meeting is taking place.
TIPTOE TIPTOE
TIPTOE TIPTOE
TIPTOE TIPTOE
A firestorm headed for Wrenly? We haven't had one of those since I was Lucas's age.
I remember that well...the blazing winds, the constant raining fire.

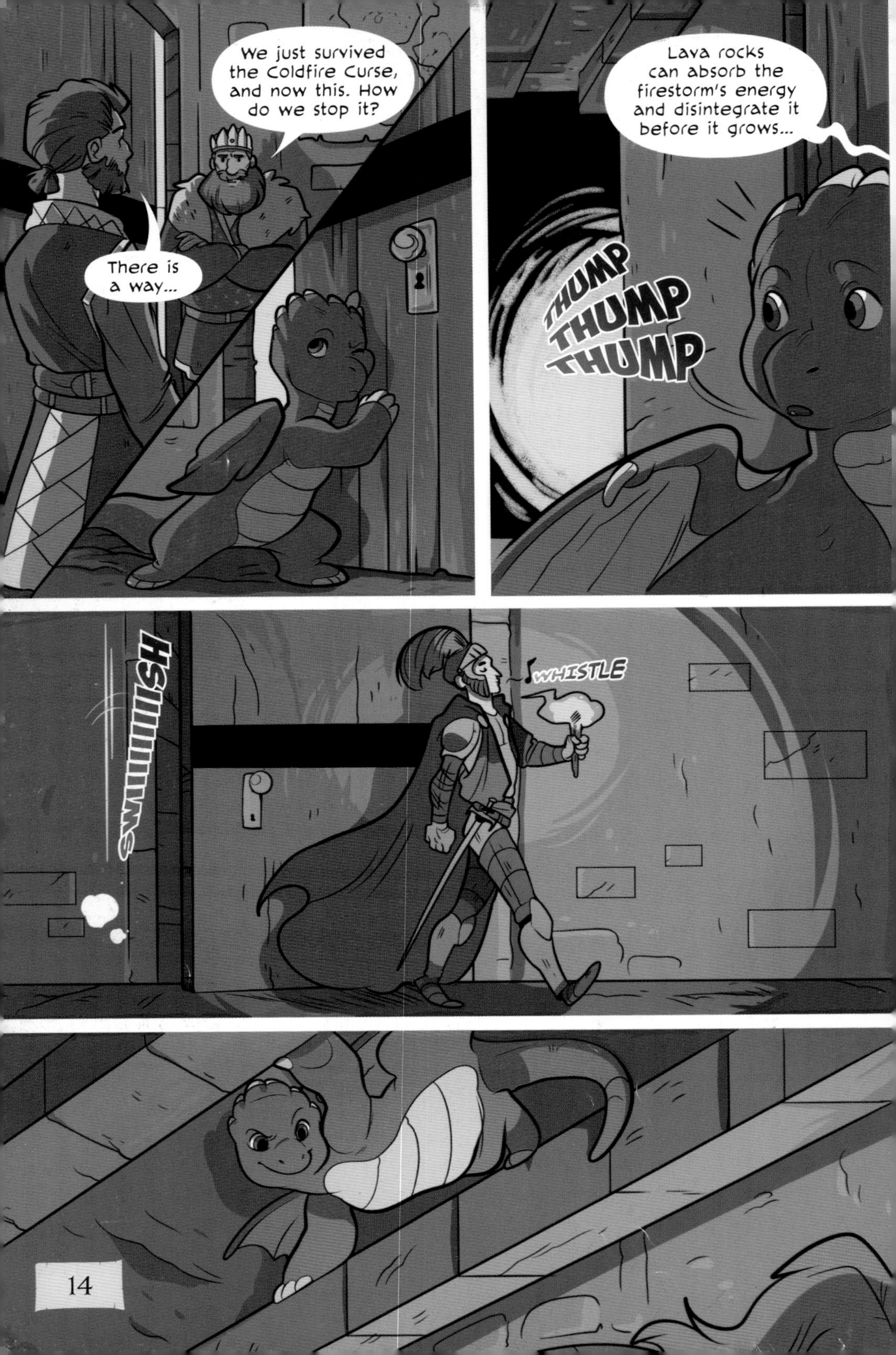

We just survived the Coldfire Curse, and now this. How do we stop it?
There is a way...
Lava rocks can absorb the firestorm's energy and disintegrate it before it grows...
THUMP THUMP THUMP
WHISTLE
SWIIIIIIIIISH

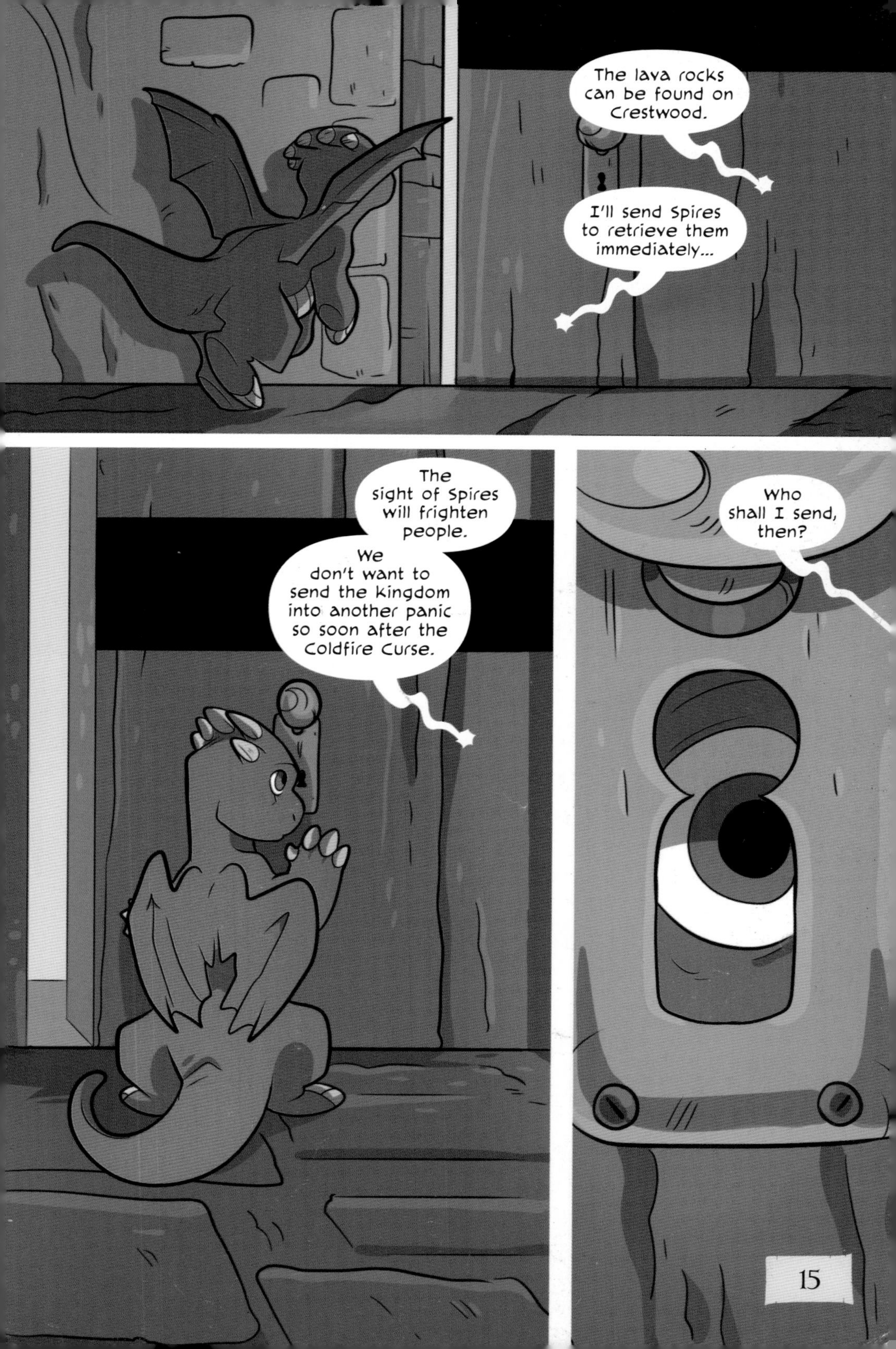
The lava rocks can be found on Crestwood.
I'll send Spires to retrieve them immediately...
The sight of Spires will frighten people.
We don't want to send the kingdom into another panic so soon after the Coldfire Curse.
Who shall I send, then?

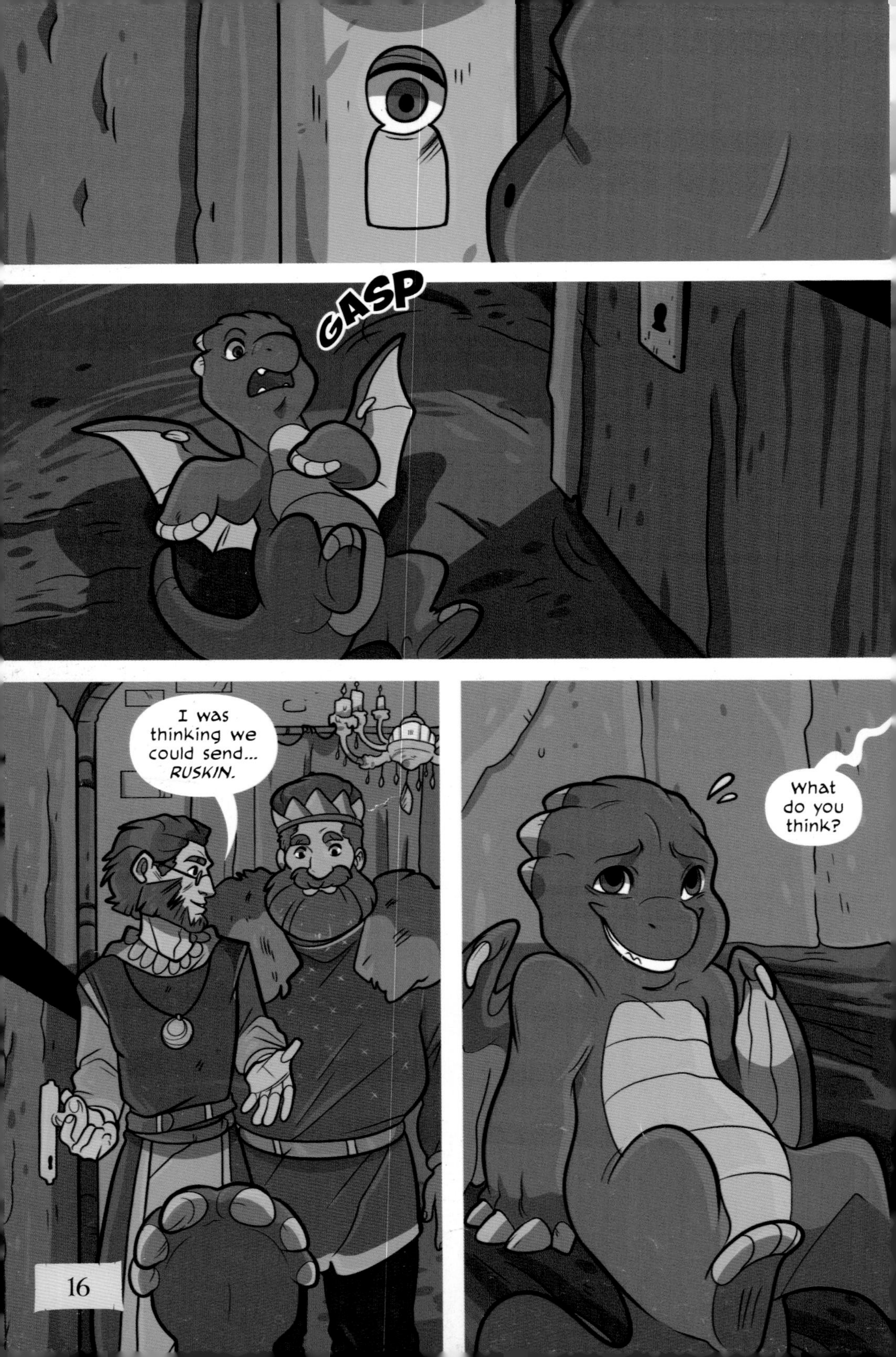
GASP
I was thinking we could send... *RUSKIN.*
What do you think?

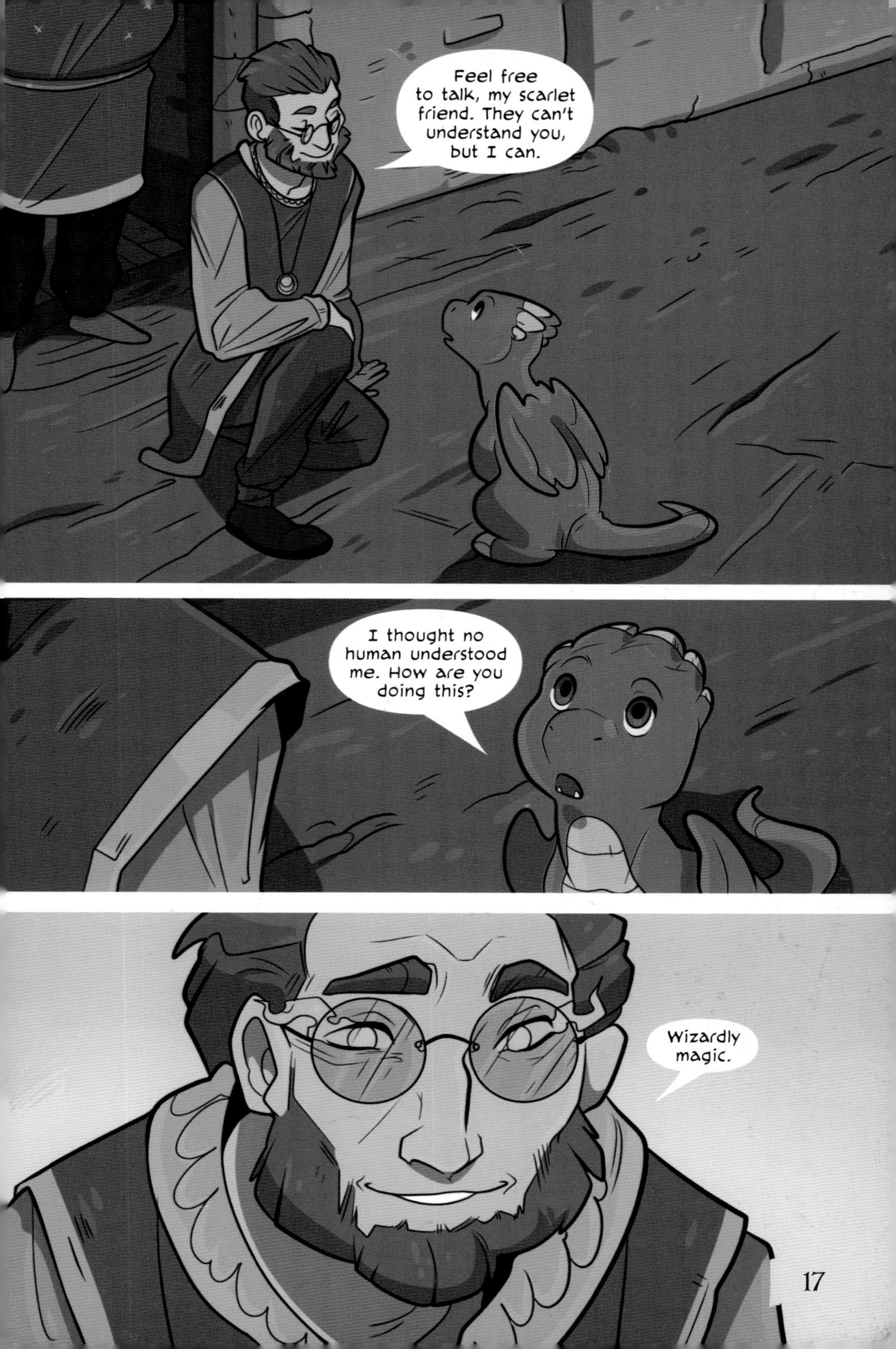
Feel free to talk, my scarlet friend. They can't understand you, but I can.
I thought no human understood me. How are you doing this?
Wizardly magic.

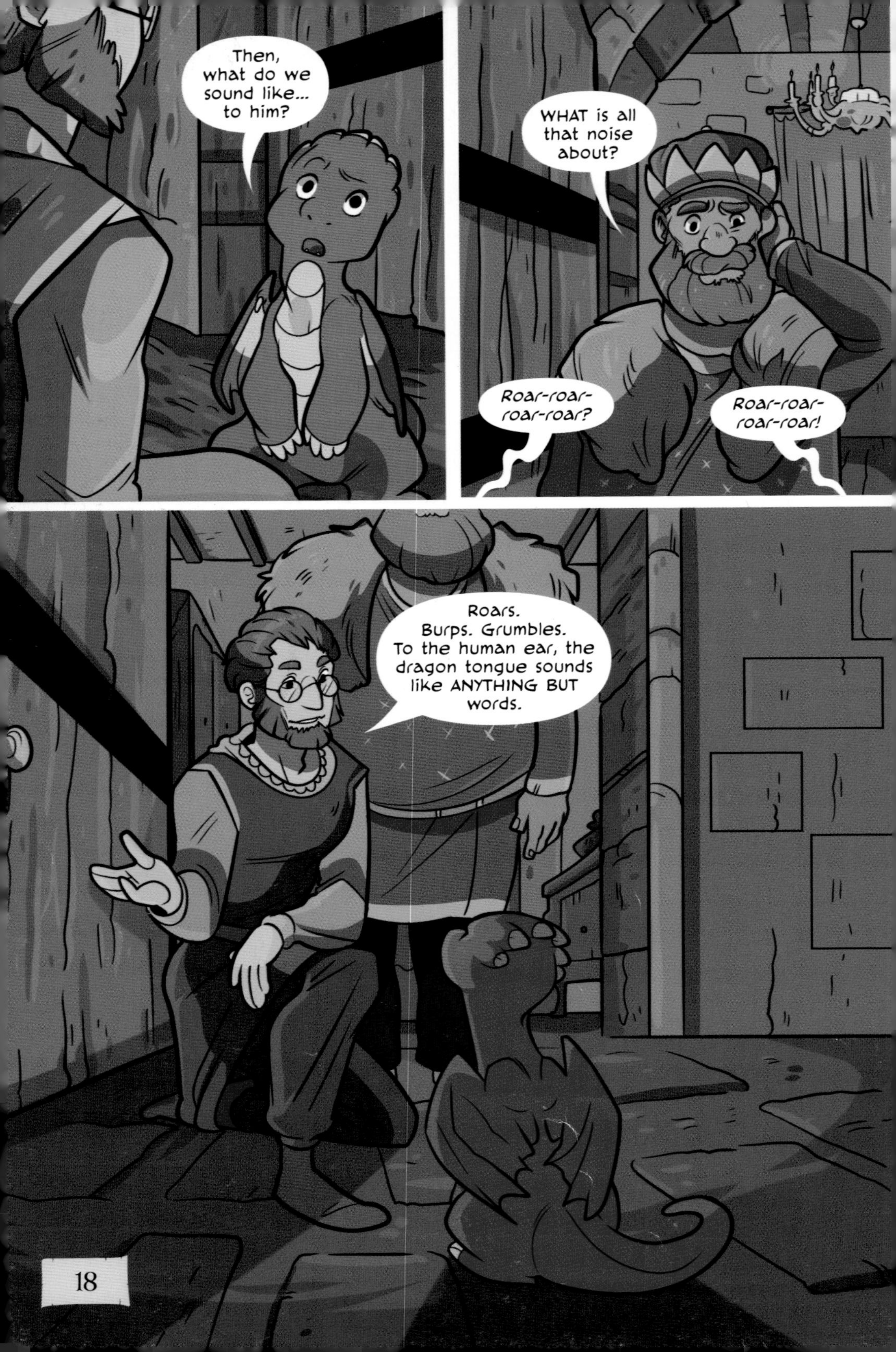
Then, what do we sound like... to him?
WHAT is all that noise about?
Roar-roar-roar-roar?
Roar-roar-roar-roar!
Roars. Burps. Grumbles. To the human ear, the dragon tongue sounds like ANYTHING BUT words.

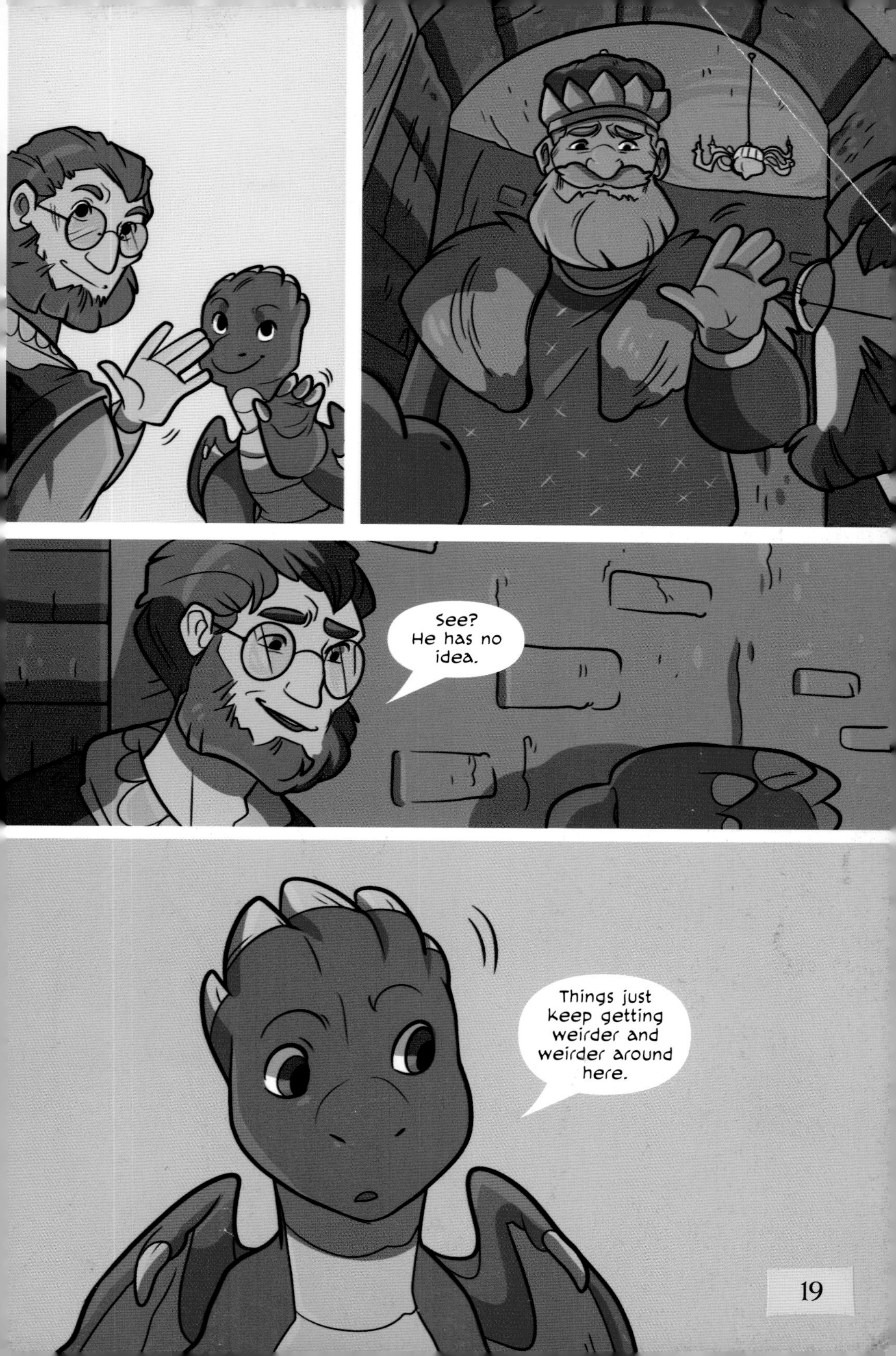
See? He has no idea.
Things just keep getting weirder and weirder around here.

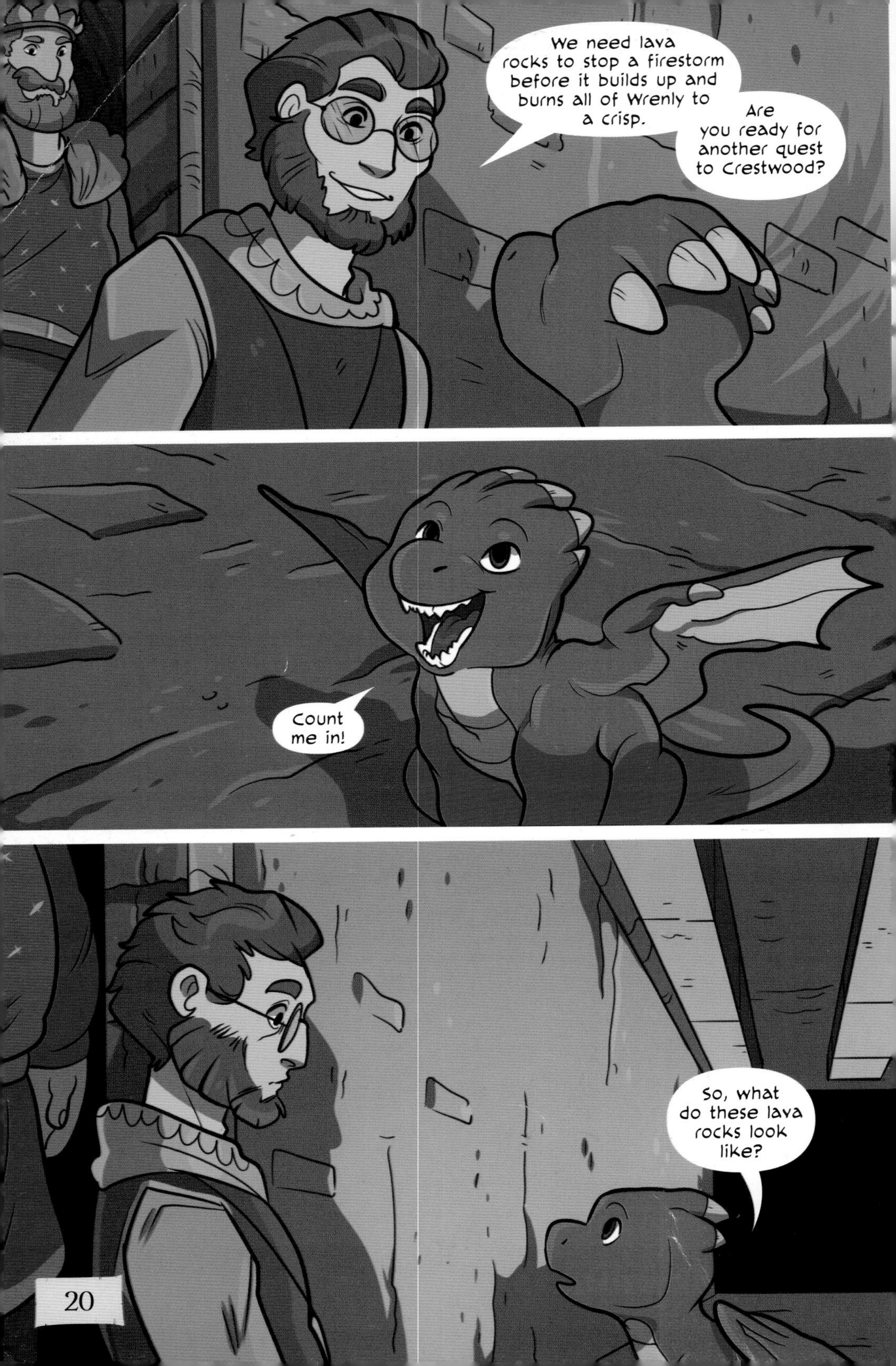
We need lava rocks to stop a firestorm before it builds up and burns all of Wrenly to a crisp.
Are you ready for another quest to Crestwood?
Count me in!
So, what do these lava rocks look like?

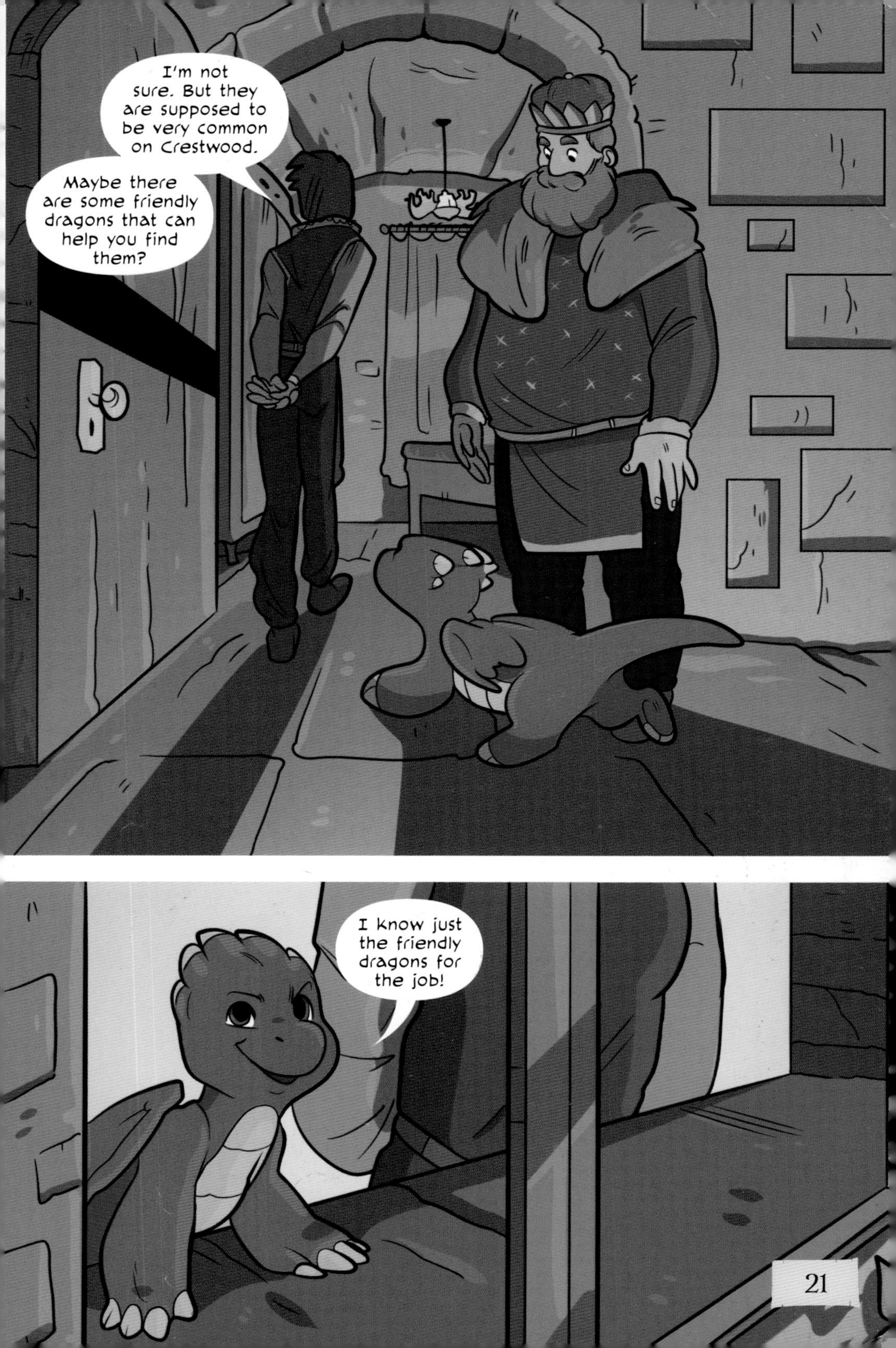
I'm not sure. But they are supposed to be very common on Crestwood.
Maybe there are some friendly dragons that can help you find them?
I know just the friendly dragons for the job!

Chapter 2

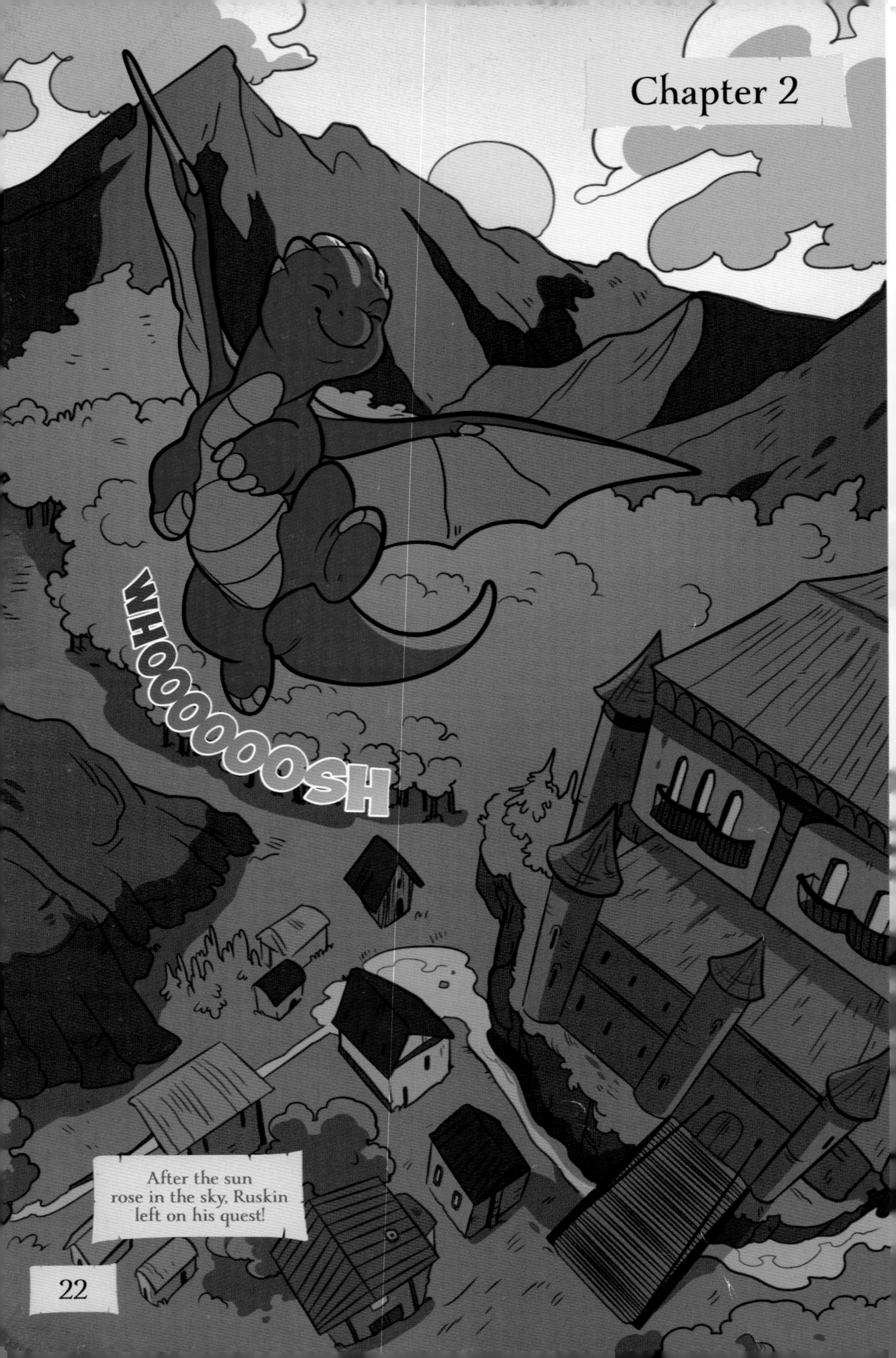
WHOOOOOOSH
After the sun rose in the sky, Ruskin left on his quest!

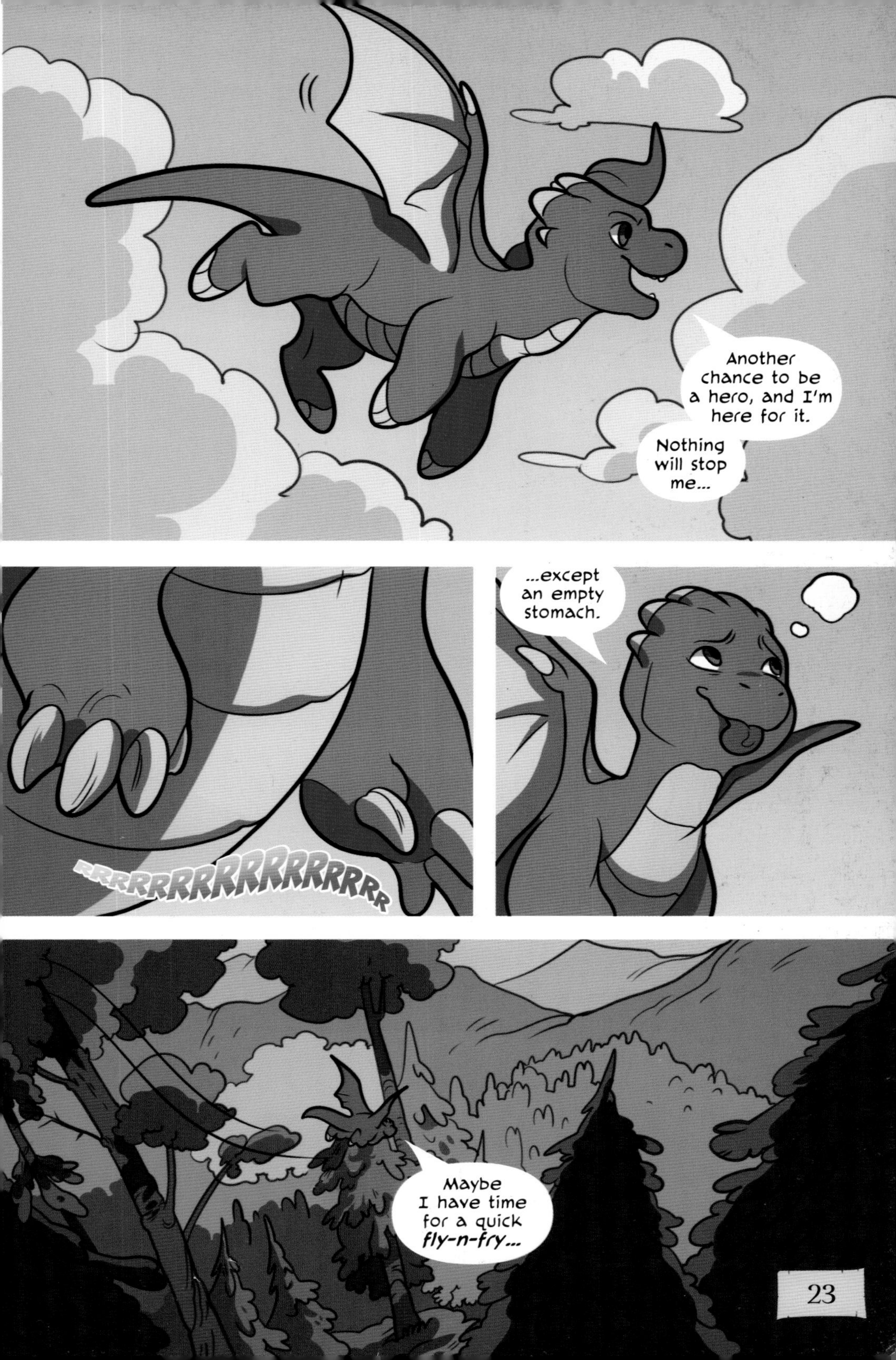
Another chance to be a hero, and I'm here for it.
Nothing will stop me...
RRRRRRRRRRRRRRRRRR
...except an empty stomach.
Maybe I have time for a quick *fly-n-fry...*

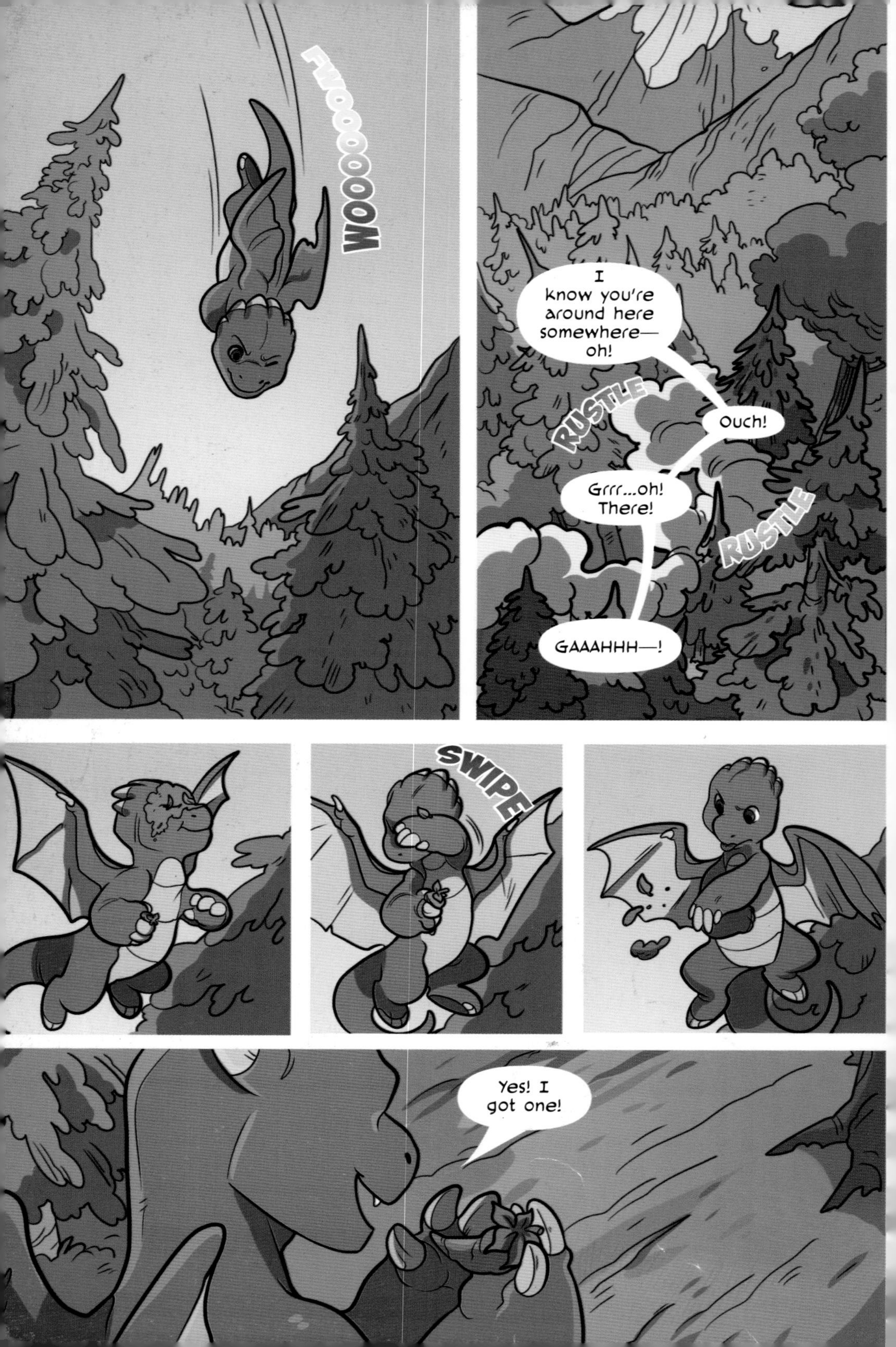
FWOOOOOOM
I know you're around here somewhere—oh!
RUSTLE
Ouch!
Grrr...oh! There!
RUSTLE
GAAAHHH—!
SWIPE
Yes! I got one!

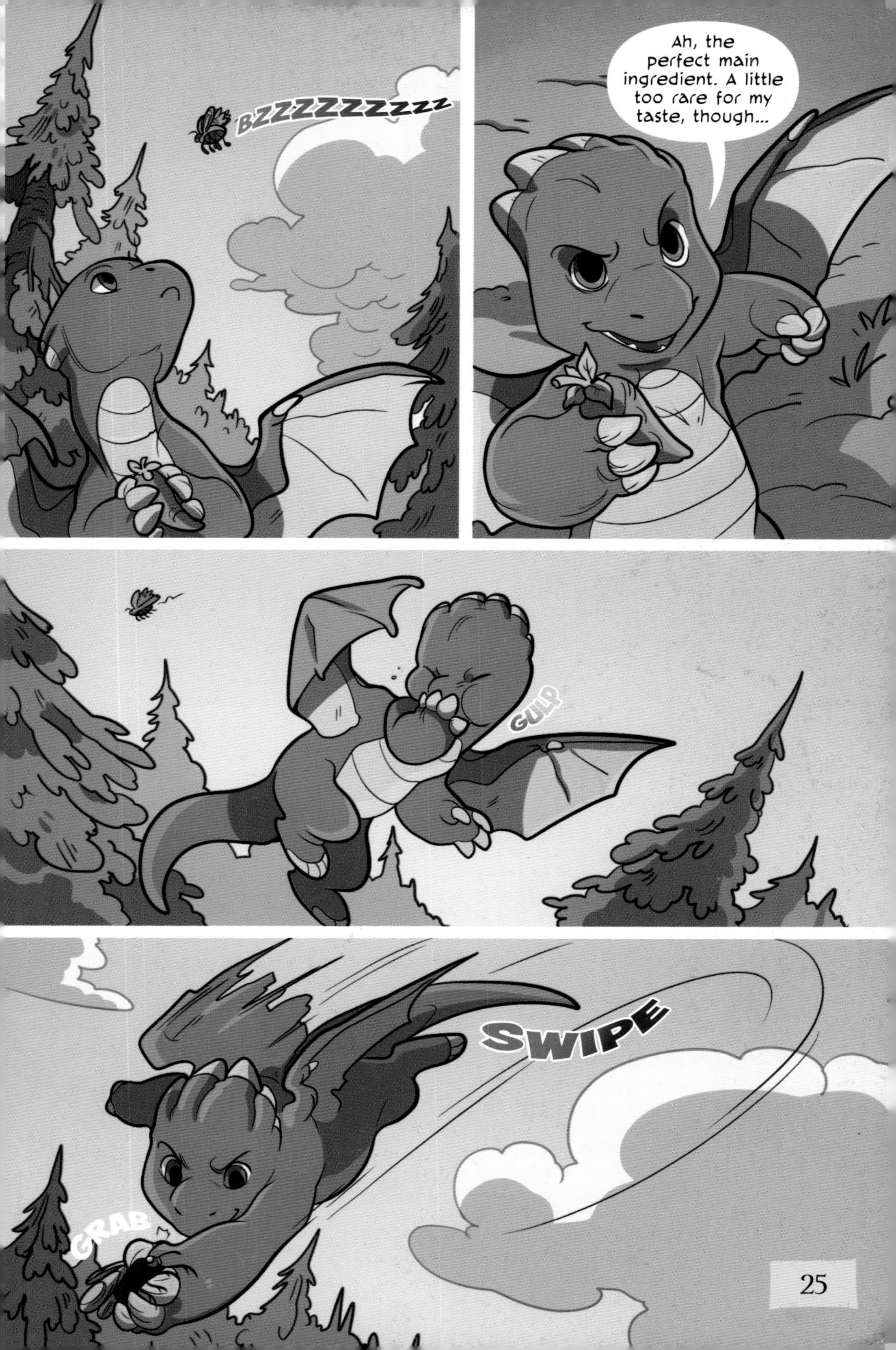
BZZZZZZZZZ
Ah, the perfect main ingredient. A little too rare for my taste, though...
GULP
SWIPE
GRAB

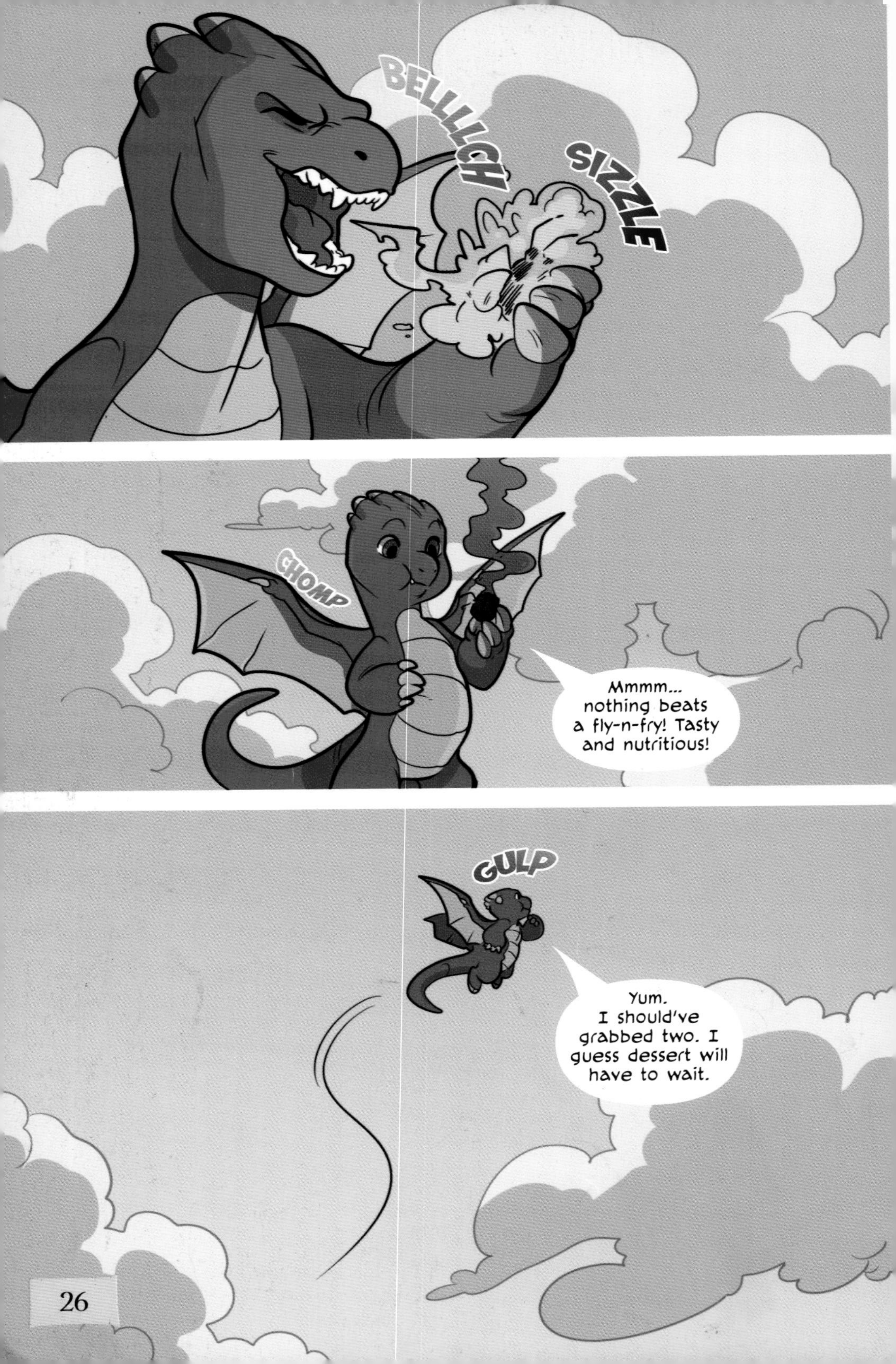
BELLLLGH
SIZZLE
CHOMP
Mmmm... nothing beats a fly-n-fry! Tasty and nutritious!
GULP
Yum. I should've grabbed two. I guess dessert will have to wait.

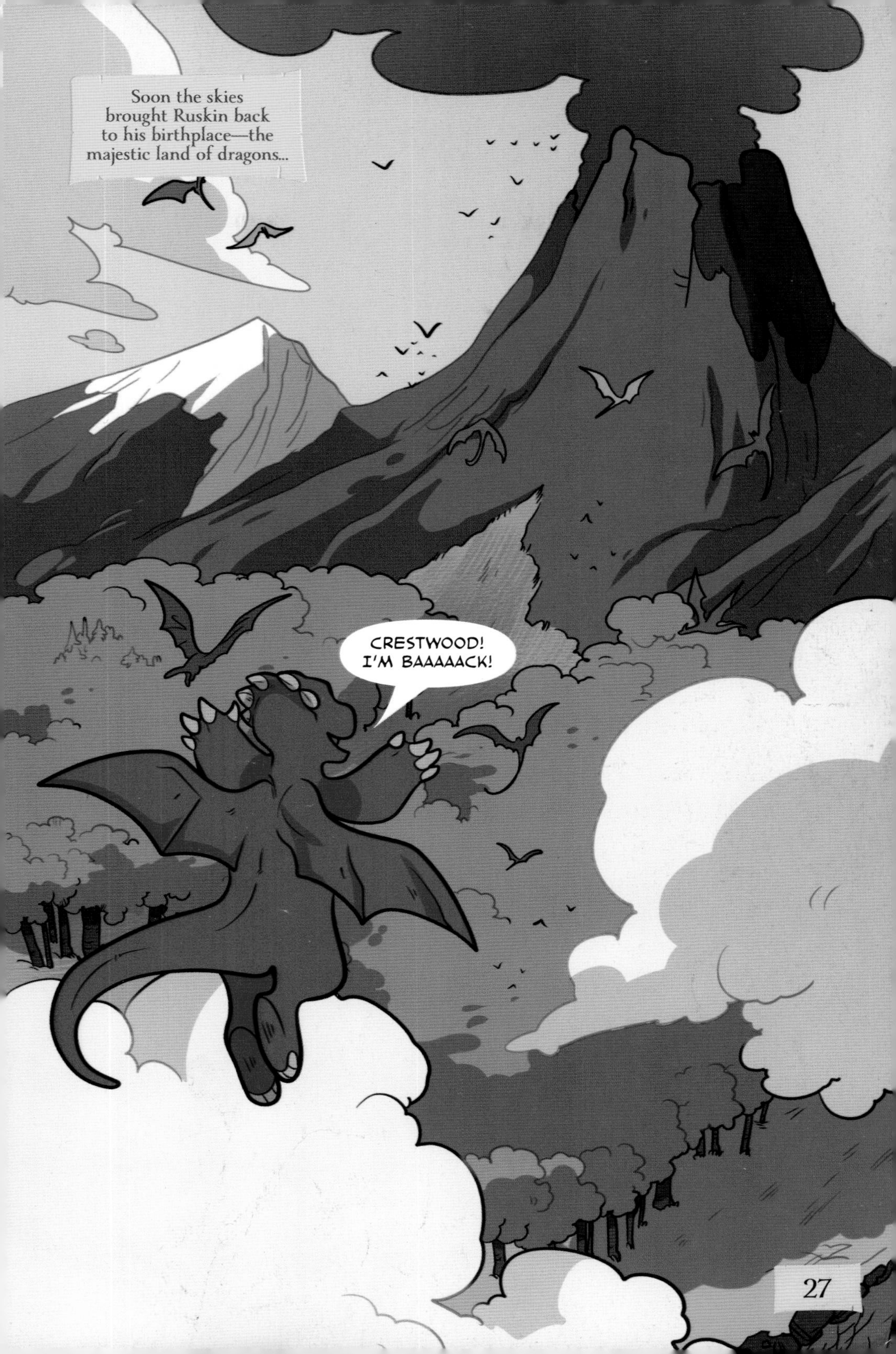
Soon the skies brought Ruskin back to his birthplace—the majestic land of dragons...
CRESTWOOD! I'M BAAAAACK!

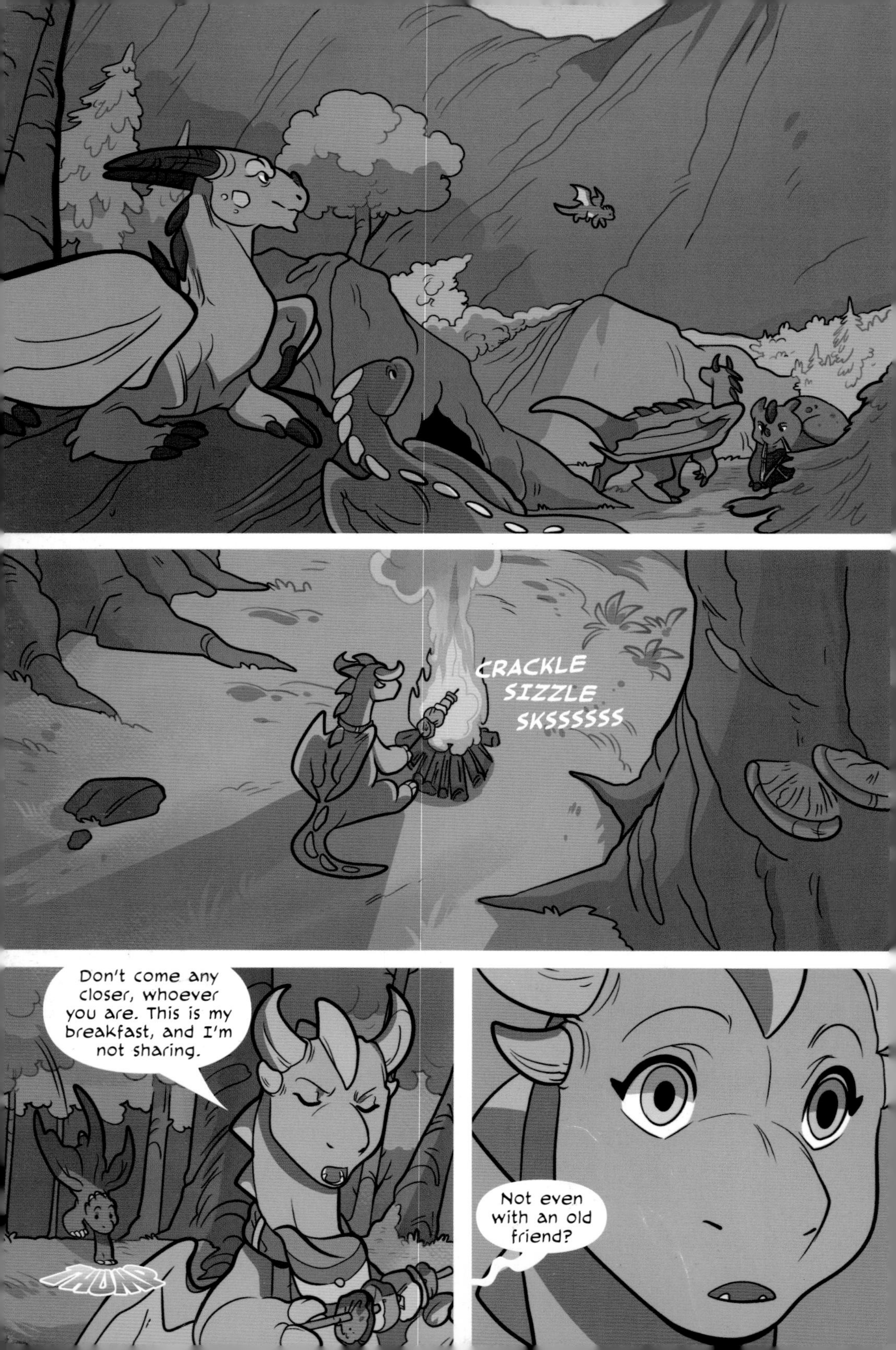
CRACKLE
SIZZLE
SKSSSSSS
Don't come any closer, whoever you are. This is my breakfast, and I'm not sharing.
THUMP
Not even with an old friend?

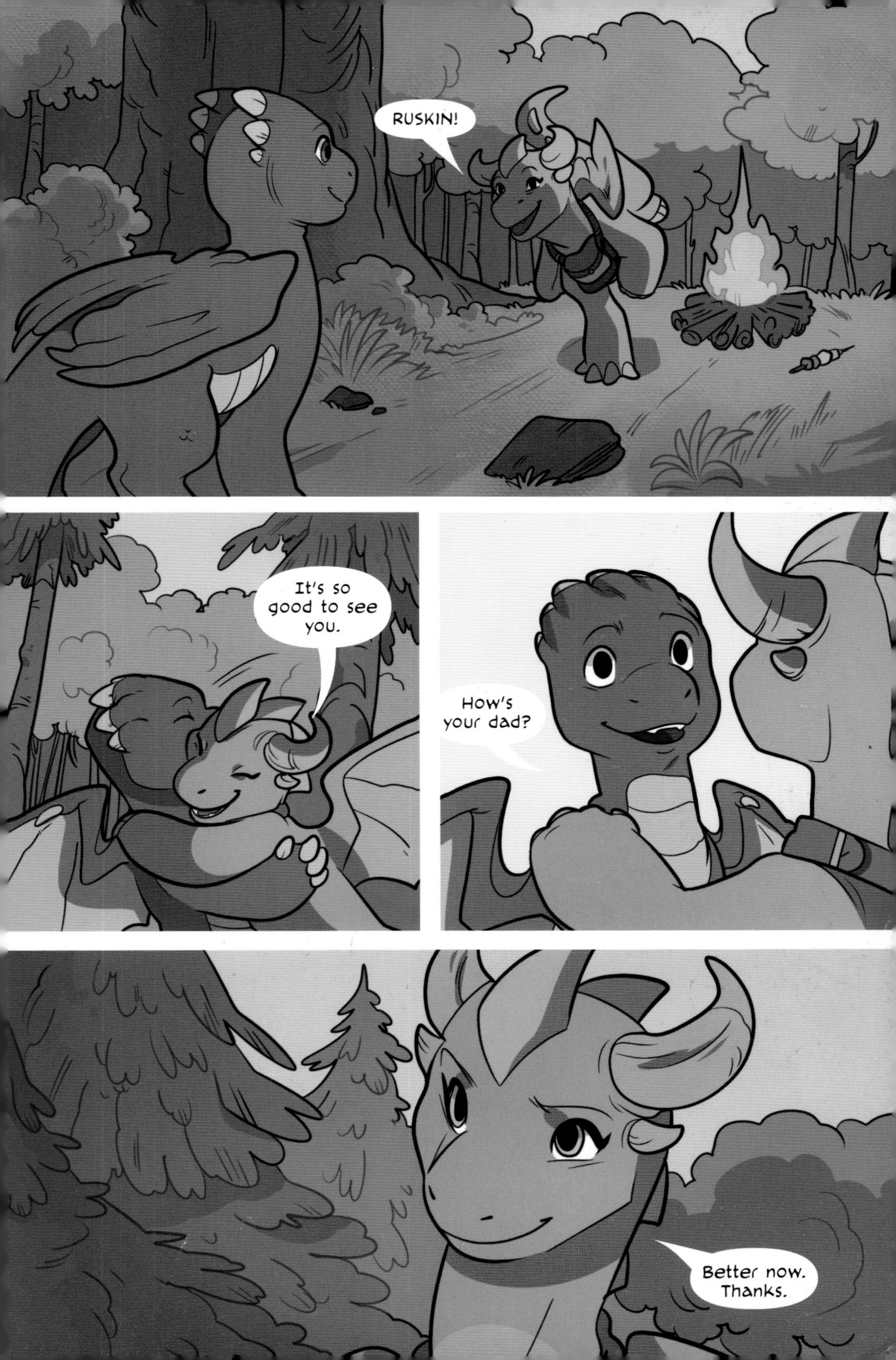
RUSKIN!
It's so good to see you.
How's your dad?
Better now. Thanks.

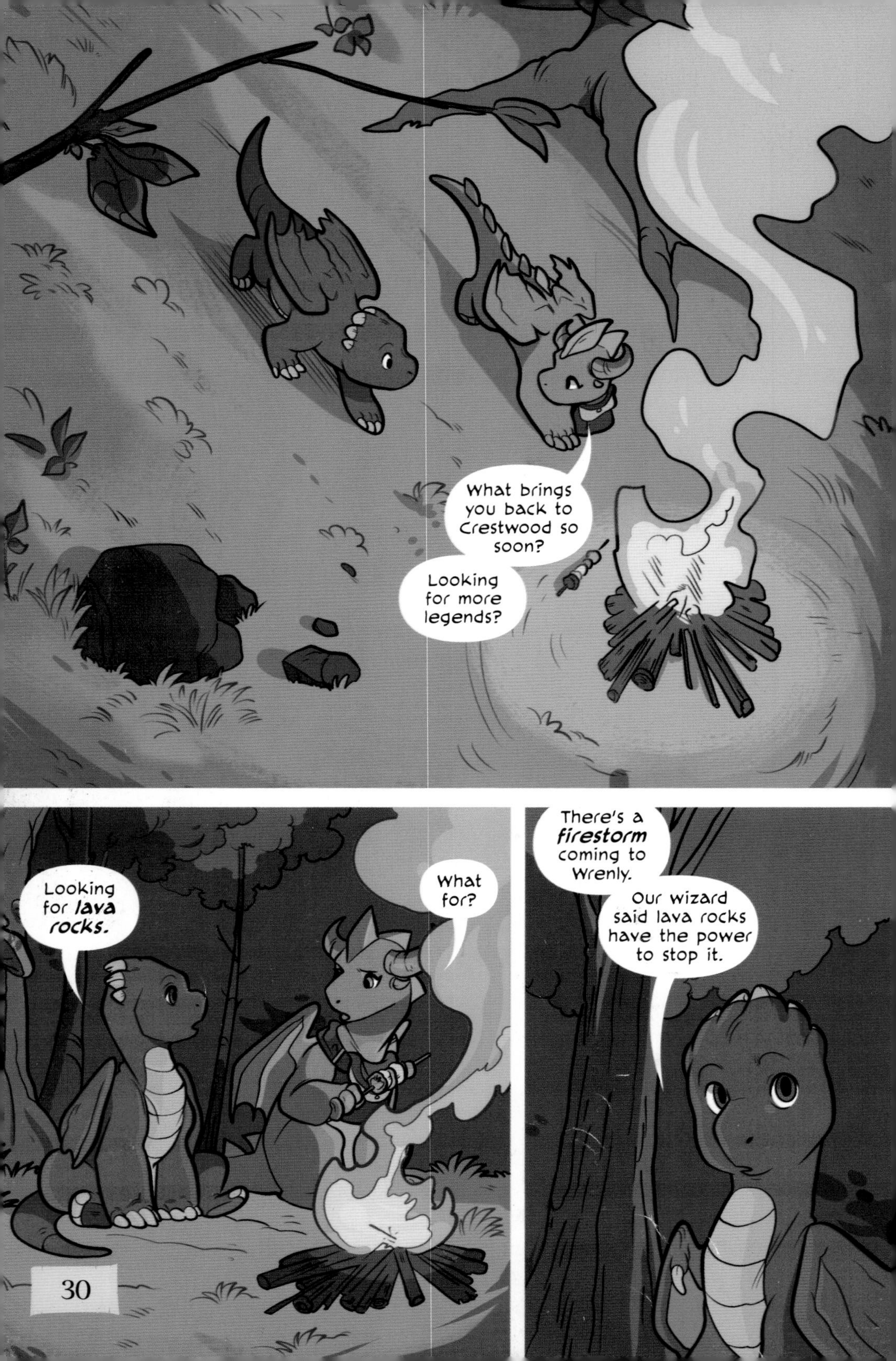
What brings you back to Crestwood so soon?
Looking for more legends?
Looking for *lava rocks.*
What for?
There's a *firestorm* coming to Wrenly.
Our wizard said lava rocks have the power to stop it.

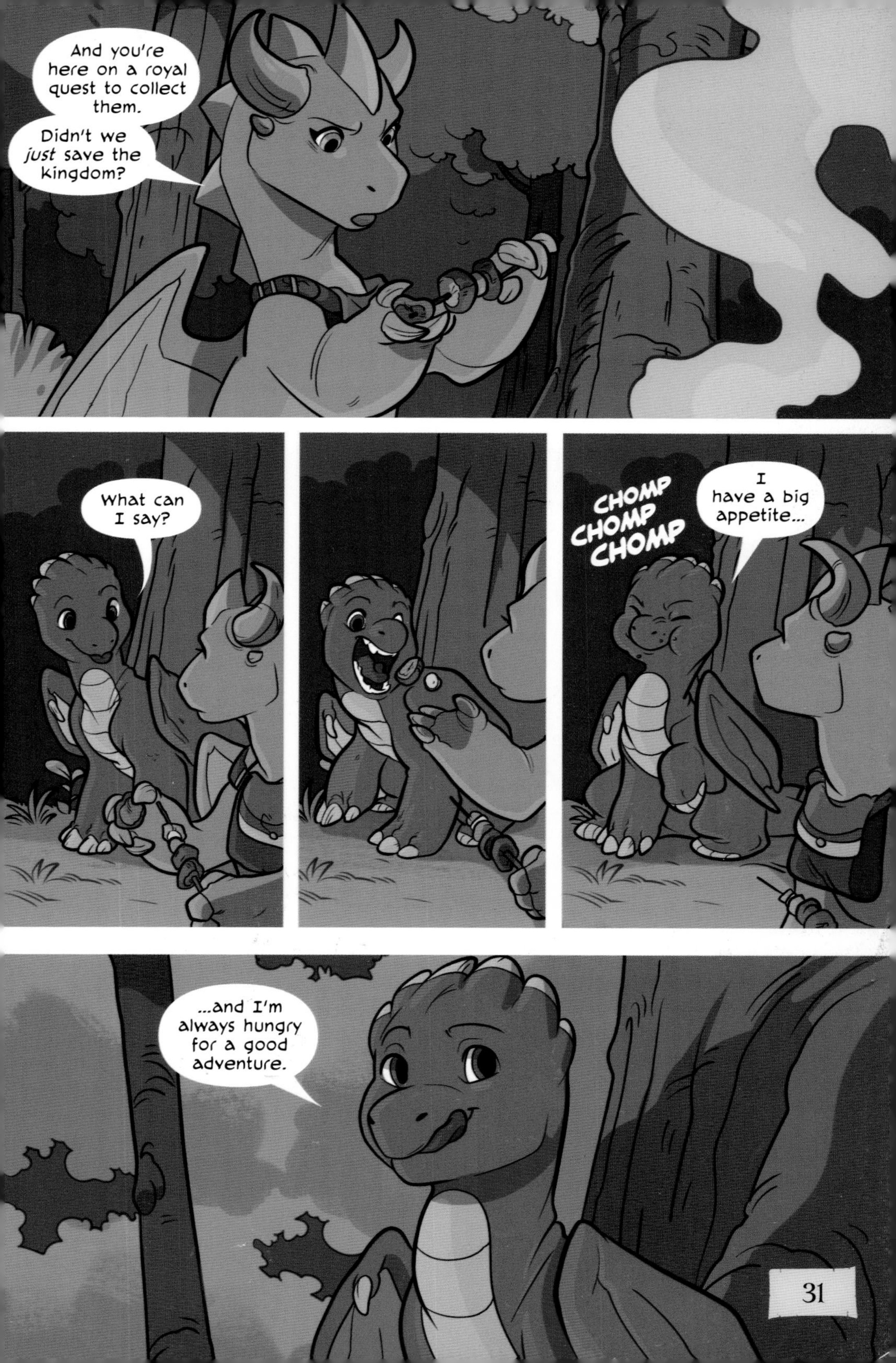
And you're here on a royal quest to collect them.
Didn't we *just* save the kingdom?
What can I say?
CHOMP CHOMP CHOMP
I have a big appetite...
...and I'm always hungry for a good adventure.

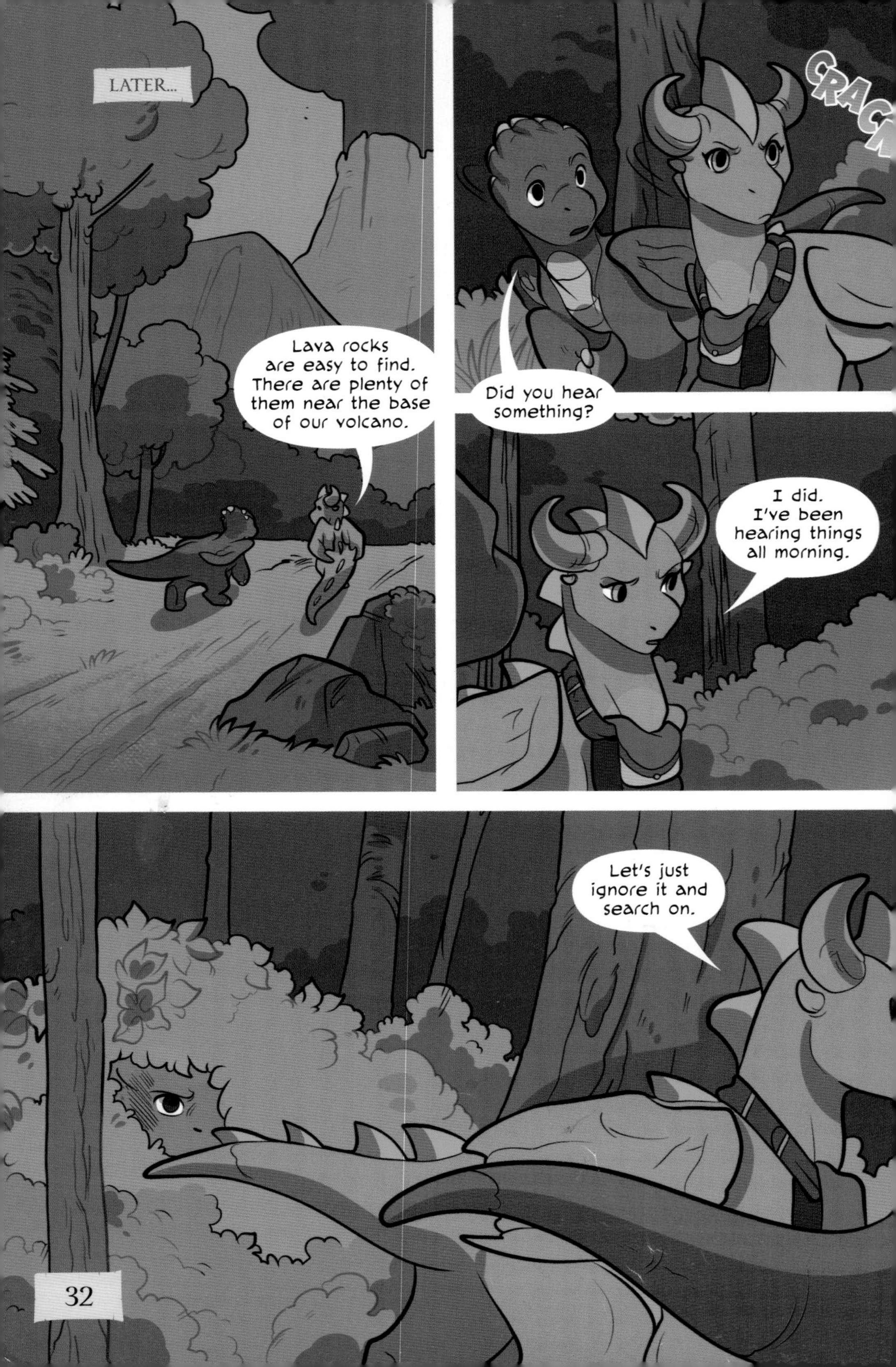

LATER...
Lava rocks are easy to find. There are plenty of them near the base of our volcano.
CRACK
Did you hear something?
I did. I've been hearing things all morning.
Let's just ignore it and search on.

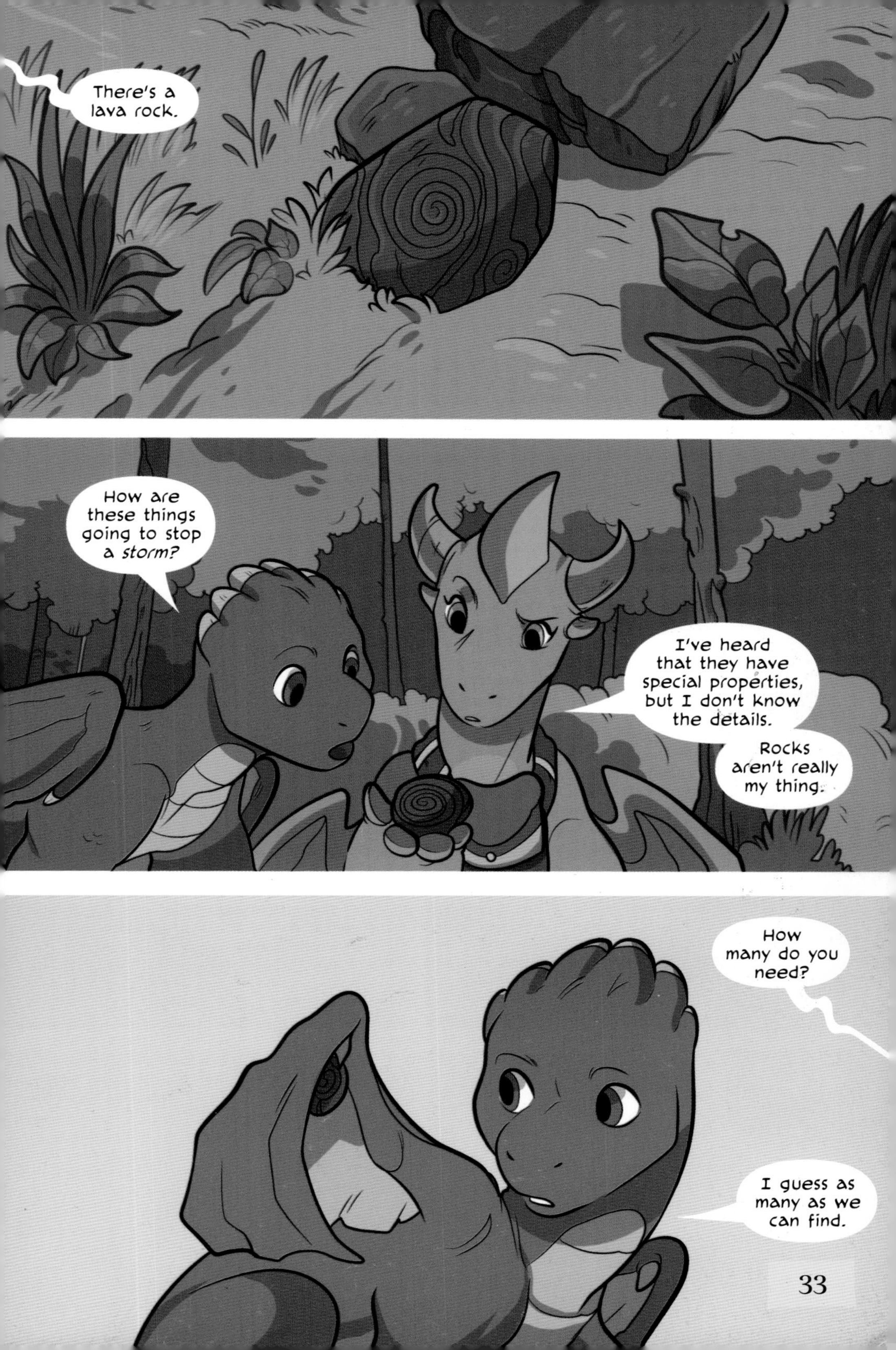
There's a lava rock.
How are these things going to stop a *storm?*
I've heard that they have special properties, but I don't know the details.
Rocks aren't really my thing.
How many do you need?
I guess as many as we can find.

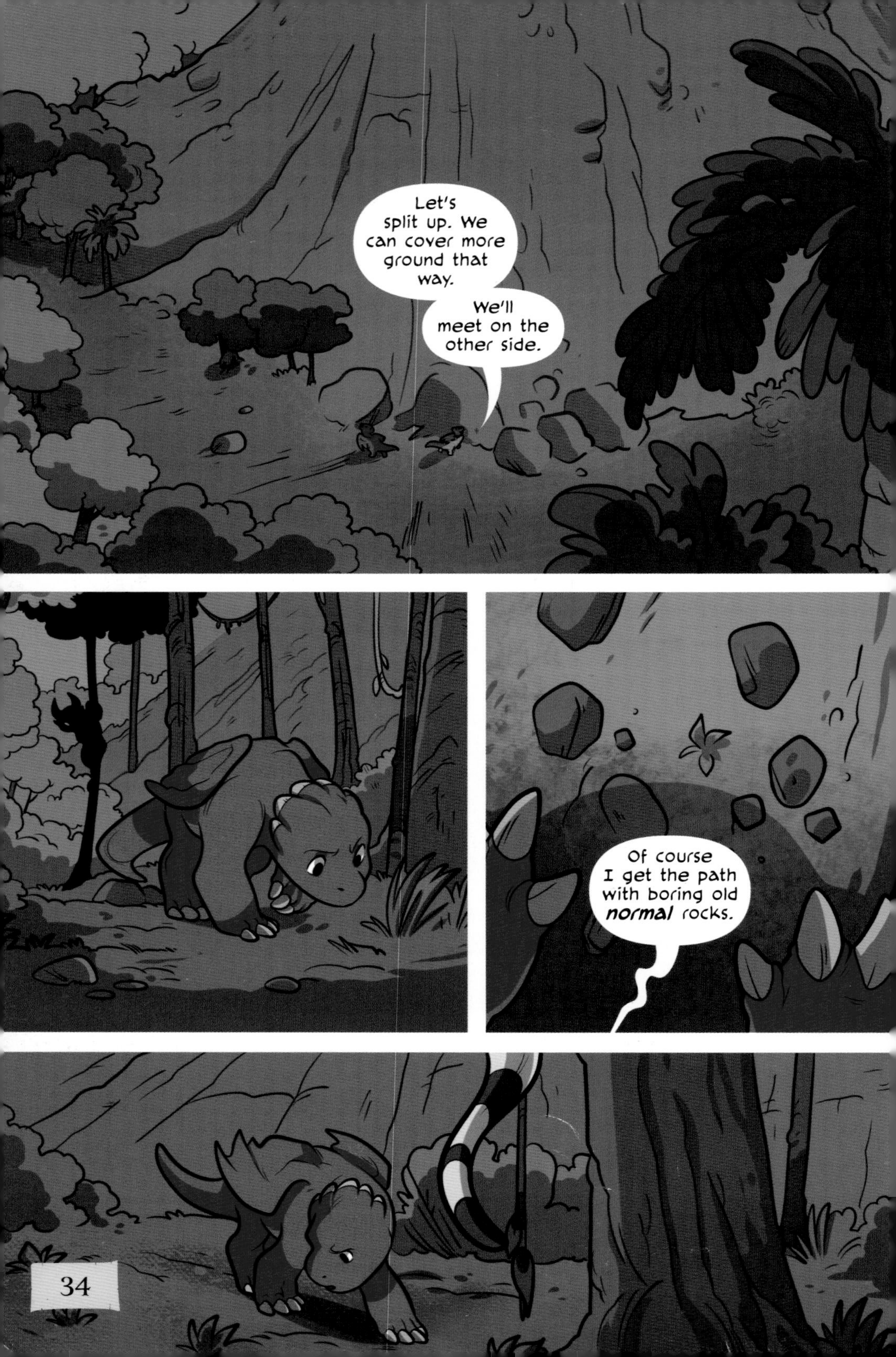
Let's split up. We can cover more ground that way.
We'll meet on the other side.
Of course I get the path with boring old ***normal*** rocks.

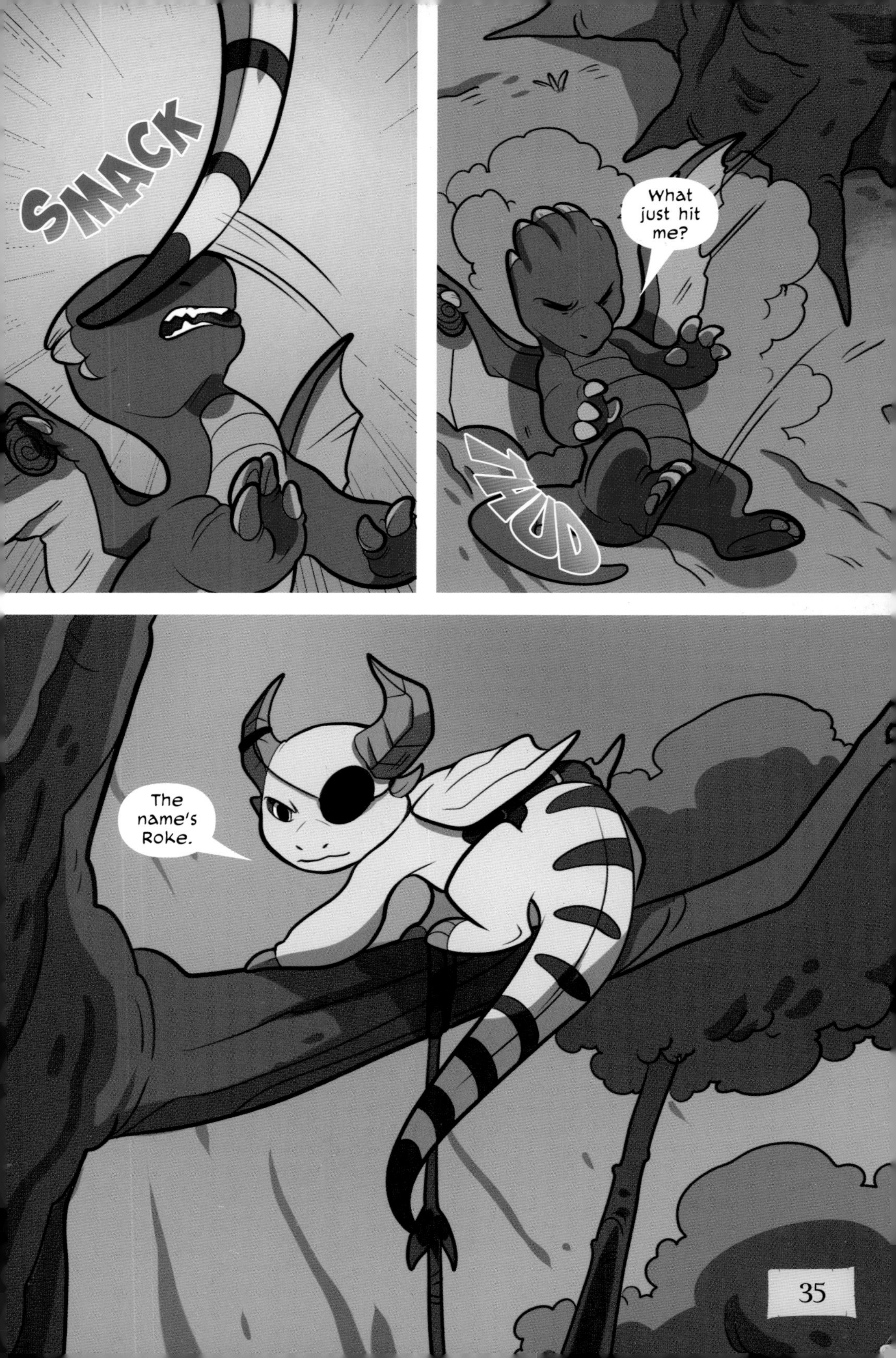
SMACK
What just hit me?
THUD
The name's Roke.

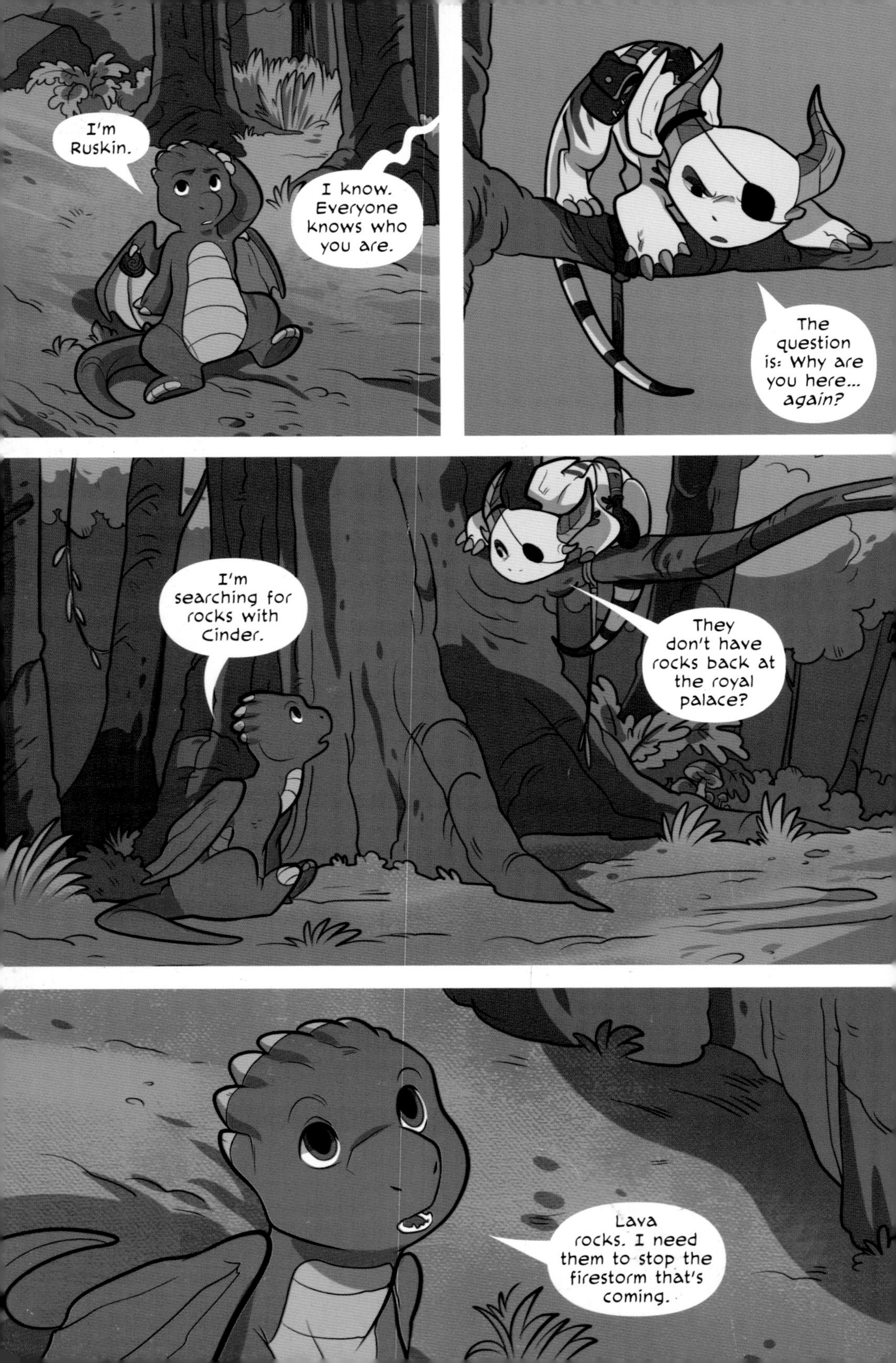
I'm Ruskin.
I know. Everyone knows who you are.
The question is: Why are you here... *again?*
I'm searching for rocks with Cinder.
They don't have rocks back at the royal palace?
Lava rocks. I need them to stop the firestorm that's coming.

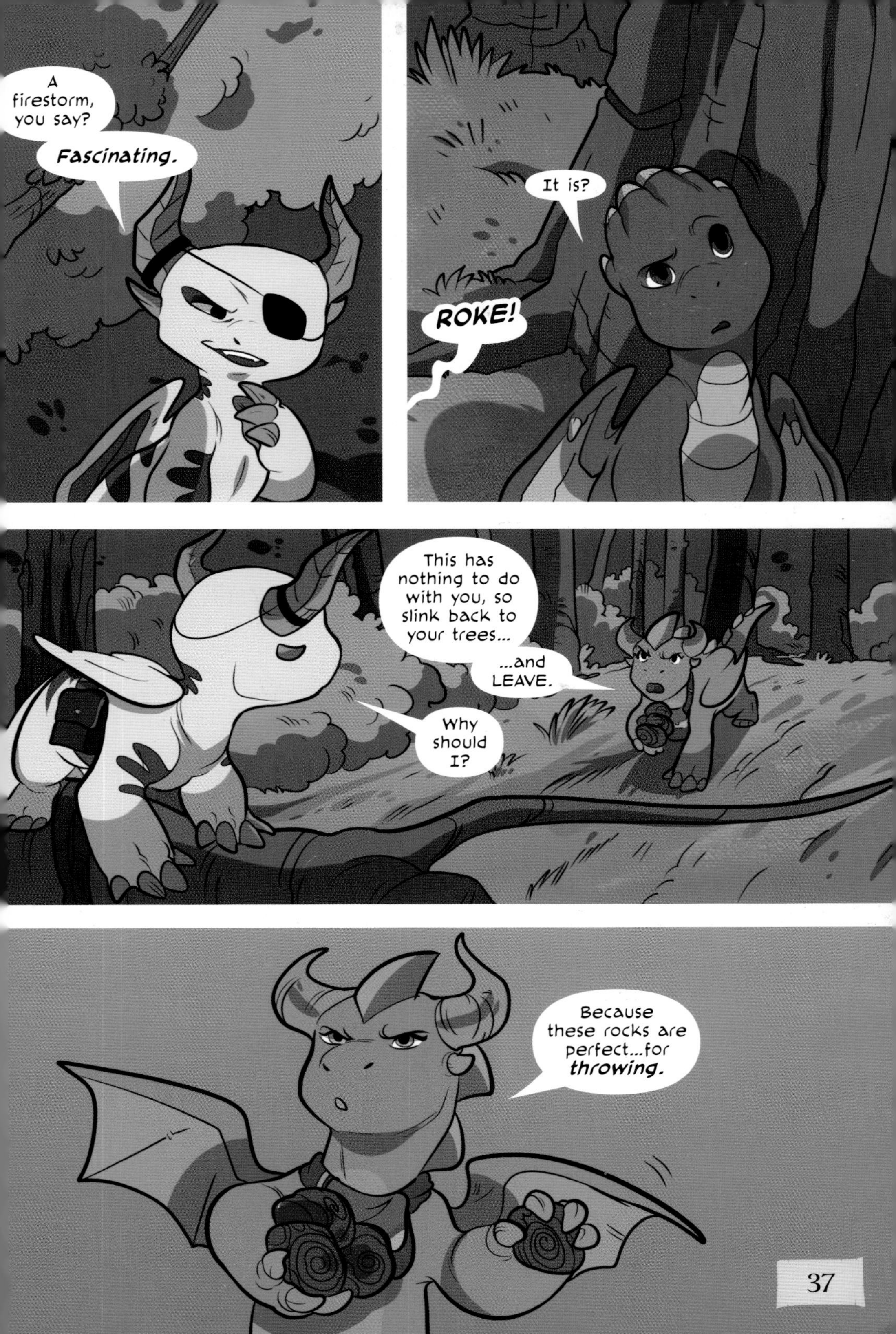
A firestorm, you say?
Fascinating.
It is?
ROKE!
This has nothing to do with you, so slink back to your trees...
...and LEAVE.
Why should I?
Because these rocks are perfect...for *throwing.*

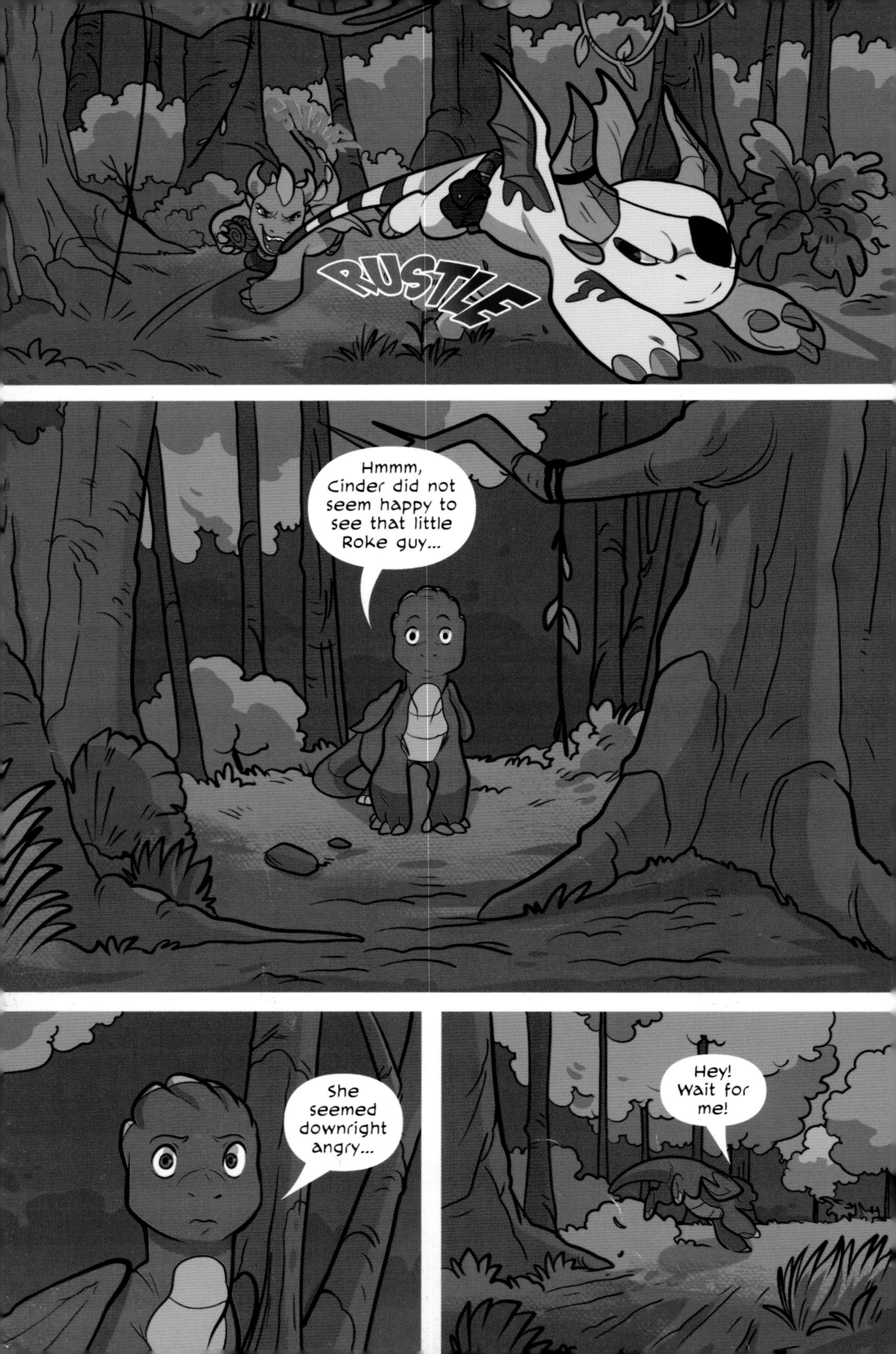
RUSTLE
Hmmm, Cinder did not seem happy to see that little Roke guy...
She seemed downright angry...
Hey! Wait for me!

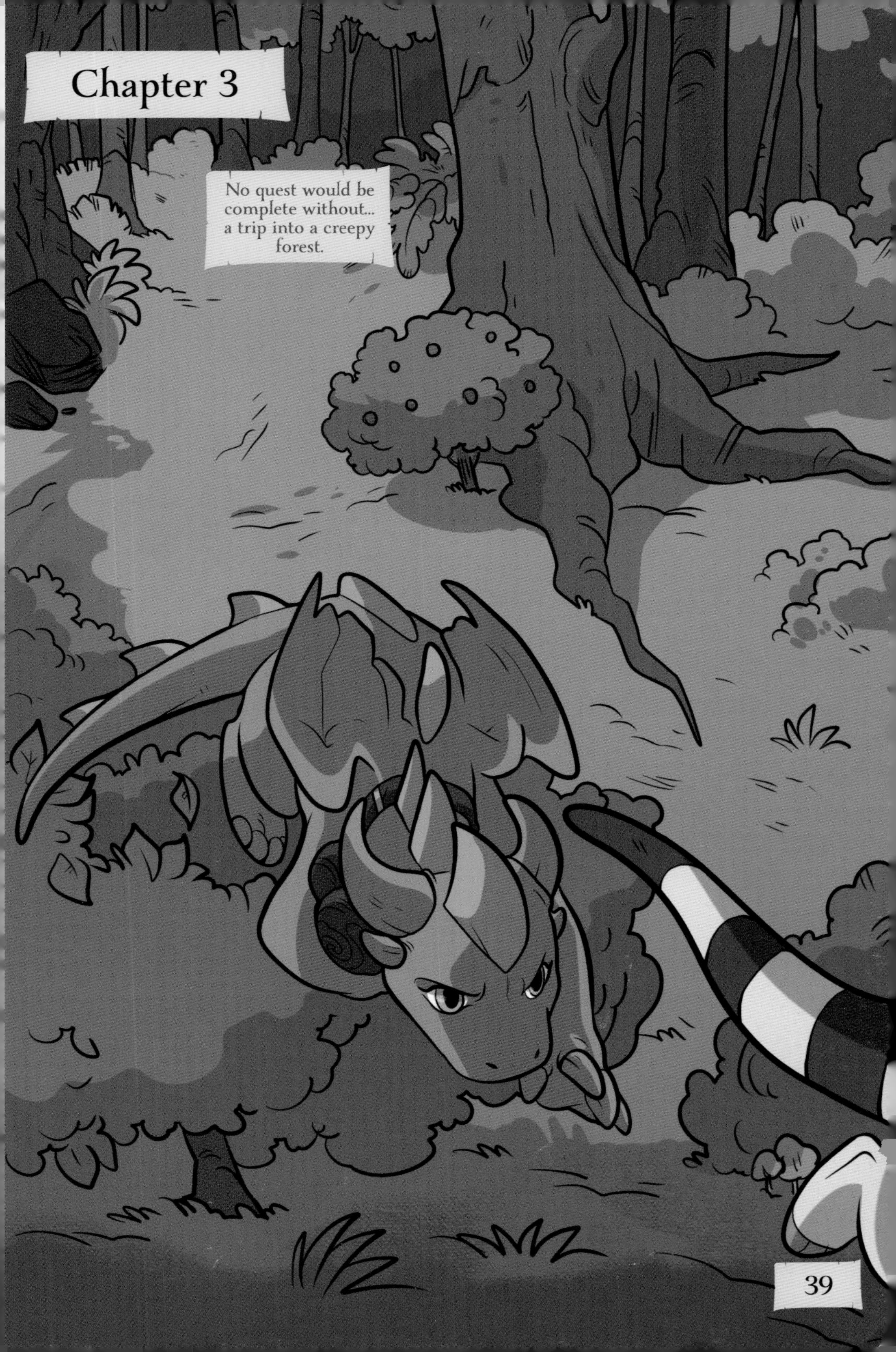
Chapter 3
No quest would be complete without... a trip into a creepy forest.
39

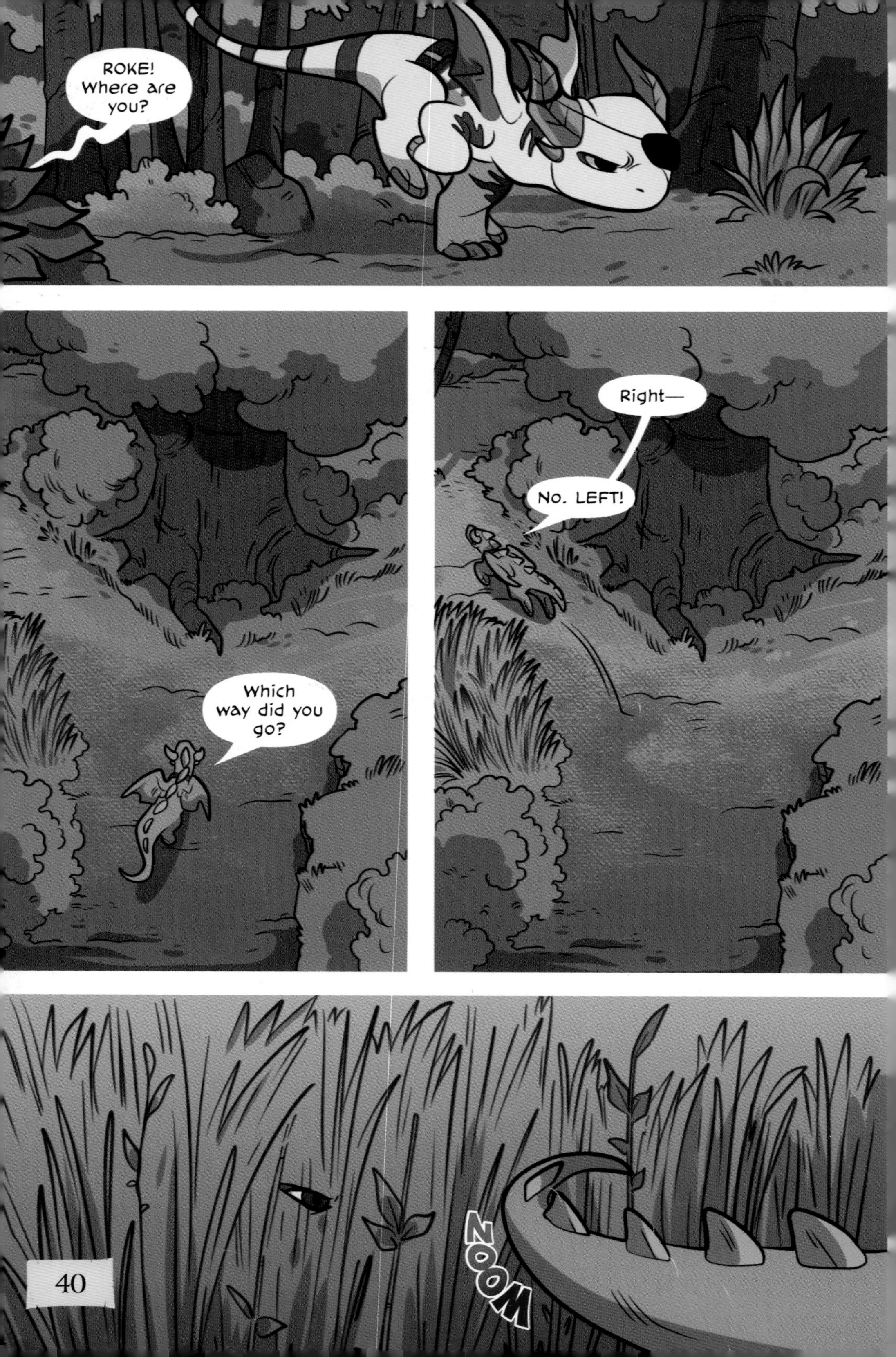
ROKE! Where are you?
Which way did you go?
Right—
No. LEFT!
ZOOM

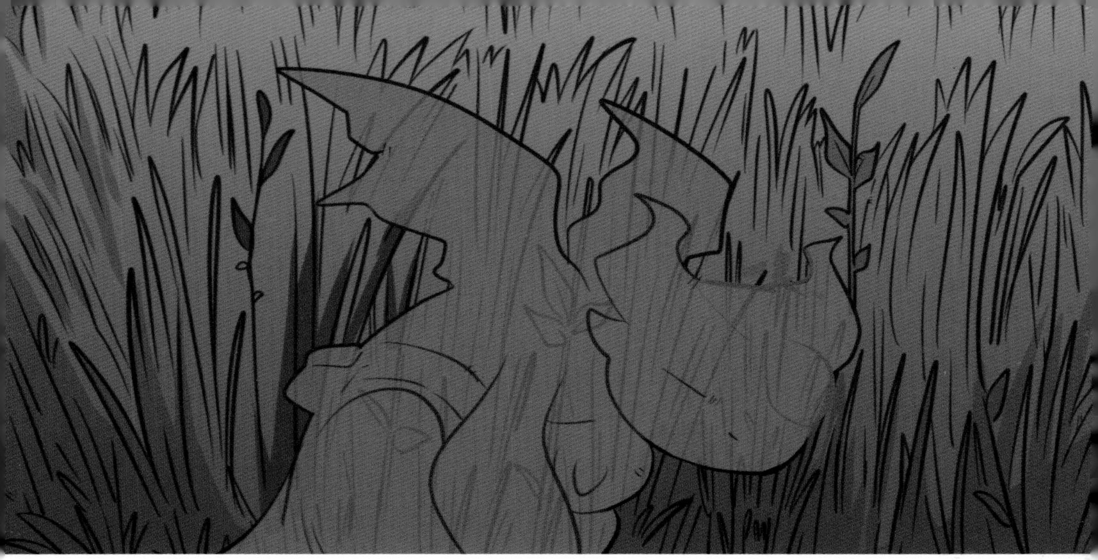

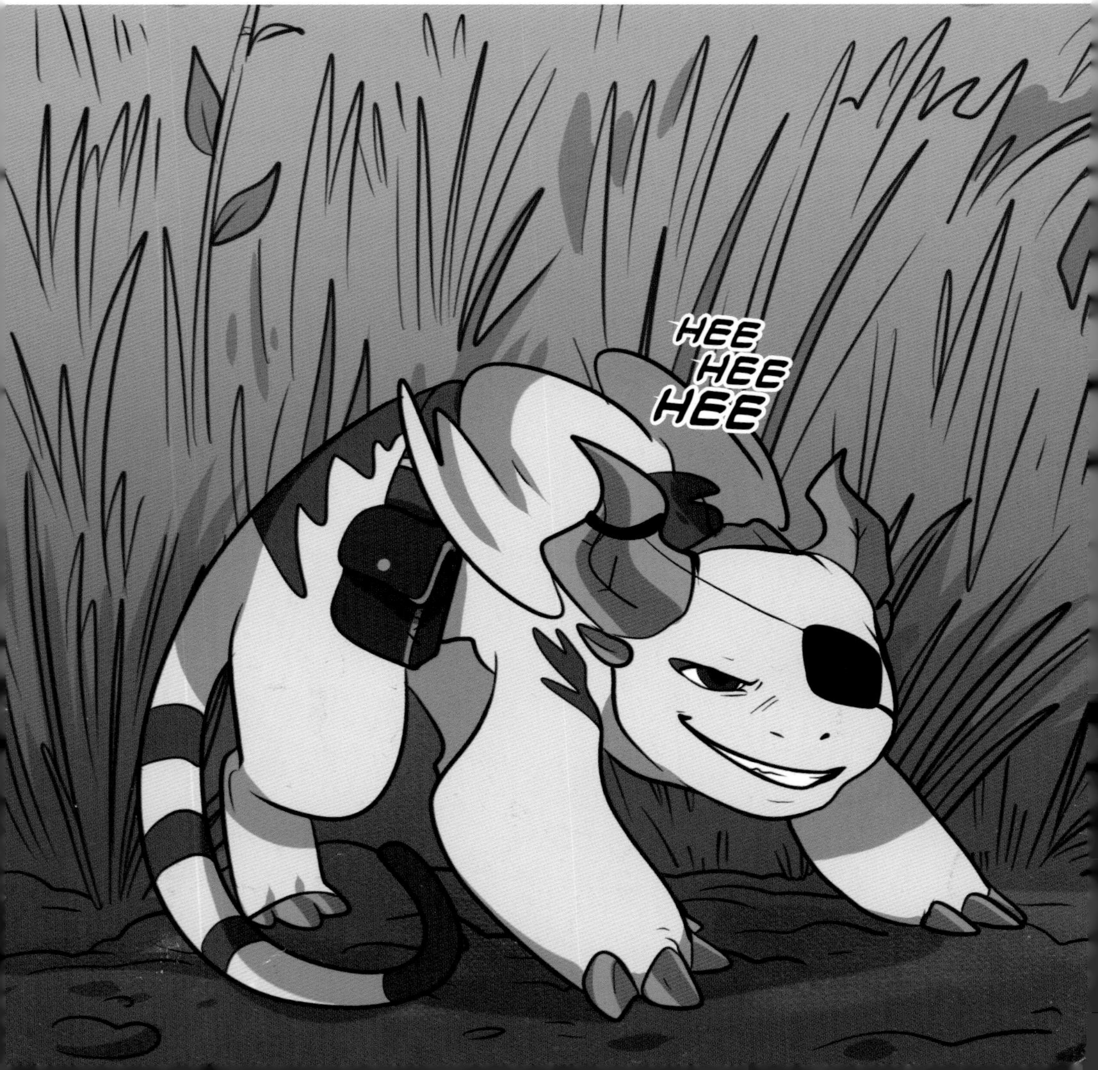
HEE
HEE
HEE

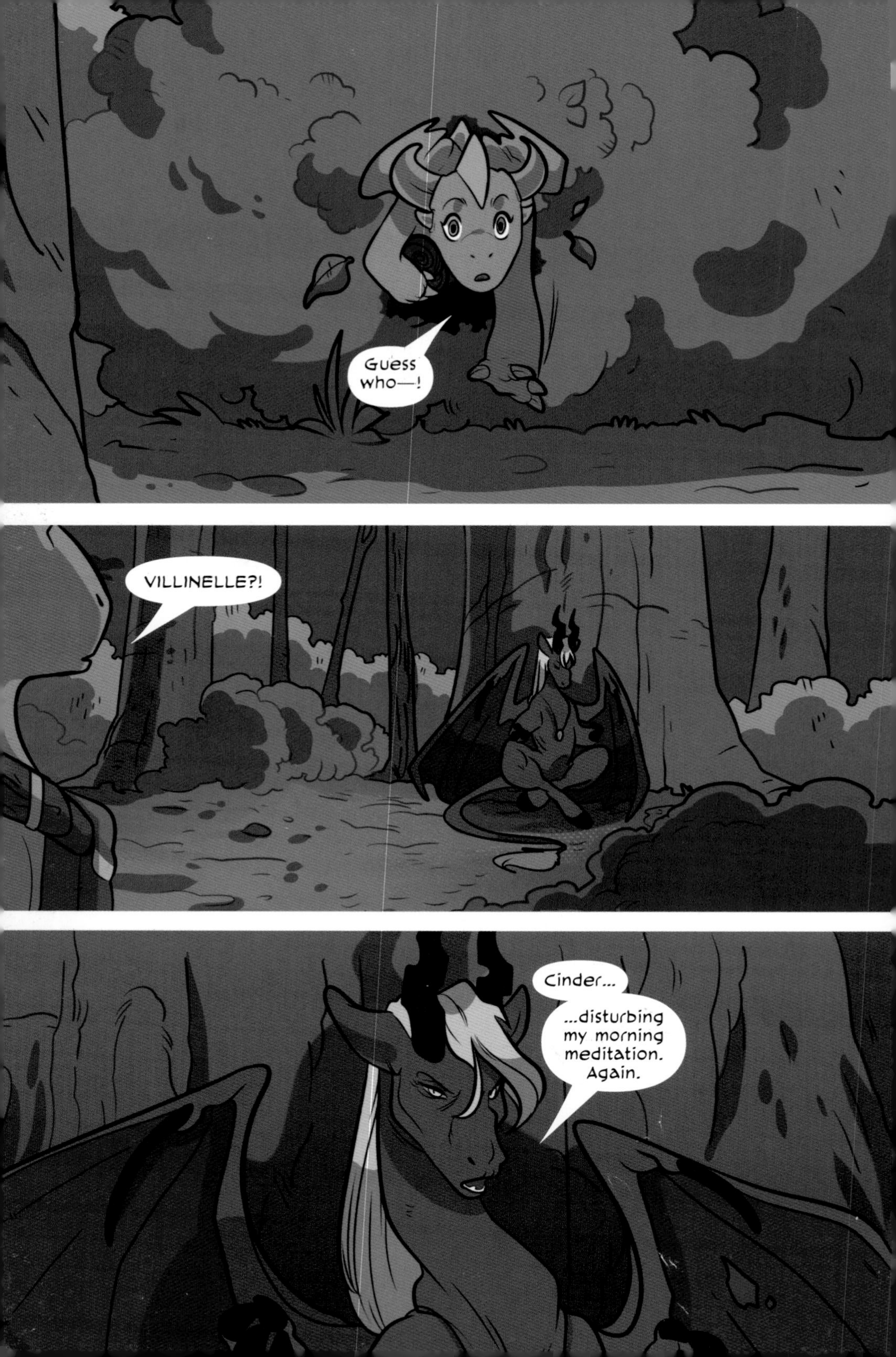
Guess who—!
VILLINELLE?!
Cinder...
...disturbing my morning meditation. Again.

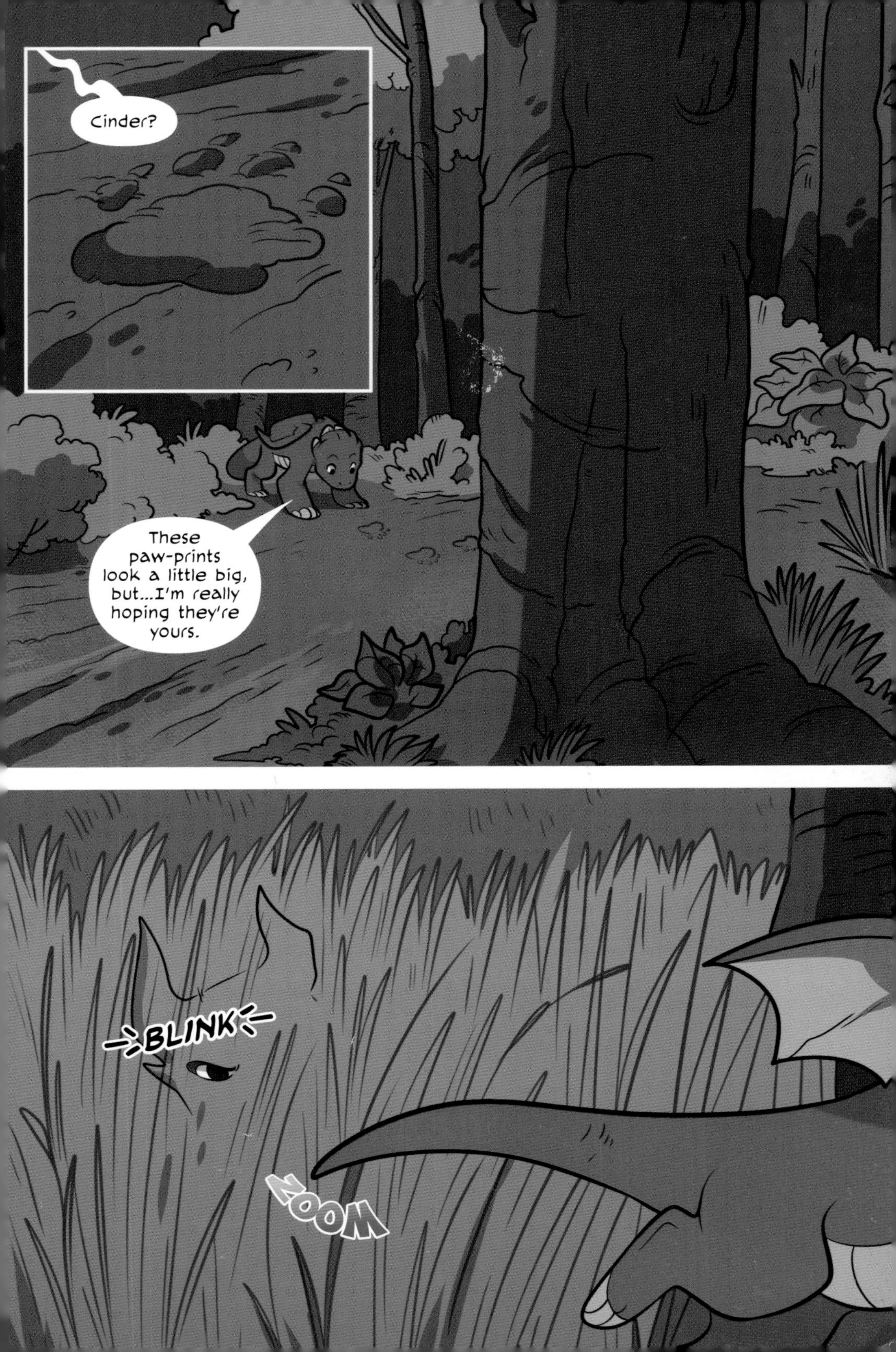
Cinder?
These paw-prints look a little big, but...I'm really hoping they're yours.
BLINK
ZOOM

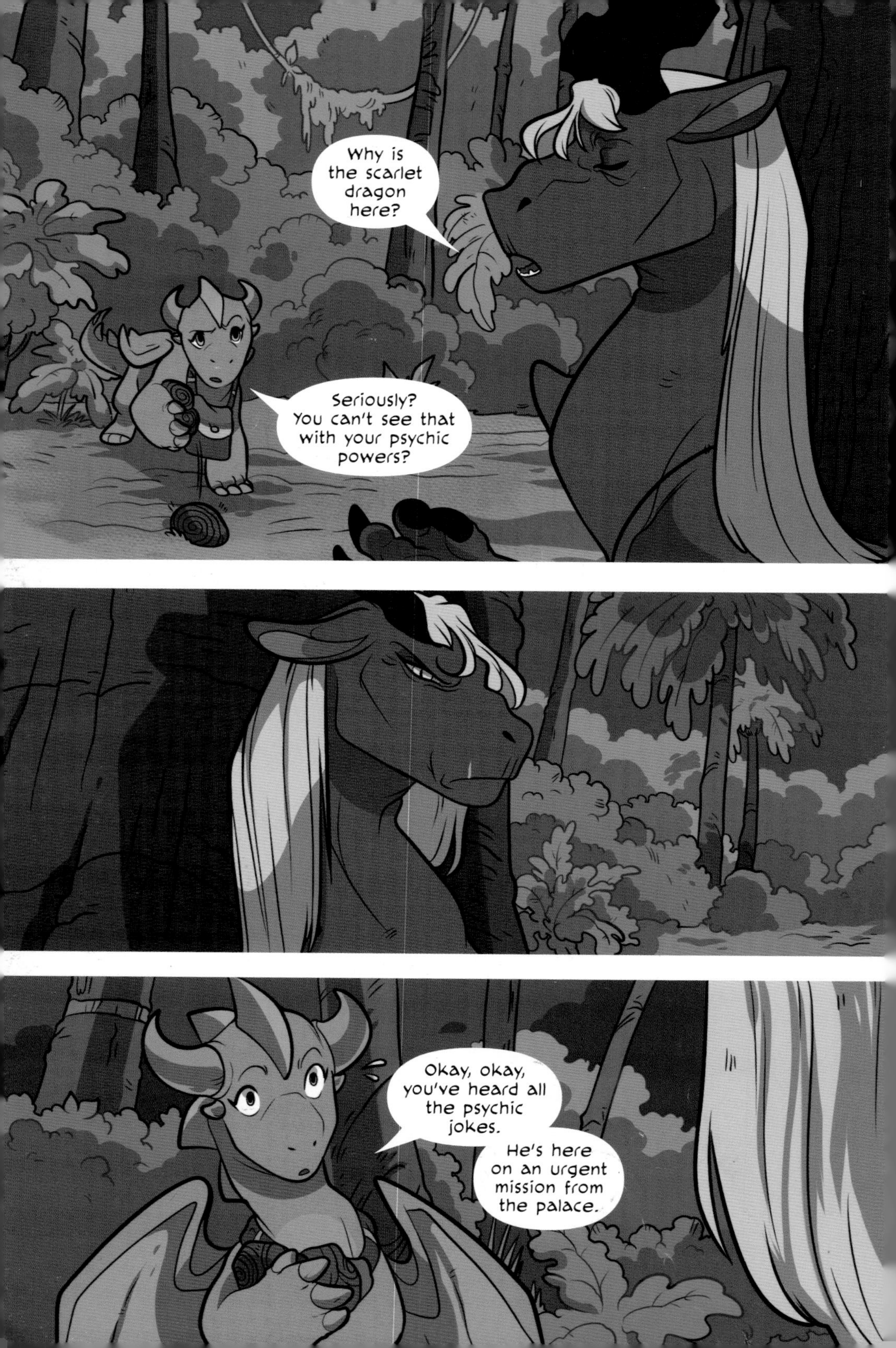
Why is the scarlet dragon here?
Seriously? You can't see that with your psychic powers?
Okay, okay, you've heard all the psychic jokes.
He's here on an urgent mission from the palace.

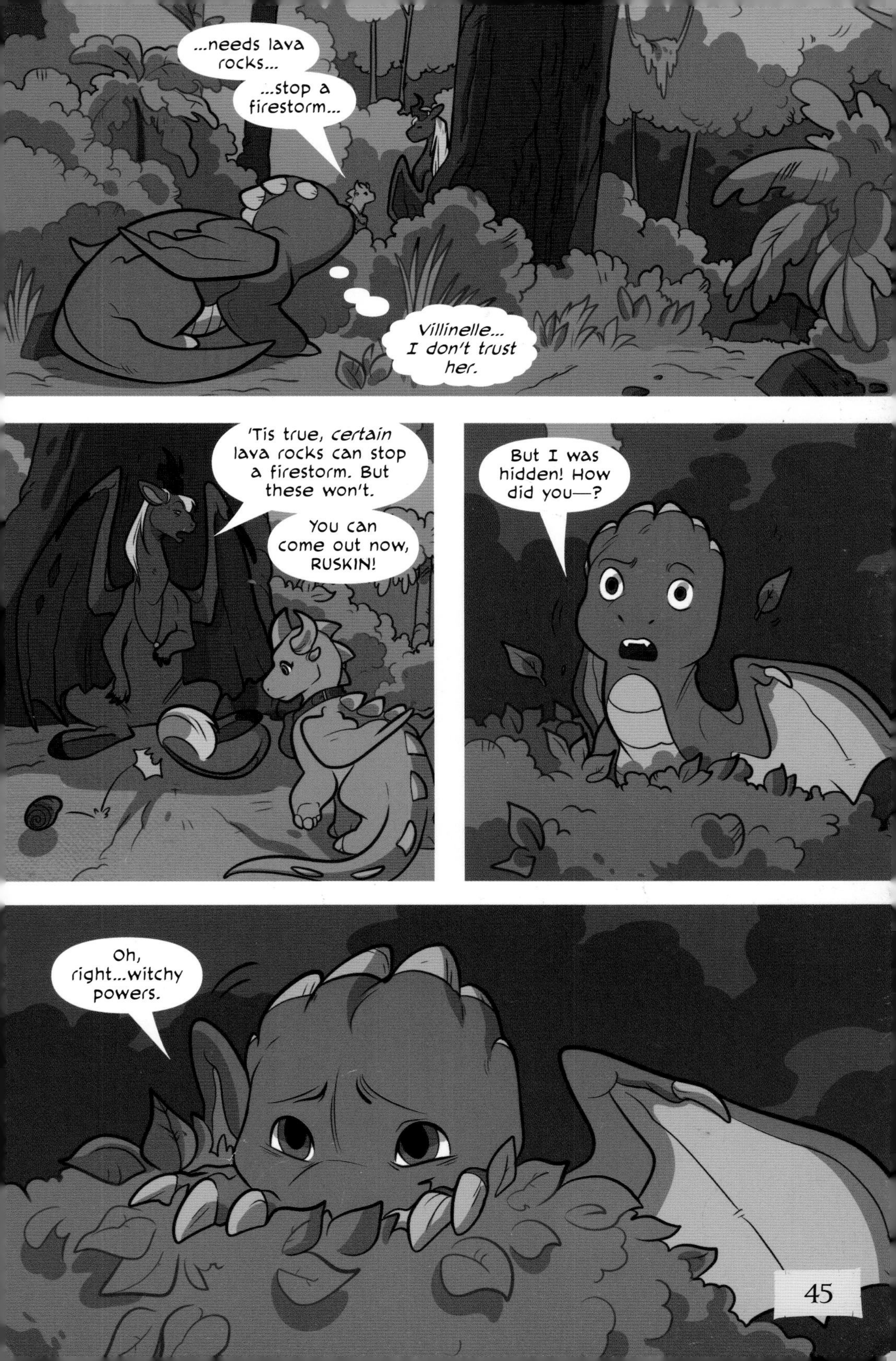
...needs lava rocks...
...stop a firestorm...
Villinelle... I don't trust her.
'Tis true, *certain* lava rocks can stop a firestorm. But these won't.
You can come out now, RUSKIN!
But I was hidden! How did you—?
Oh, right...witchy powers.

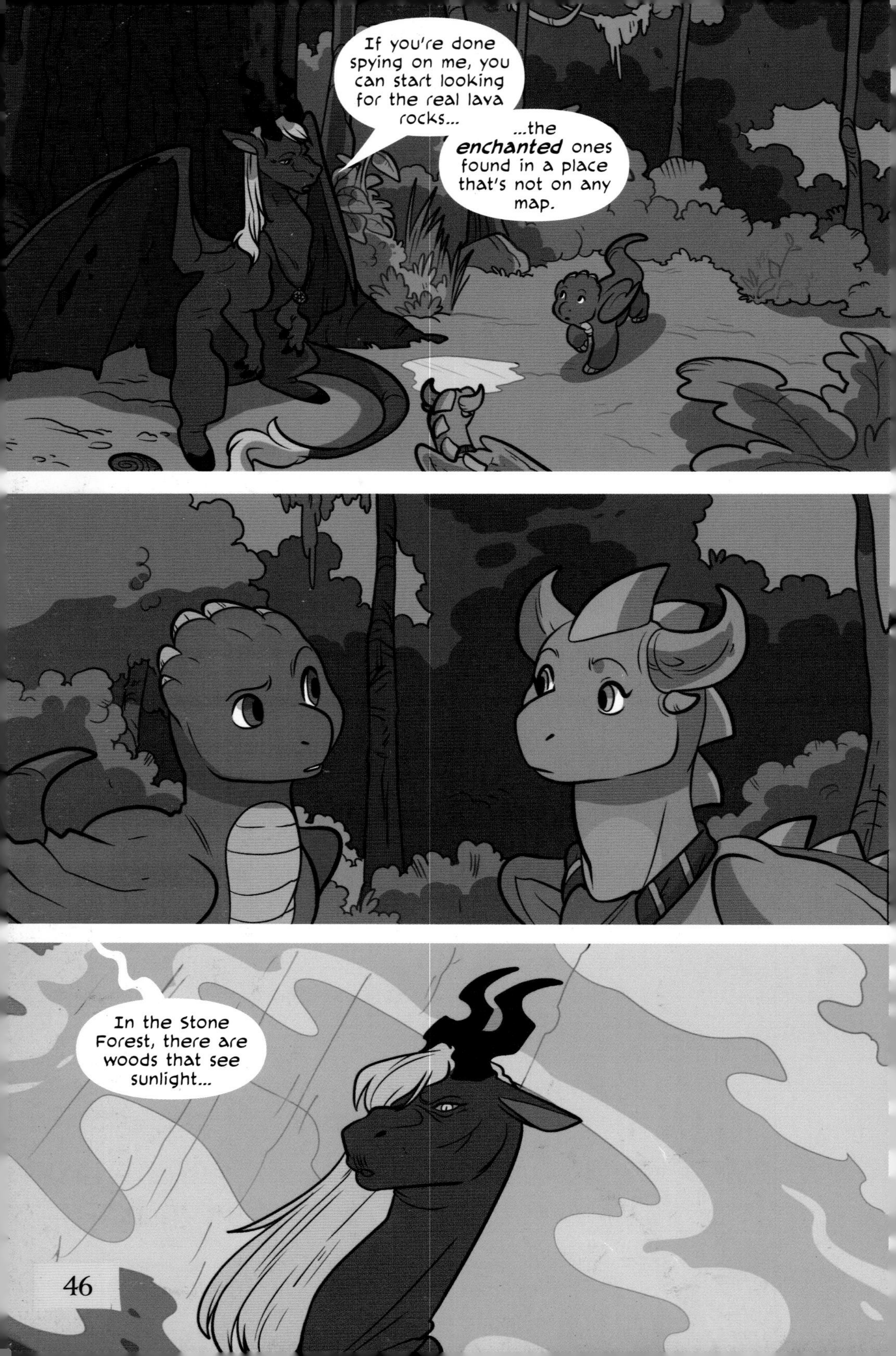
If you're done spying on me, you can start looking for the real lava rocks...
...the *enchanted* ones found in a place that's not on any map.
In the Stone Forest, there are woods that see sunlight...

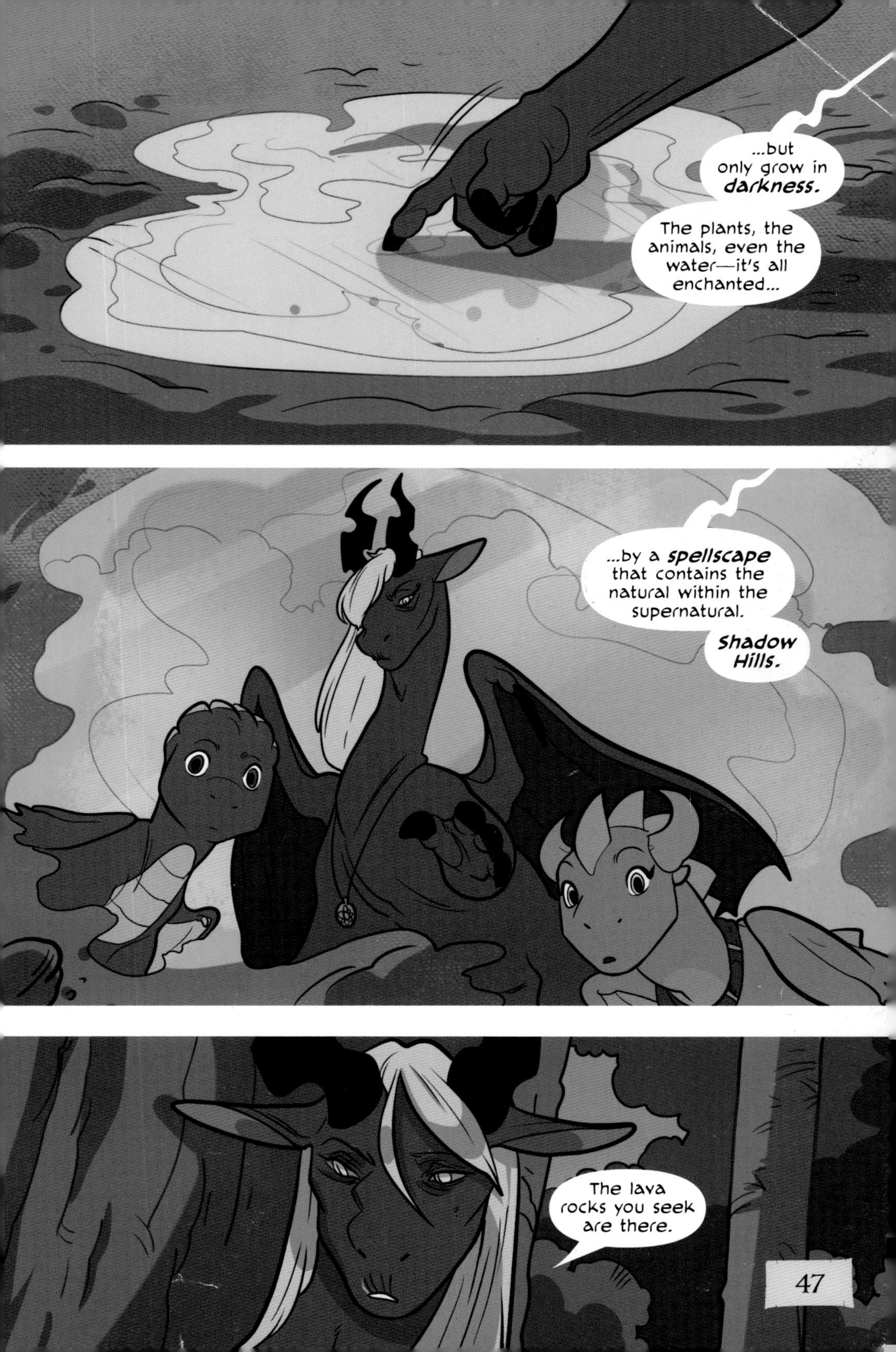
...but only grow in darkness.
The plants, the animals, even the water—it's all enchanted...
...by a spellscape that contains the natural within the supernatural.
Shadow Hills.
The lava rocks you seek are there.

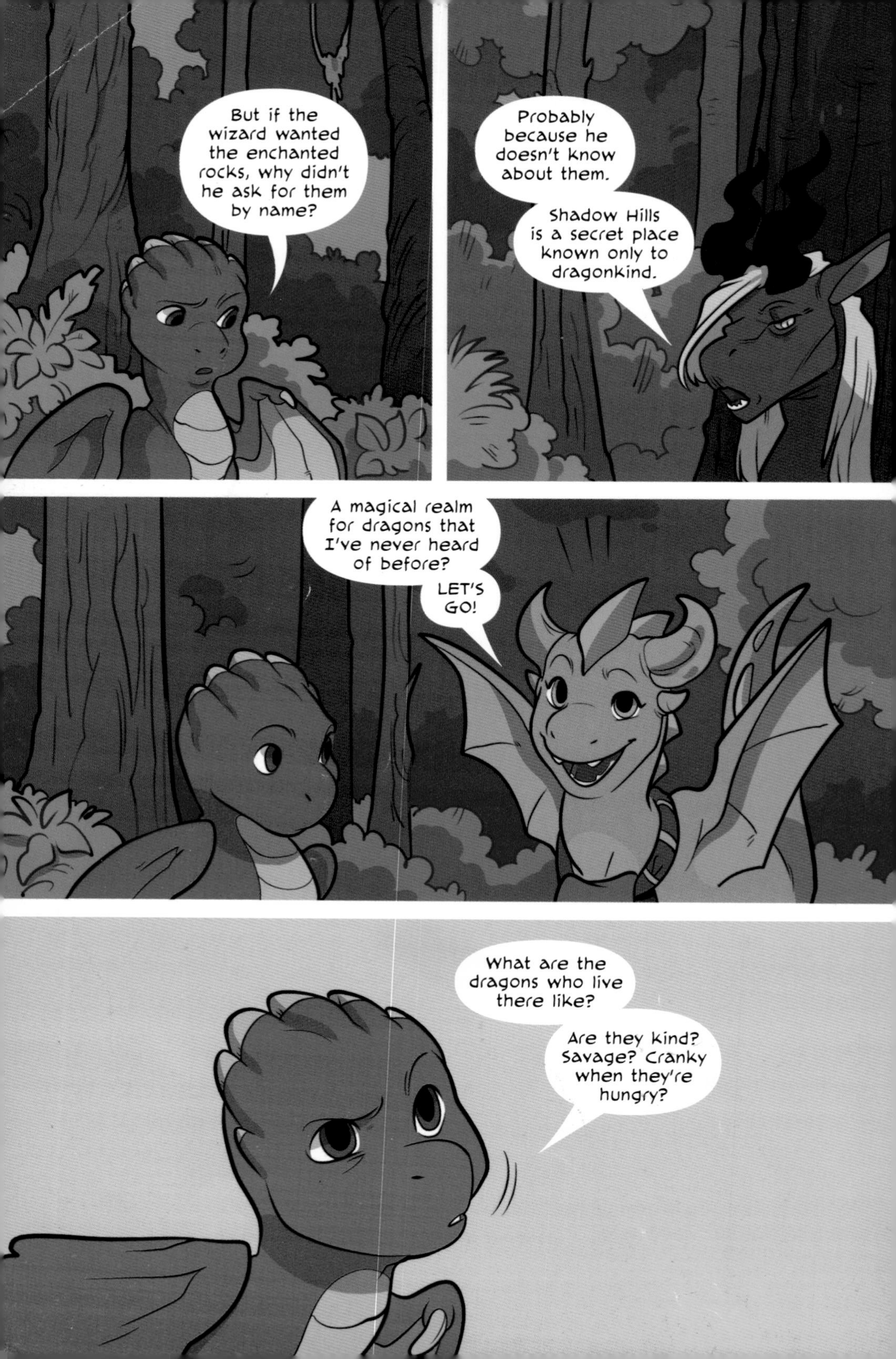
But if the wizard wanted the enchanted rocks, why didn't he ask for them by name?
Probably because he doesn't know about them.
Shadow Hills is a secret place known only to dragonkind.
A magical realm for dragons that I've never heard of before?
LET'S GO!
What are the dragons who live there like?
Are they kind? Savage? Cranky when they're hungry?

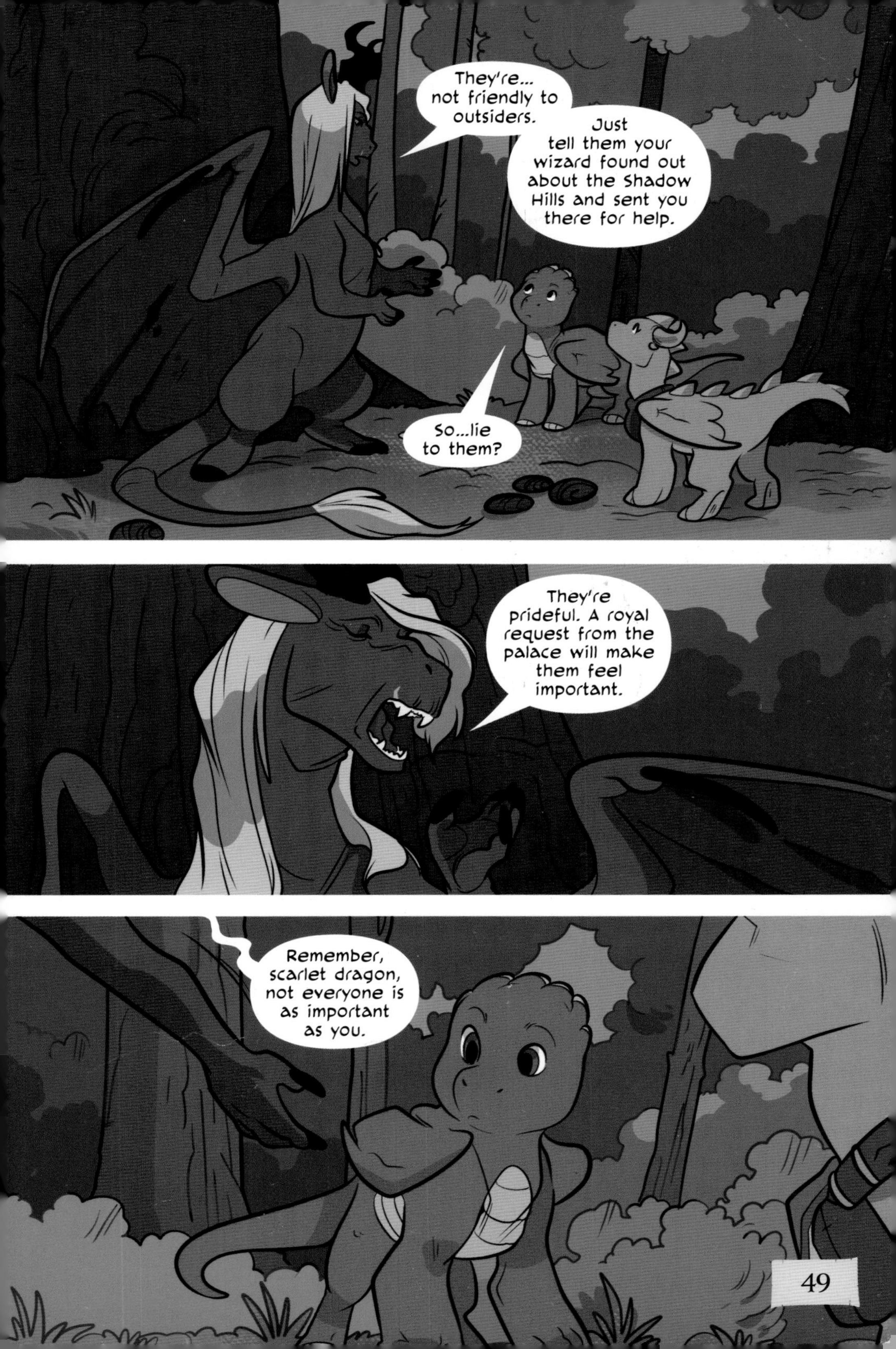
They're... not friendly to outsiders.
Just tell them your wizard found out about the Shadow Hills and sent you there for help.
So...lie to them?
They're prideful. A royal request from the palace will make them feel important.
Remember, scarlet dragon, not everyone is as important as you.

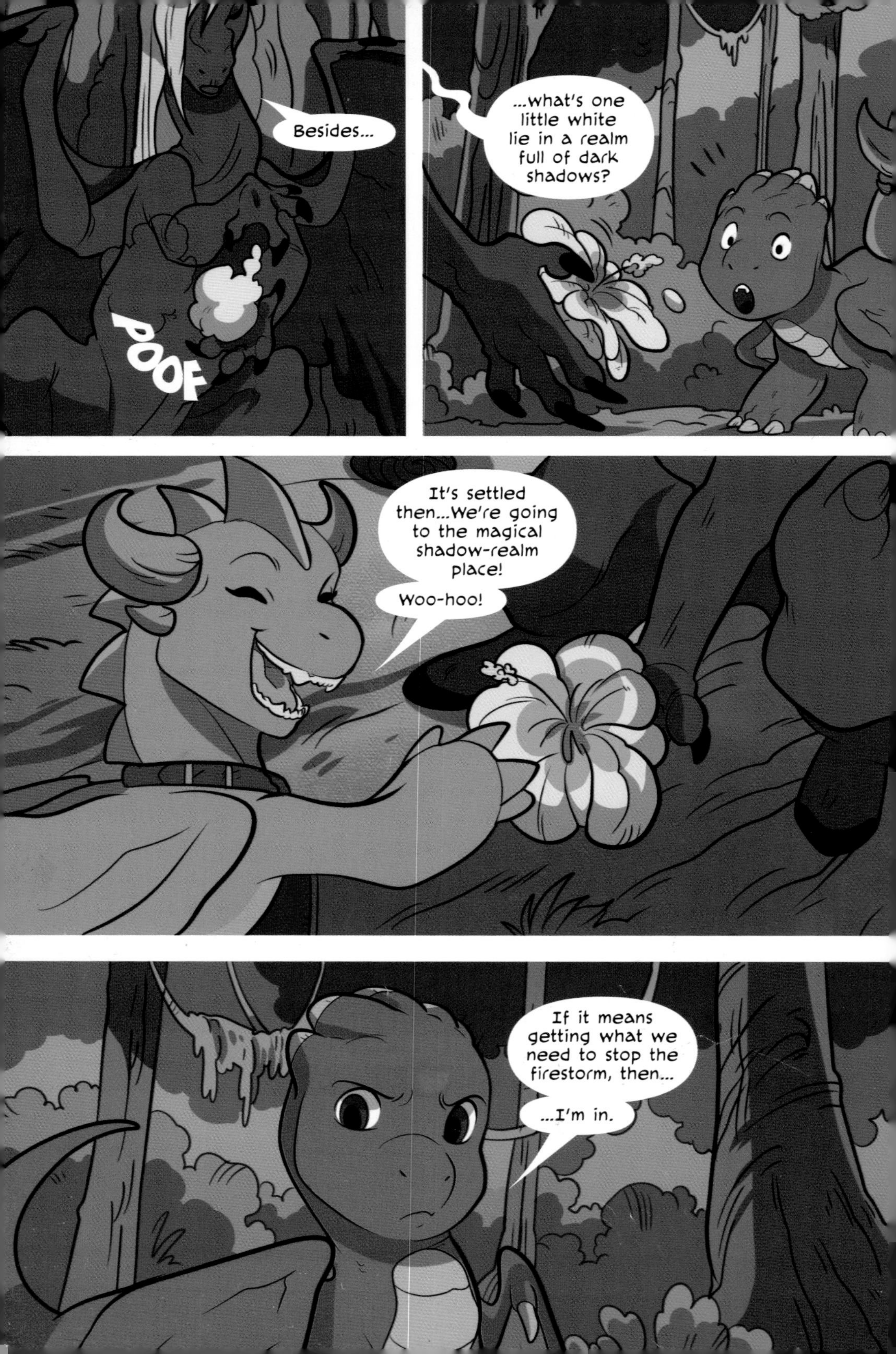
Besides...
POOF
...what's one little white lie in a realm full of dark shadows?
It's settled then...We're going to the magical shadow-realm place!
Woo-hoo!
If it means getting what we need to stop the firestorm, then...
...I'm in.

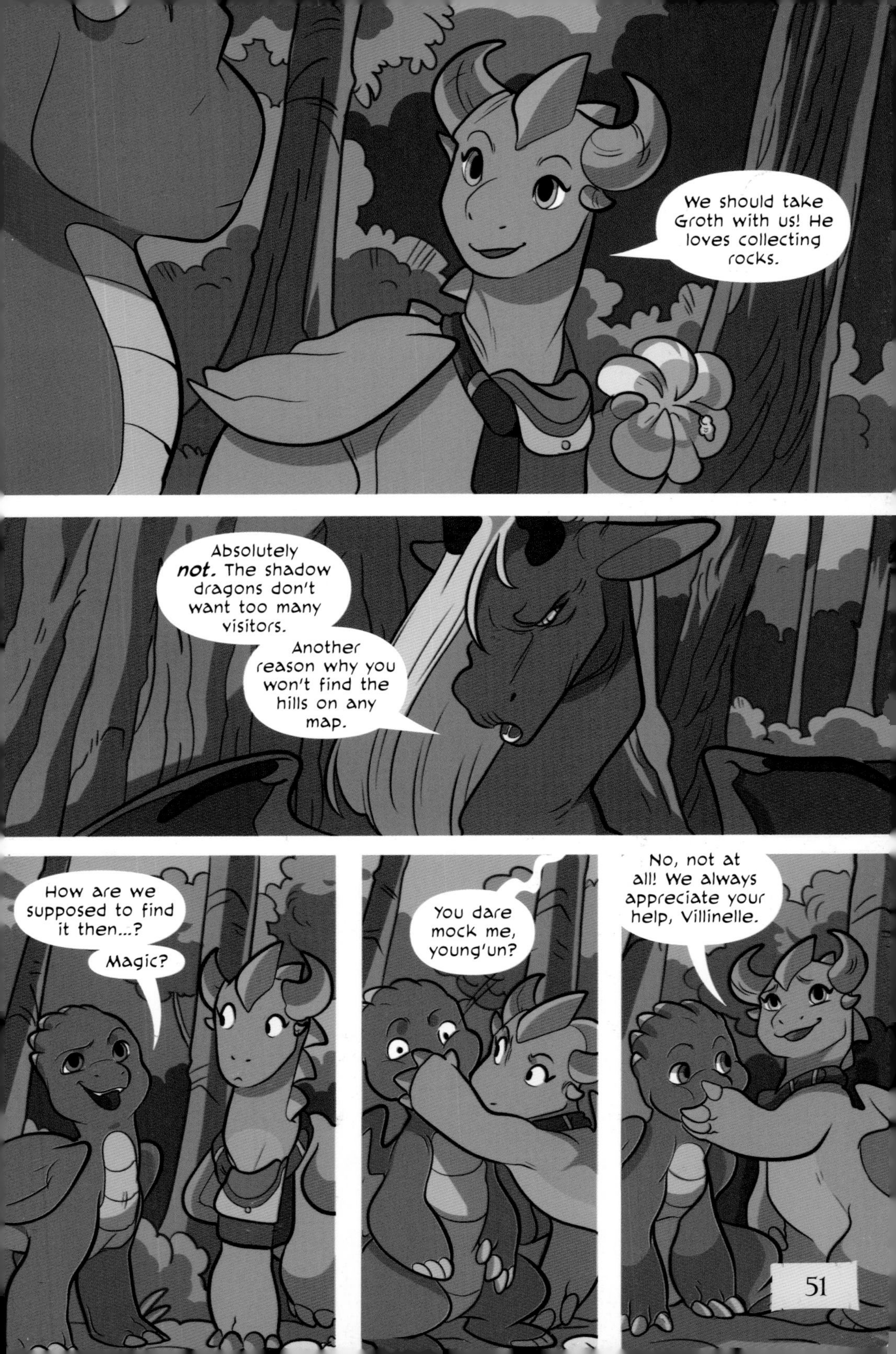
We should take Groth with us! He loves collecting rocks.
Absolutely **not.** The shadow dragons don't want too many visitors.
Another reason why you won't find the hills on any map.
How are we supposed to find it then...?
Magic?
You dare mock me, young'un?
No, not at all! We always appreciate your help, Villinelle.

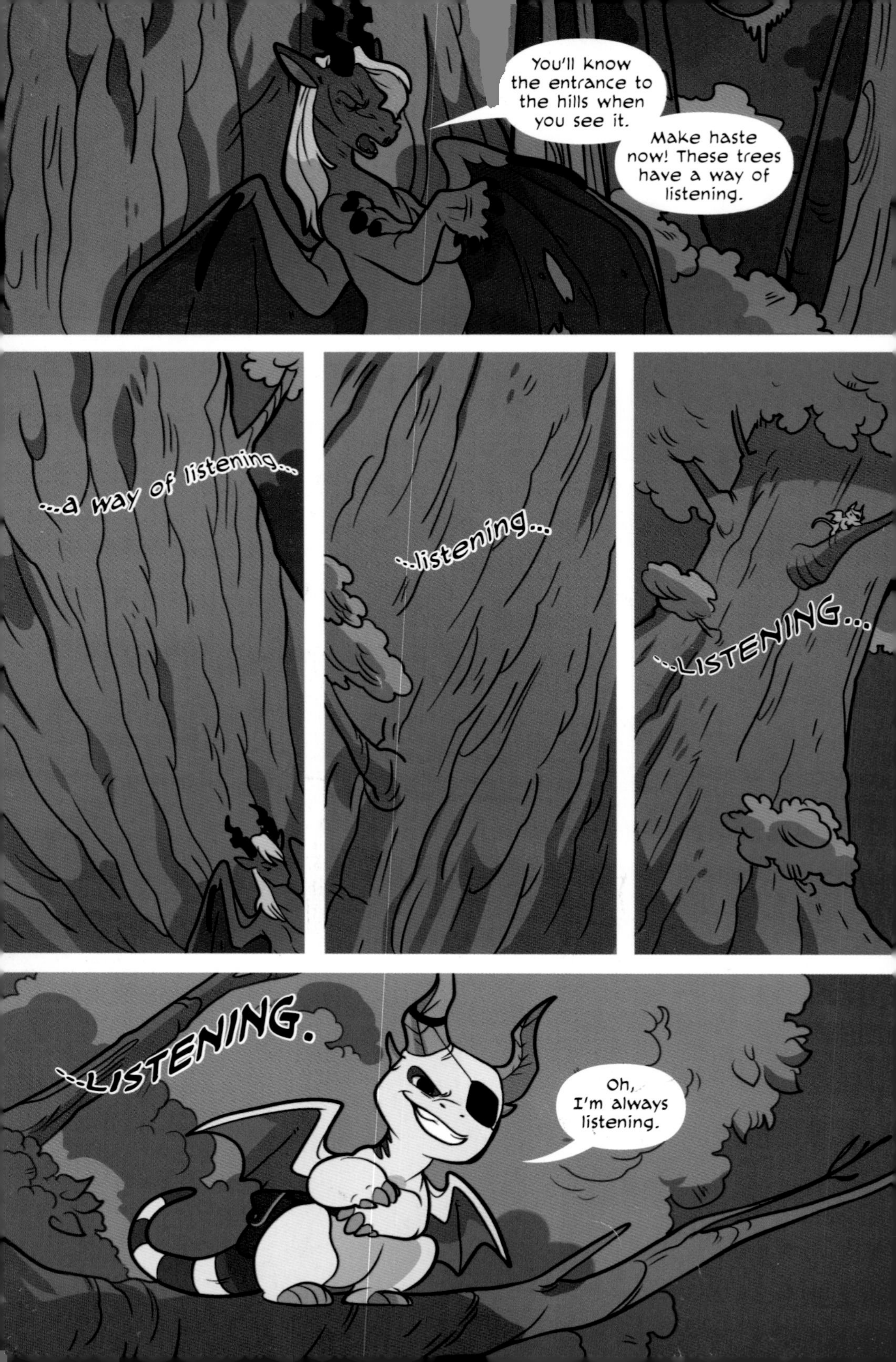

You'll know the entrance to the hills when you see it.
Make haste now! These trees have a way of listening.
...a way of listening...
...listening...
...LISTENING...
...LISTENING.
Oh, I'm always listening.

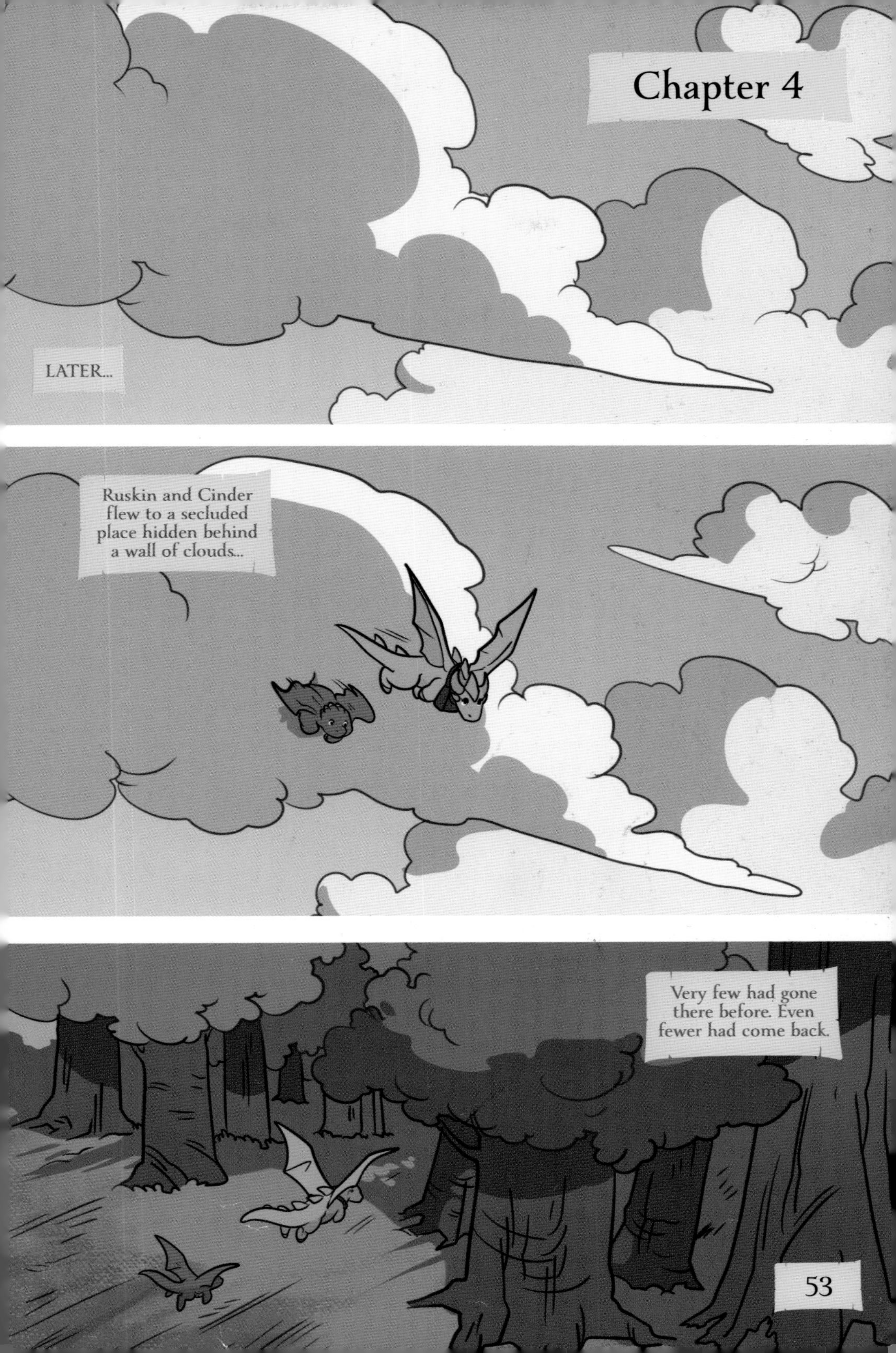
Chapter 4
LATER...
Ruskin and Cinder flew to a secluded place hidden behind a wall of clouds...
Very few had gone there before. Even fewer had come back.

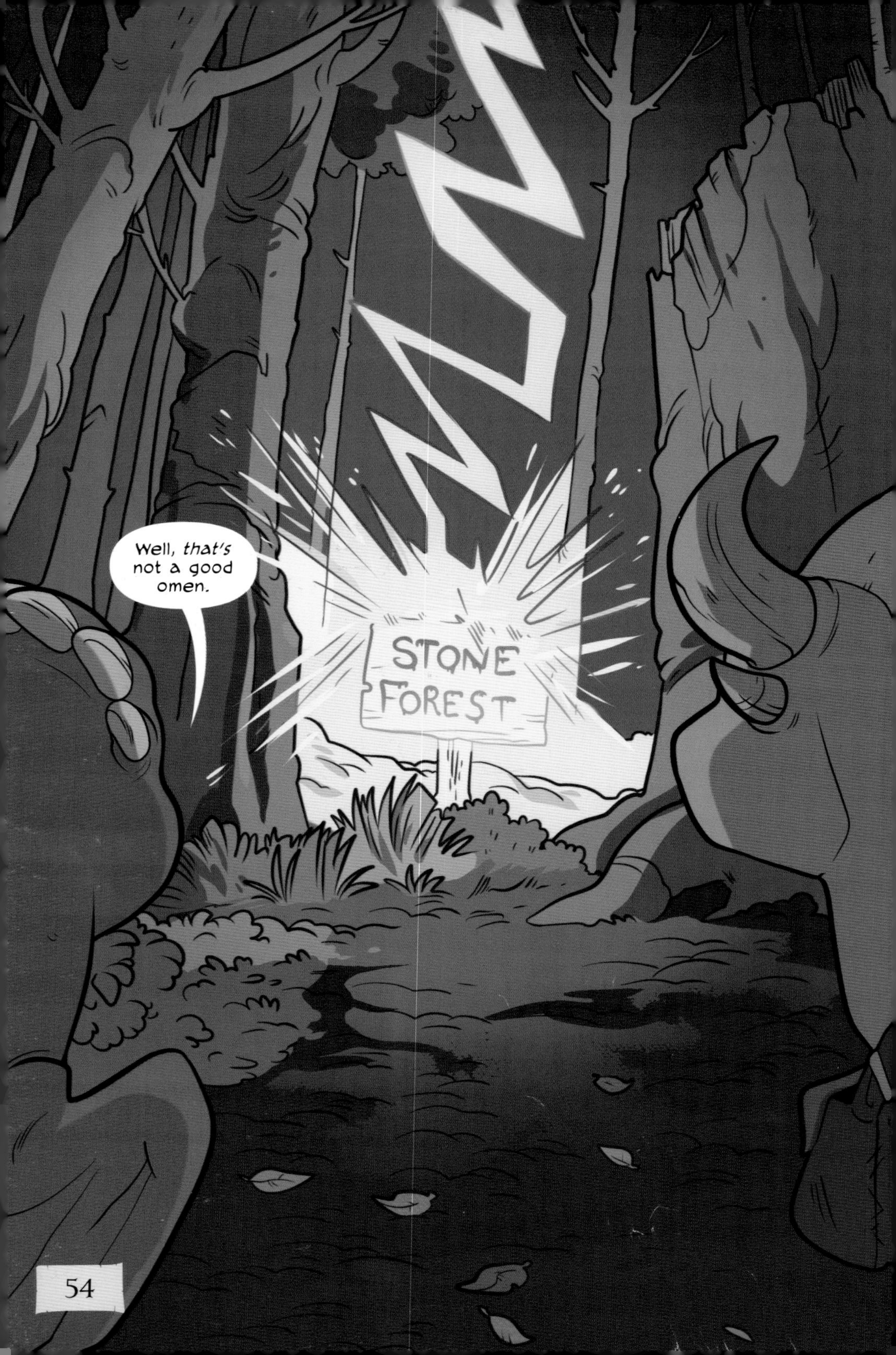
Well, *that's* not a good omen.
STONE FOREST

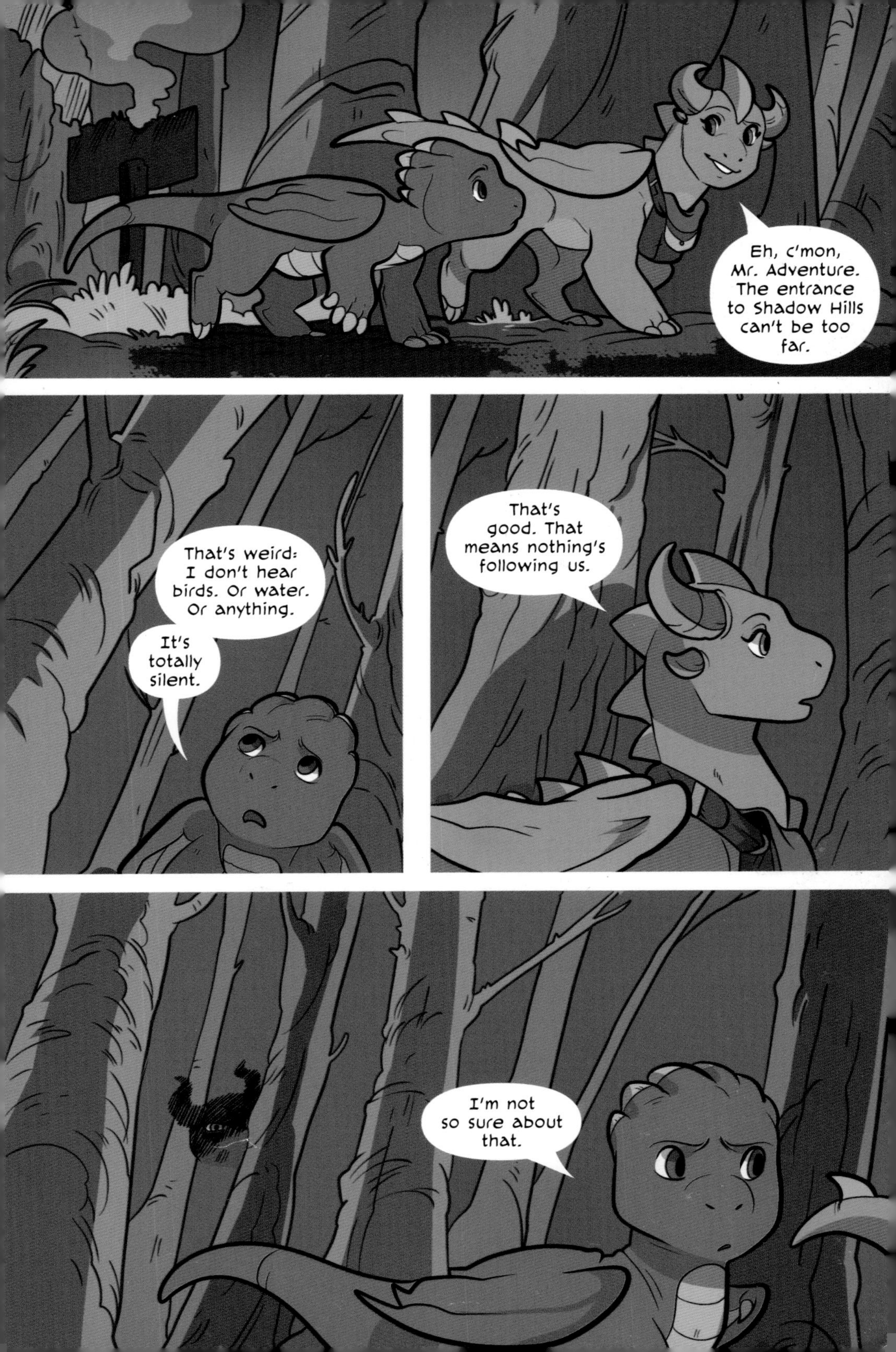
Eh, c'mon, Mr. Adventure. The entrance to Shadow Hills can't be too far.
That's weird: I don't hear birds. Or water. Or anything.
It's totally silent.
That's good. That means nothing's following us.
I'm not so sure about that.

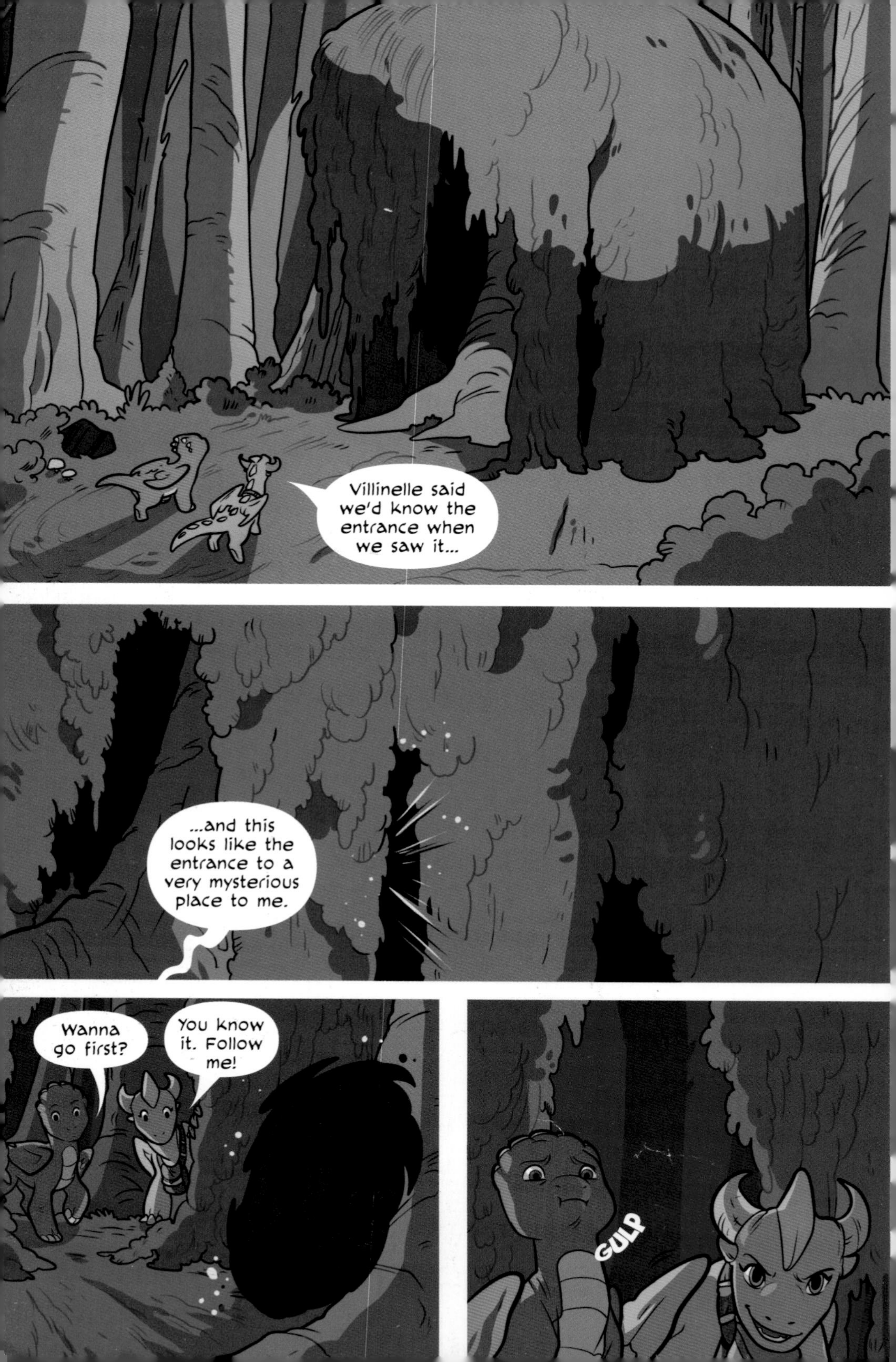
Villinelle said we'd know the entrance when we saw it...
...and this looks like the entrance to a very mysterious place to me.
Wanna go first?
You know it. Follow me!
GULP

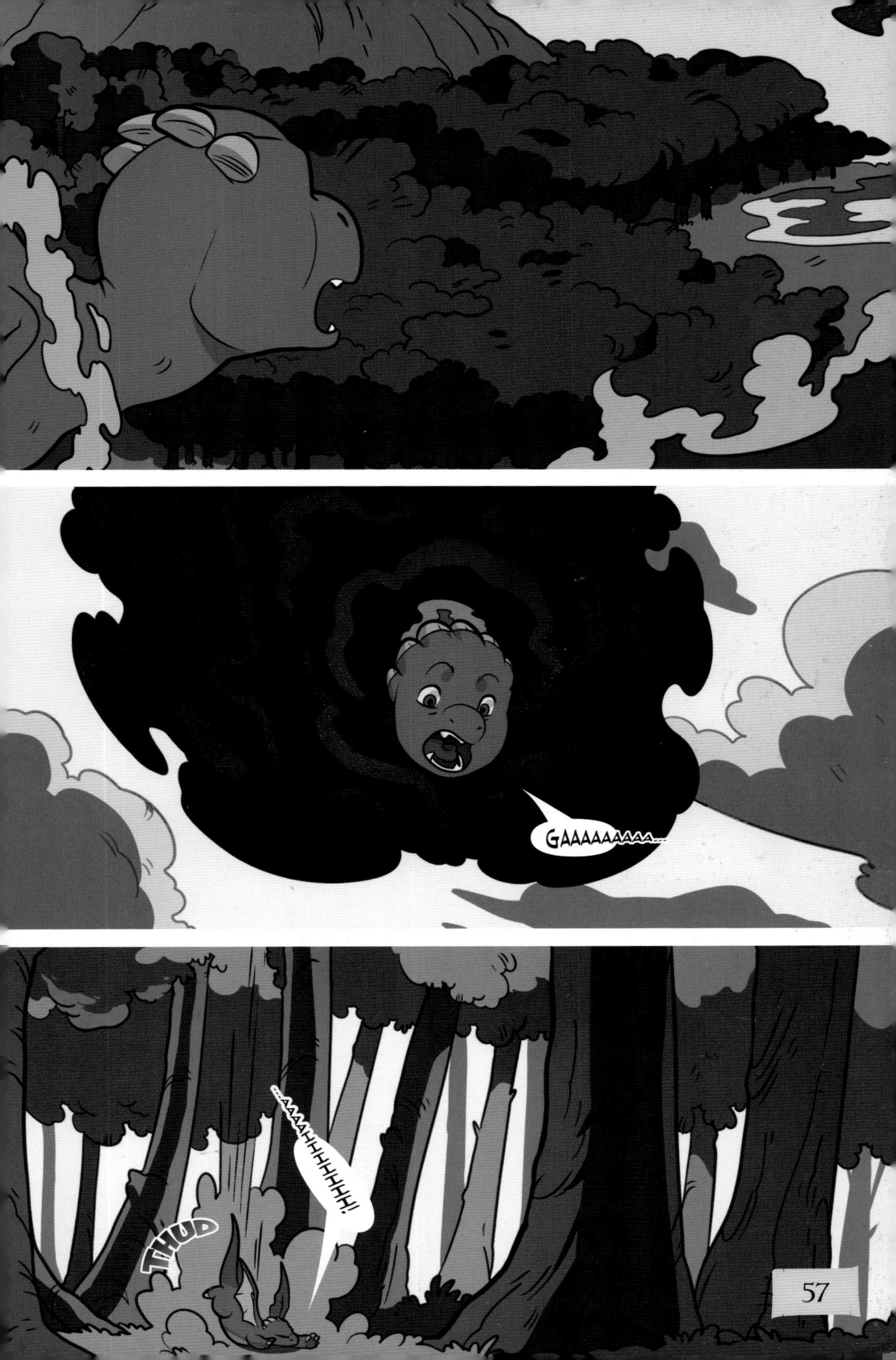
GAAAAAAAAA...
...AAAAIIIIIIIH!
THUD

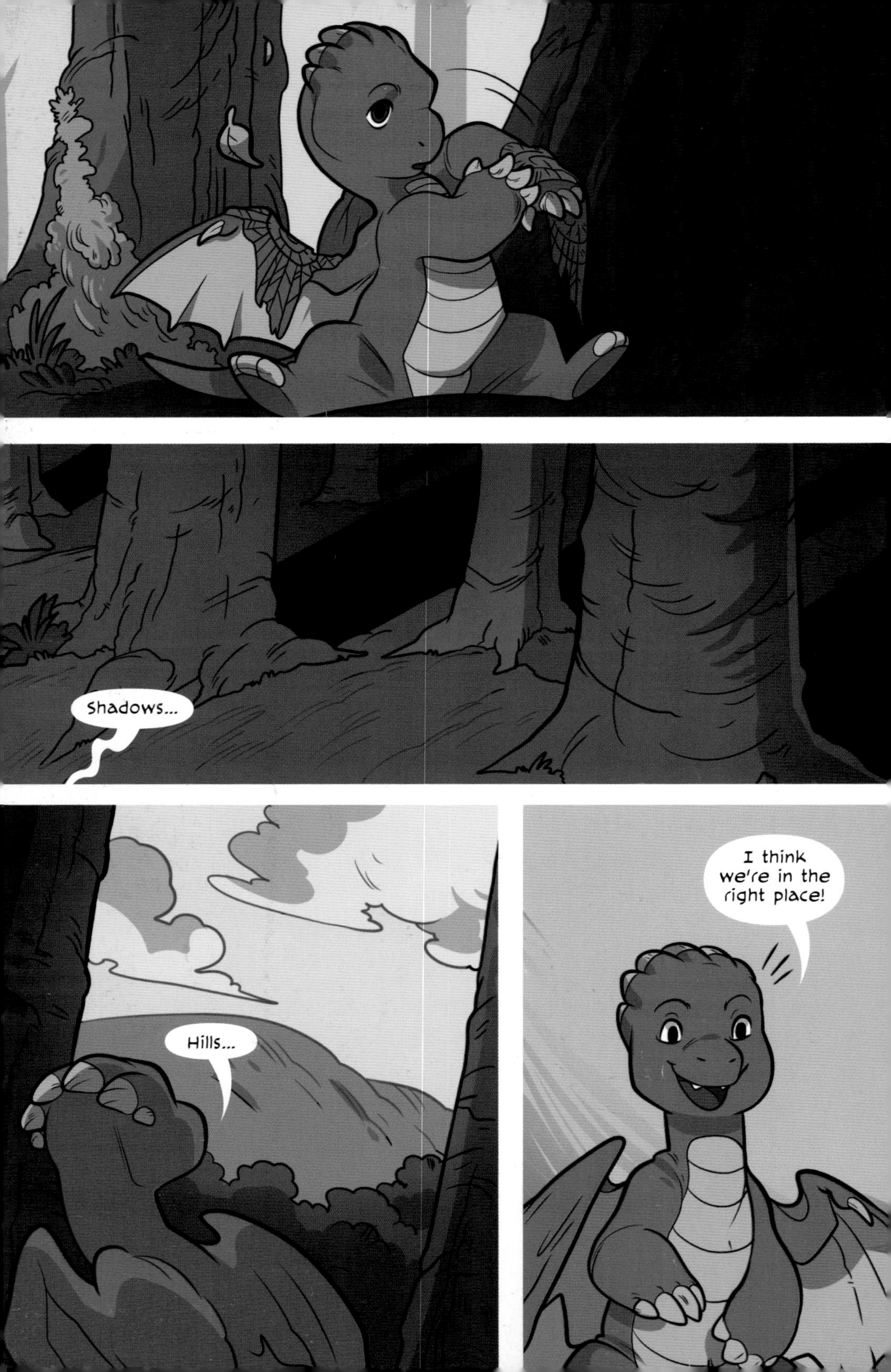
Shadows...
Hills...
I think we're in the right place!

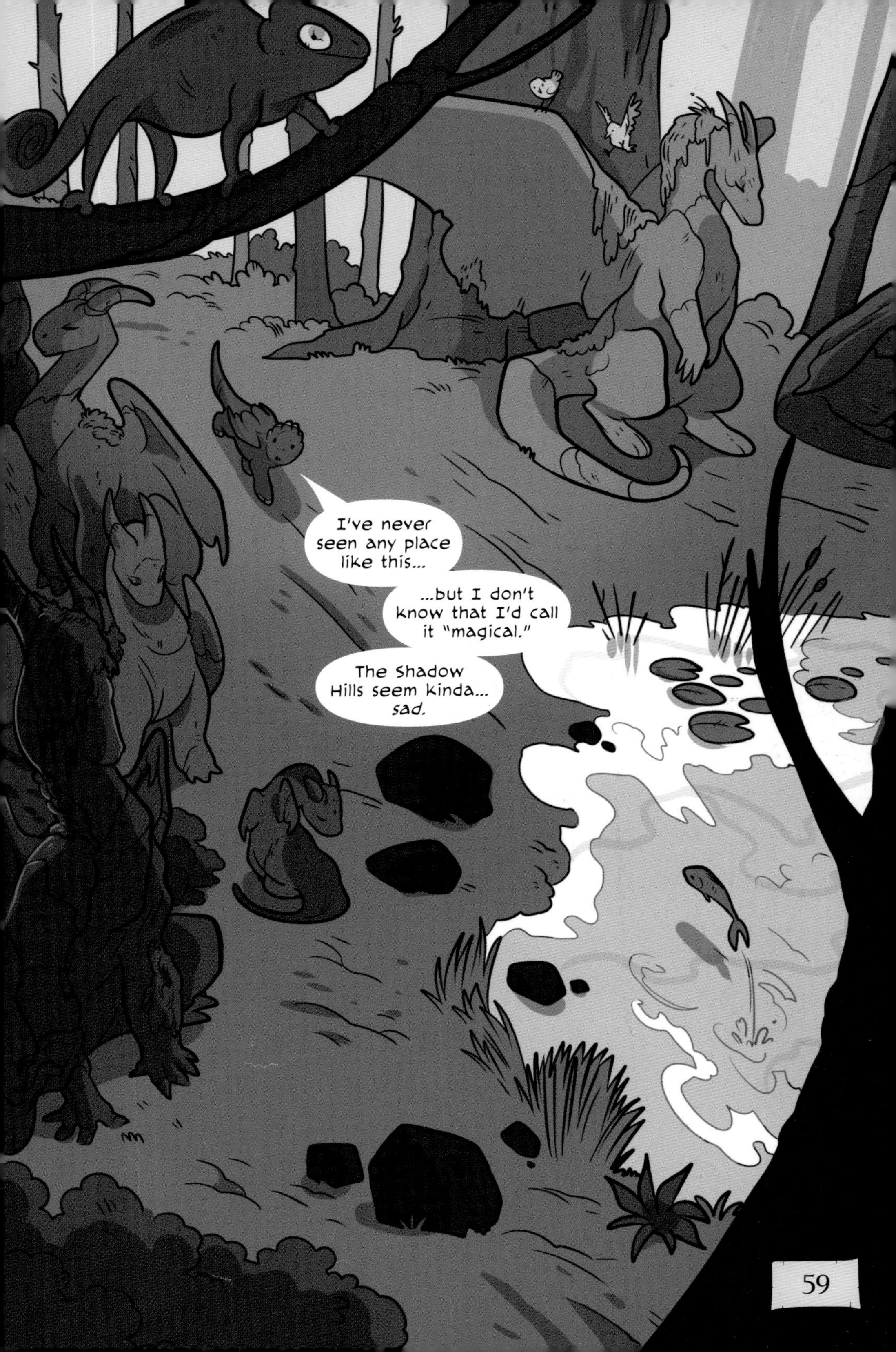
I've never seen any place like this...
...but I don't know that I'd call it "magical."
The Shadow Hills seem kinda... sad.

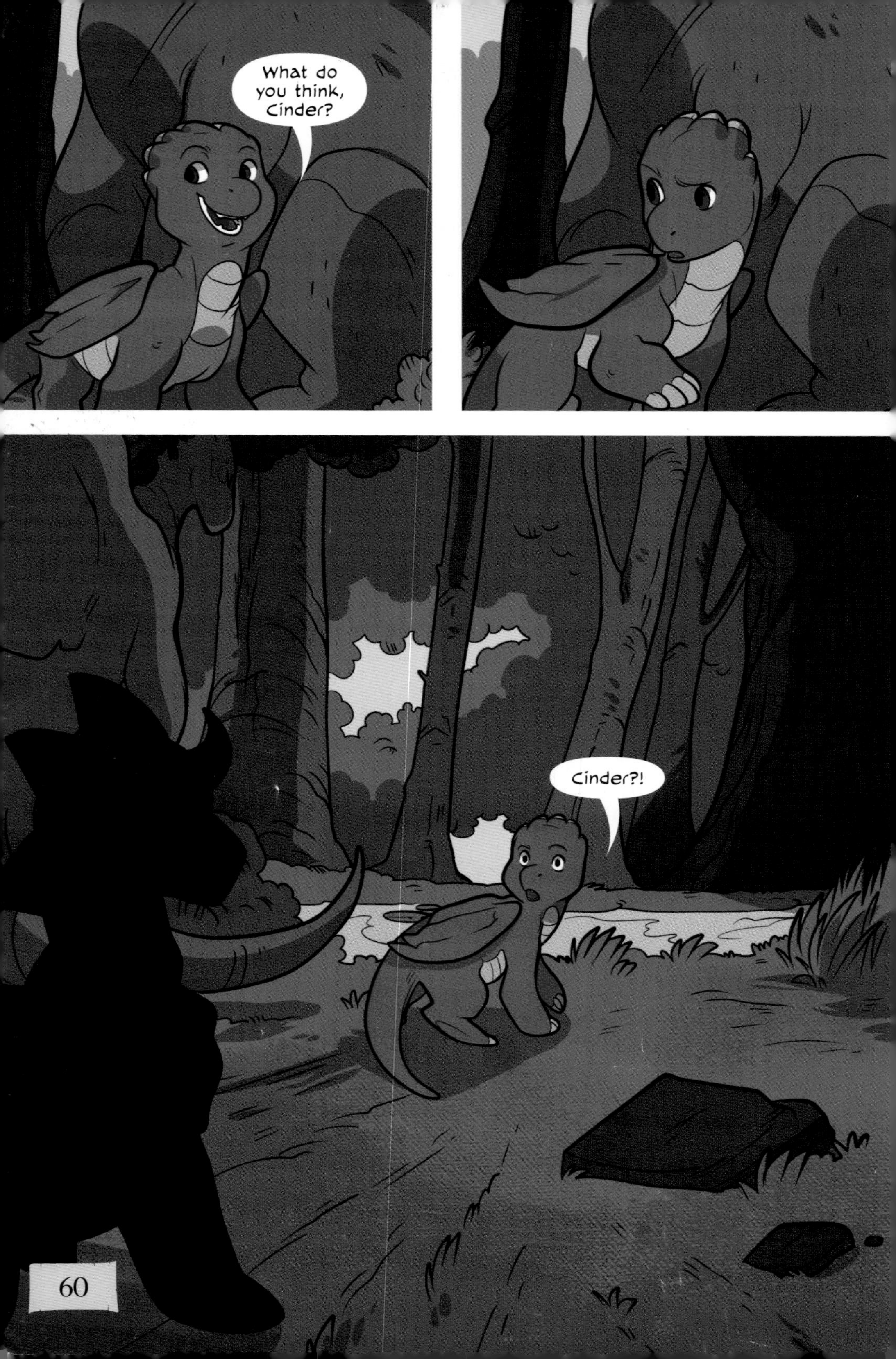
What do you think, Cinder?
Cinder?!

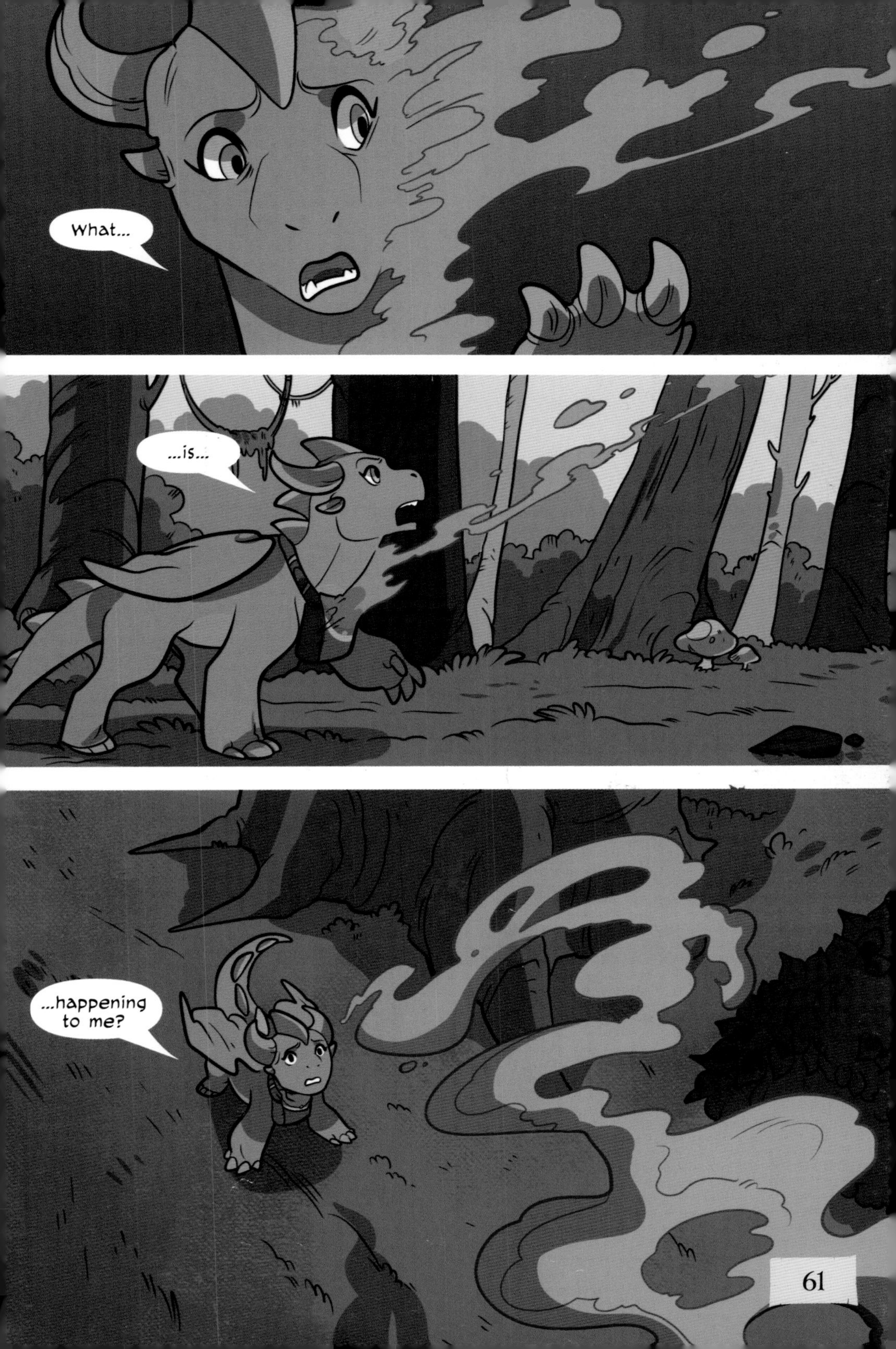
What...
...is...
...happening to me?

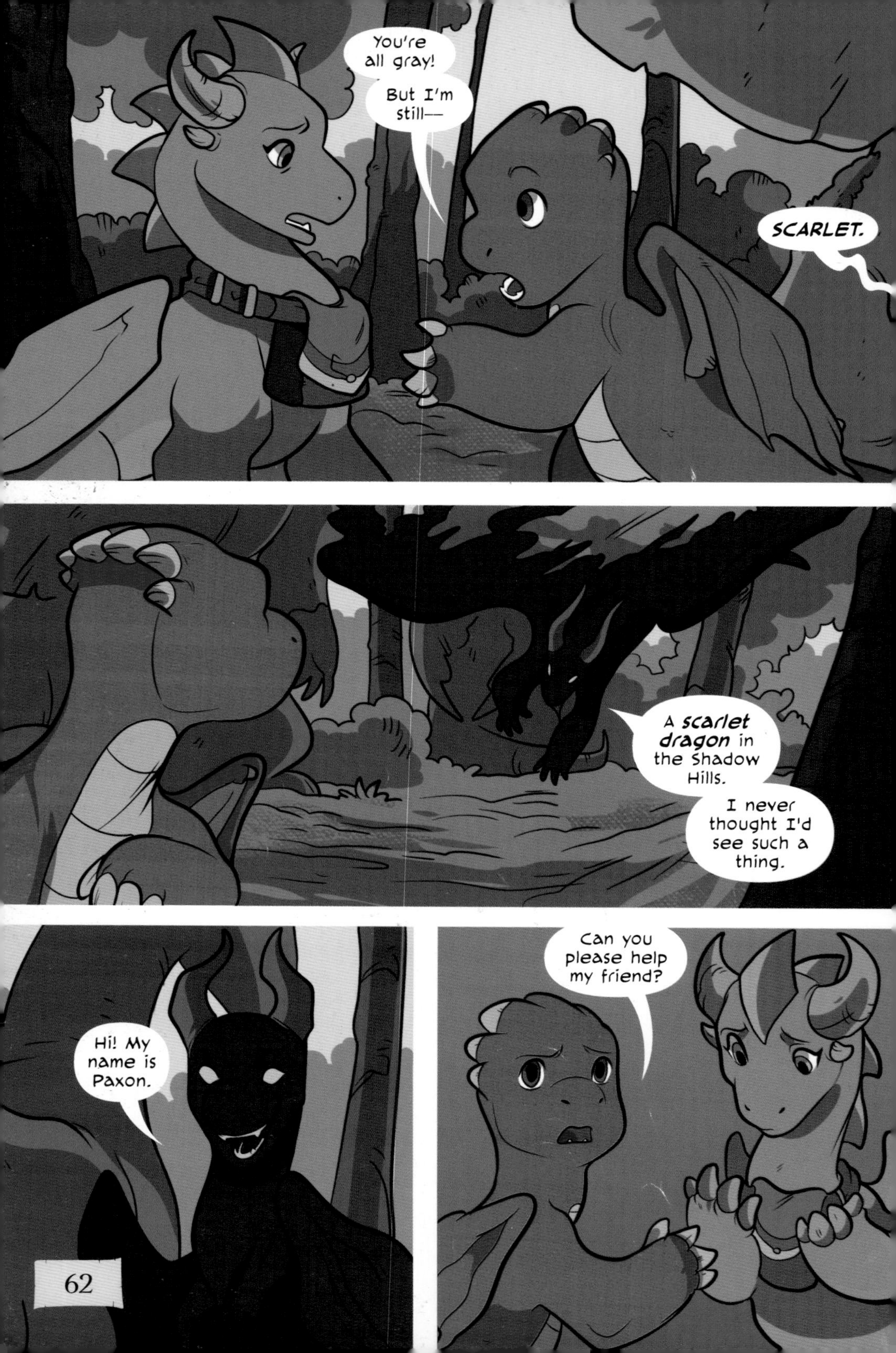
You're all gray!
But I'm still—
SCARLET.
A *scarlet dragon* in the Shadow Hills.
I never thought I'd see such a thing.
Hi! My name is Paxon.
Can you please help my friend?

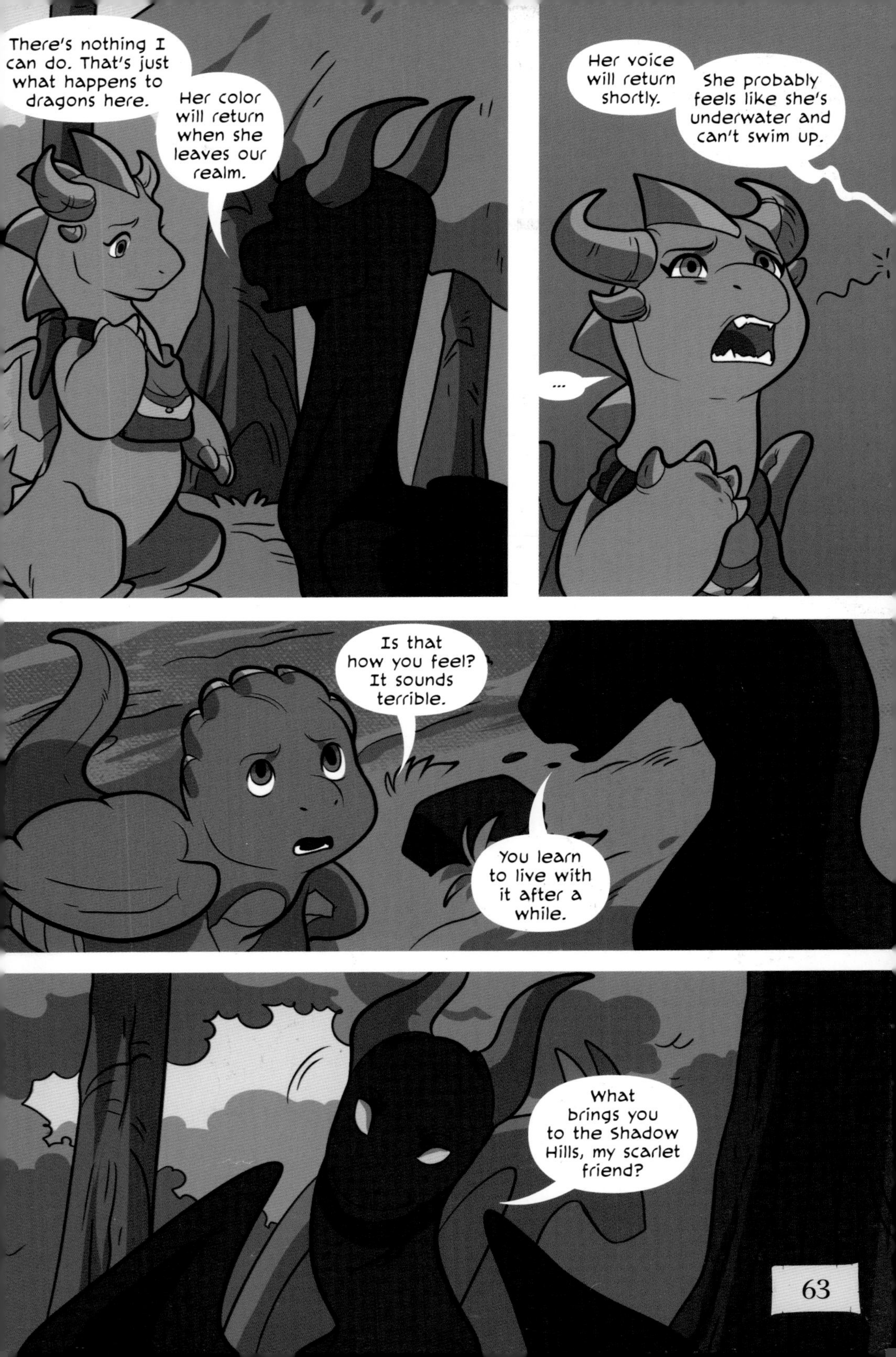
There's nothing I can do. That's just what happens to dragons here.
Her color will return when she leaves our realm.
Her voice will return shortly.
She probably feels like she's underwater and can't swim up.
...
Is that how you feel? It sounds terrible.
You learn to live with it after a while.
What brings you to the Shadow Hills, my scarlet friend?

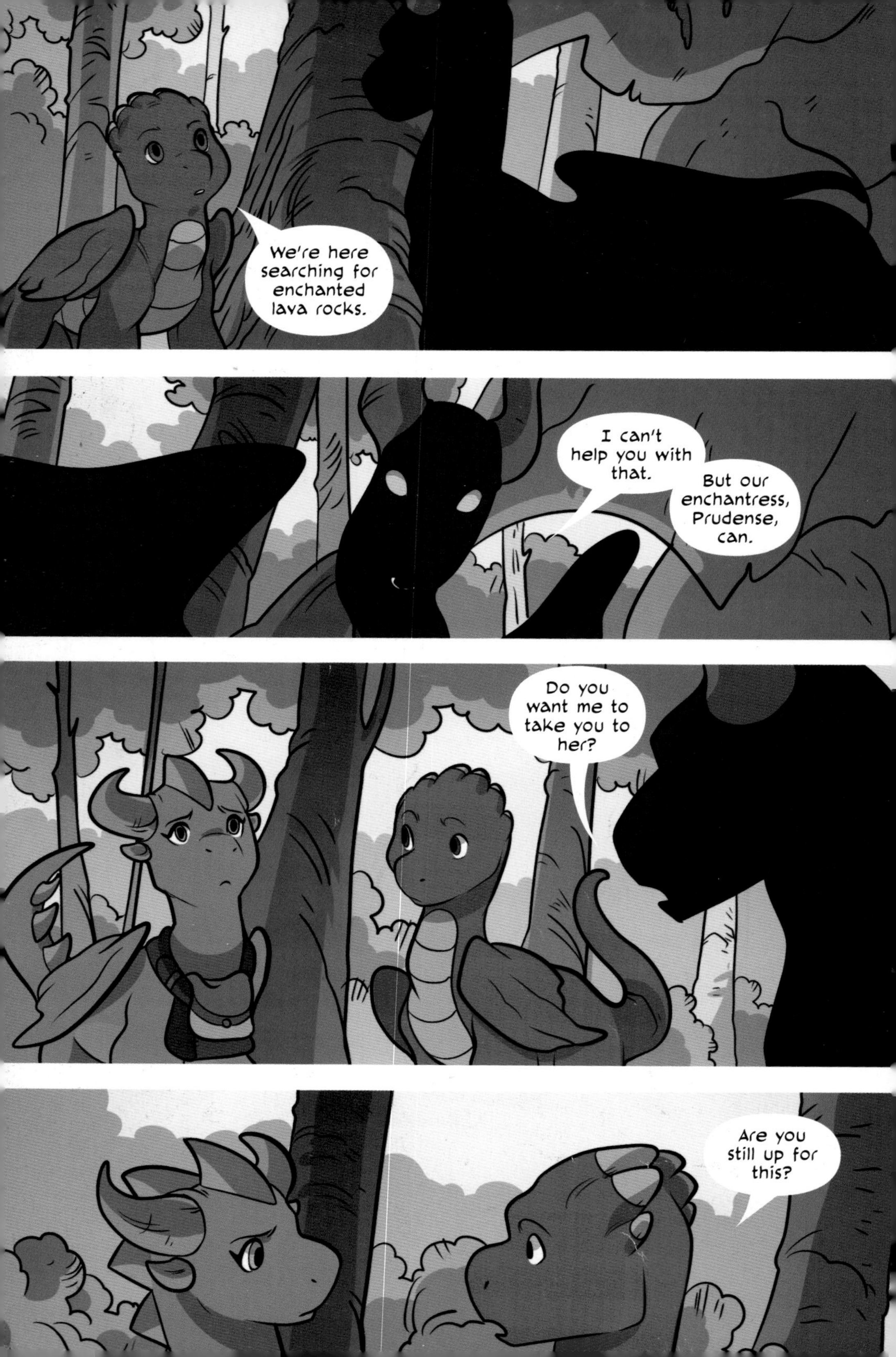
We're here searching for enchanted lava rocks.
I can't help you with that.
But our enchantress, Prudense, can.
Do you want me to take you to her?
Are you still up for this?

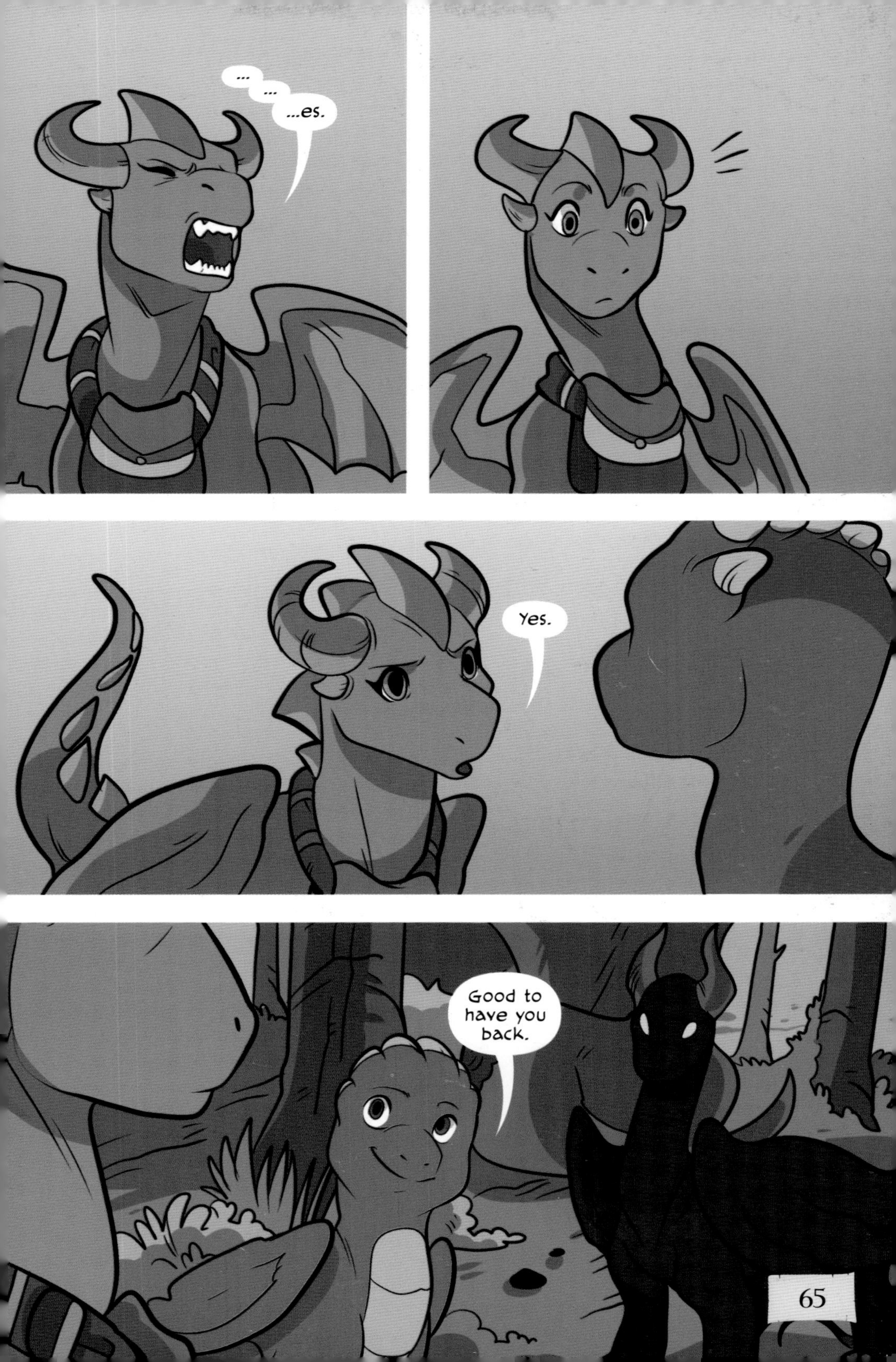
...
...
...es.
Yes.
Good to have you back.

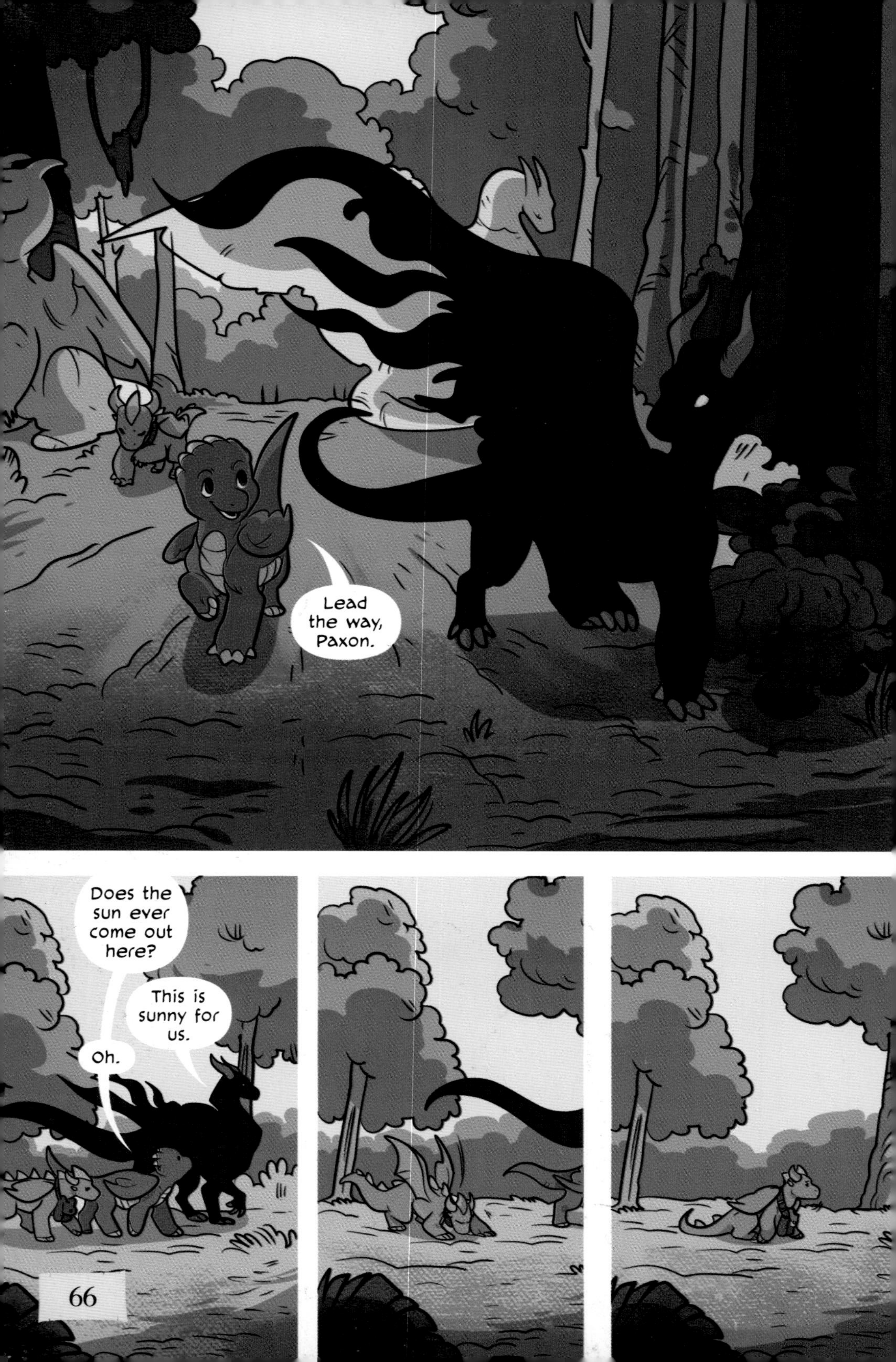
Lead the way, Paxon.
Does the sun ever come out here?
This is sunny for us.
Oh.

Chapter 5

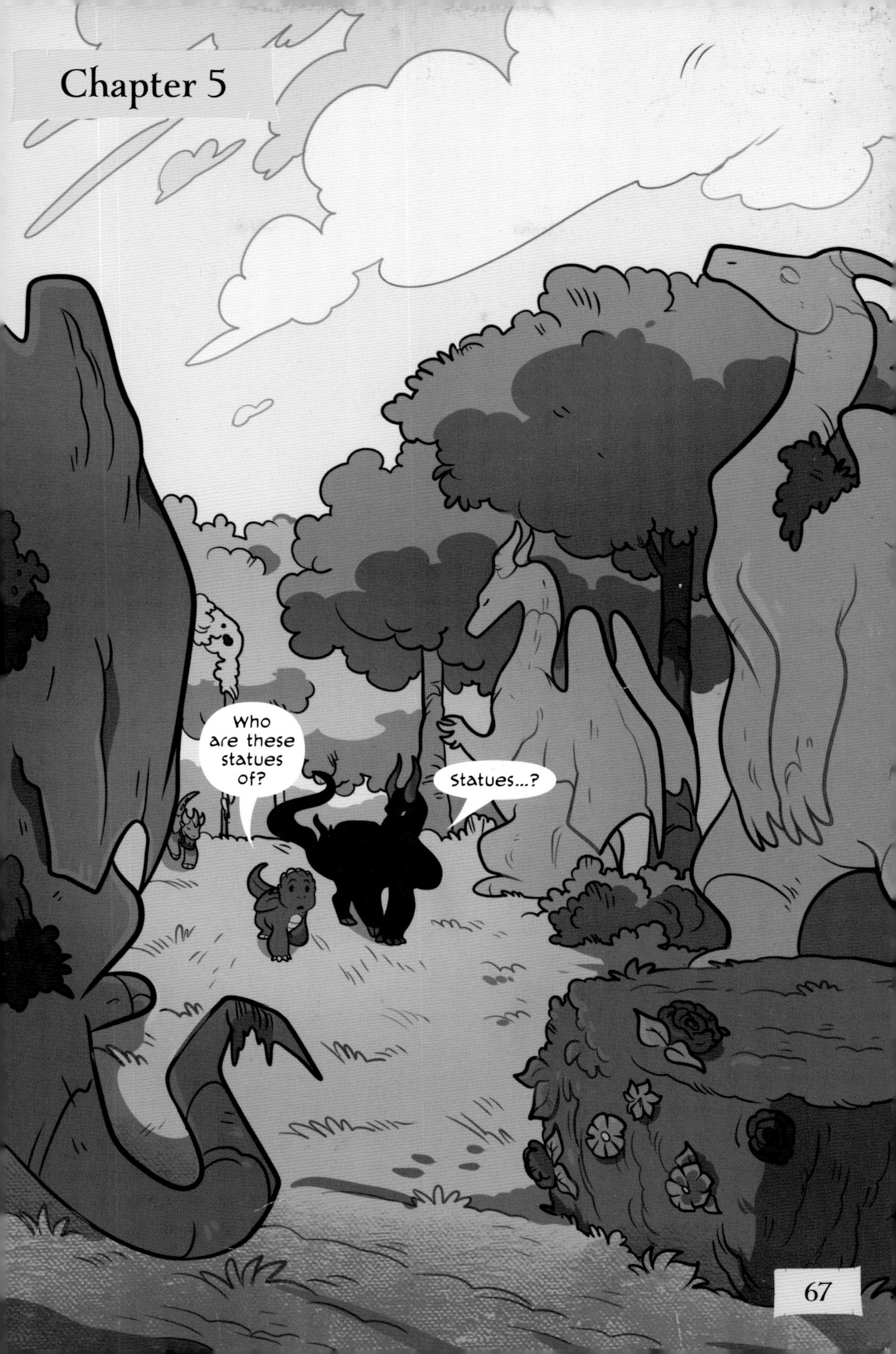
Who are these statues of?
Statues...?

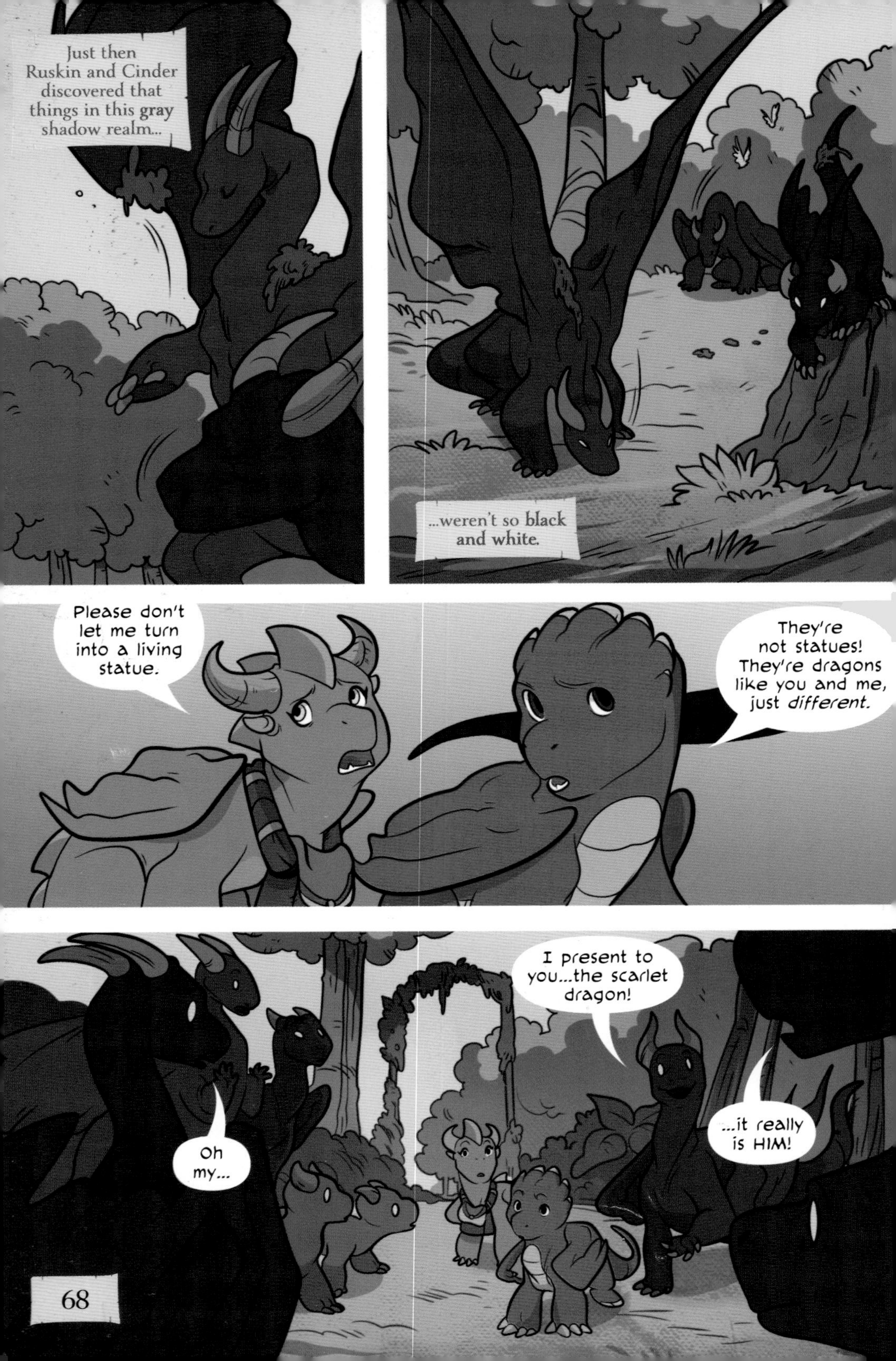
Just then Ruskin and Cinder discovered that things in this gray shadow realm...
...weren't so black and white.
Please don't let me turn into a living statue.
They're not statues! They're dragons like you and me, just *different.*
I present to you...the scarlet dragon!
Oh my...
...it really is HIM!

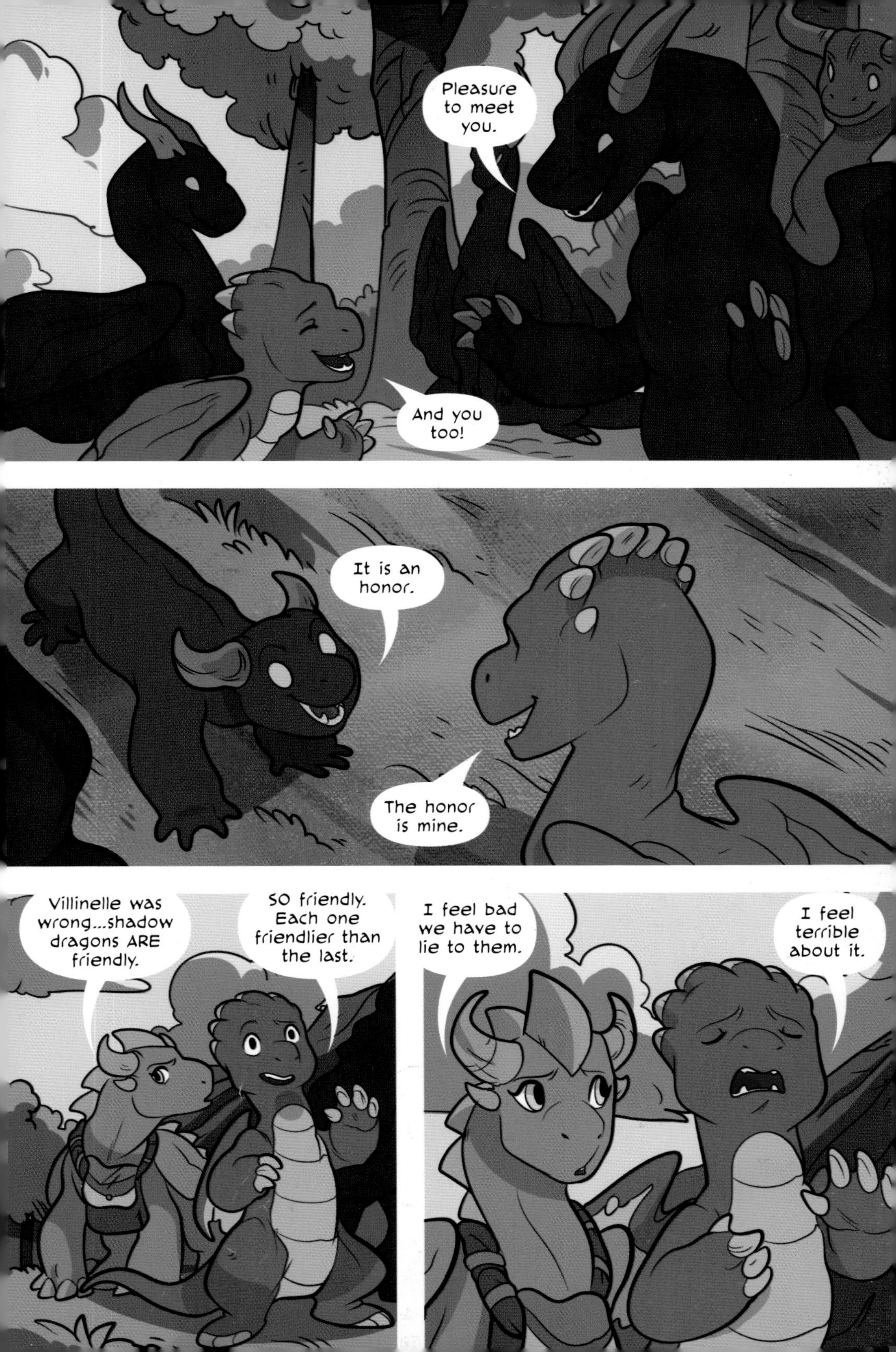
Pleasure to meet you.
And you too!
It is an honor.
The honor is mine.
Villinelle was wrong...shadow dragons ARE friendly.
SO friendly. Each one friendlier than the last.
I feel bad we have to lie to them.
I feel terrible about it.

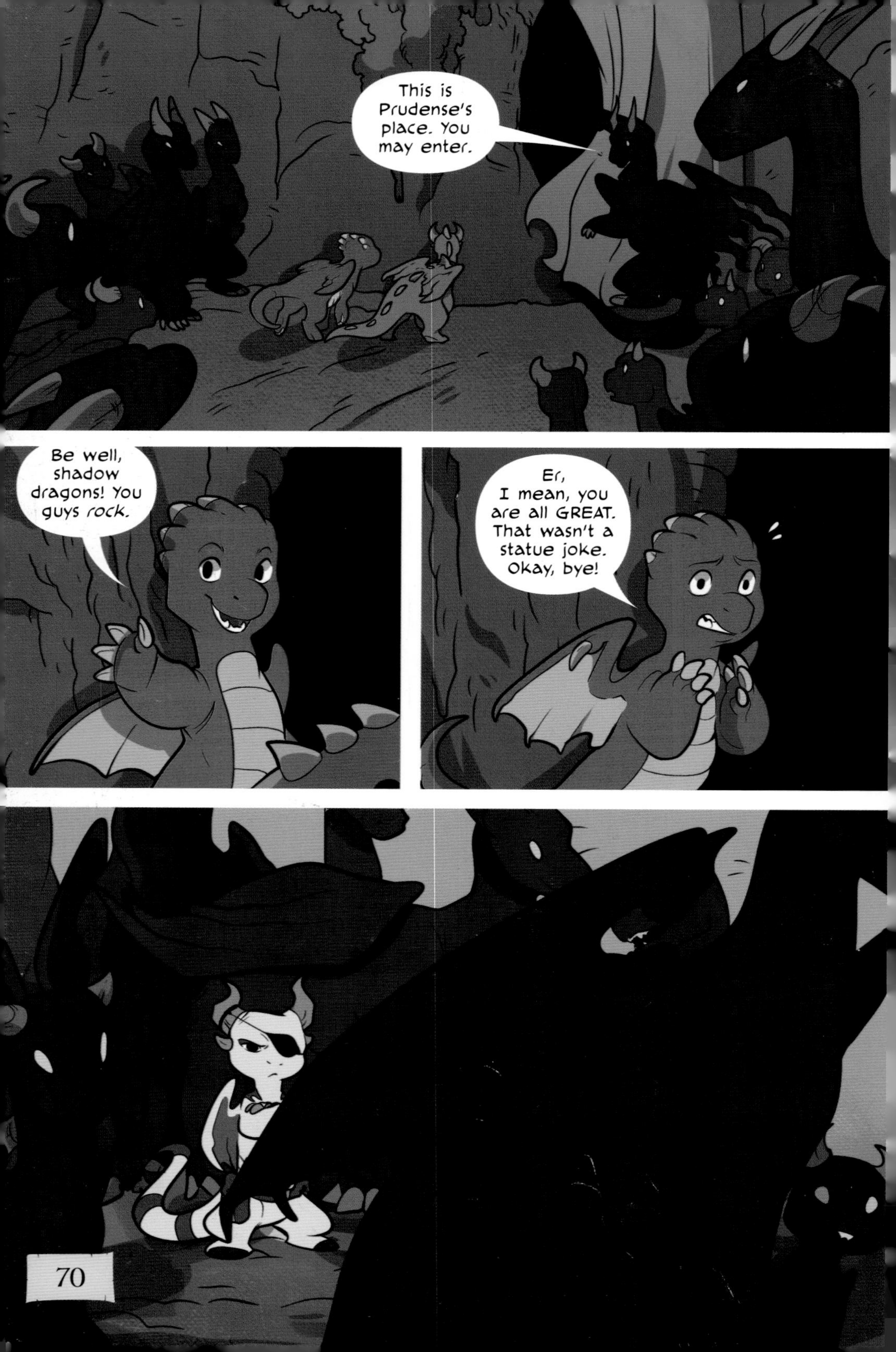
This is Prudense's place. You may enter.
Be well, shadow dragons! You guys *rock*.
Er, I mean, you are all GREAT. That wasn't a statue joke. Okay, bye!

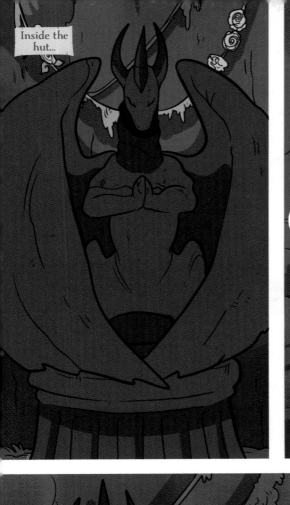

Inside the hut...

Greetings, I am Ruskin of Wrenly.

Why are you talking to my stone idol?

I am the one they call Prudense.

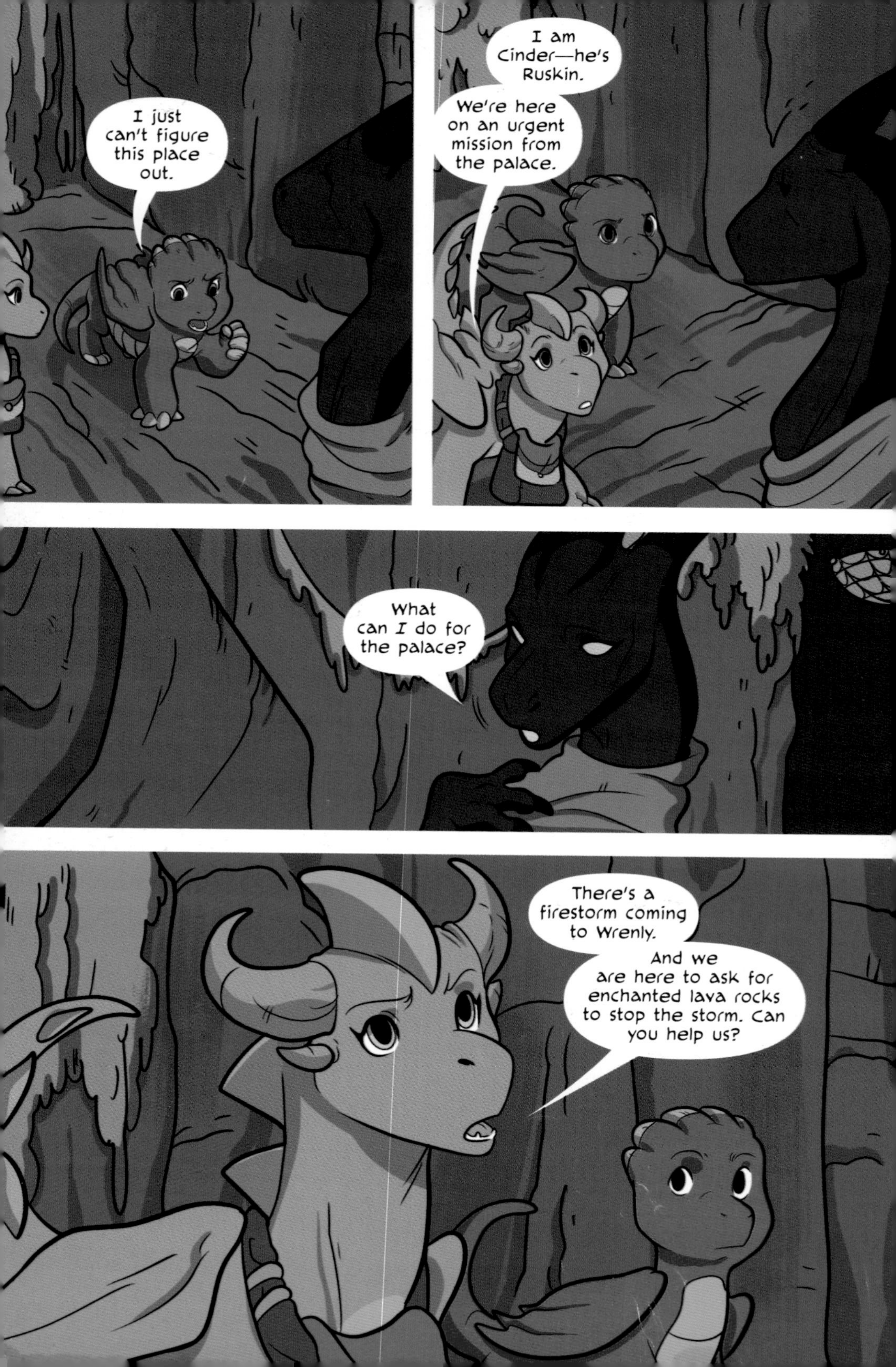
I just can't figure this place out.
I am Cinder—he's Ruskin.
We're here on an urgent mission from the palace.
What can *I* do for the palace?
There's a firestorm coming to Wrenly.
And we are here to ask for enchanted lava rocks to stop the storm. Can you help us?

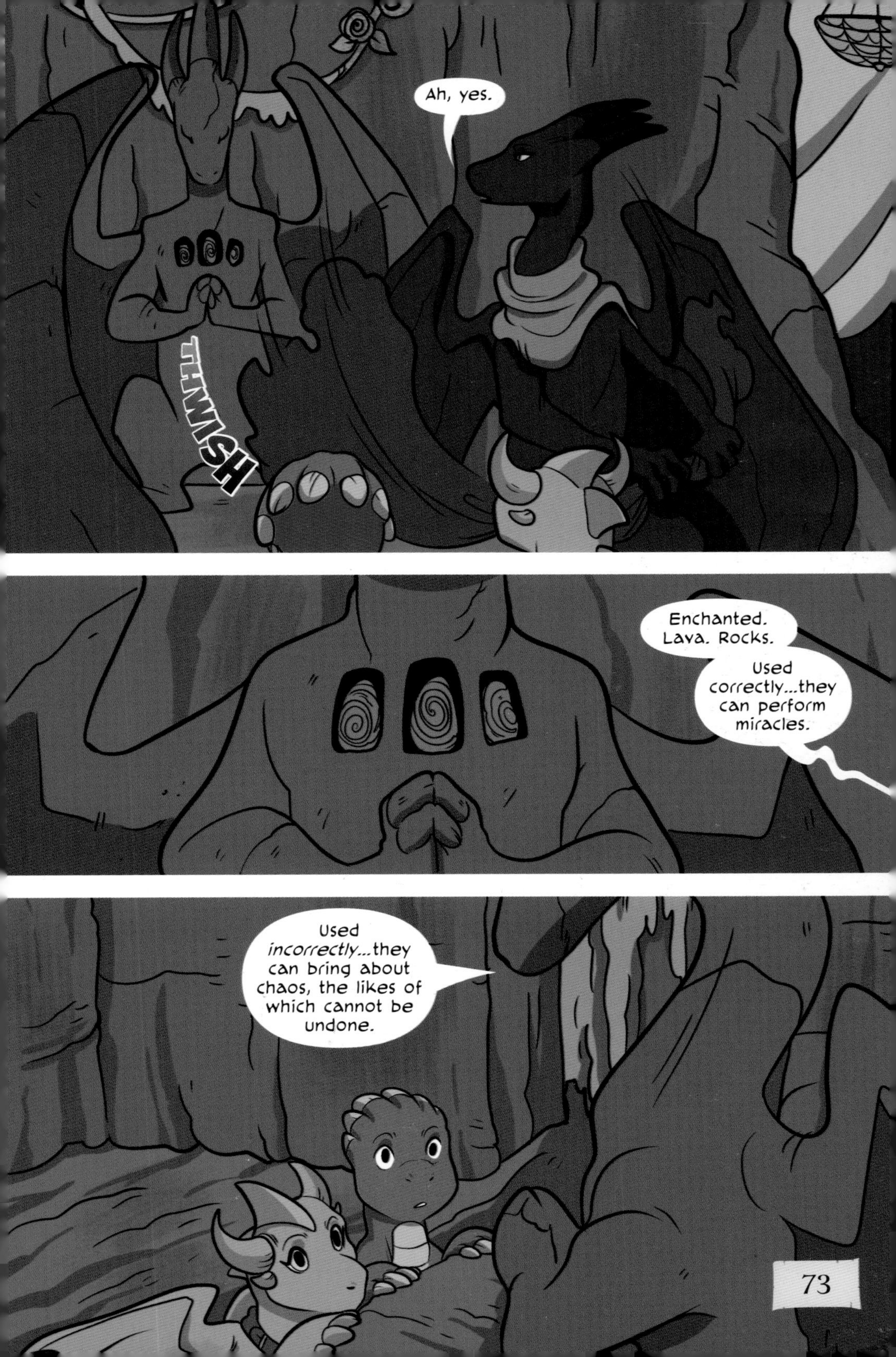
Ah, yes.
THWISH
Enchanted. Lava. Rocks.
Used correctly...they can perform miracles.
Used *incorrectly*...they can bring about chaos, the likes of which cannot be undone.

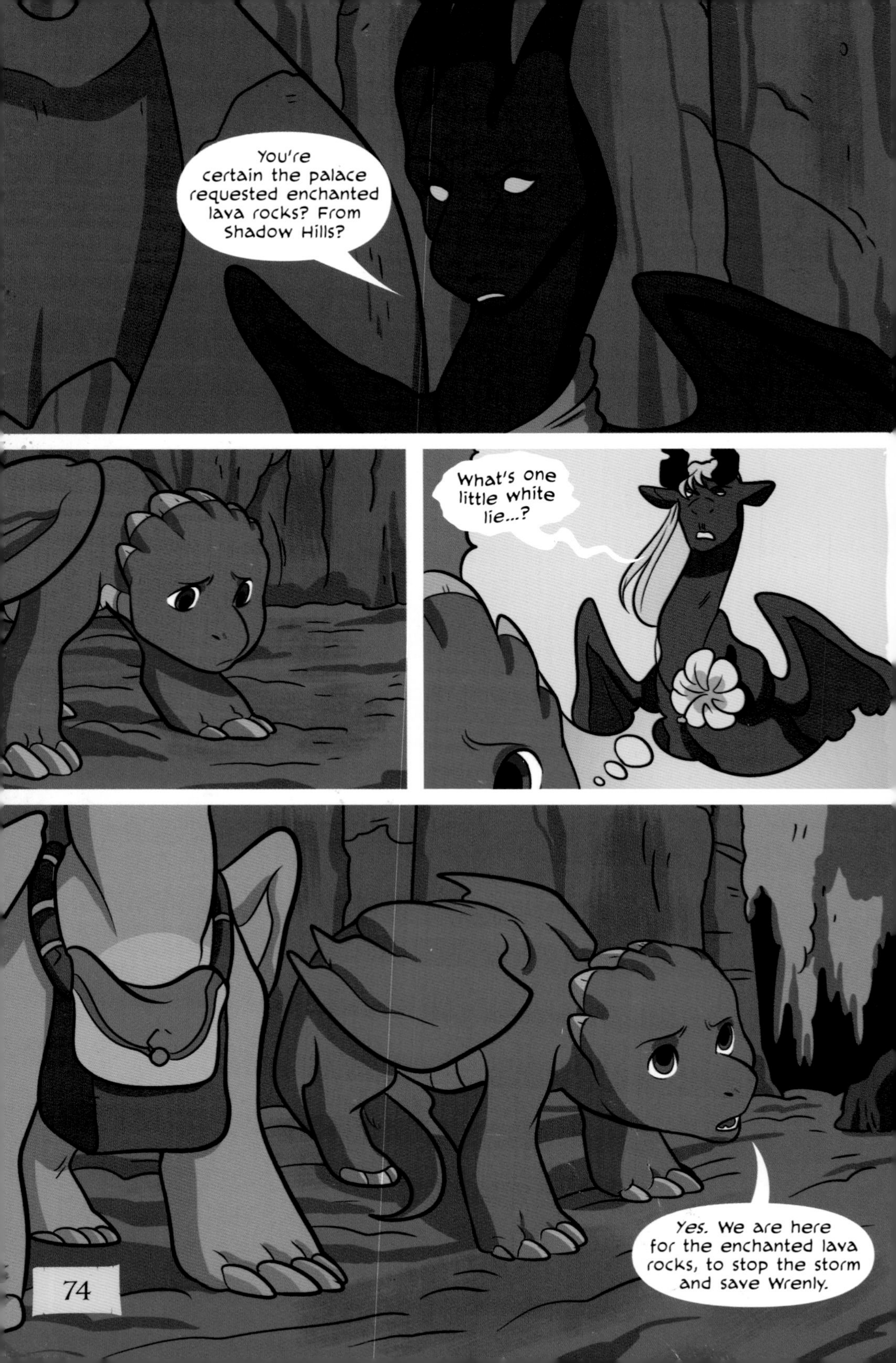
You're certain the palace requested enchanted lava rocks? From Shadow Hills?
What's one little white lie...?
Yes. We are here for the enchanted lava rocks, to stop the storm and save Wrenly.

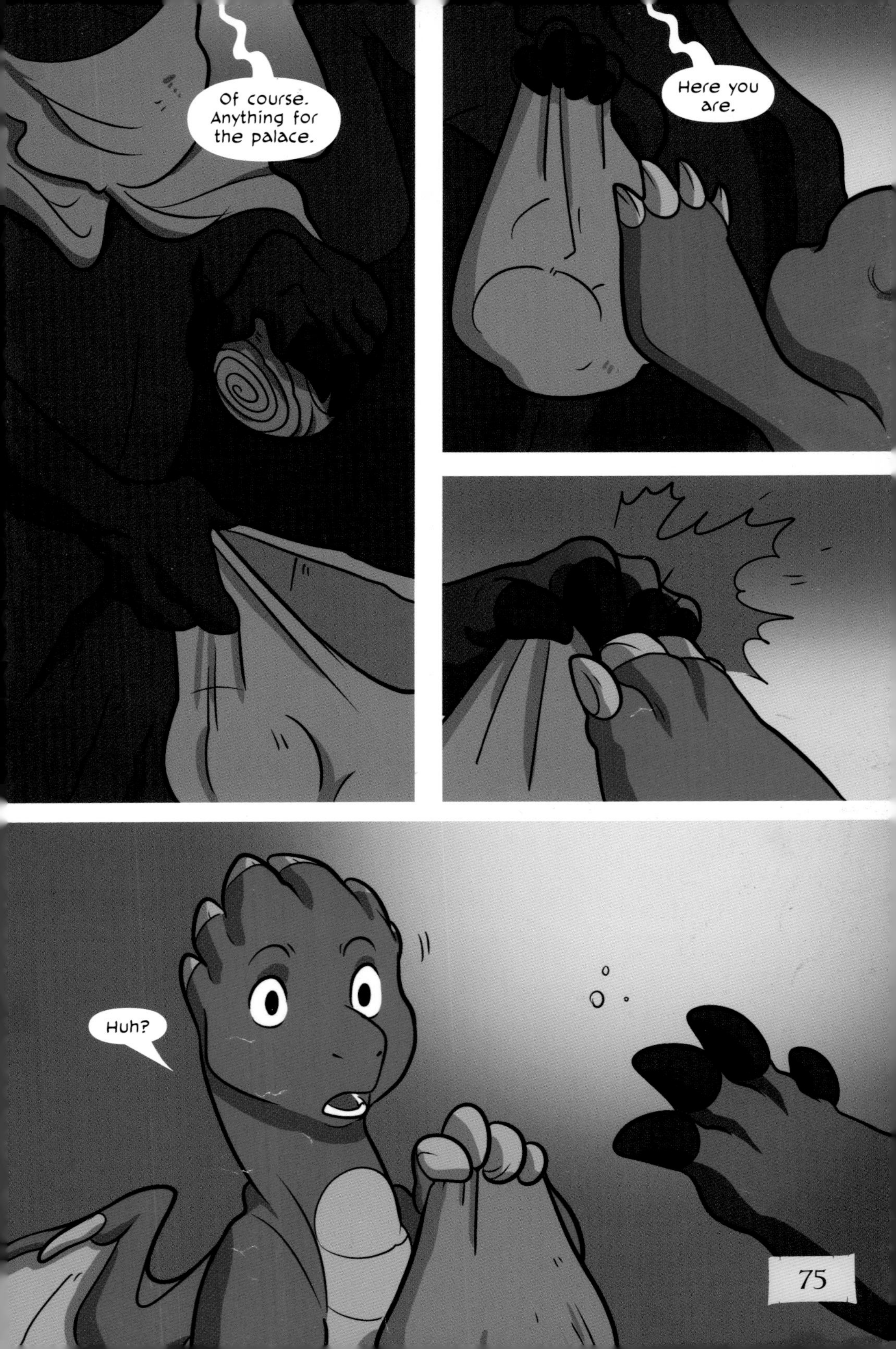
Of course. Anything for the palace.
Here you are.
Huh?

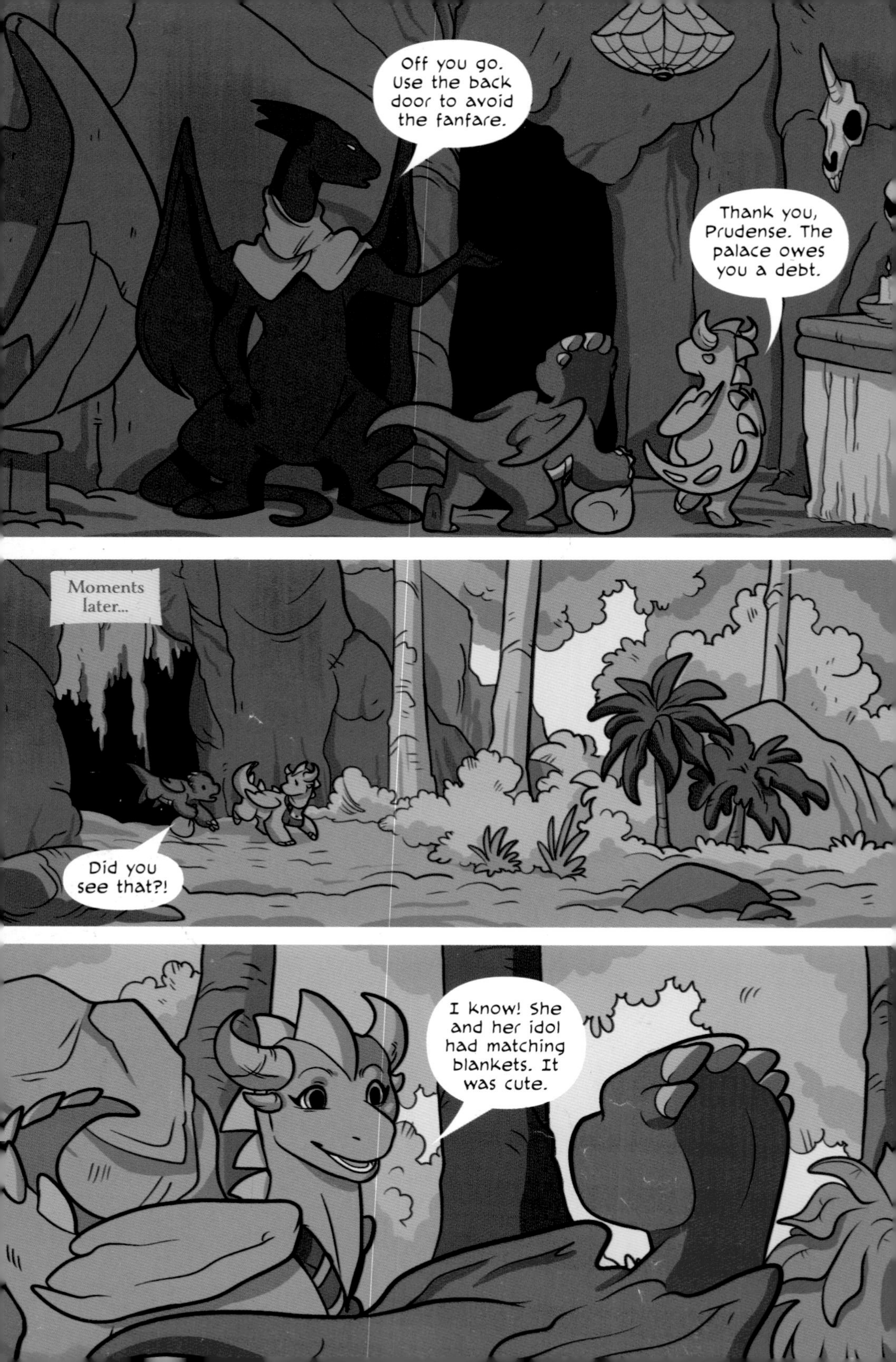
Off you go. Use the back door to avoid the fanfare.
Thank you, Prudense. The palace owes you a debt.
Moments later...
Did you see that?!
I know! She and her idol had matching blankets. It was cute.

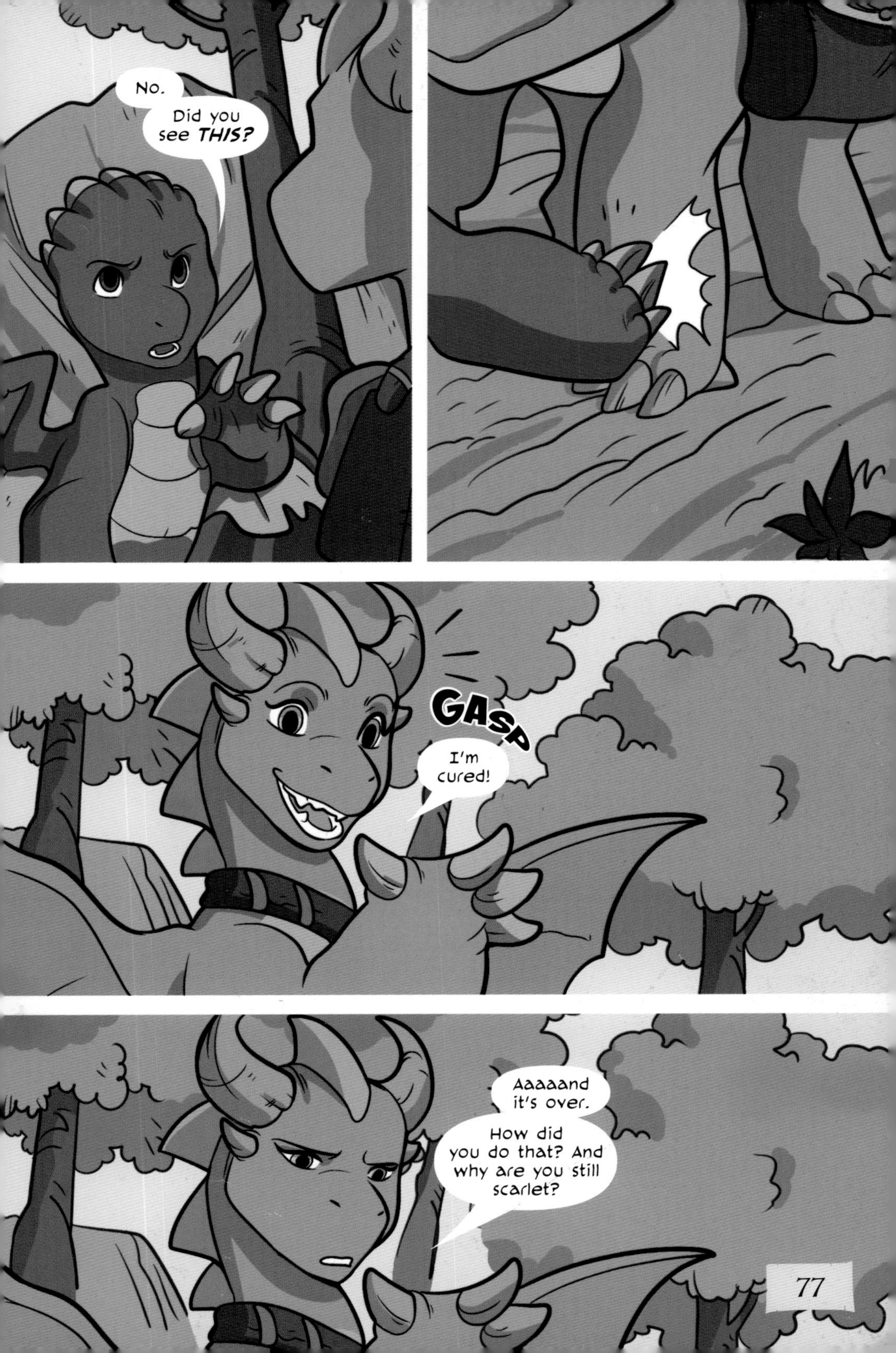
No.
Did you see *THIS?*
GASP
I'm cured!
Aaaaand it's over.
How did you do that? And why are you still scarlet?

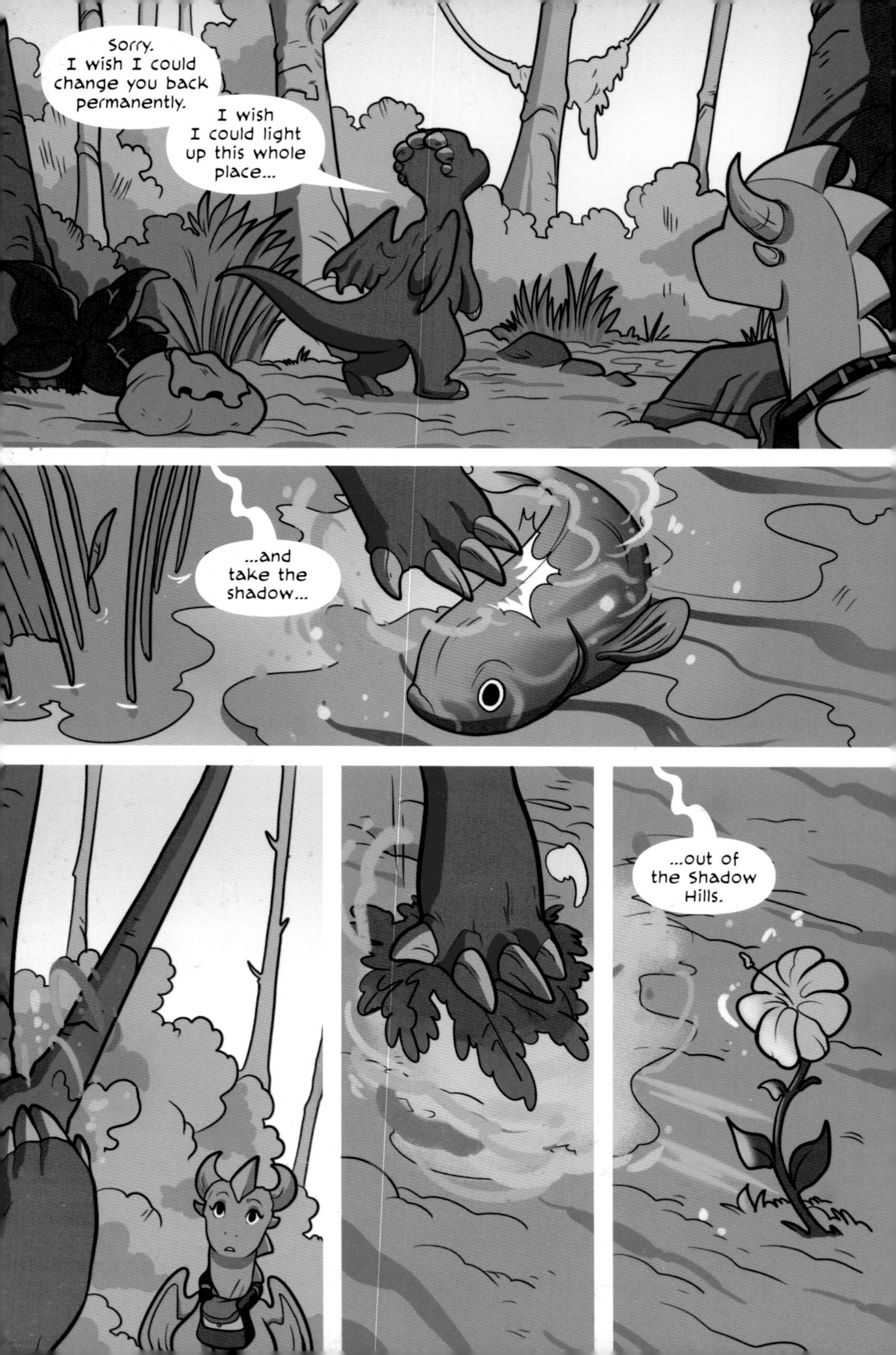
Sorry. I wish I could change you back permanently.
I wish I could light up this whole place...
...and take the shadow...
...out of the Shadow Hills.

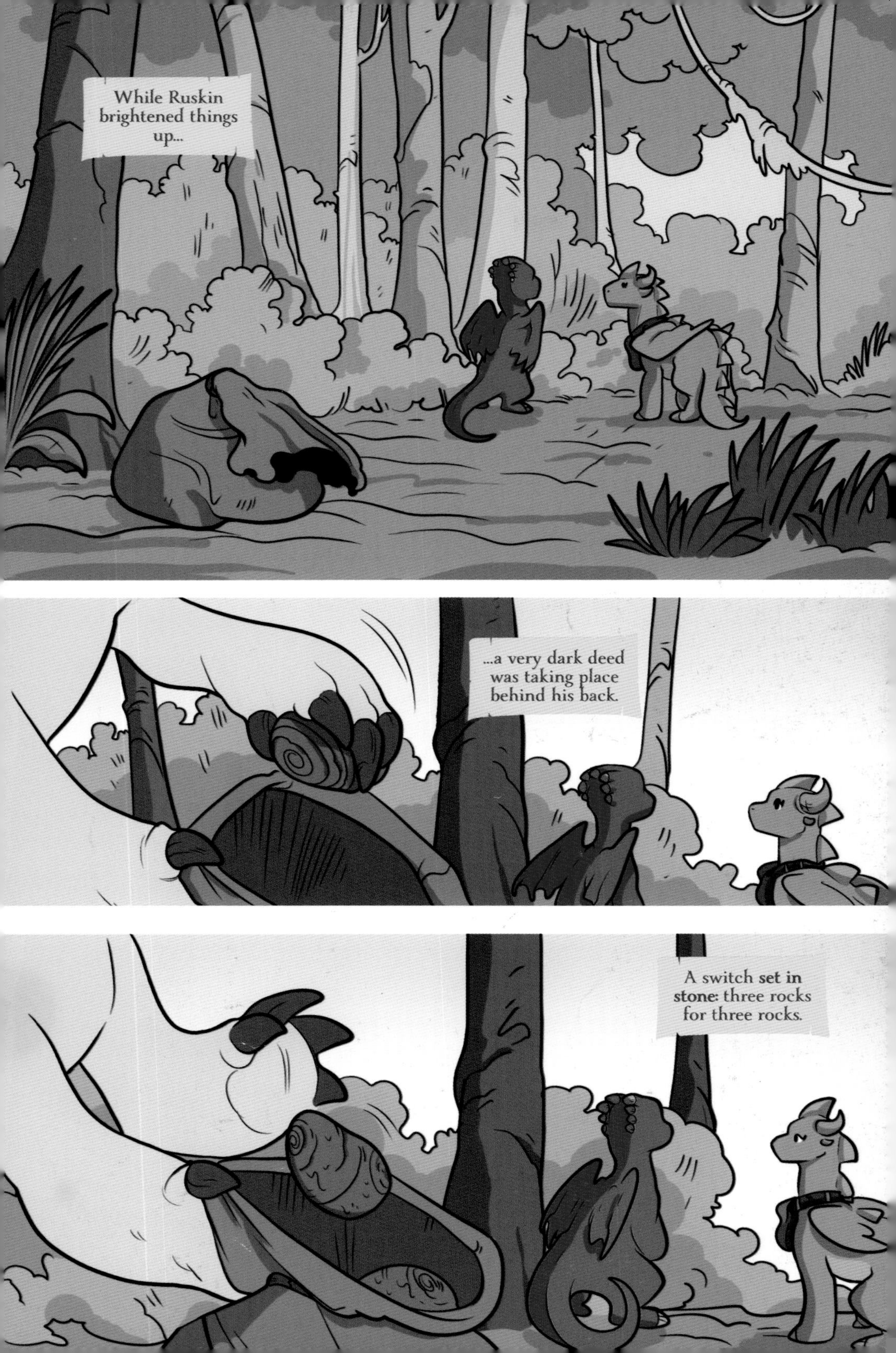
While Ruskin brightened things up...
...a very dark deed was taking place behind his back.
A switch set in stone: three rocks for three rocks.

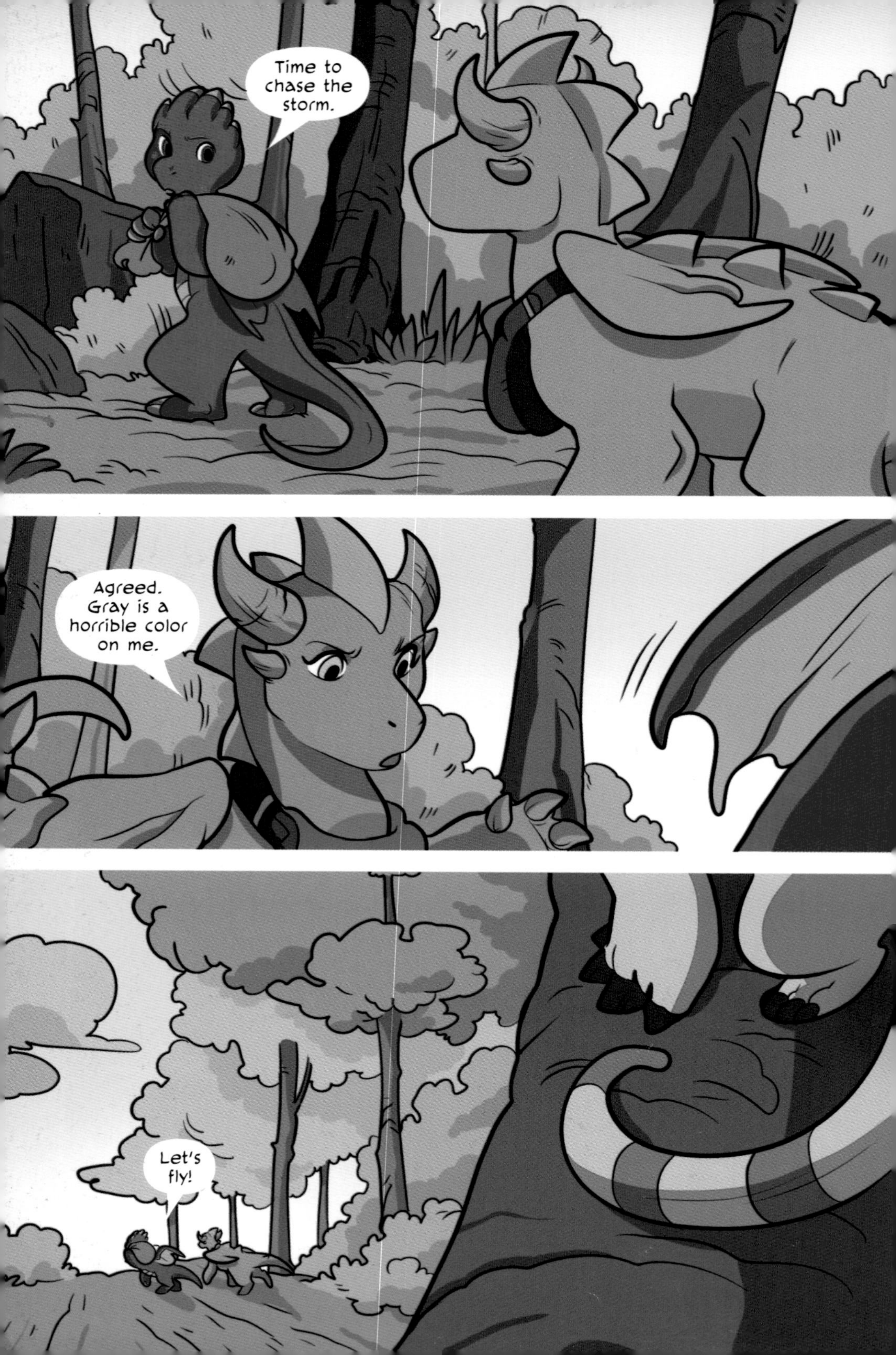
Time to chase the storm.
Agreed. Gray is a horrible color on me.
Let's fly!

Chapter 6

See you on the other side!

Ow!

THUD

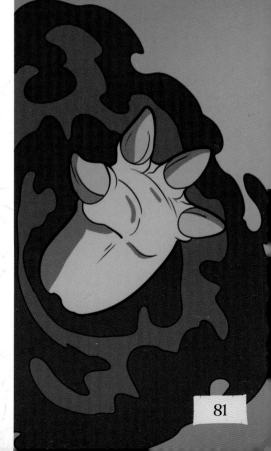

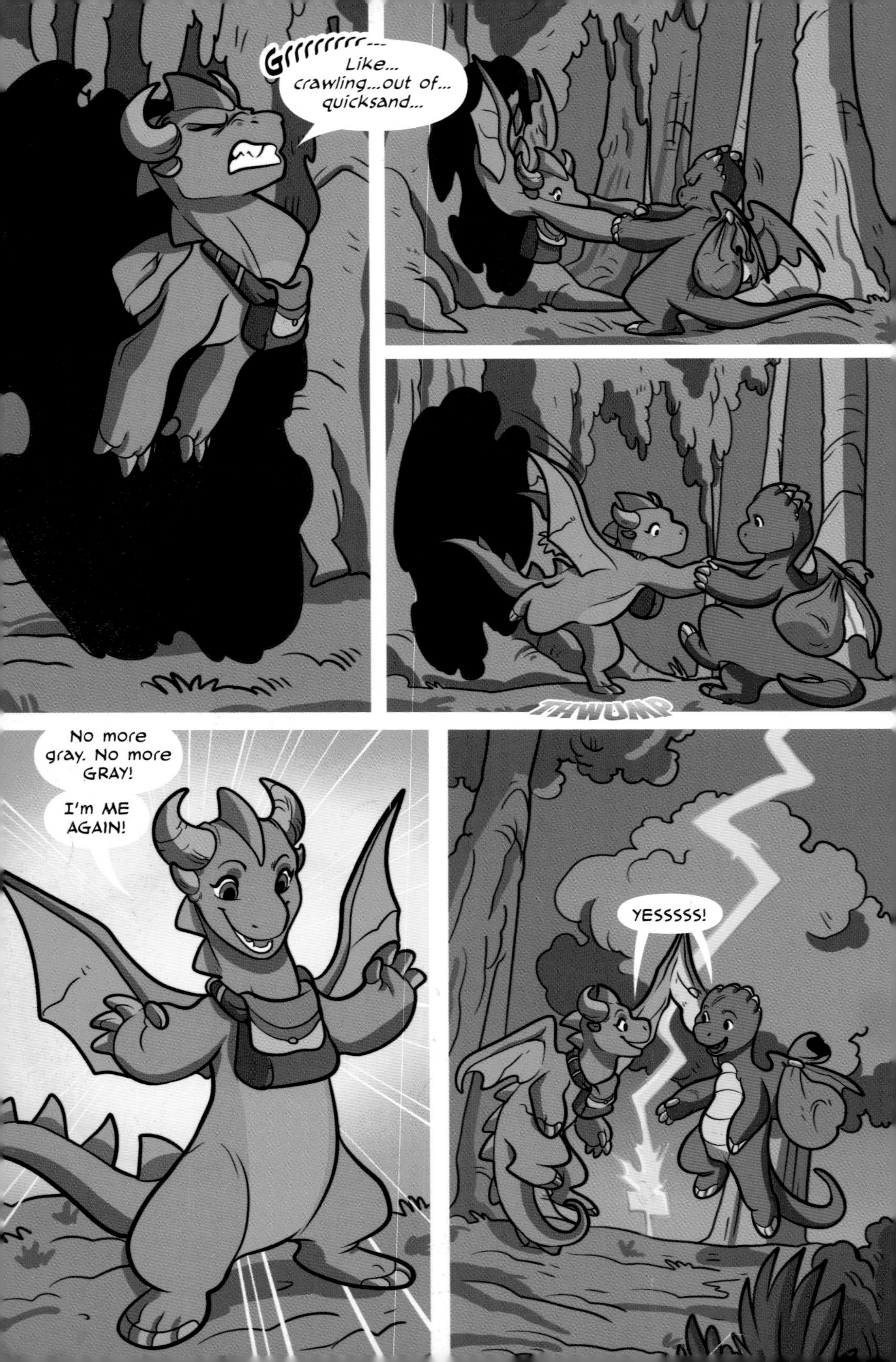
Grrrrrrrr...
Like... crawling...out of... quicksand...
THWUMP
No more gray. No more GRAY!
I'm ME AGAIN!
YESSSSS!

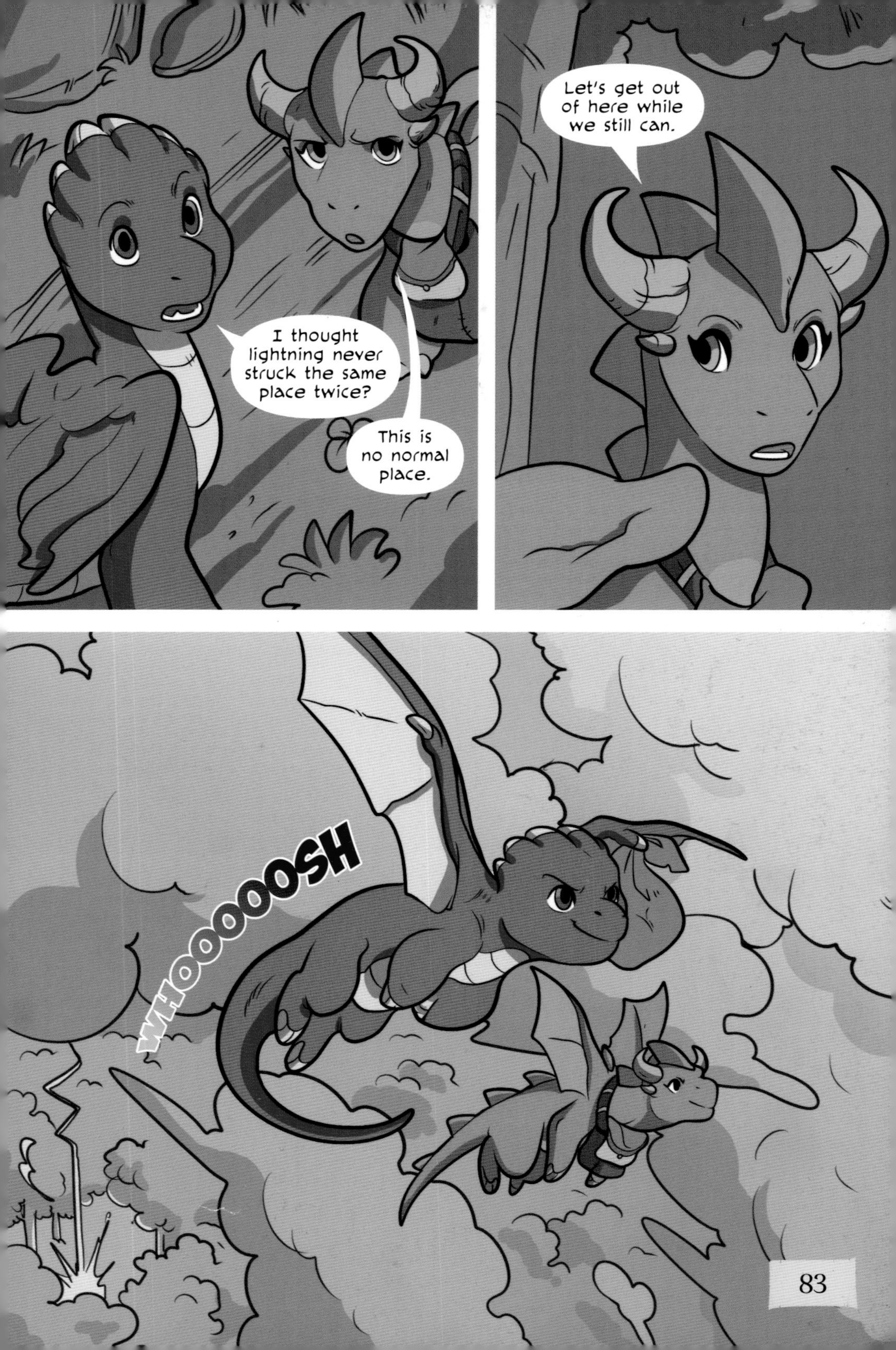
I thought lightning never struck the same place twice?
This is no normal place.
Let's get out of here while we still can.
WHOOOOOOSH

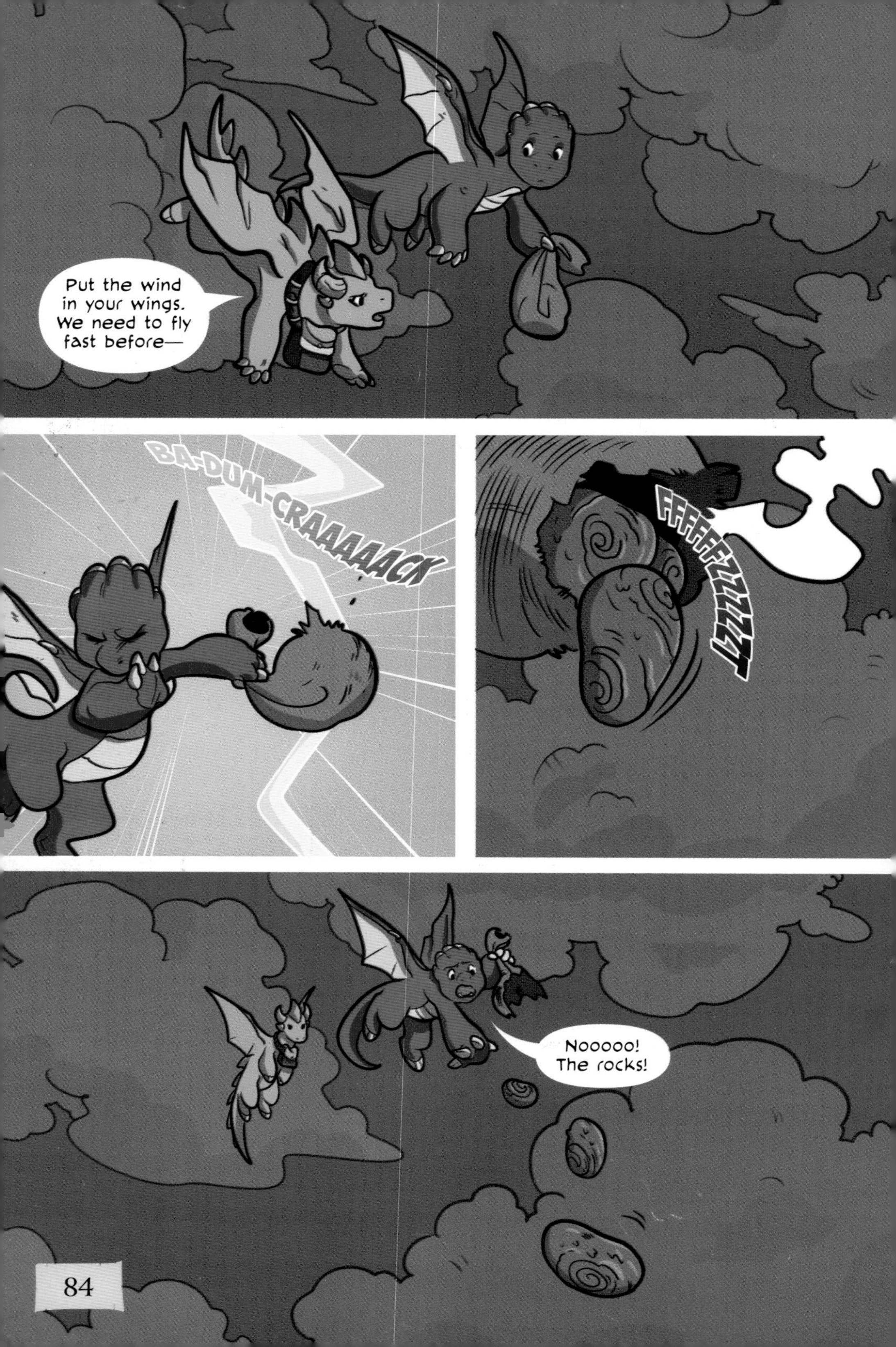
Put the wind in your wings. We need to fly fast before—
BA-DUM-CRAAAAAACK
FFFFFFZZZZZZT
Nooooo! The rocks!

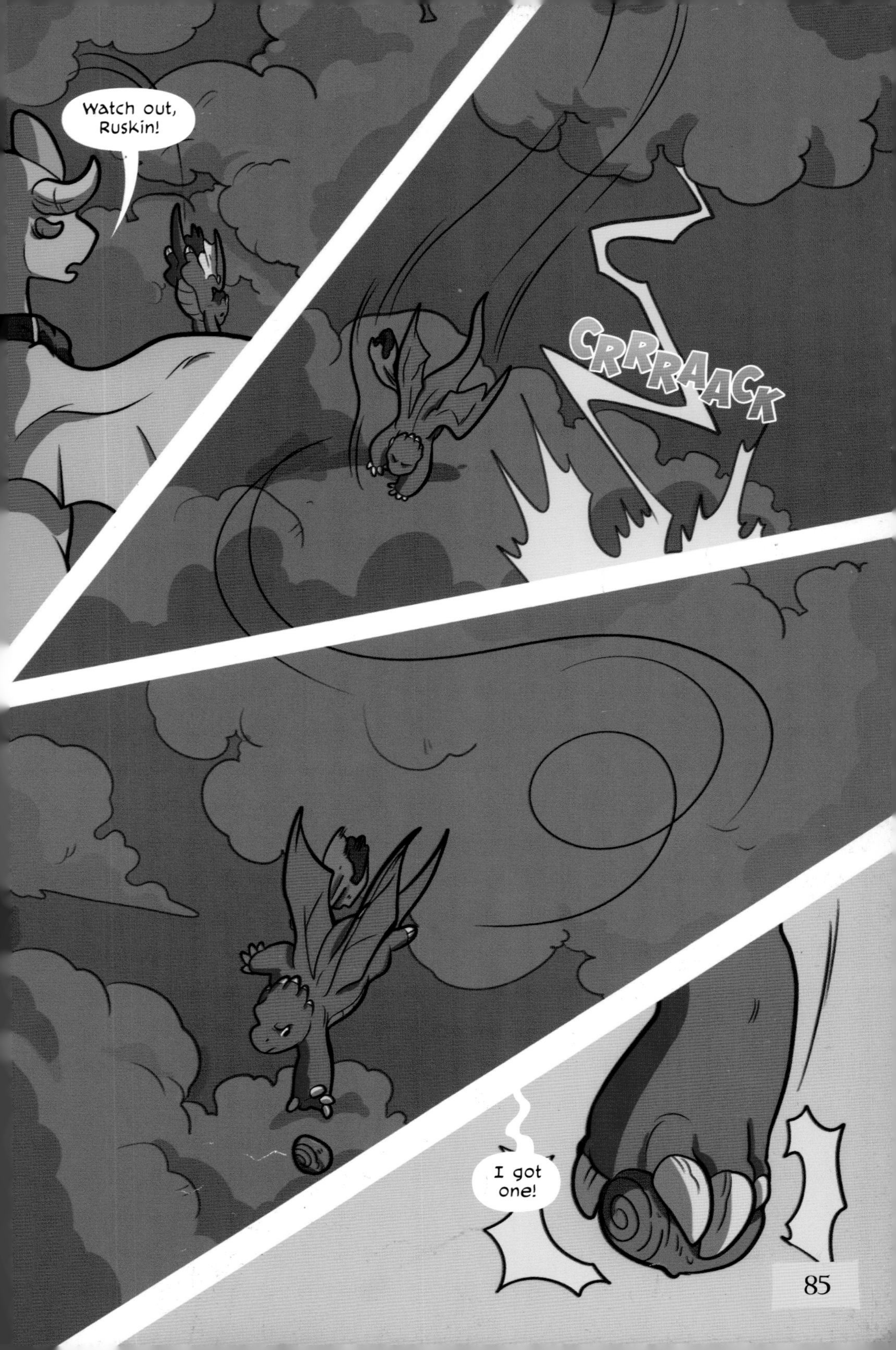
Watch out, Ruskin!
CRRRAACK
I got one!

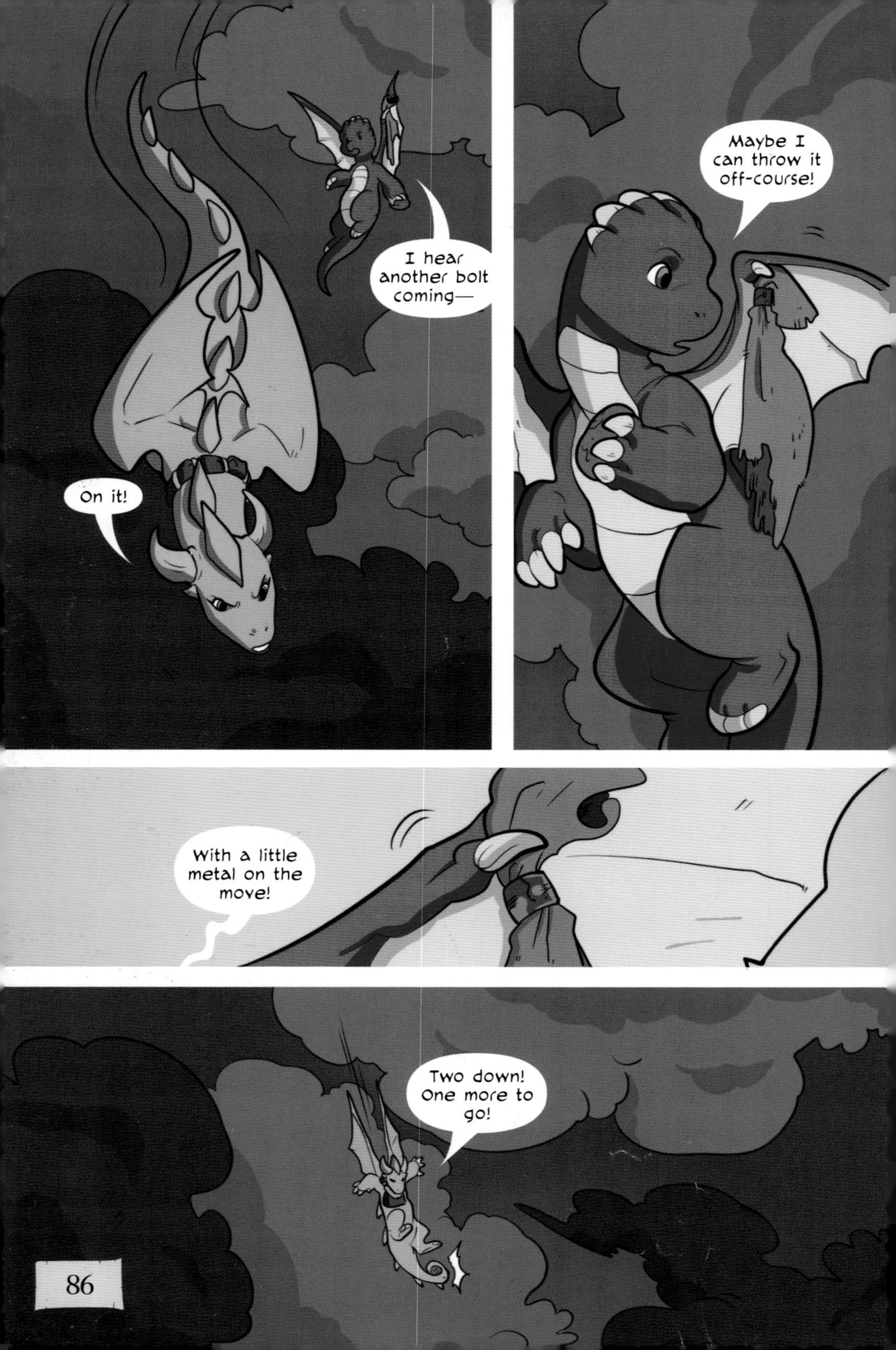
I hear another bolt coming—
On it!
Maybe I can throw it off-course!
With a little metal on the move!
Two down! One more to go!

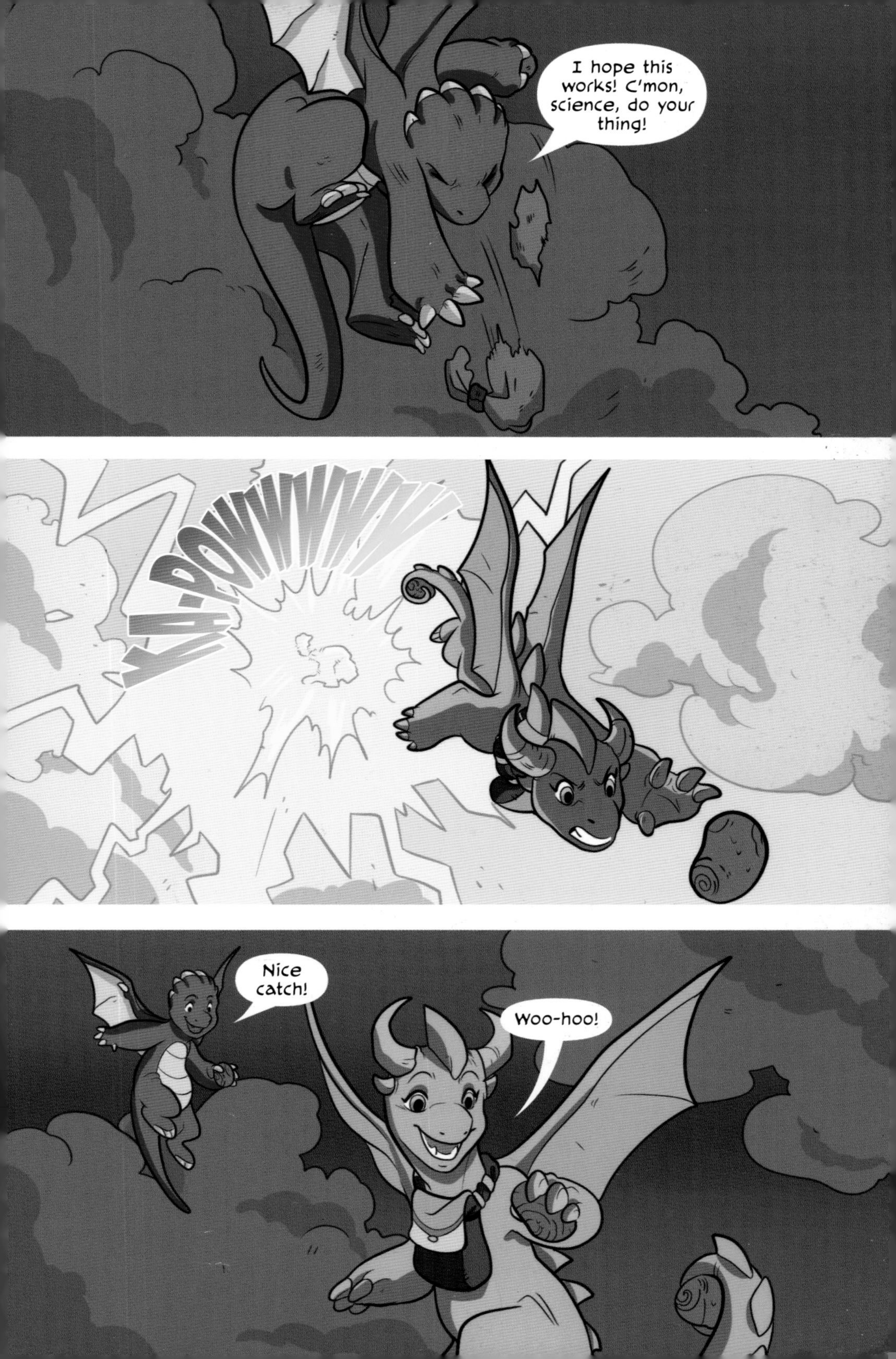
I hope this works! C'mon, science, do your thing!
KA-POWWWWW
Nice catch!
Woo-hoo!

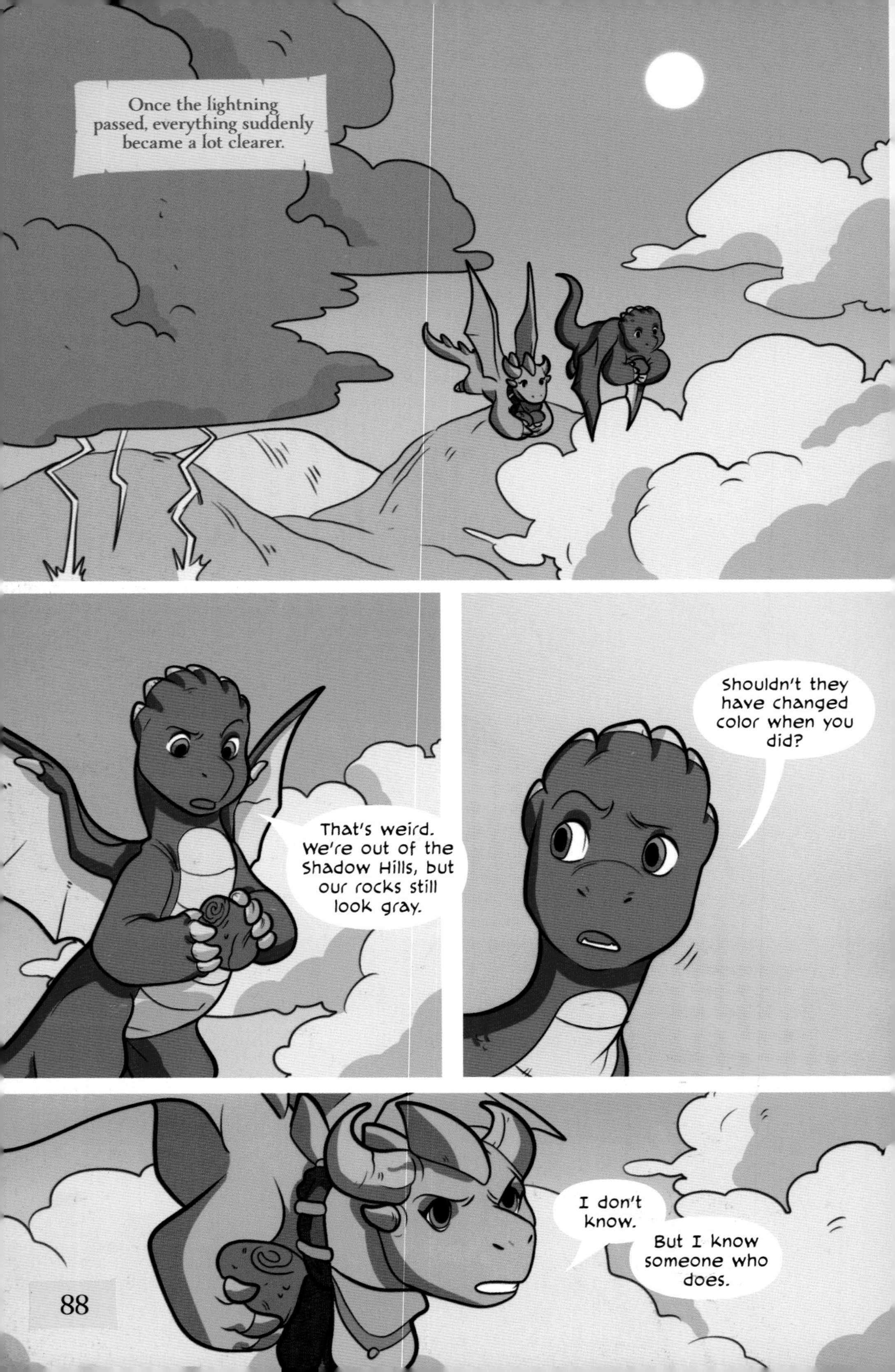
Once the lightning passed, everything suddenly became a lot clearer.
That's weird. We're out of the Shadow Hills, but our rocks still look gray.
Shouldn't they have changed color when you did?
I don't know.
But I know someone who does.

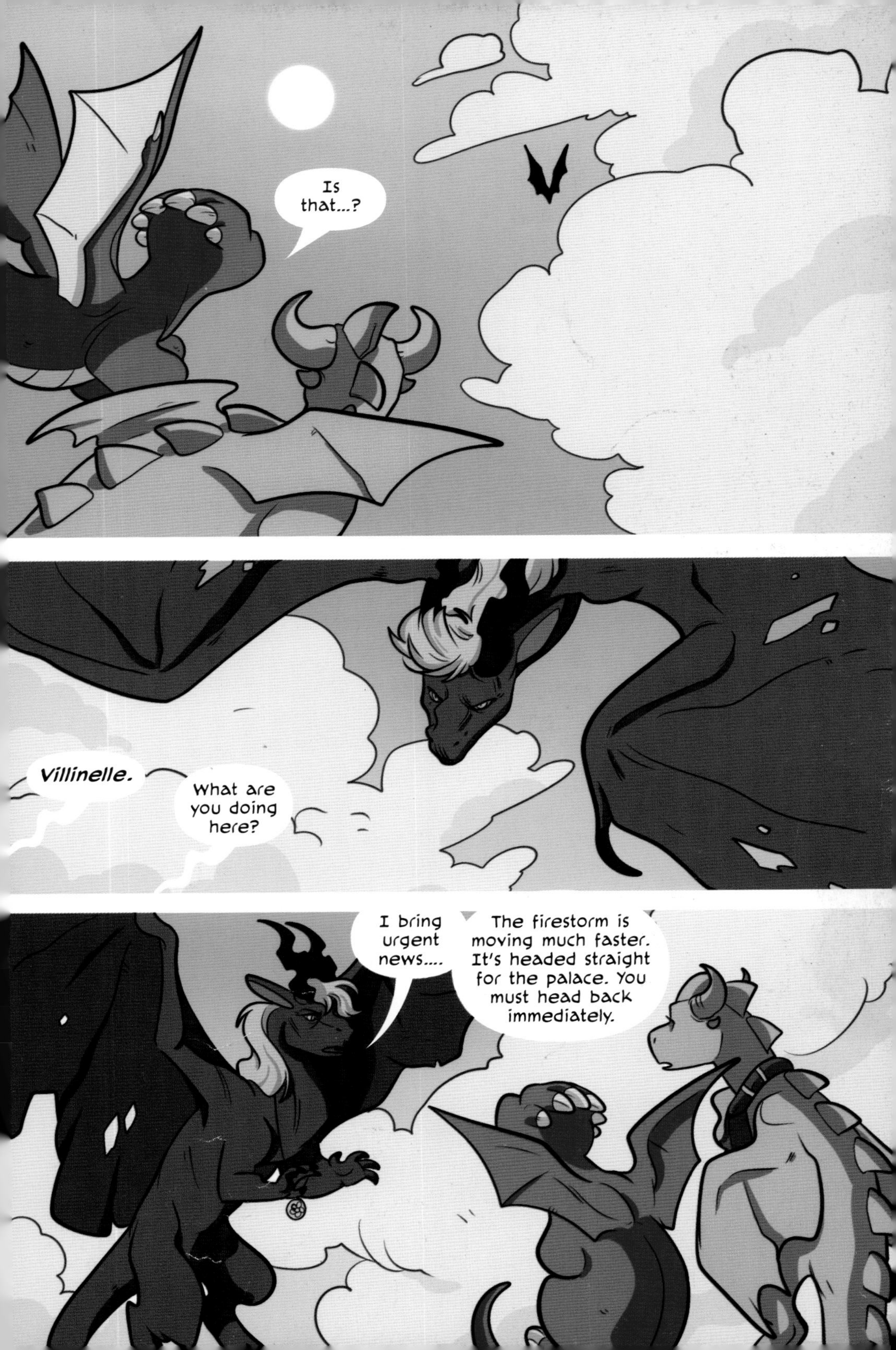
Is that...?
Villinelle.
What are you doing here?
I bring urgent news....
The firestorm is moving much faster. It's headed straight for the palace. You must head back immediately.

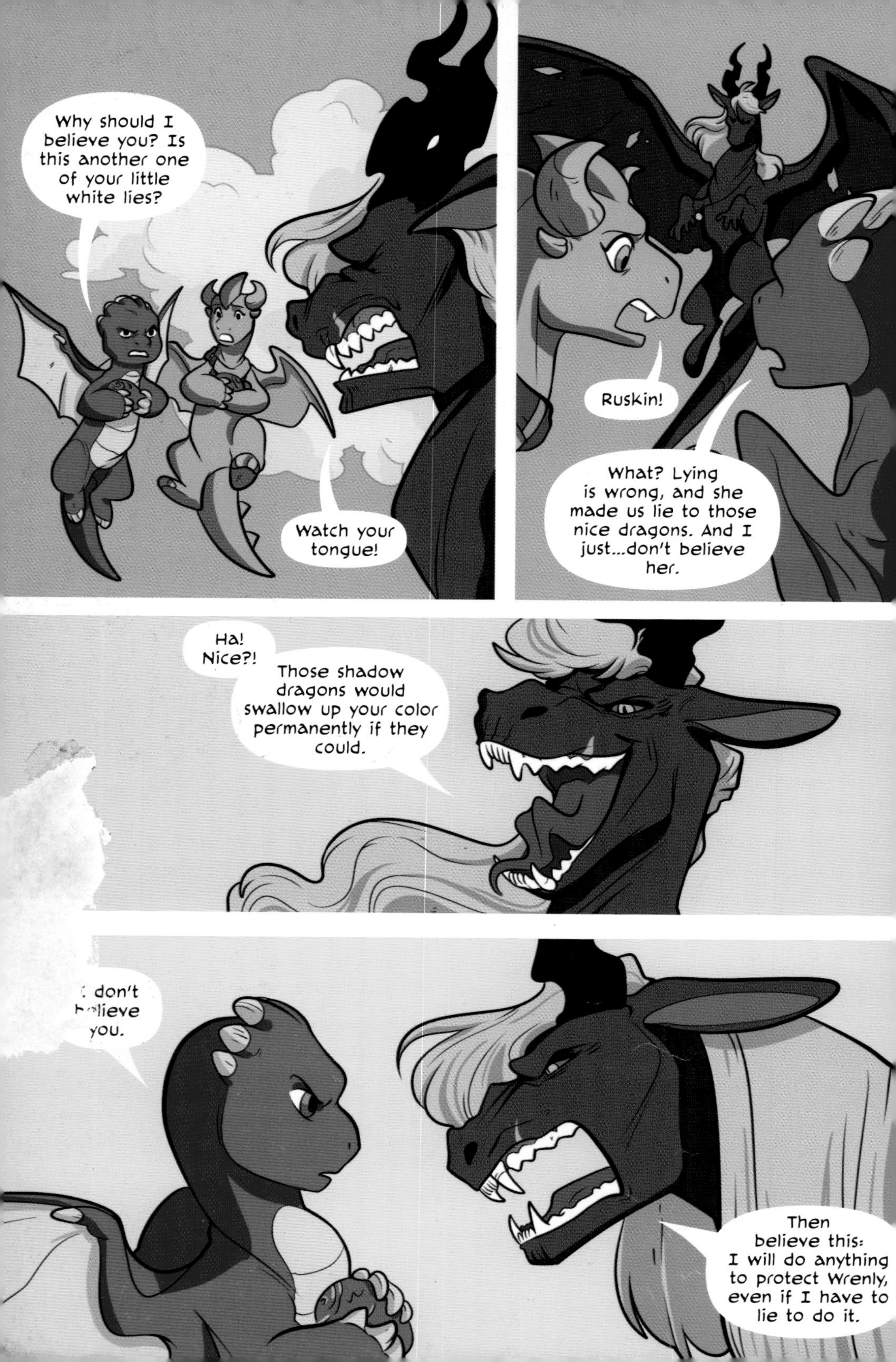
Why should I believe you? Is this another one of your little white lies?
Watch your tongue!
Ruskin!
What? Lying is wrong, and she made us lie to those nice dragons. And I just...don't believe her.
Ha! Nice?!
Those shadow dragons would swallow up your color permanently if they could.
don't
you.
Then believe this: I will do anything to protect Wrenly, even if I have to lie to do it.

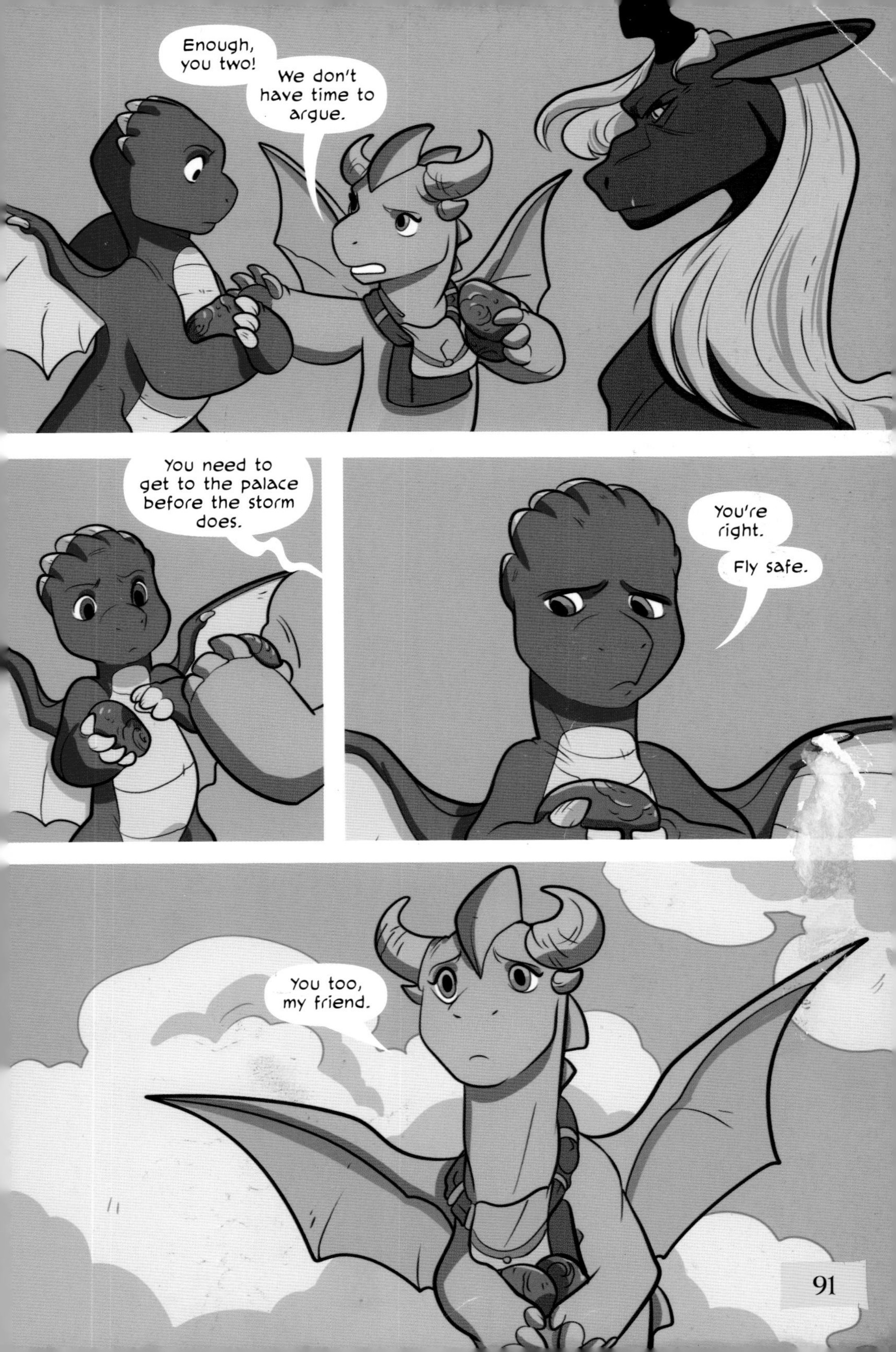
Enough, you two!
We don't have time to argue.
You need to get to the palace before the storm does.
You're right.
Fly safe.
You too, my friend.

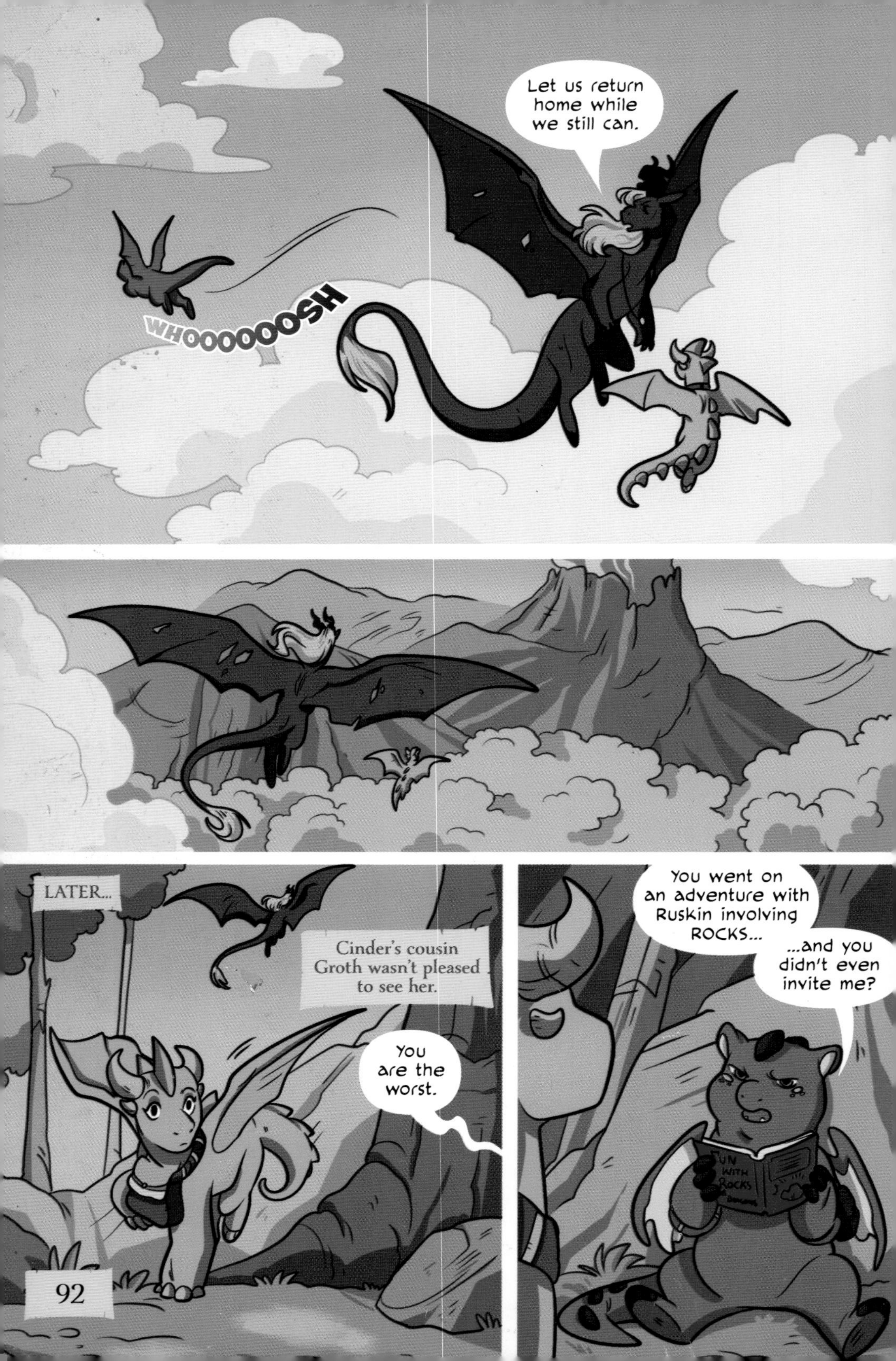
Let us return home while we still can.
WHOOOOOOOSH
LATER...
Cinder's cousin Groth wasn't pleased to see her.
You are the worst.
You went on an adventure with Ruskin involving ROCKS...
...and you didn't even invite me?
FUN WITH ROCKS

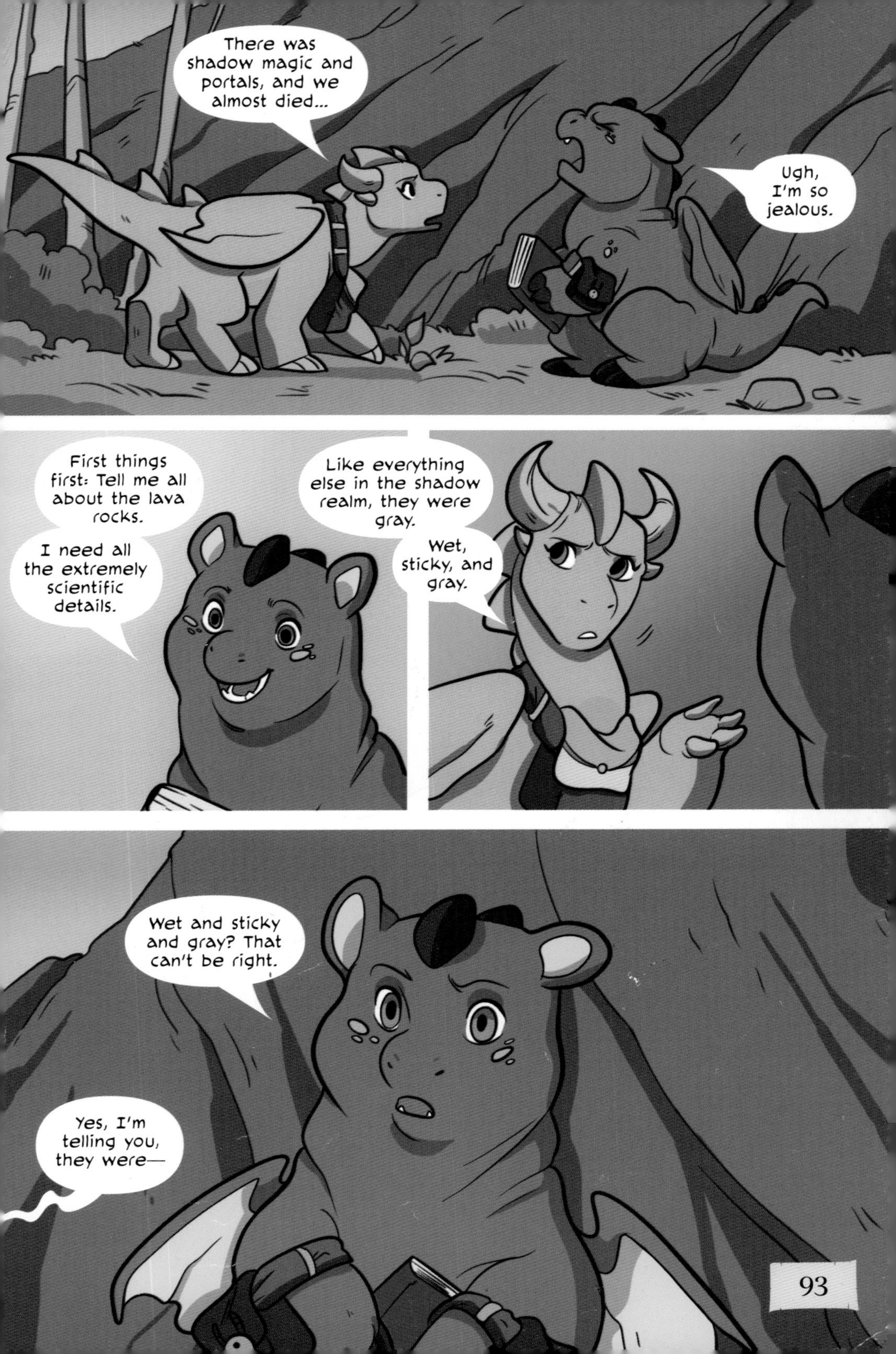
There was shadow magic and portals, and we almost died...
Ugh, I'm so jealous.
First things first: Tell me all about the lava rocks.
I need all the extremely scientific details.
Like everything else in the shadow realm, they were gray.
Wet, sticky, and gray.
Wet and sticky and gray? That can't be right.
Yes, I'm telling you, they were—

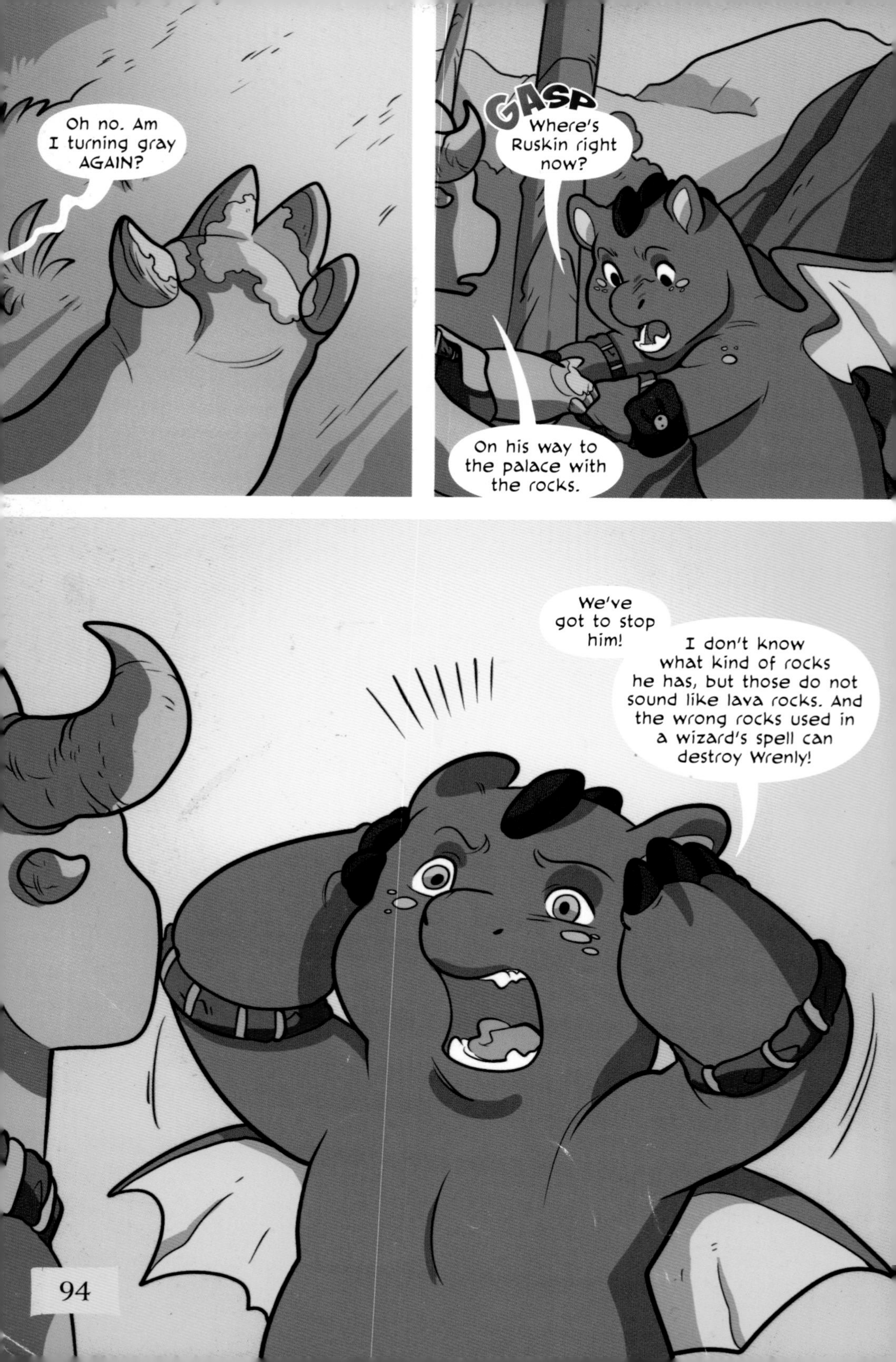
Oh no. Am I turning gray AGAIN?
GASP
Where's Ruskin right now?
On his way to the palace with the rocks.
We've got to stop him!
I don't know what kind of rocks he has, but those do not sound like lava rocks. And the wrong rocks used in a wizard's spell can destroy Wrenly!

Chapter 7

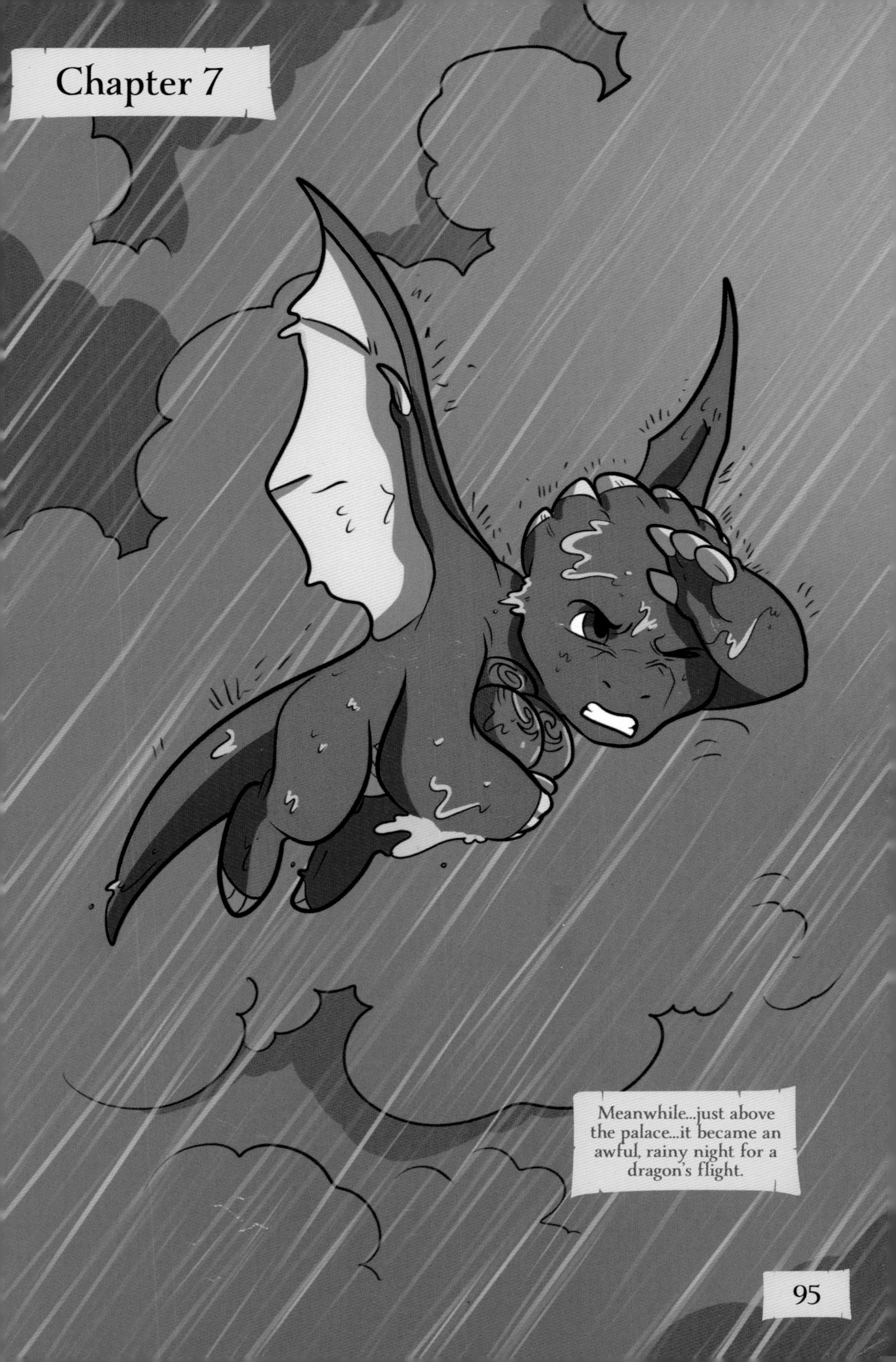
Meanwhile...just above the palace...it became an awful, rainy night for a dragon's flight.

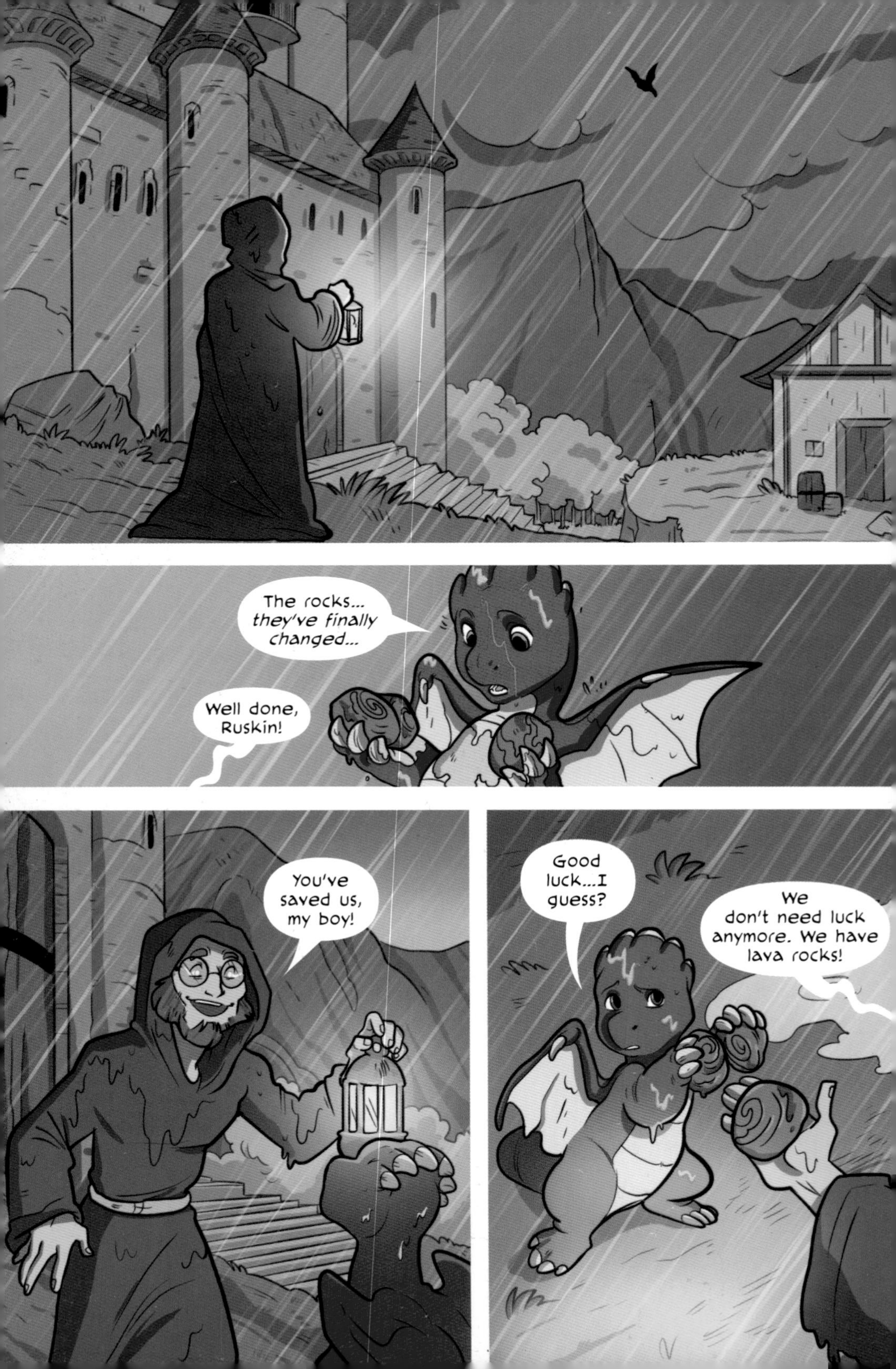

The rocks... they've finally changed...
Well done, Ruskin!
You've saved us, my boy!
Good luck...I guess?
We don't need luck anymore. We have lava rocks!

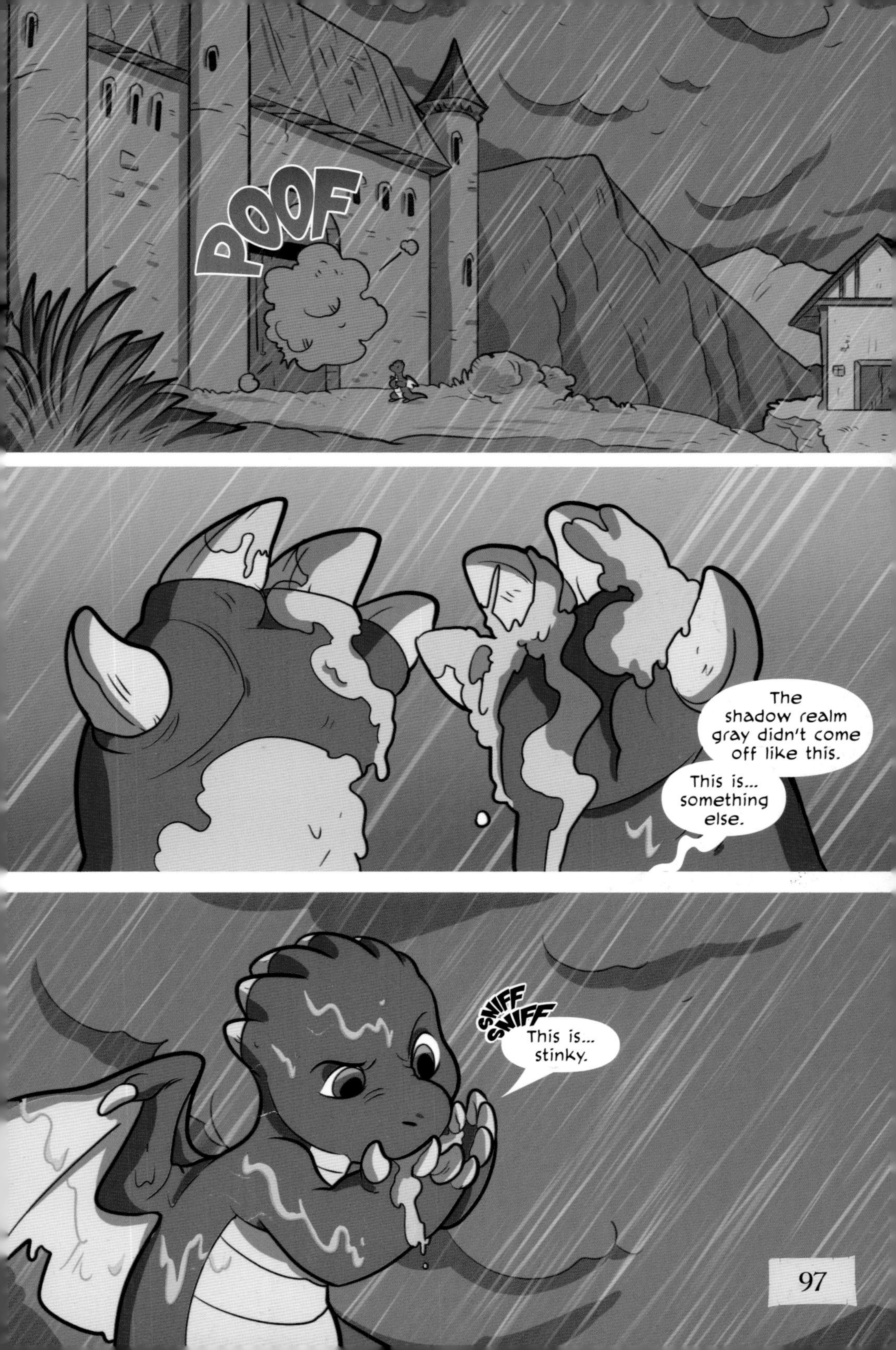
POOF
The shadow realm gray didn't come off like this.
This is... something else.
SNIFF SNIFF
This is... stinky.

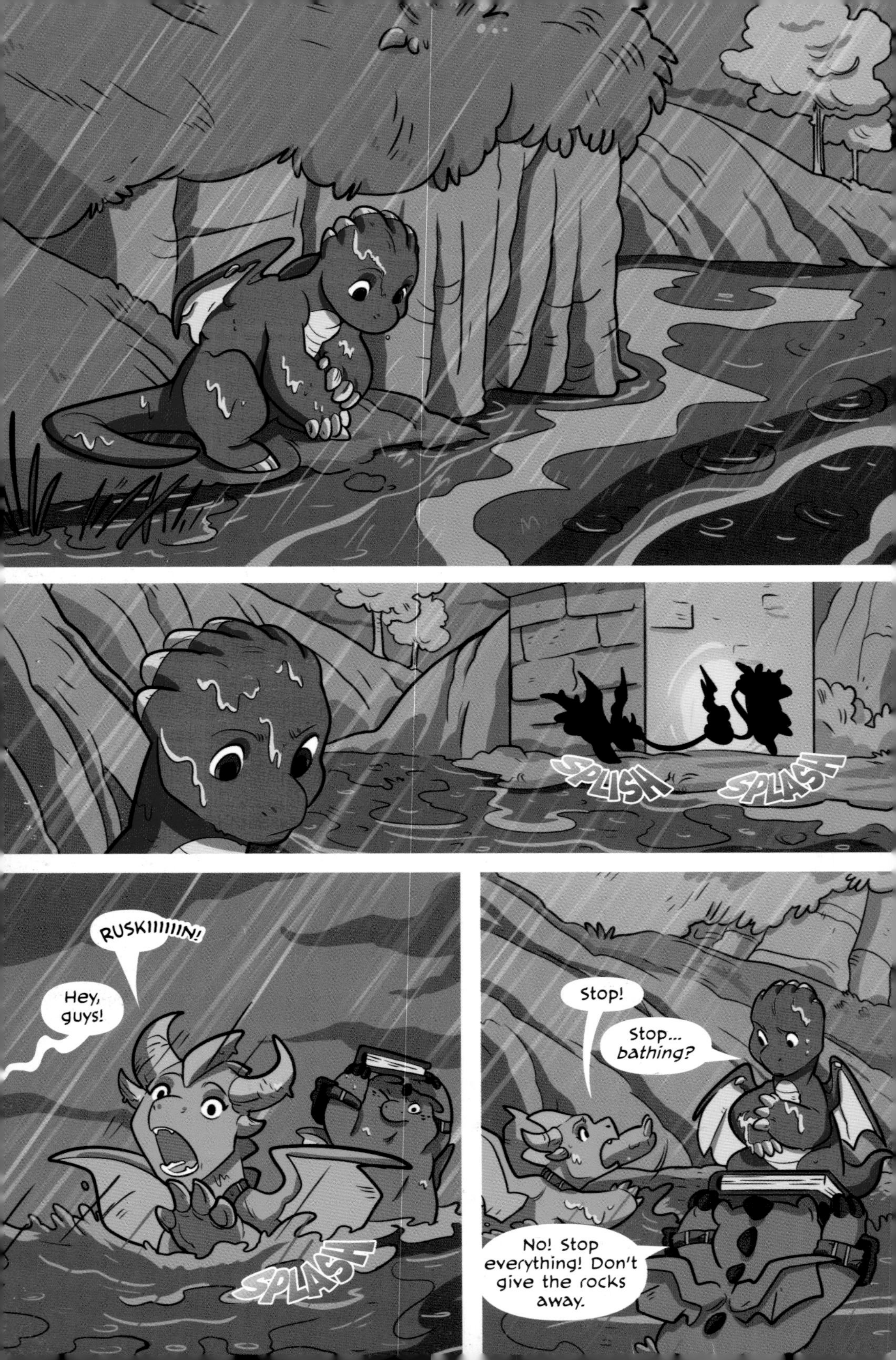

SPLISH
SPLASH
RUSKIIIIIIIN!
Hey, guys!
SPLASH
Stop!
Stop... *bathing?*
No! Stop everything! Don't give the rocks away.

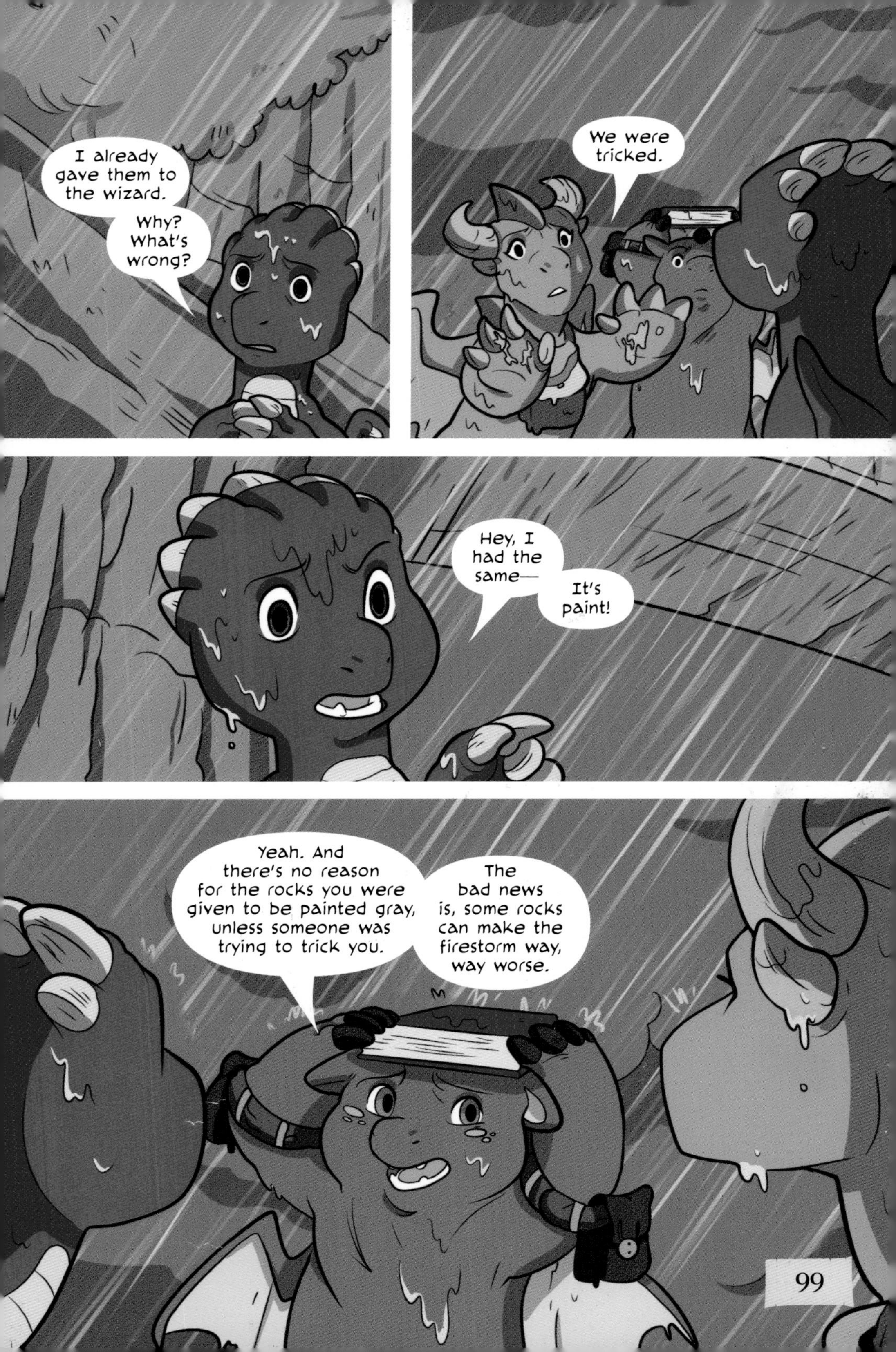
I already gave them to the wizard.
Why? What's wrong?
We were tricked.
Hey, I had the same—
It's paint!
Yeah. And there's no reason for the rocks you were given to be painted gray, unless someone was trying to trick you.
The bad news is, some rocks can make the firestorm way, way worse.

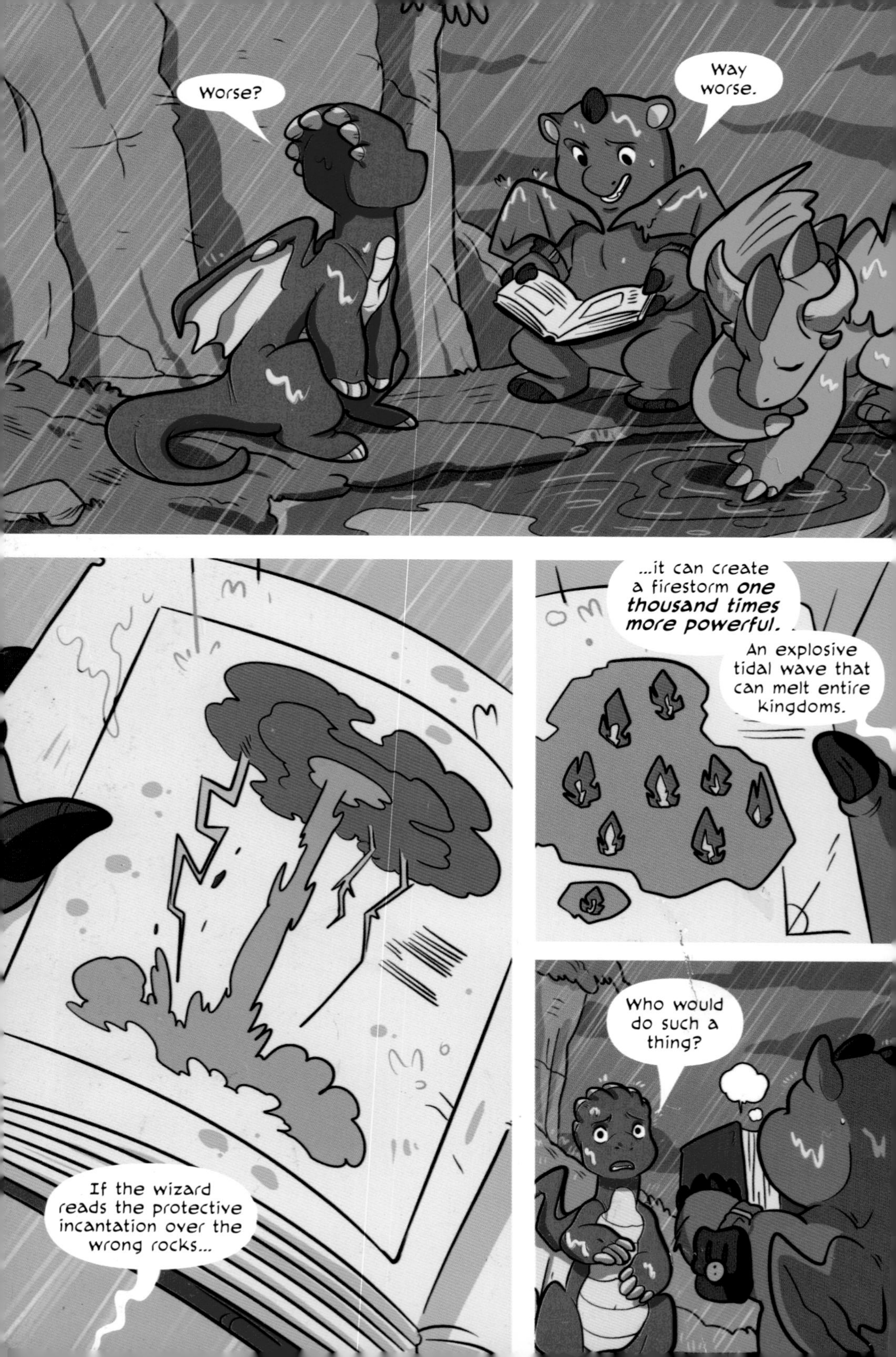
Worse?
Way worse.
If the wizard reads the protective incantation over the wrong rocks...
...it can create a firestorm **one thousand times more powerful.**
An explosive tidal wave that can melt entire kingdoms.
Who would do such a thing?

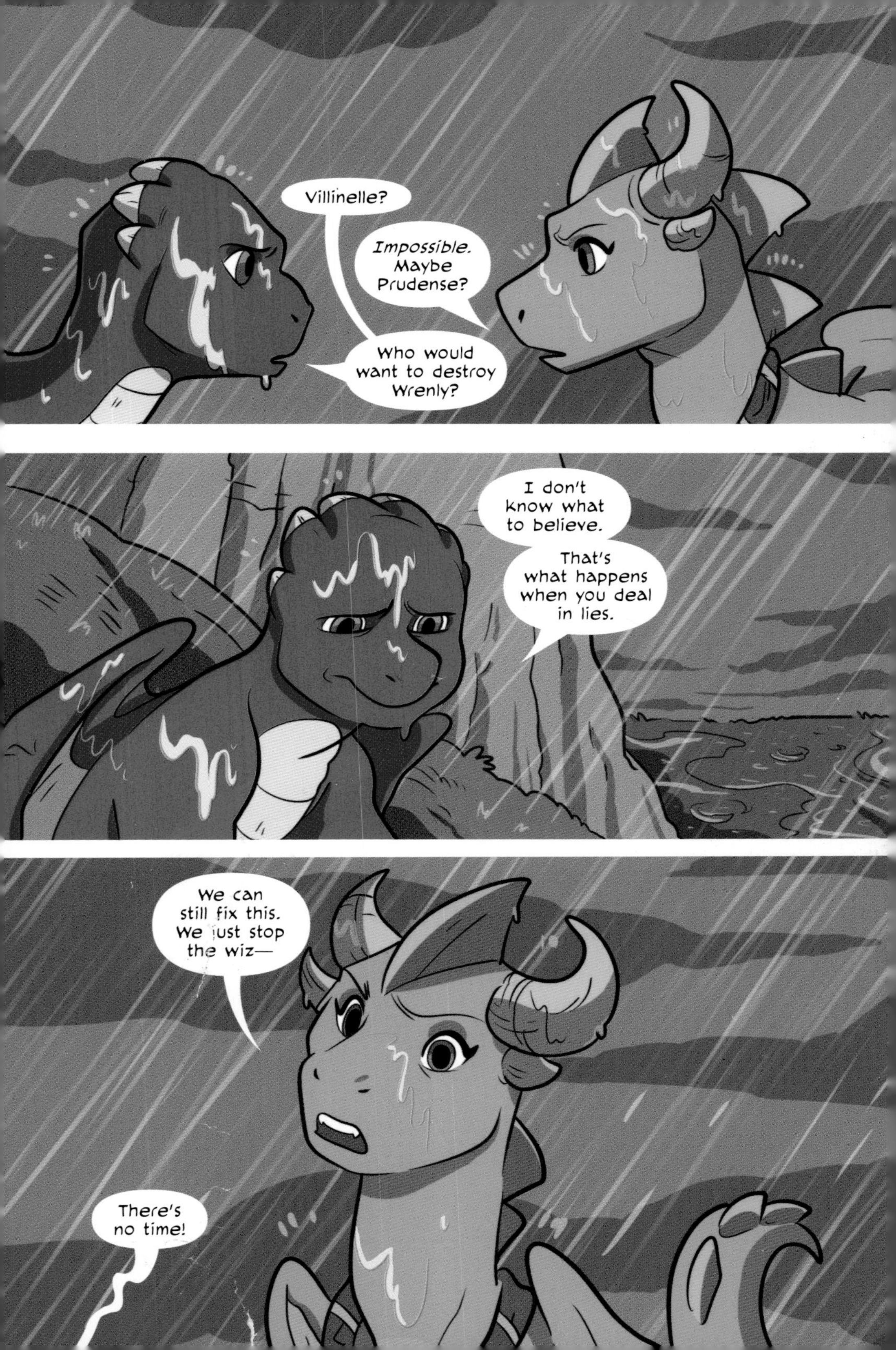
Villinelle?
Impossible. Maybe Prudense?
Who would want to destroy Wrenly?
I don't know what to believe.
That's what happens when you deal in lies.
We can still fix this. We just stop the wiz—
There's no time!

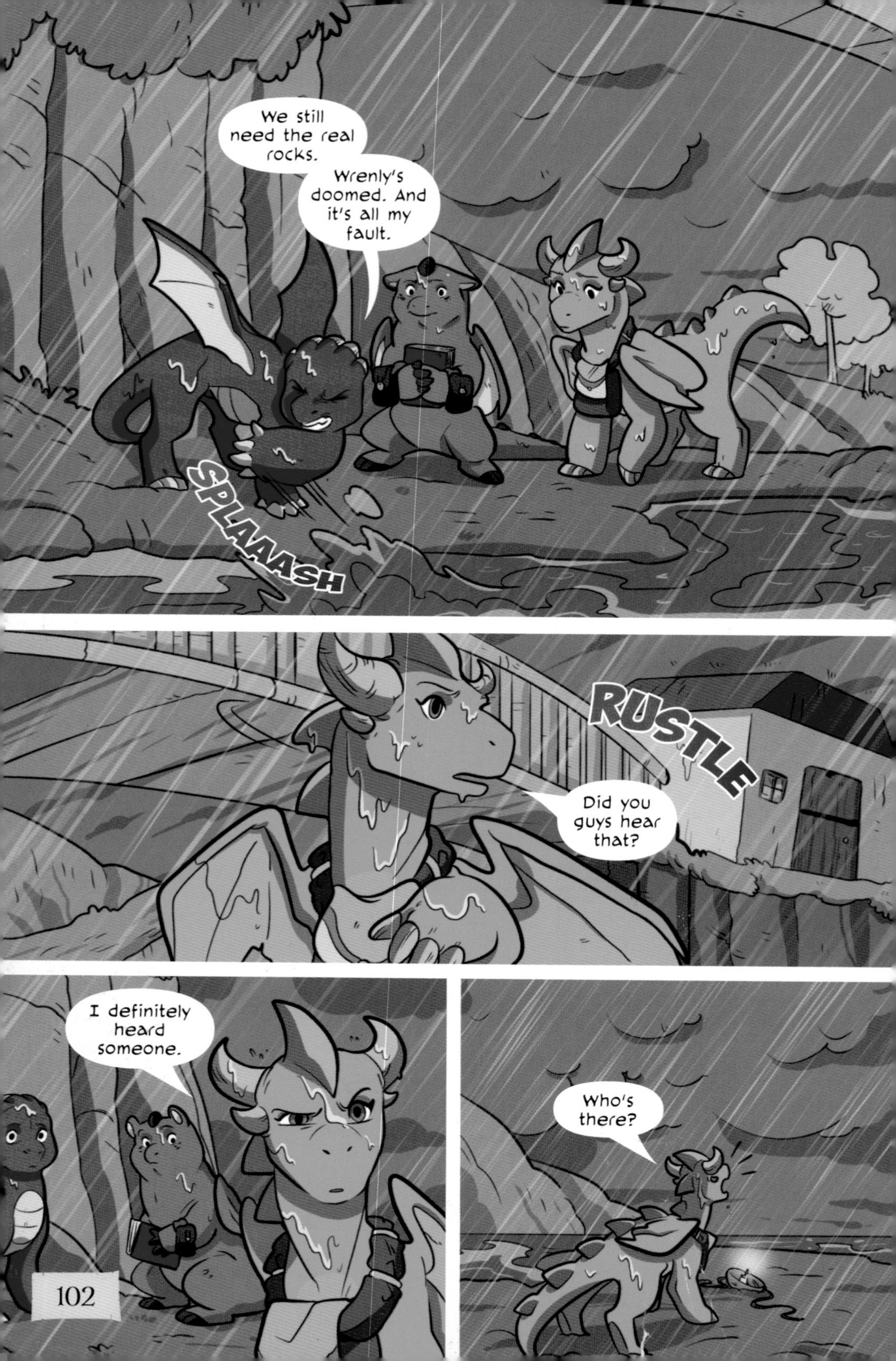
We still need the real rocks.
Wrenly's doomed. And it's all my fault.
SPLAAAASH
RUSTLE
Did you guys hear that?
I definitely heard someone.
Who's there?

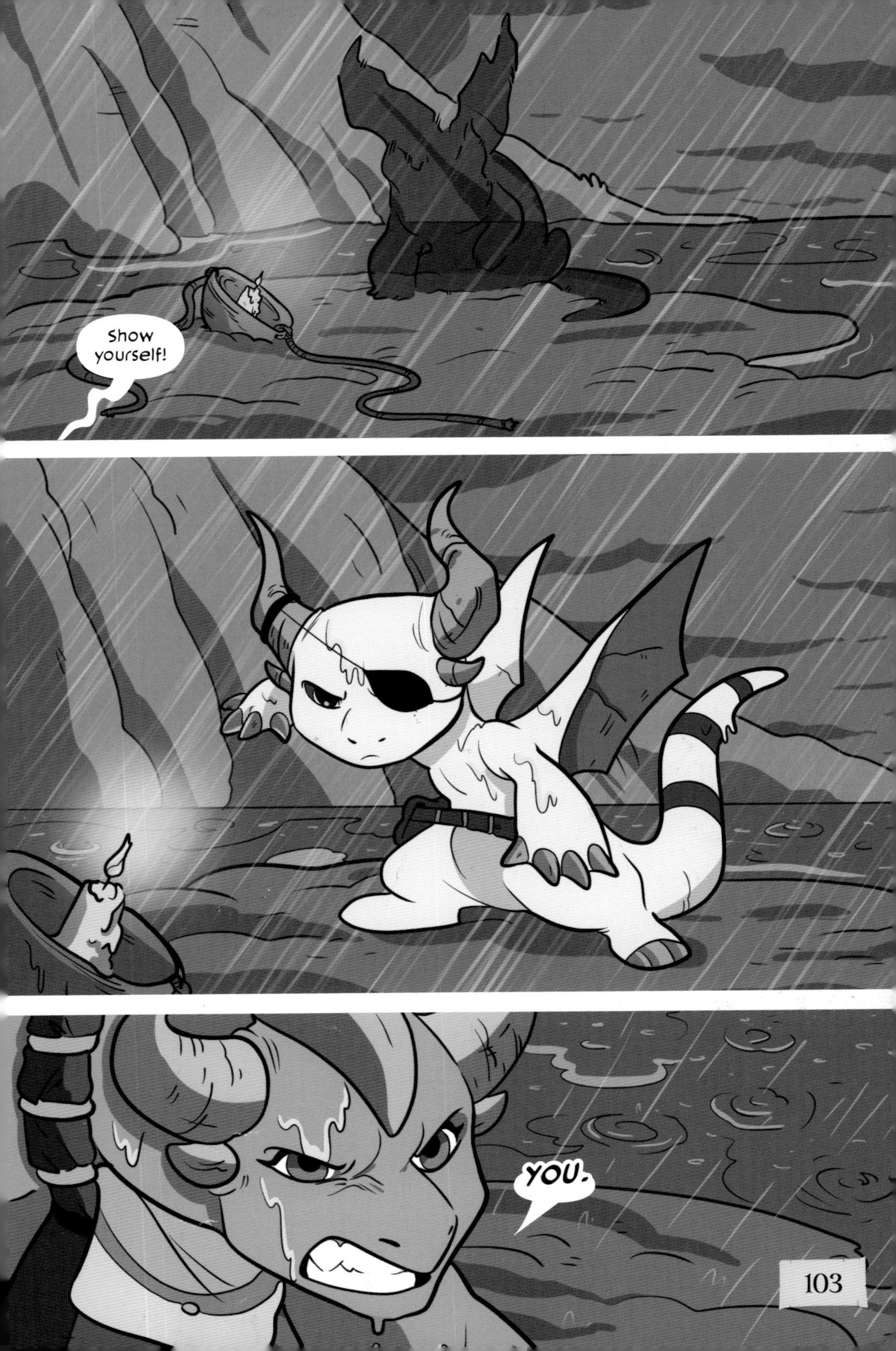
Show yourself!
YOU.

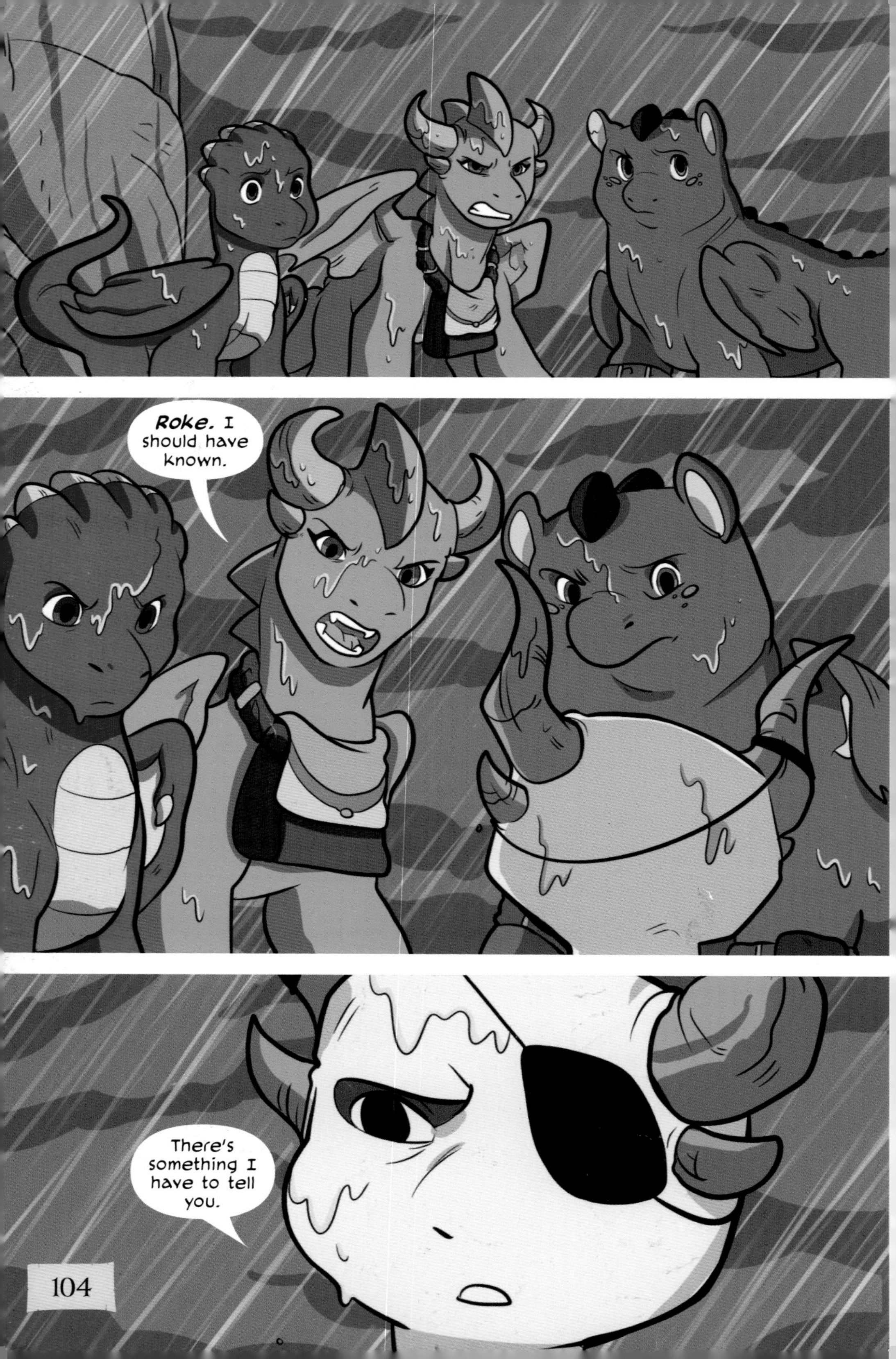
Roke. I should have known.
There's something I have to tell you.

Chapter 8

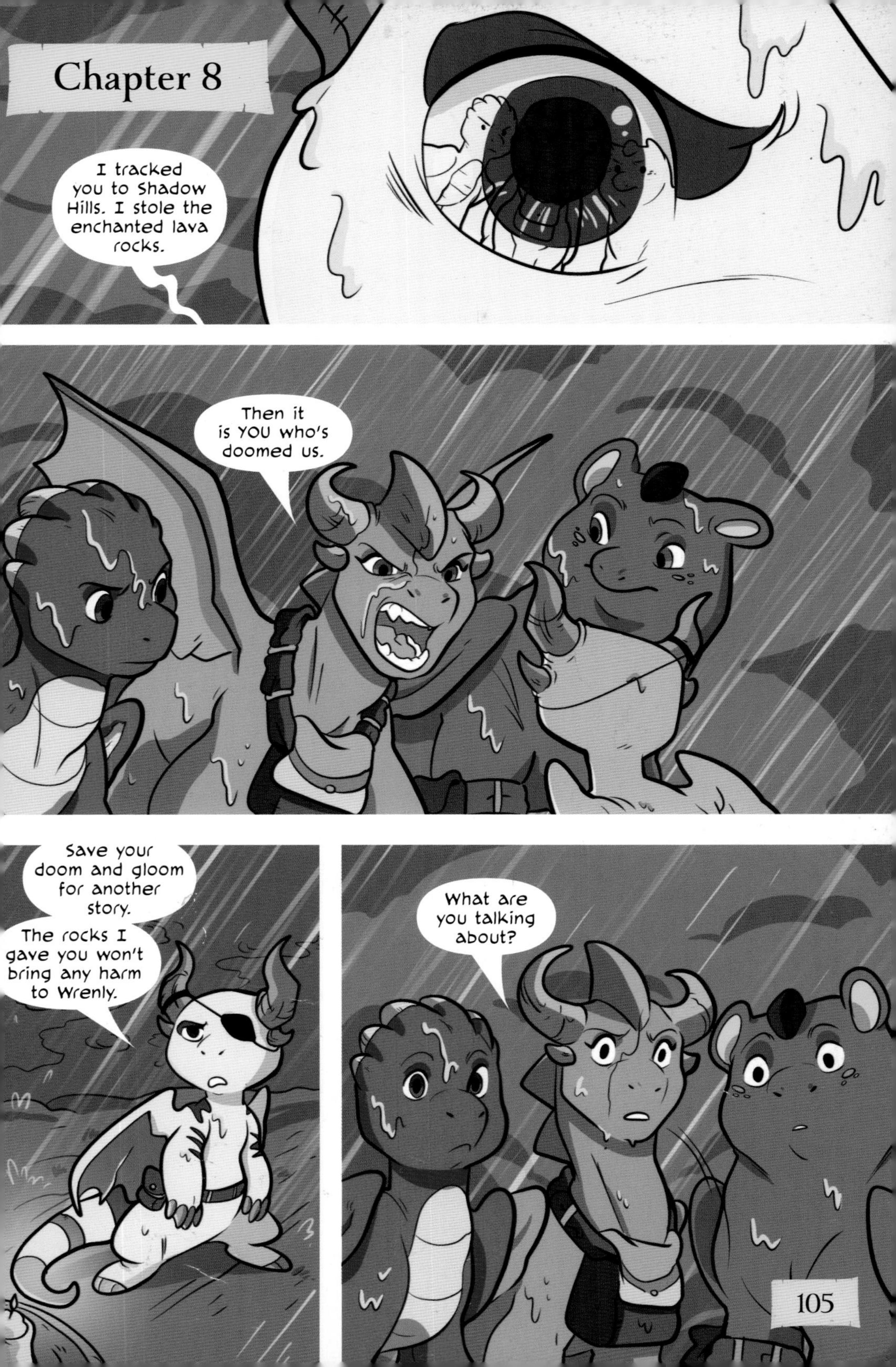

I tracked you to Shadow Hills. I stole the enchanted lava rocks.
Then it is YOU who's doomed us.
Save your doom and gloom for another story.
The rocks I gave you won't bring any harm to Wrenly.
What are you talking about?

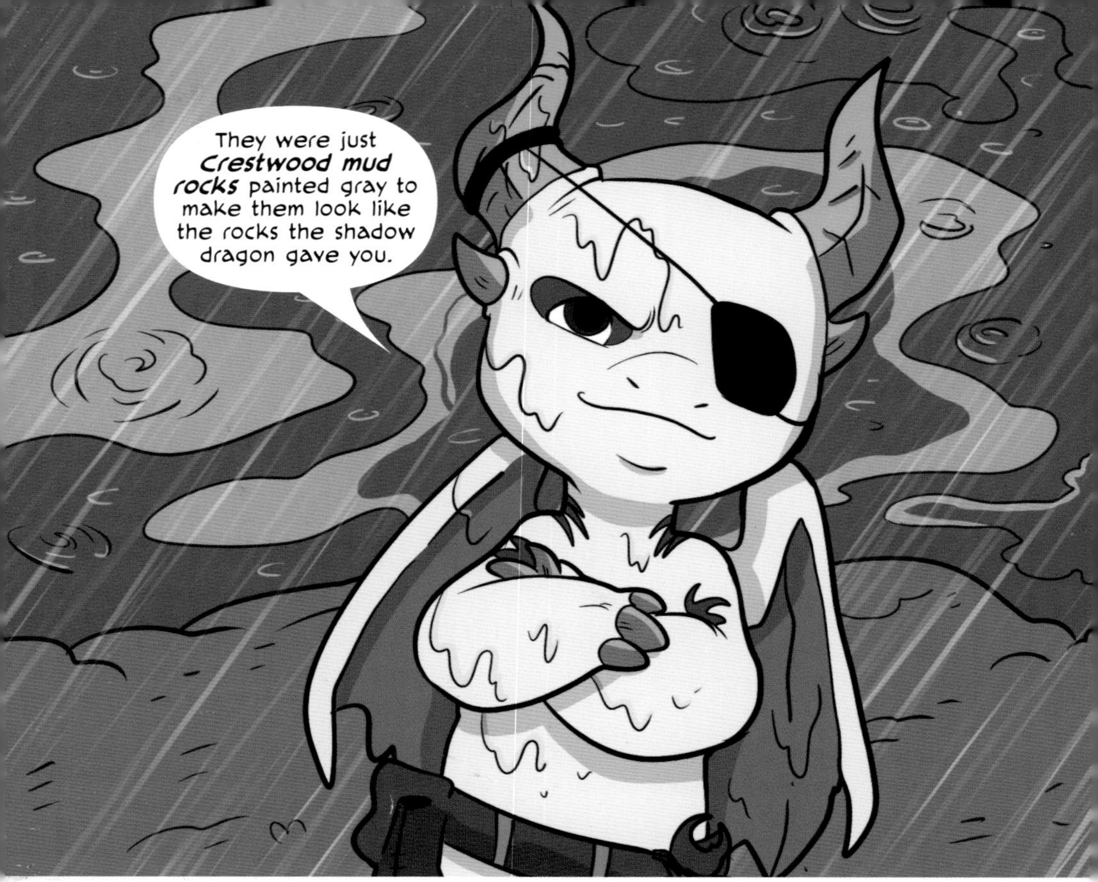
They were just *Crestwood mud rocks* painted gray to make them look like the rocks the shadow dragon gave you.

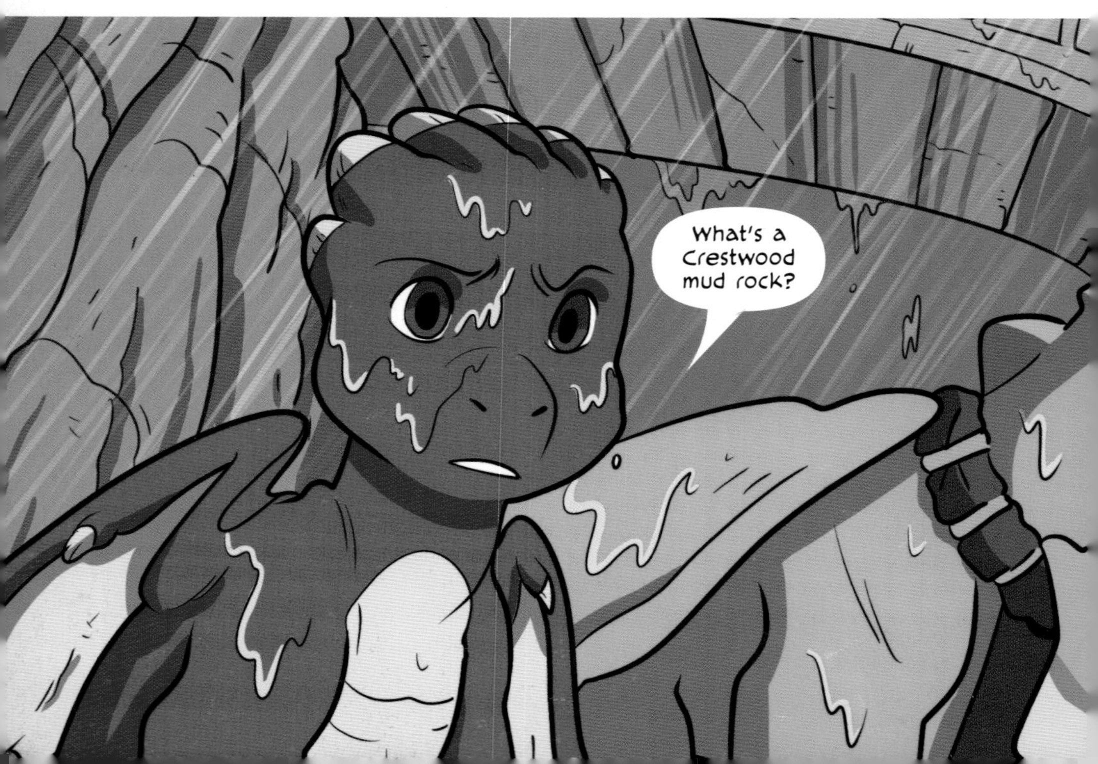
What's a Crestwood mud rock?

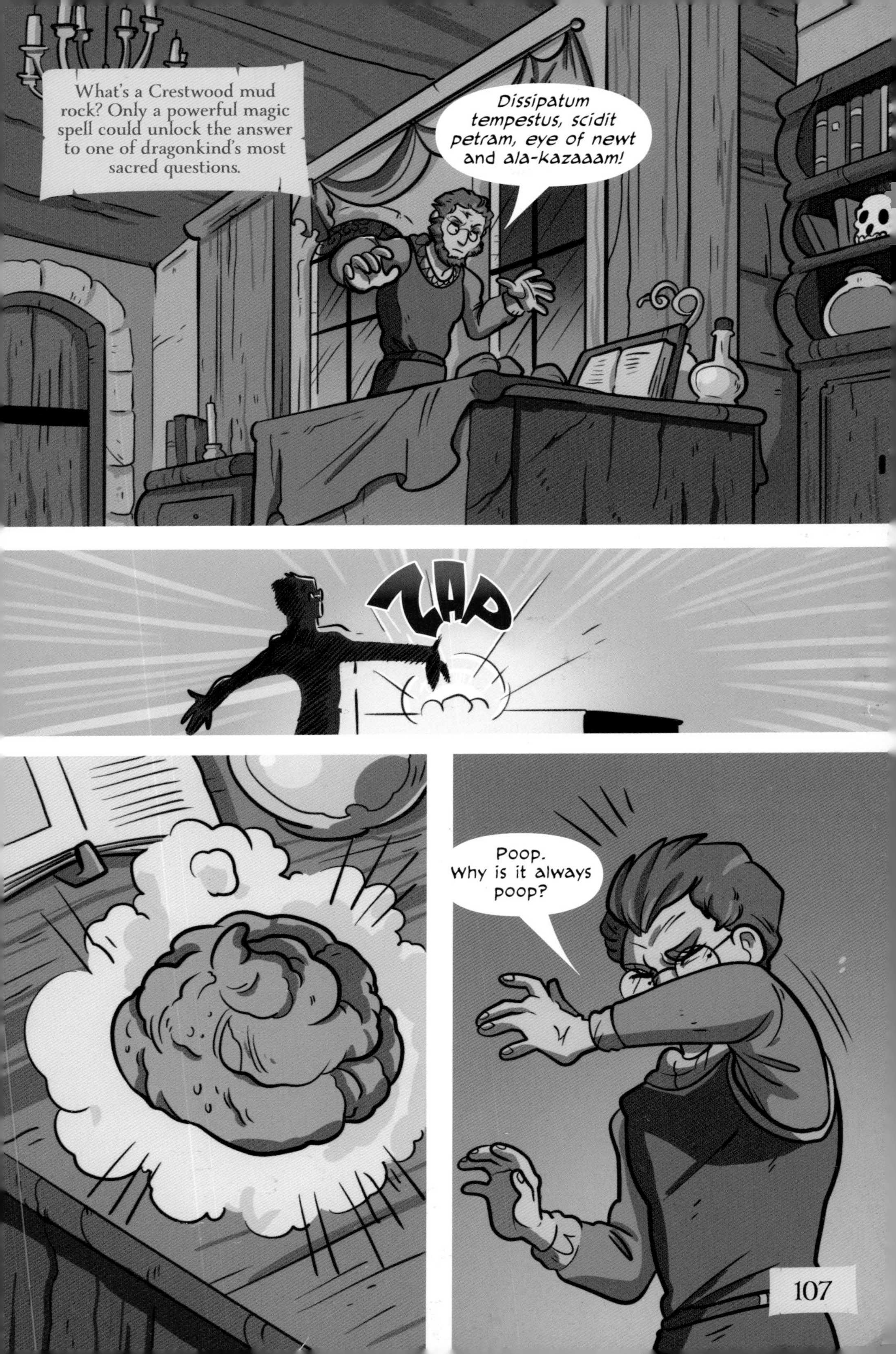
What's a Crestwood mud rock? Only a powerful magic spell could unlock the answer to one of dragonkind's most sacred questions.
Dissipatum tempestus, scidit petram, eye of newt and ala-kazaaam!
ZAP
Poop. Why is it always poop?

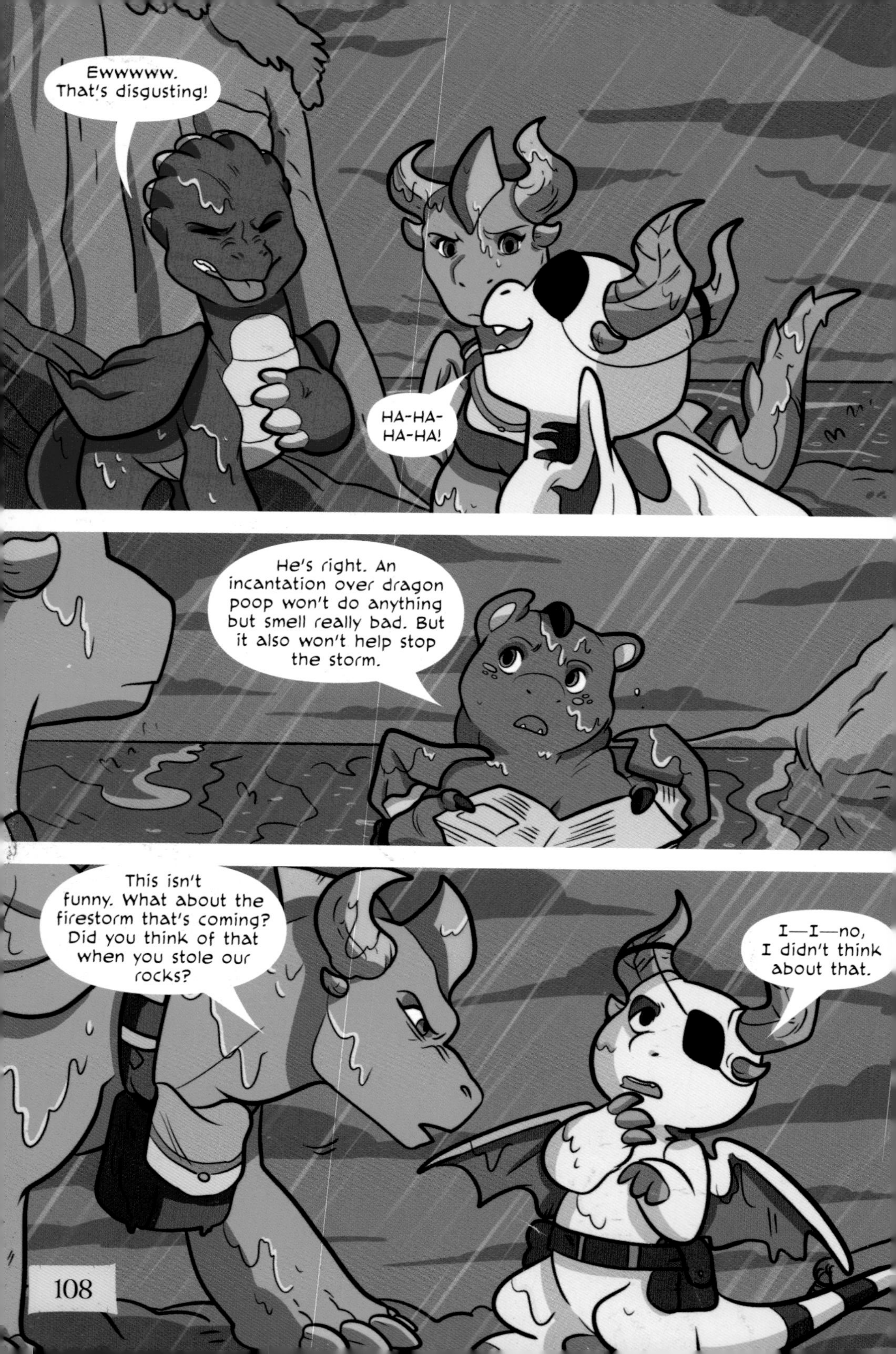
Ewwwww. That's disgusting!
HA-HA-HA-HA!
He's right. An incantation over dragon poop won't do anything but smell really bad. But it also won't help stop the storm.
This isn't funny. What about the firestorm that's coming? Did you think of that when you stole our rocks?
I—I—no, I didn't think about that.

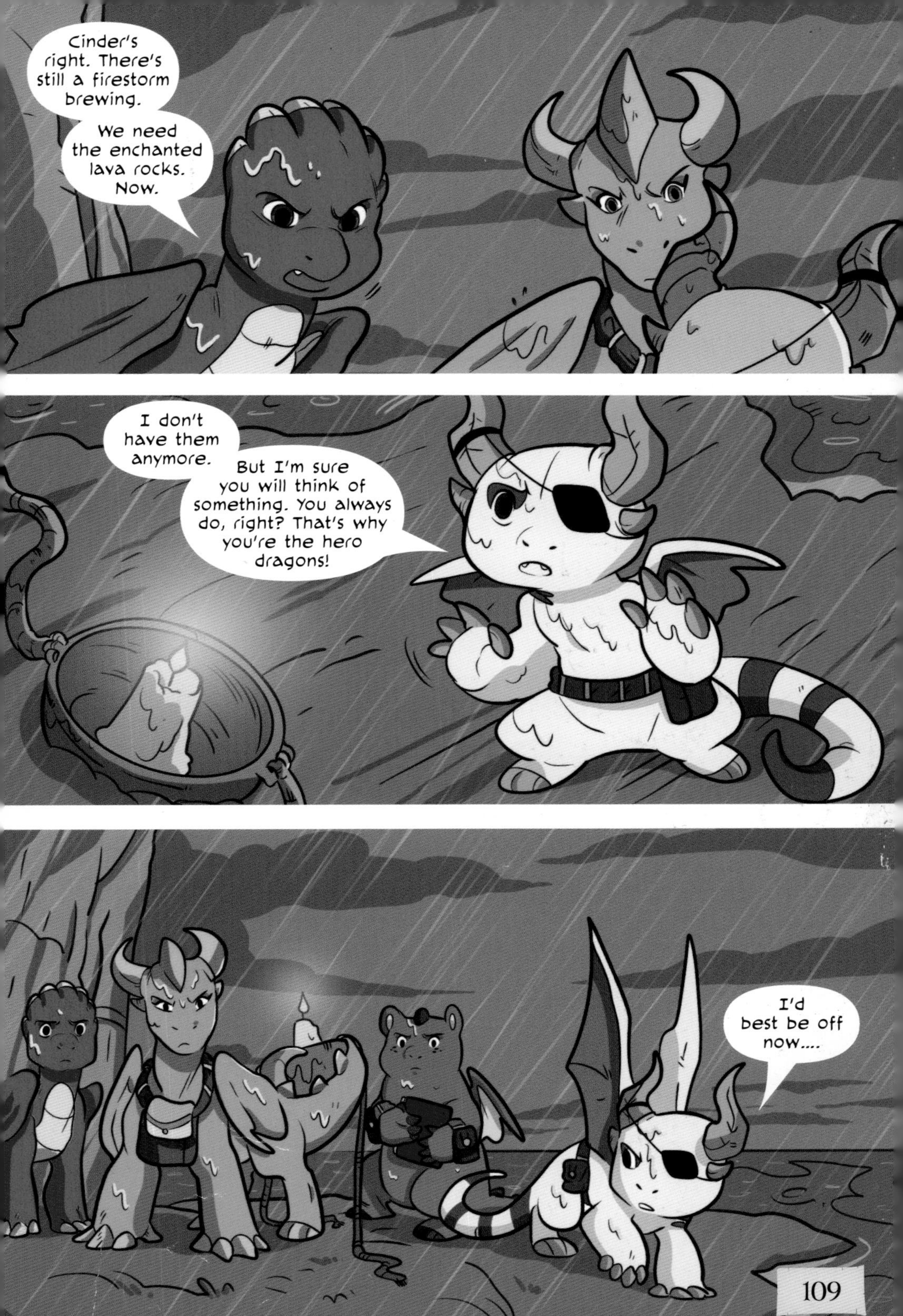
Cinder's right. There's still a firestorm brewing.
We need the enchanted lava rocks. Now.
I don't have them anymore.
But I'm sure you will think of something. You always do, right? That's why you're the hero dragons!
I'd best be off now....

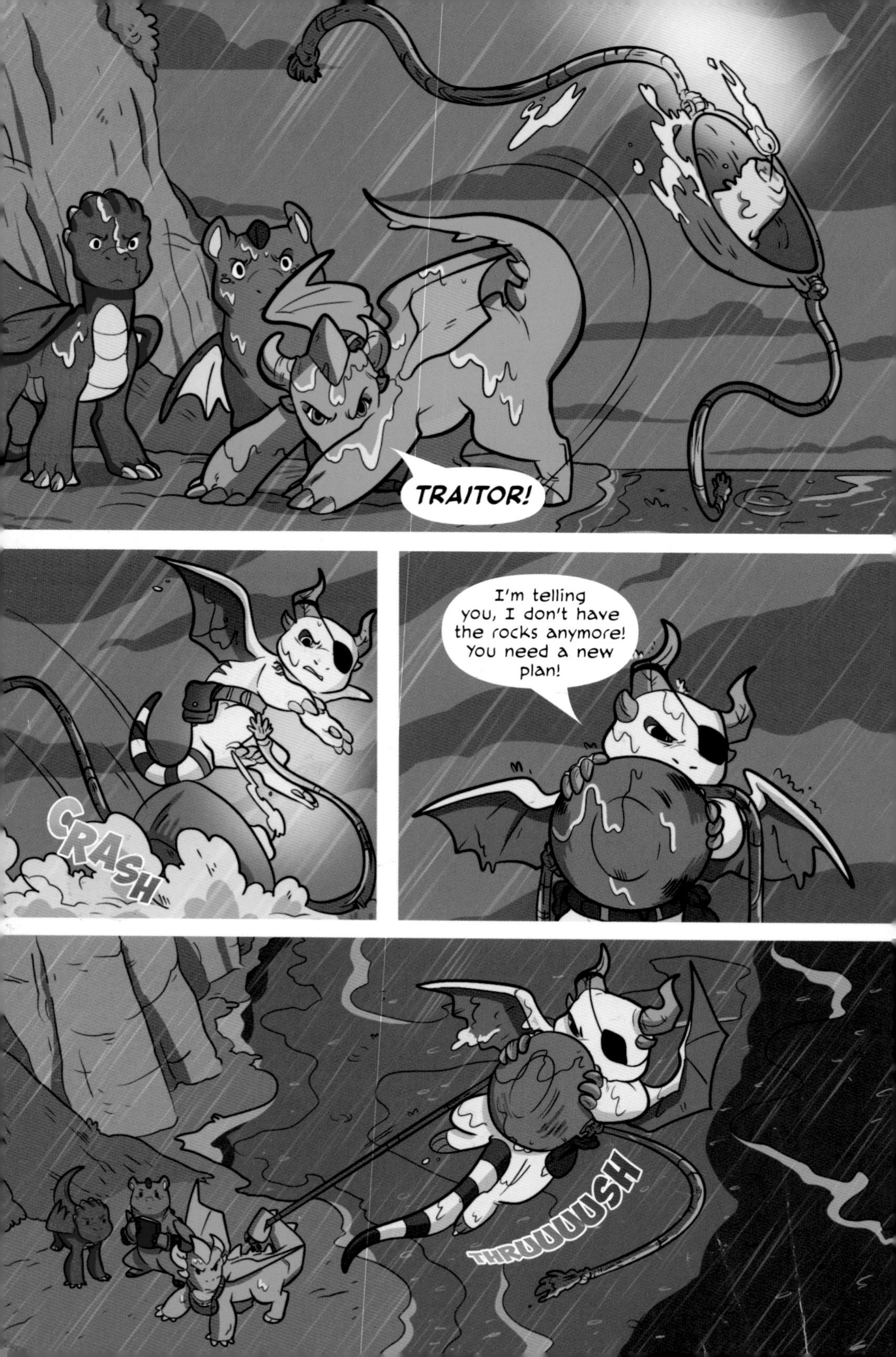

TRAITOR!
CRASH
I'm telling you, I don't have the rocks anymore! You need a new plan!
THRUUUUSH

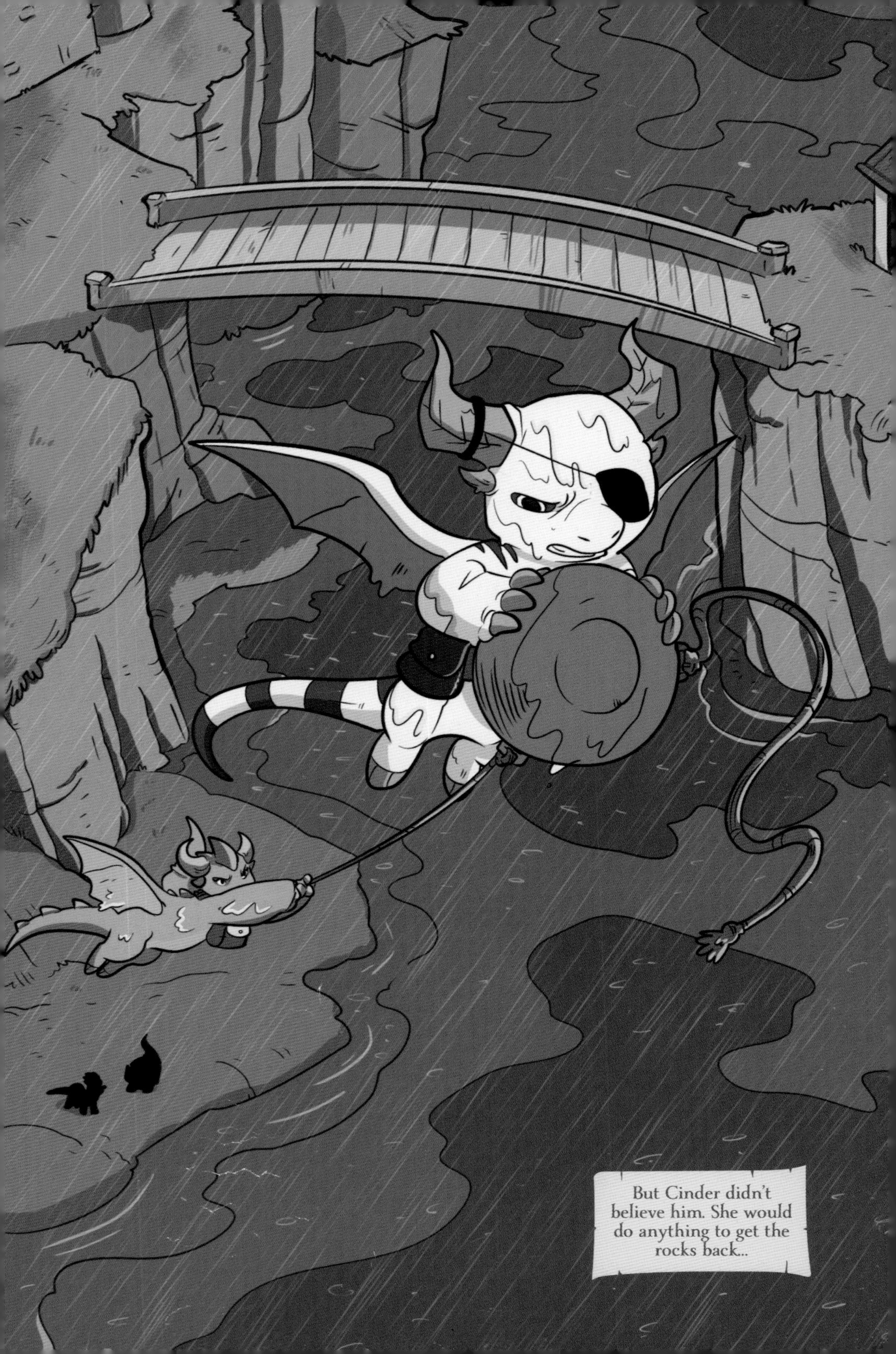
But Cinder didn't believe him. She would do anything to get the rocks back...

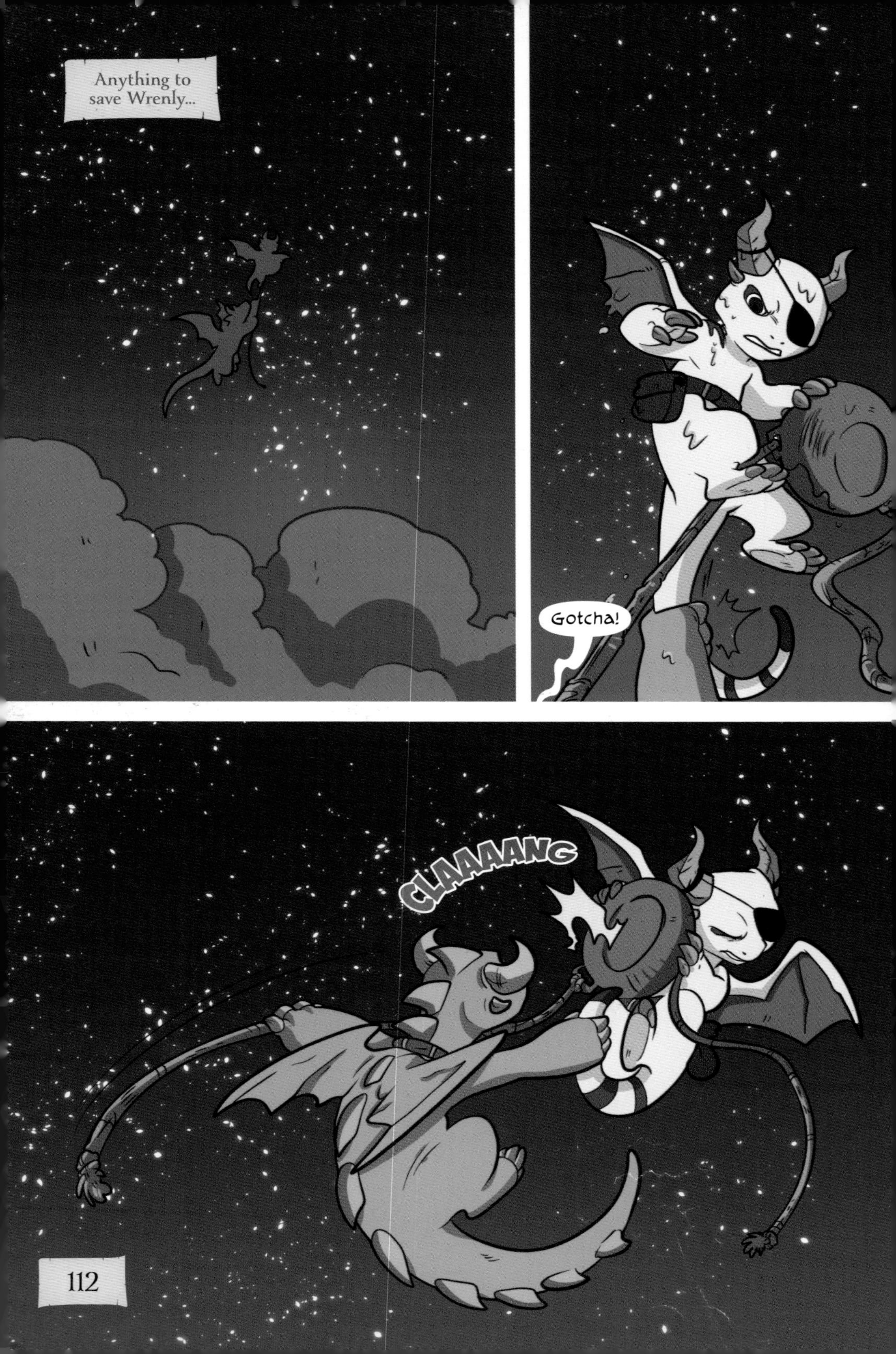
Anything to save Wrenly...
Gotcha!
CLAAAAANG

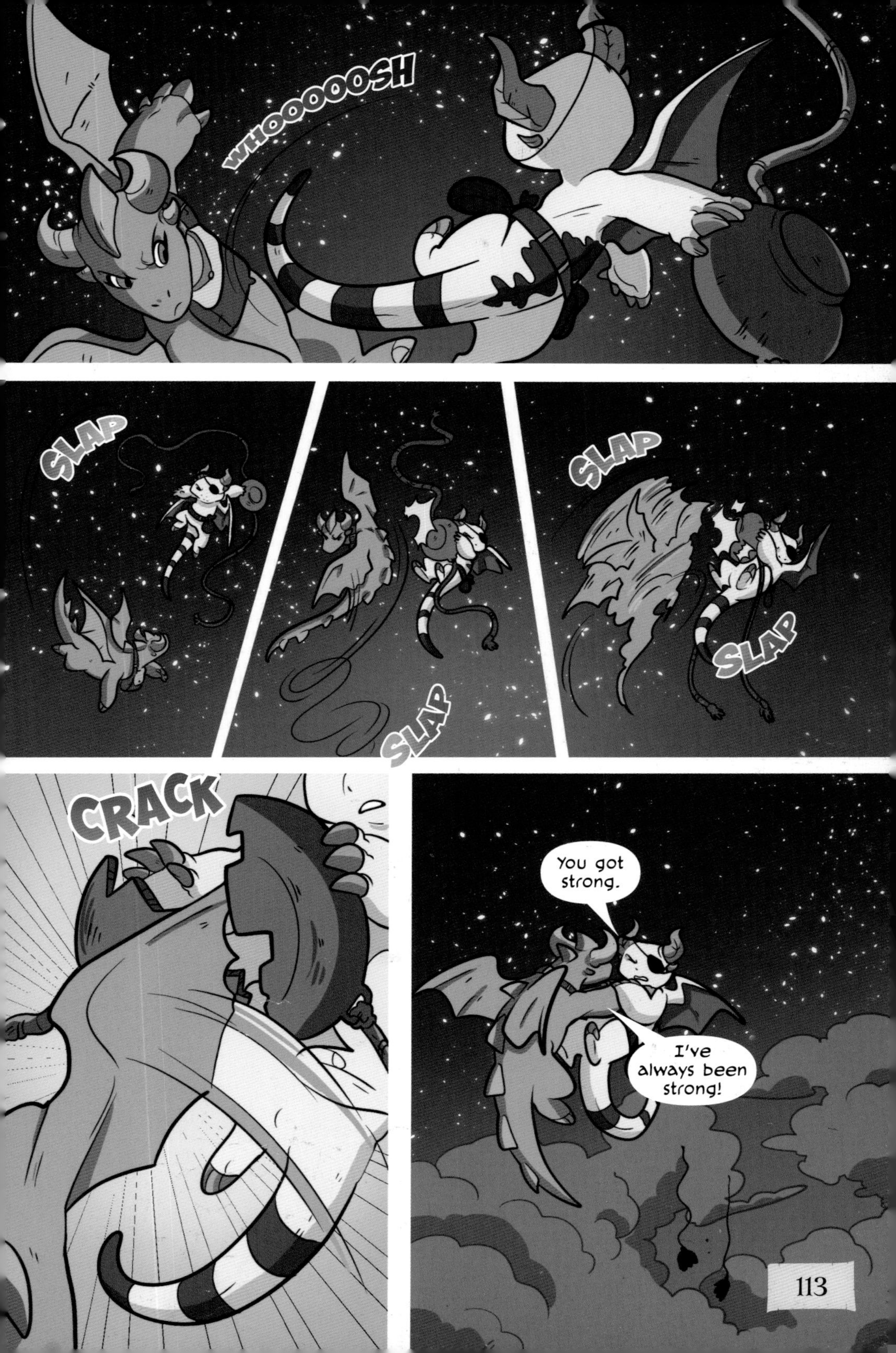
WHOOOOOOSH
SLAP
SLAP
SLAP
SLAP
CRACK
You got strong.
I've always been strong!

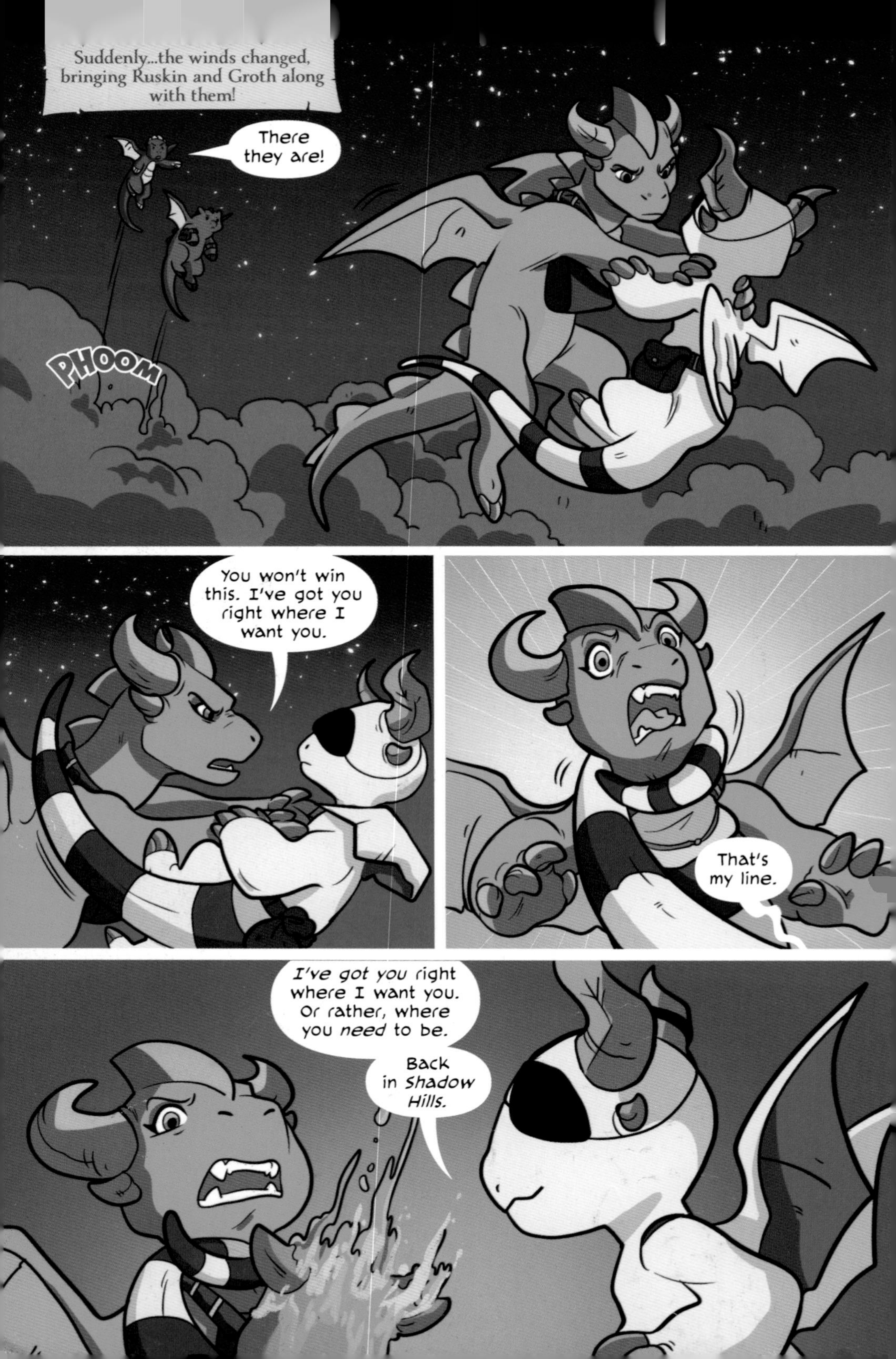
Suddenly...the winds changed, bringing Ruskin and Groth along with them!
There they are!
PHOOM
You won't win this. I've got you right where I want you.
That's my line.
I've got you right where I want you. Or rather, where you *need* to be.
Back in Shadow Hills.

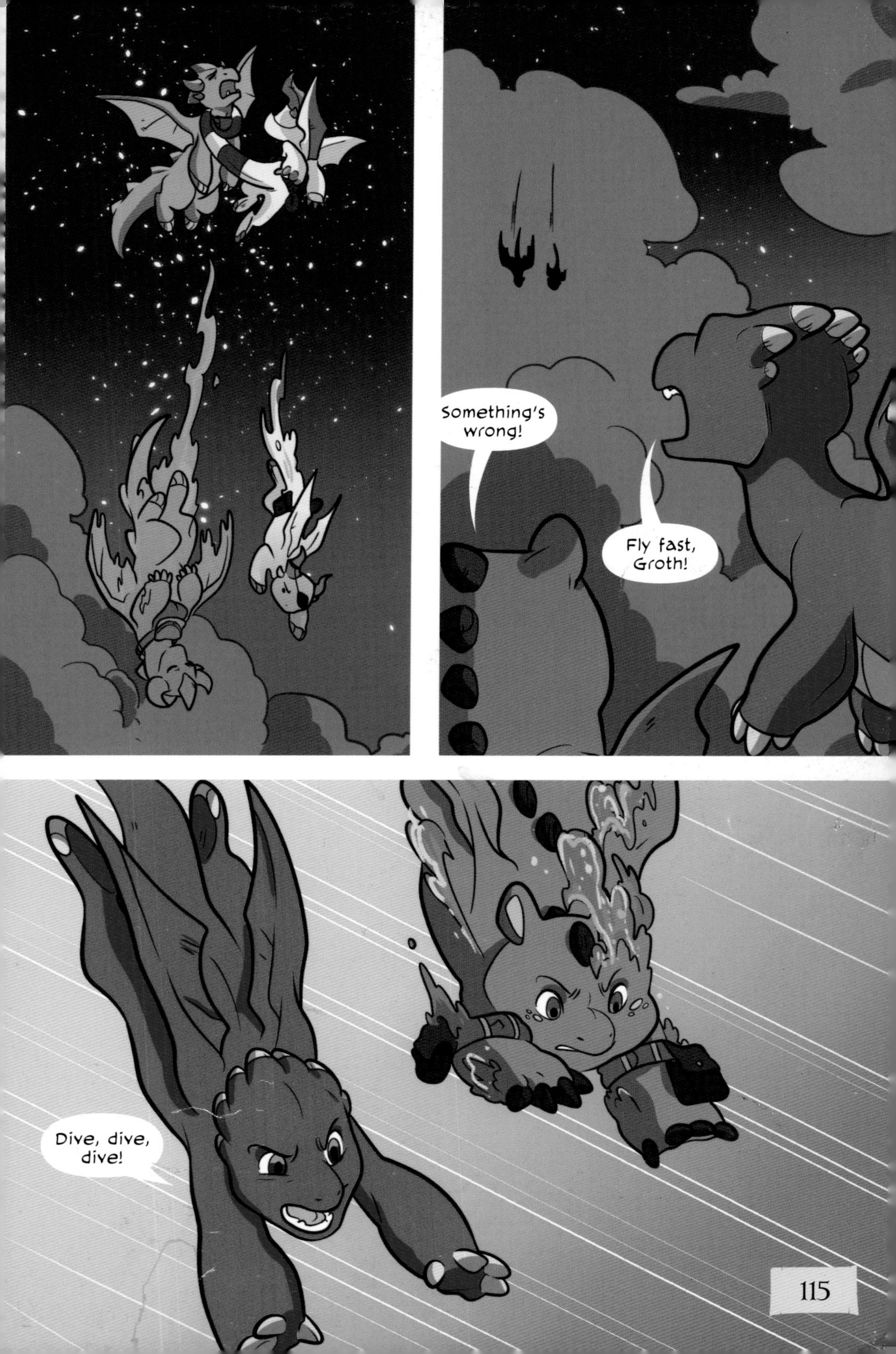
Something's wrong!
Fly fast, Groth!
Dive, dive, dive!

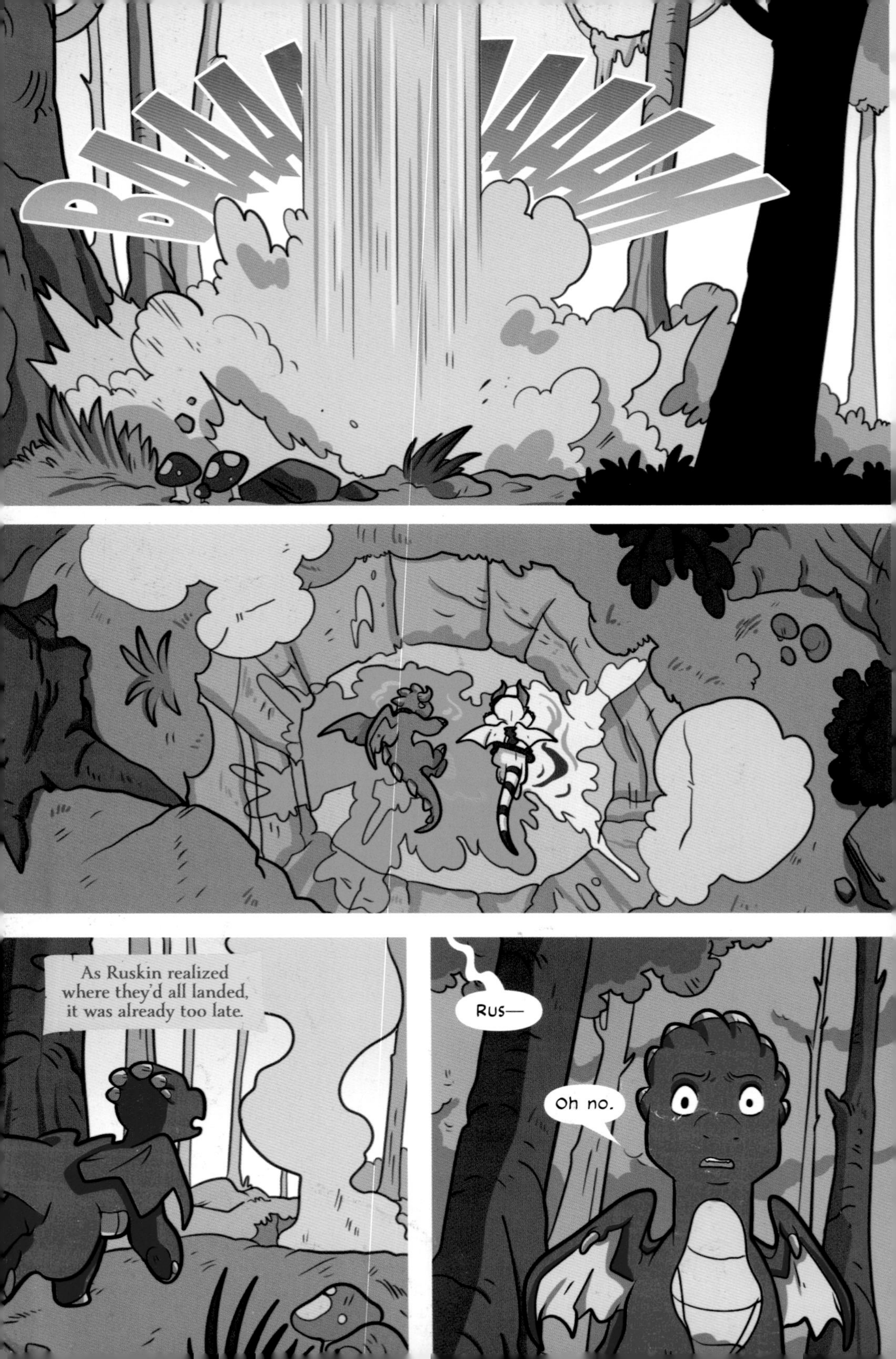
BAAAAAAAM
As Ruskin realized where they'd all landed, it was already too late.
Rus—
Oh no.

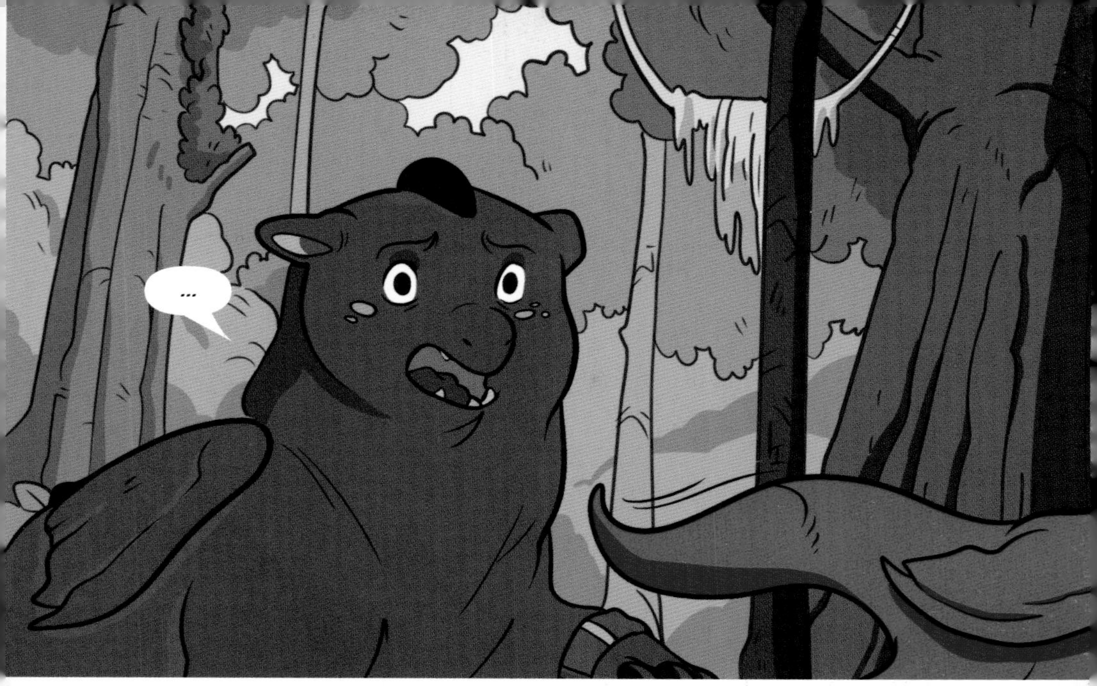
...

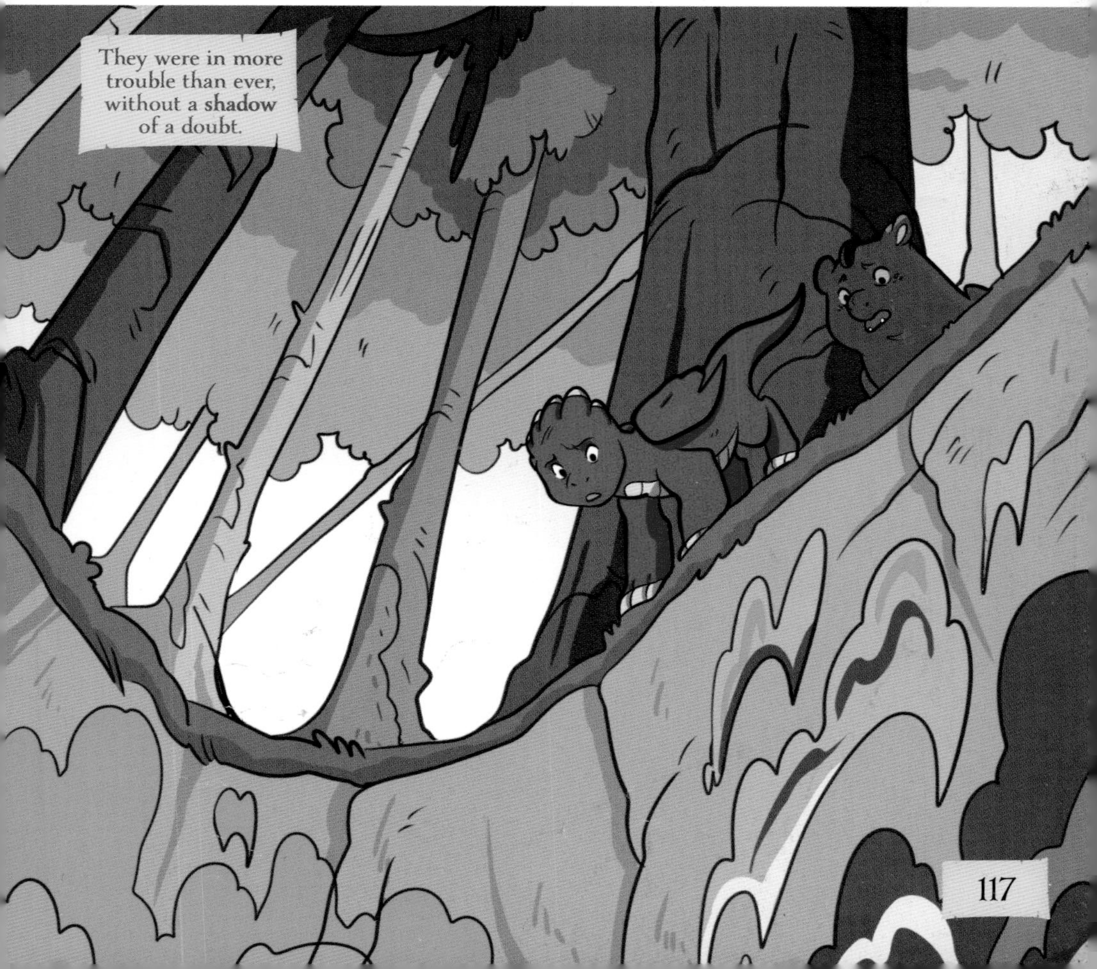
They were in more trouble than ever, without a **shadow** of a doubt.

Chapter 9

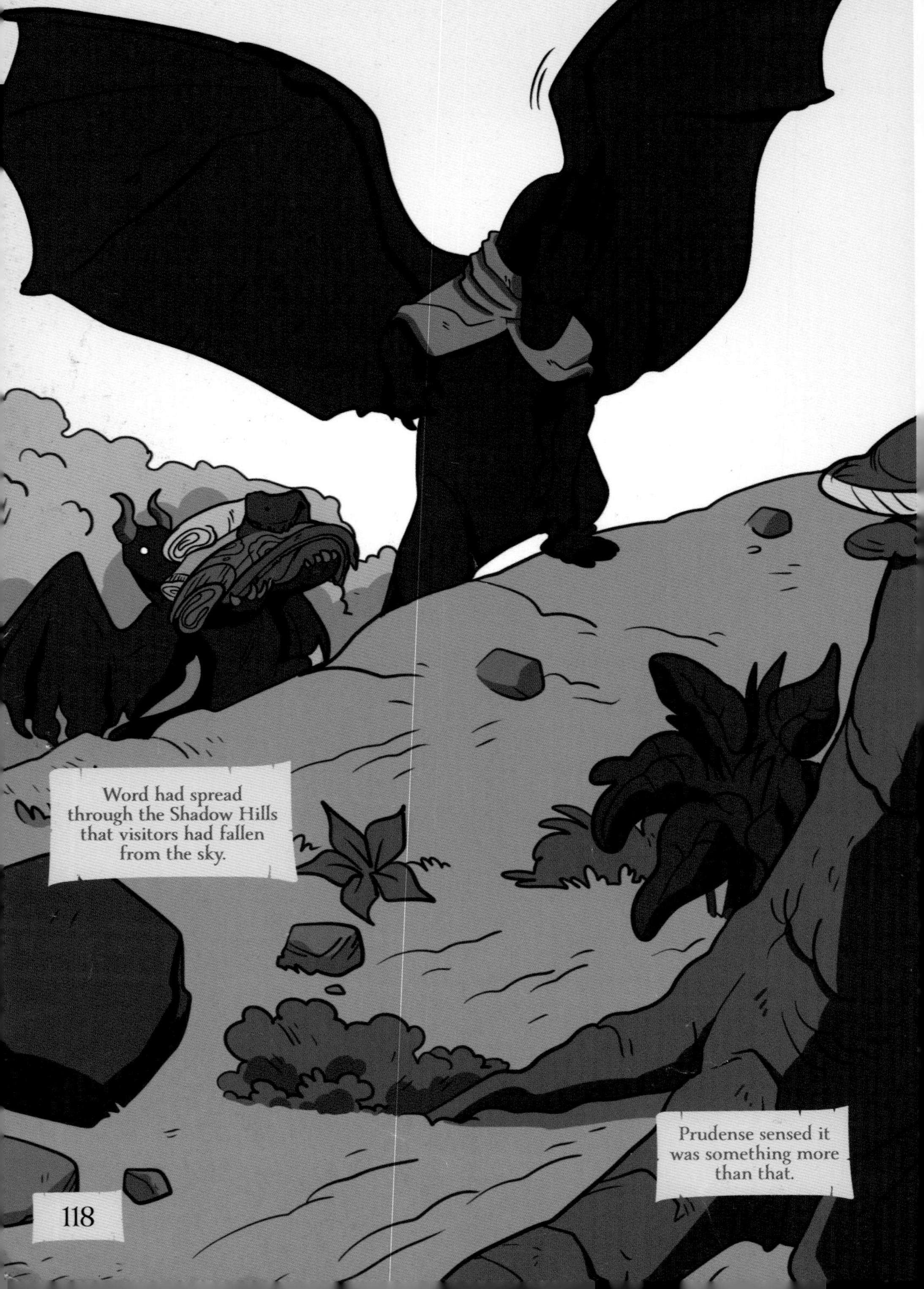
Word had spread through the Shadow Hills that visitors had fallen from the sky.
Prudense sensed it was something more than that.

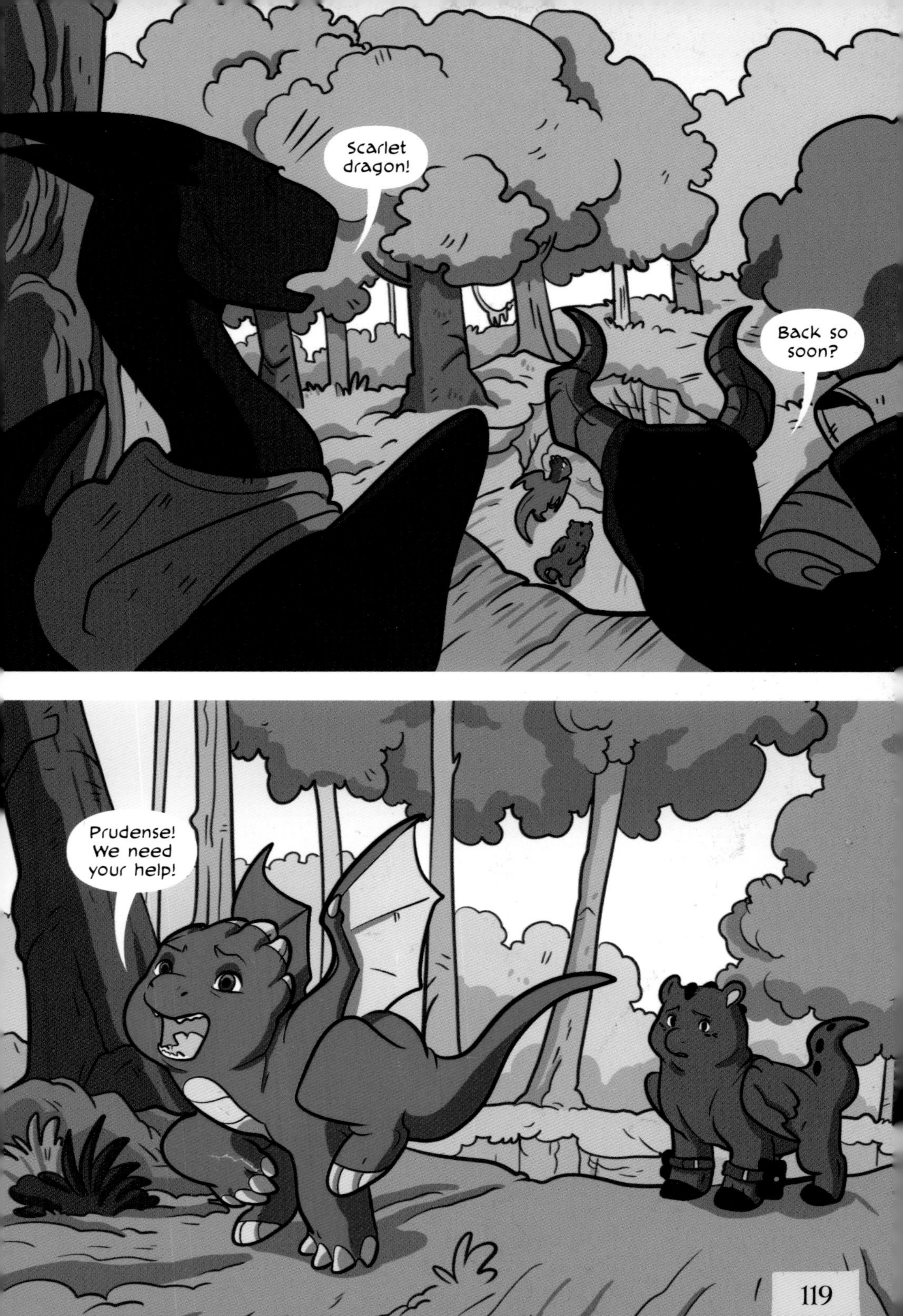
Scarlet dragon!
Back so soon?
Prudense! We need your help!

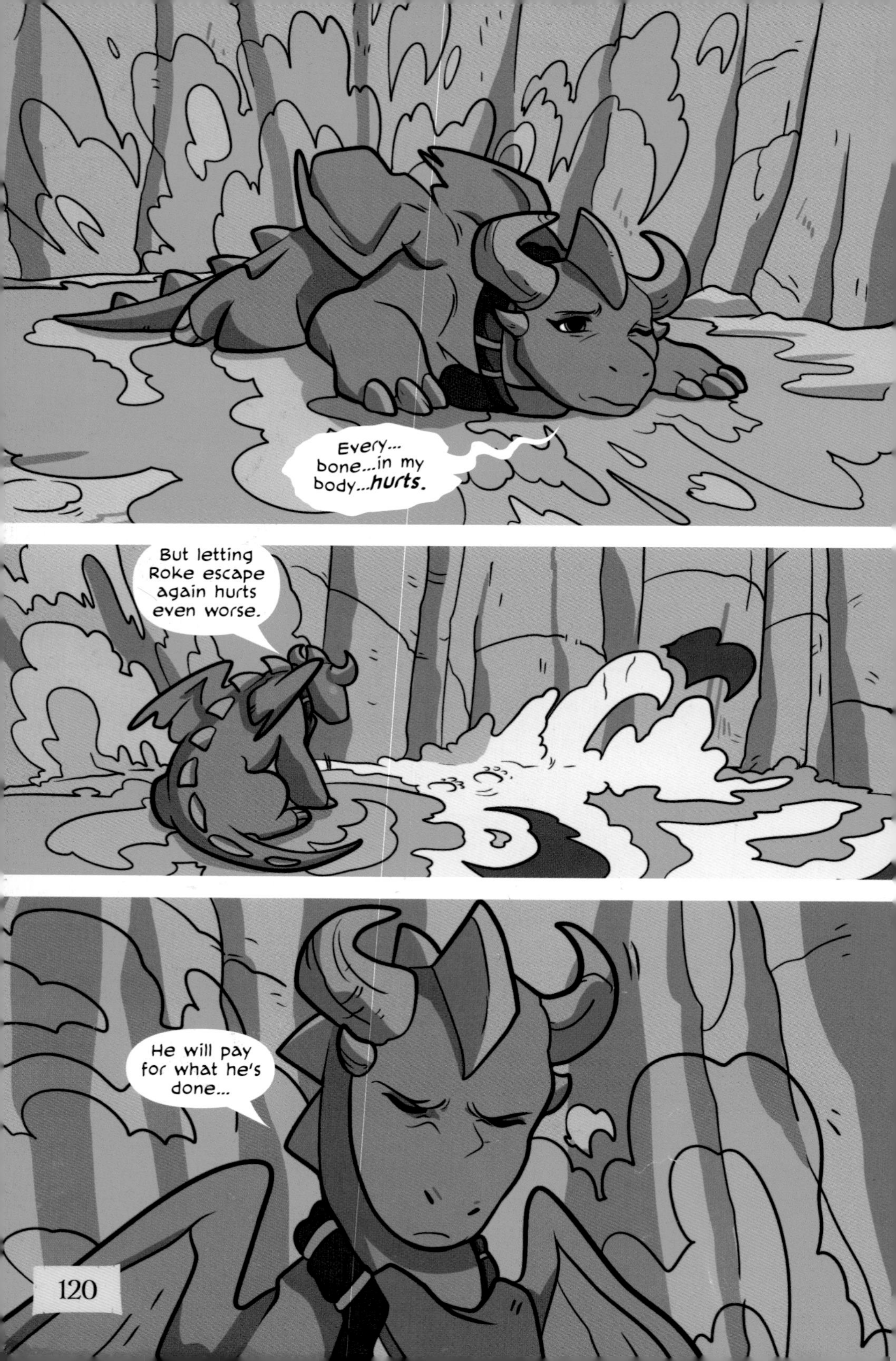
Every... bone...in my body...**hurts.**
But letting Roke escape again hurts even worse.
He will pay for what he's done...

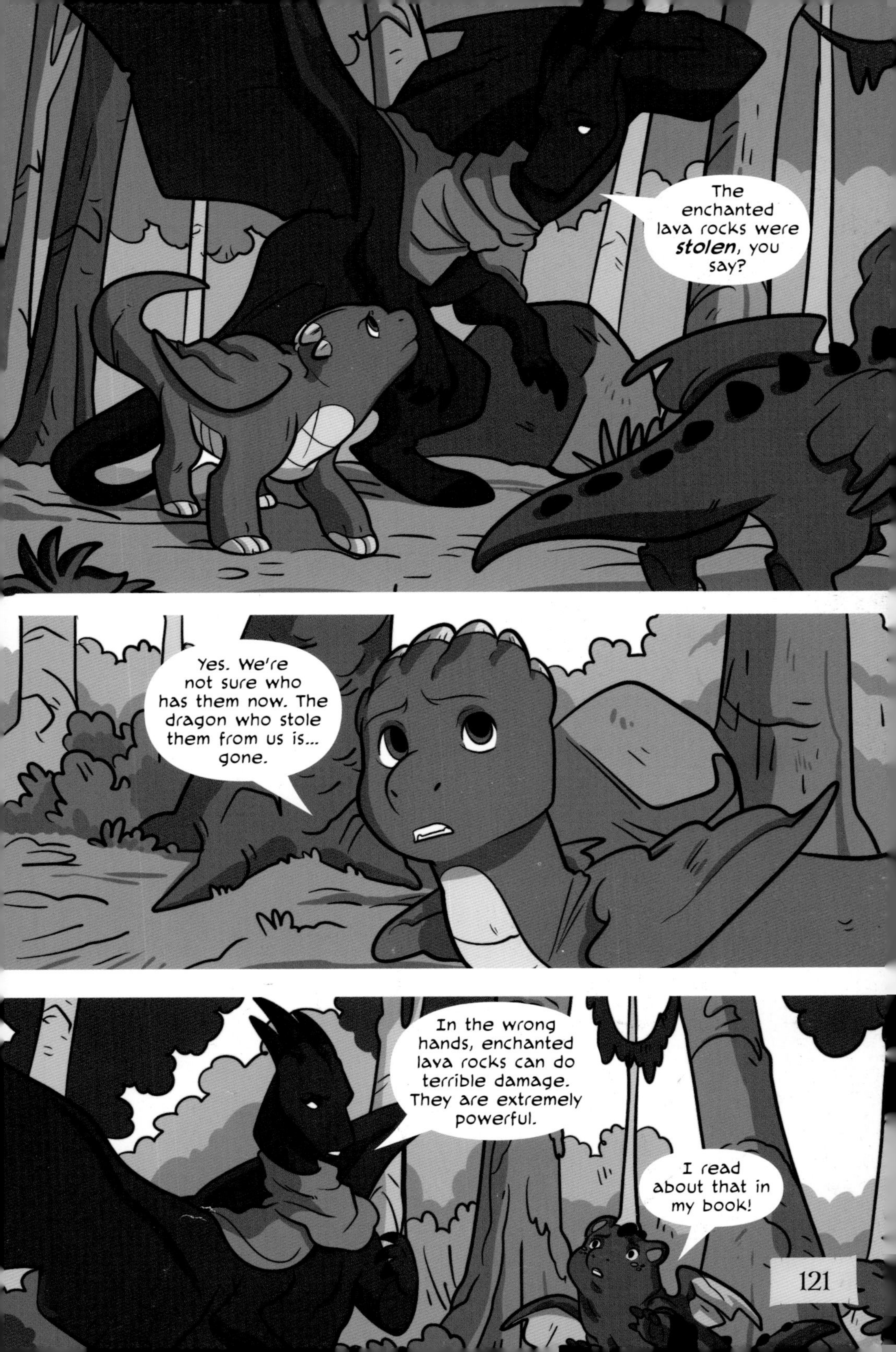
The enchanted lava rocks were stolen, you say?
Yes. We're not sure who has them now. The dragon who stole them from us is... gone.
In the wrong hands, enchanted lava rocks can do terrible damage. They are extremely powerful.
I read about that in my book!

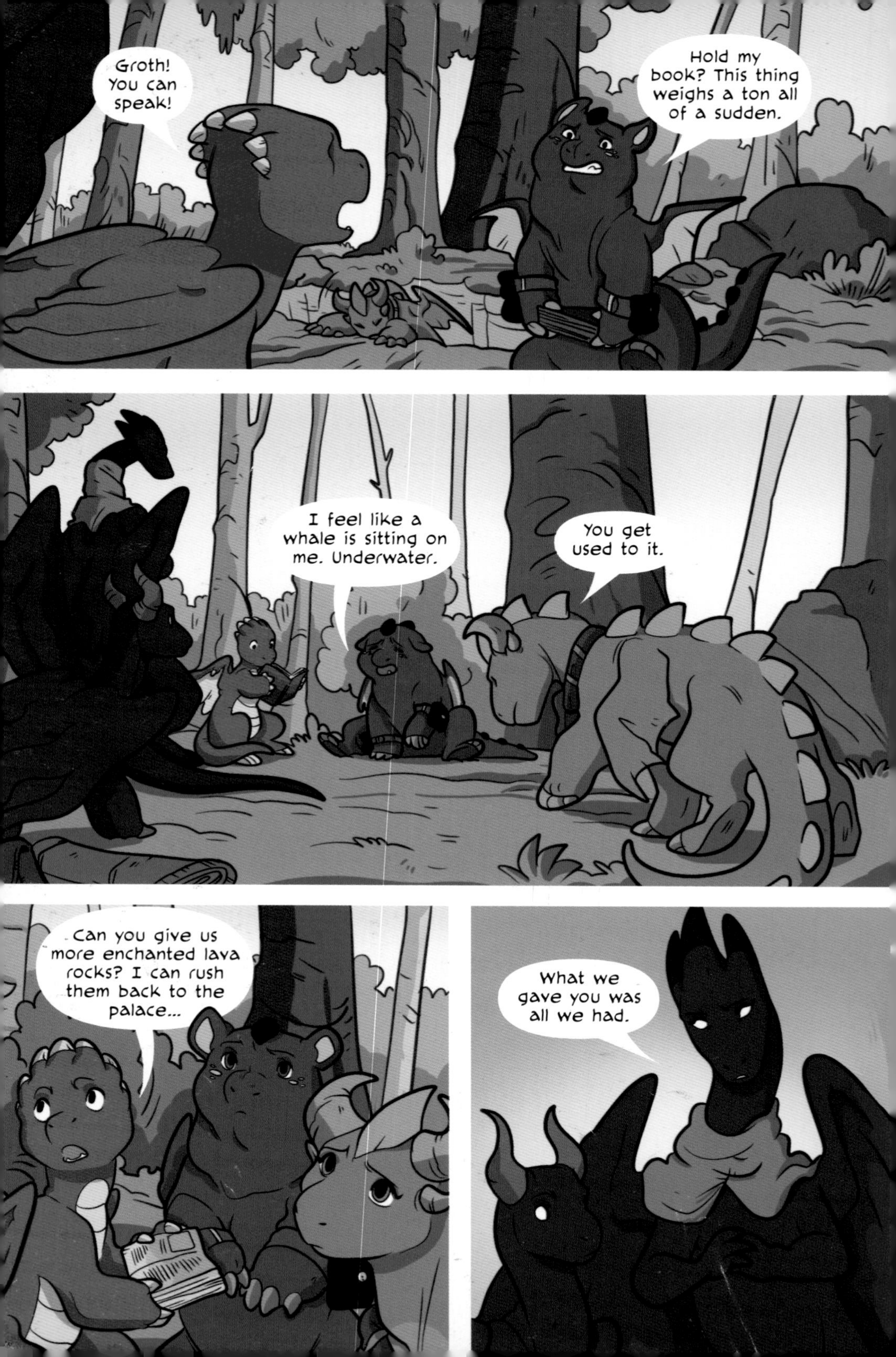
Groth! You can speak!
Hold my book? This thing weighs a ton all of a sudden.
I feel like a whale is sitting on me. Underwater.
You get used to it.
Can you give us more enchanted lava rocks? I can rush them back to the palace...
What we gave you was all we had.

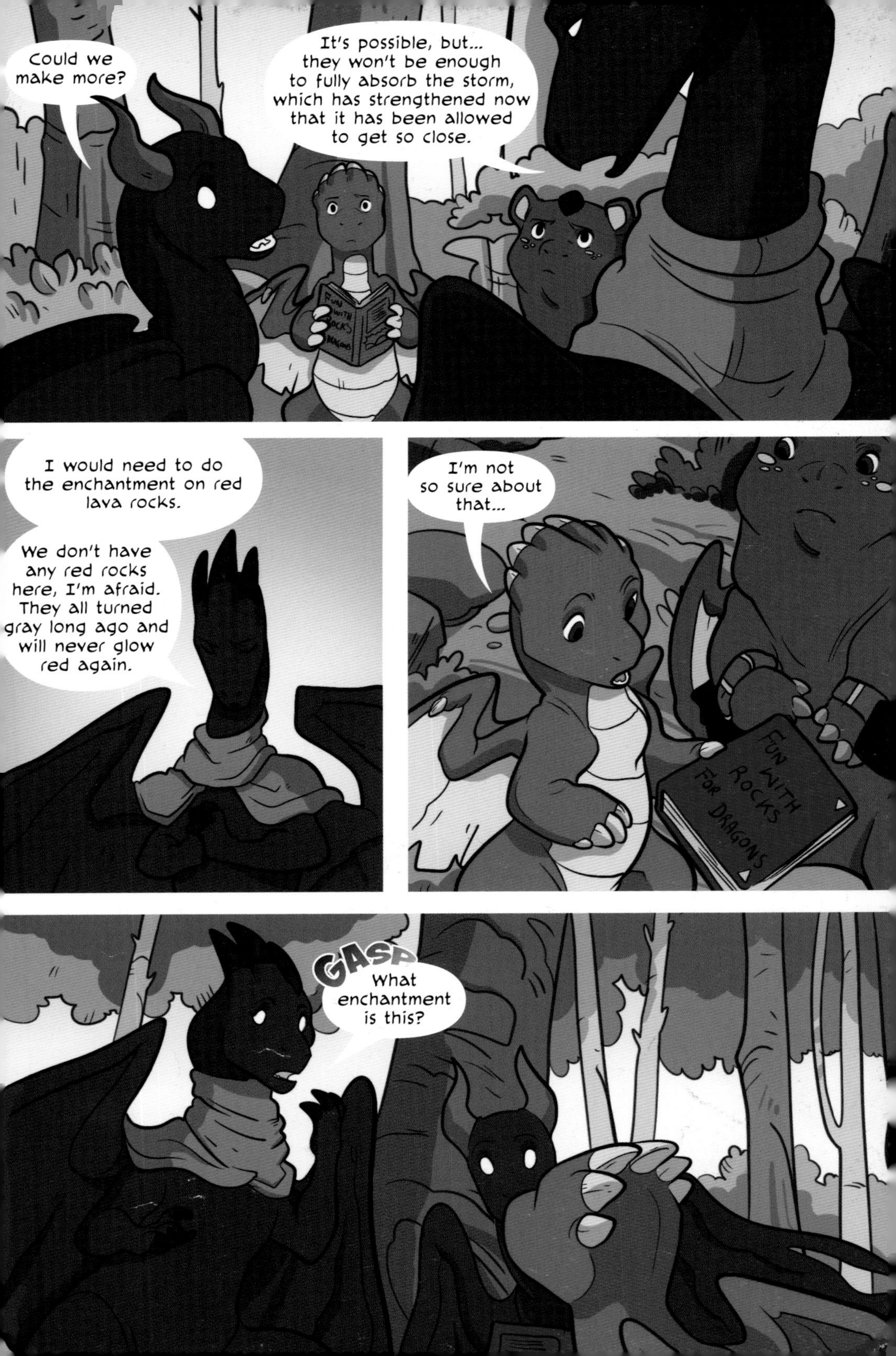
Could we make more?
It's possible, but... they won't be enough to fully absorb the storm, which has strengthened now that it has been allowed to get so close.
FUN WITH ROCKS FOR DRAGONS
I would need to do the enchantment on red lava rocks.
We don't have any red rocks here, I'm afraid. They all turned gray long ago and will never glow red again.
I'm not so sure about that...
FUN WITH ROCKS FOR DRAGONS
GASP
What enchantment is this?

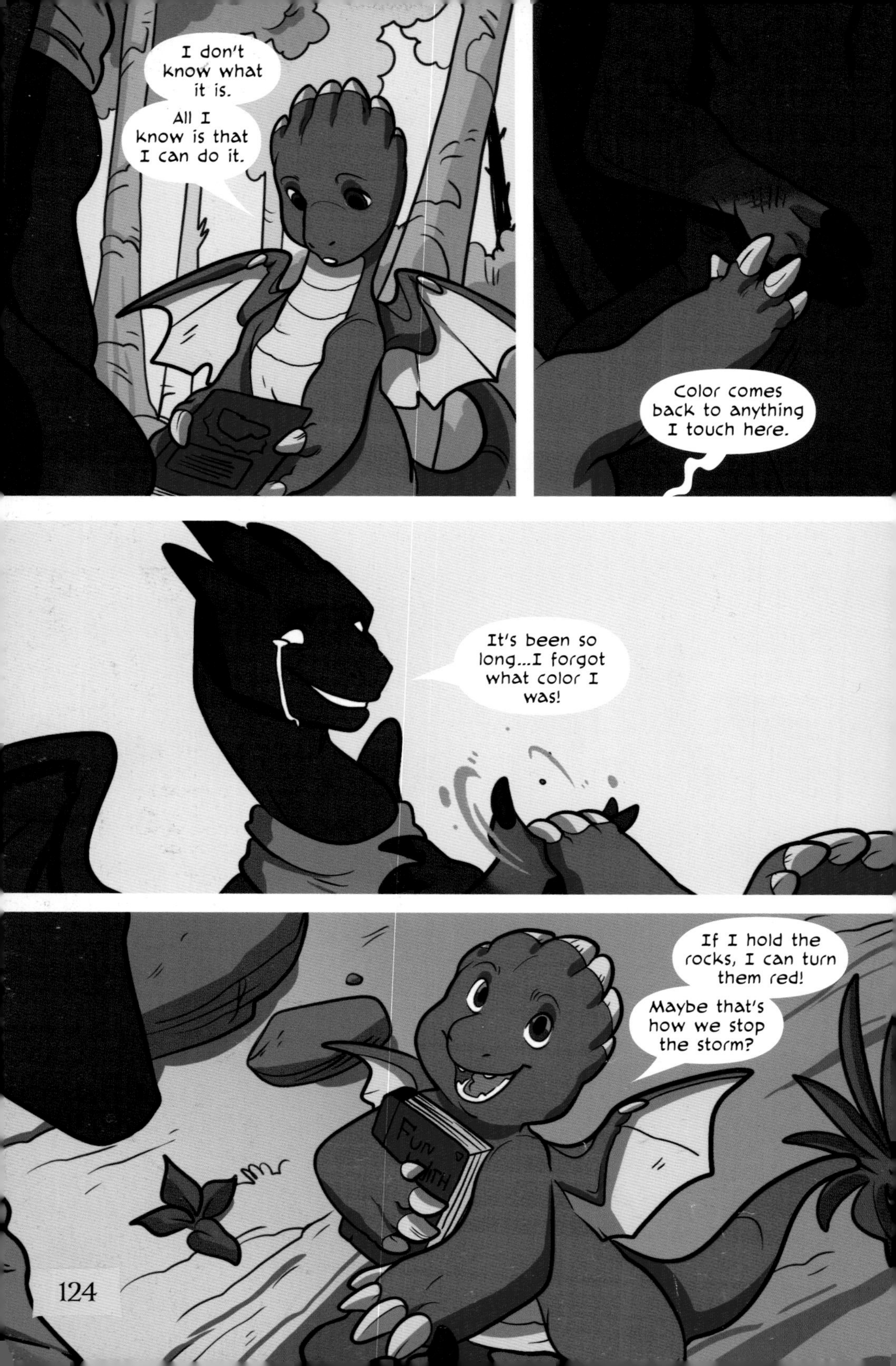
I don't know what it is.
All I know is that I can do it.
Color comes back to anything I touch here.
It's been so long...I forgot what color I was!
If I hold the rocks, I can turn them red!
Maybe that's how we stop the storm?

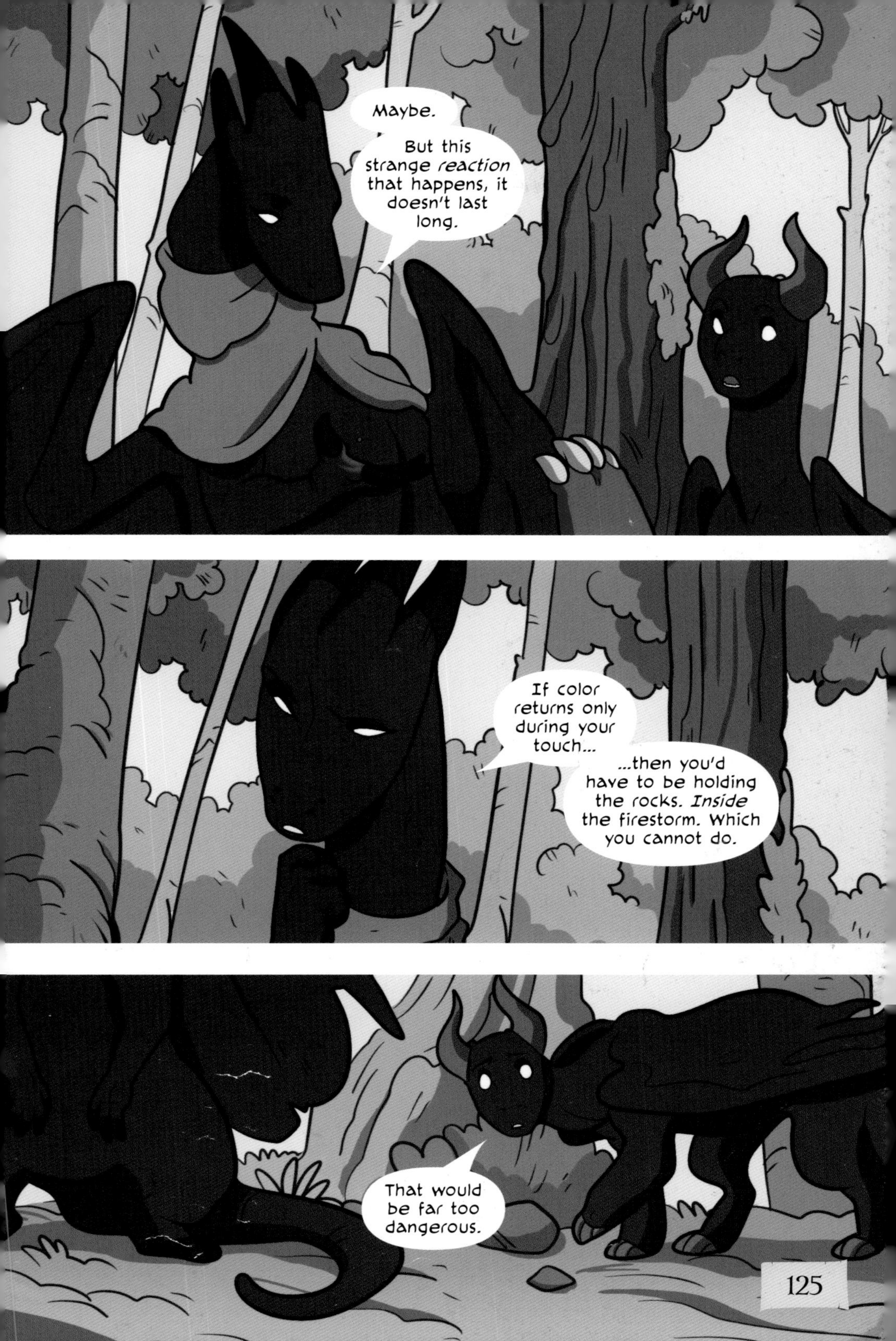
Maybe.
But this strange *reaction* that happens, it doesn't last long.
If color returns only during your touch...
...then you'd have to be holding the rocks. *Inside* the firestorm. Which you cannot do.
That would be far too dangerous.

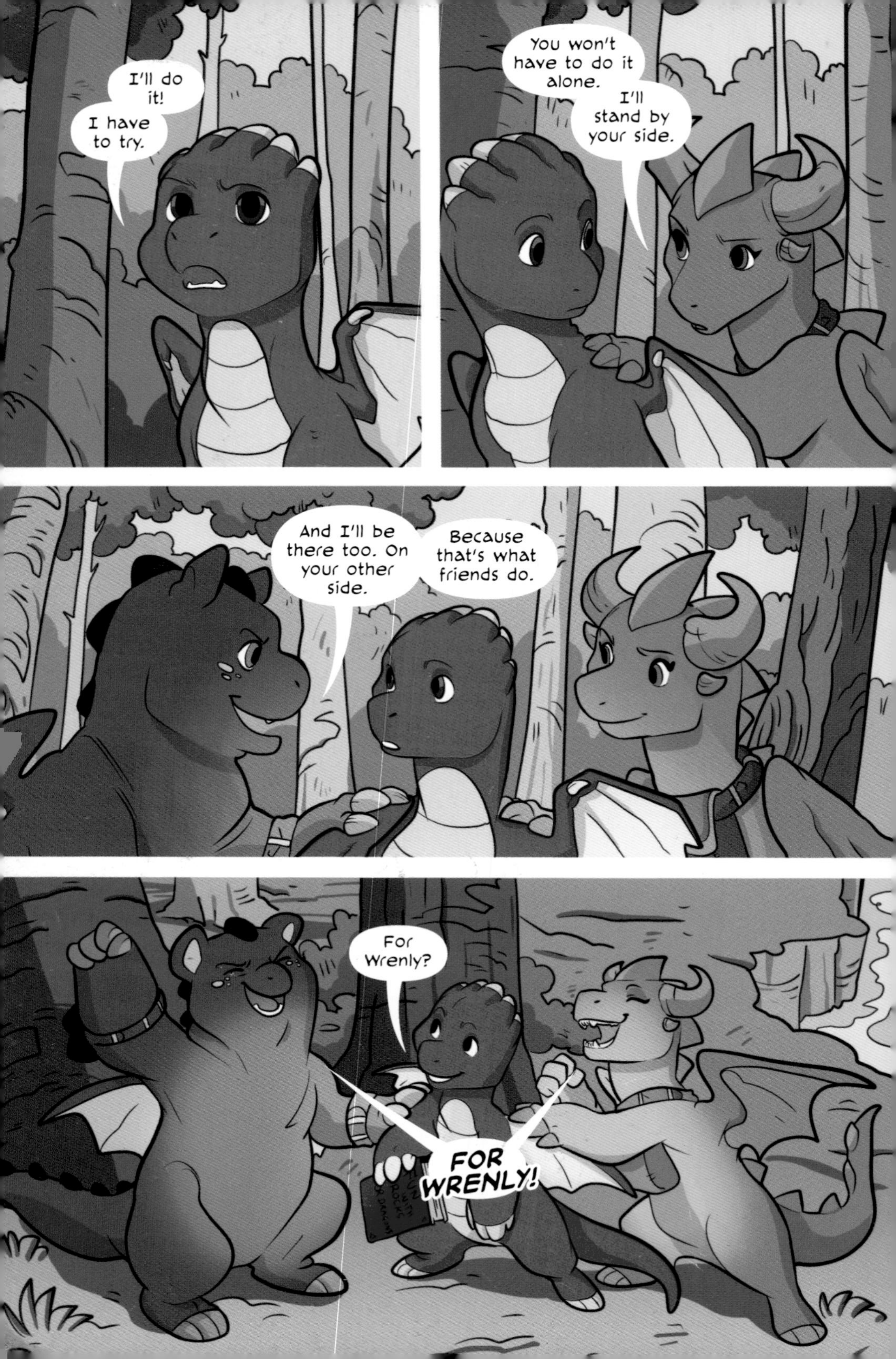

I'll do it!
I have to try.
You won't have to do it alone.
I'll stand by your side.
And I'll be there too. On your other side.
Because that's what friends do.
For Wrenly?
FOR WRENLY!

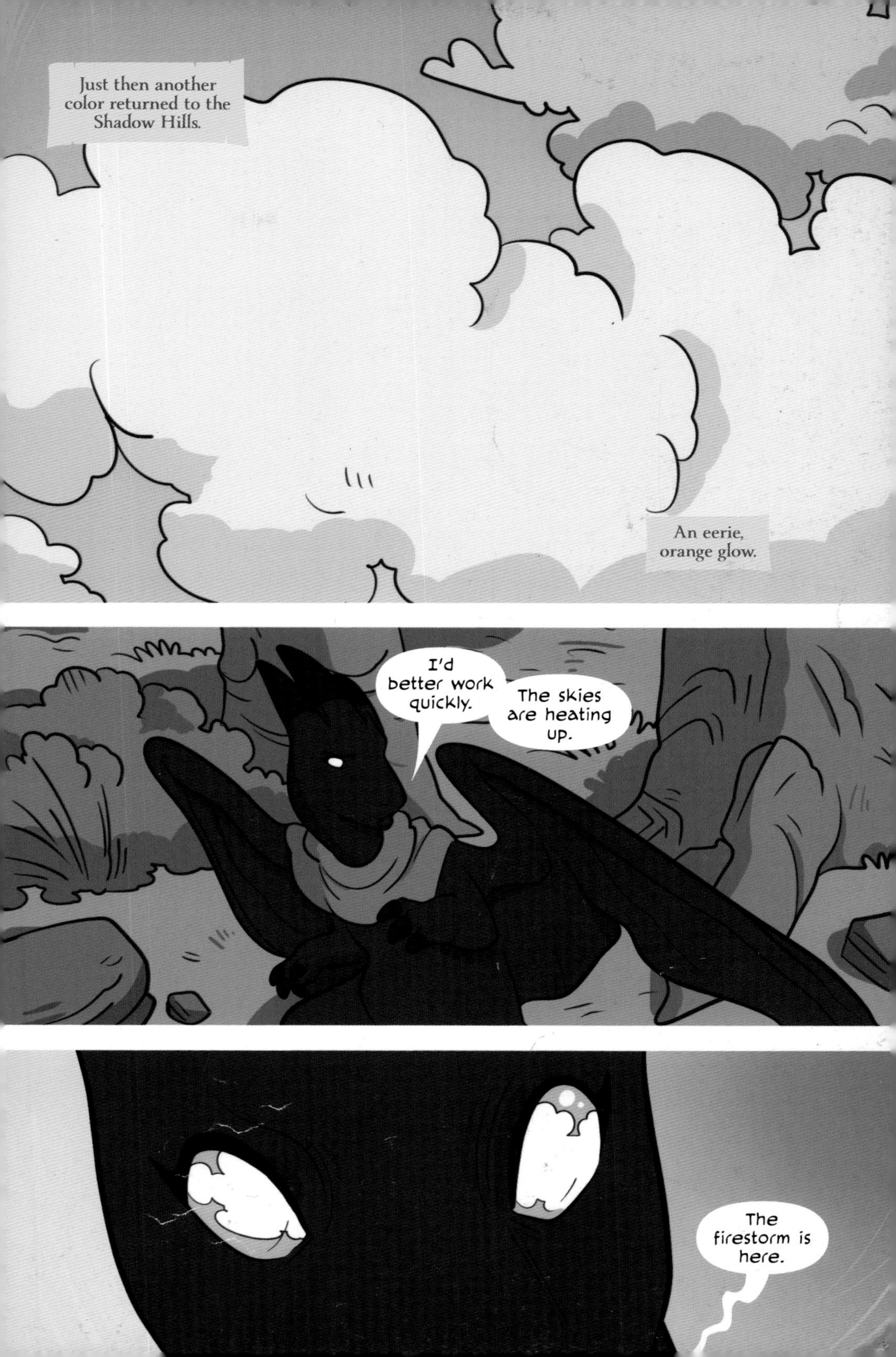
Just then another color returned to the Shadow Hills.
An eerie, orange glow.
I'd better work quickly.
The skies are heating up.
The firestorm is here.

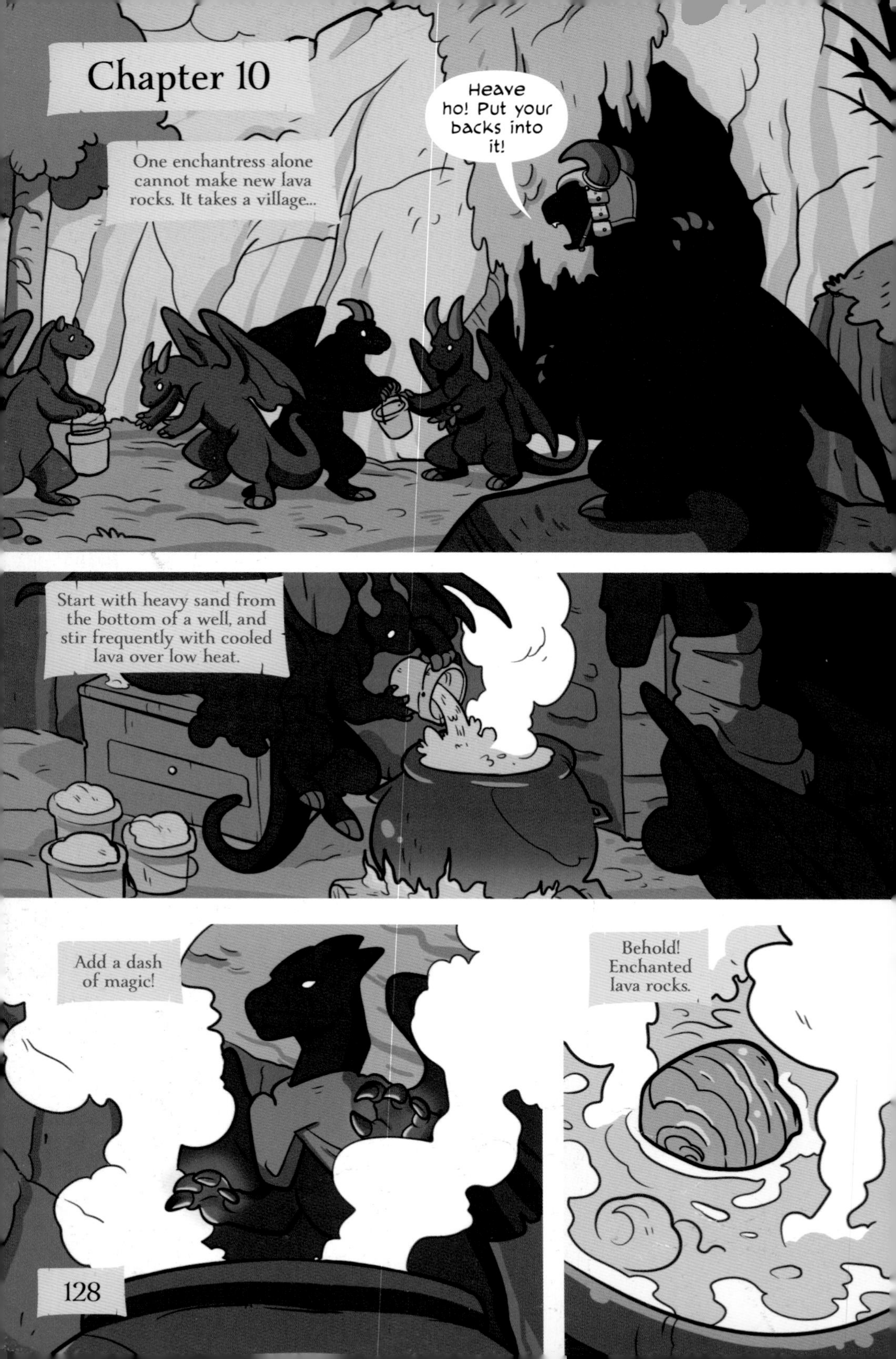
Chapter 10
One enchantress alone cannot make new lava rocks. It takes a village...
Heave ho! Put your backs into it!
Start with heavy sand from the bottom of a well, and stir frequently with cooled lava over low heat.
Add a dash of magic!
Behold! Enchanted lava rocks.

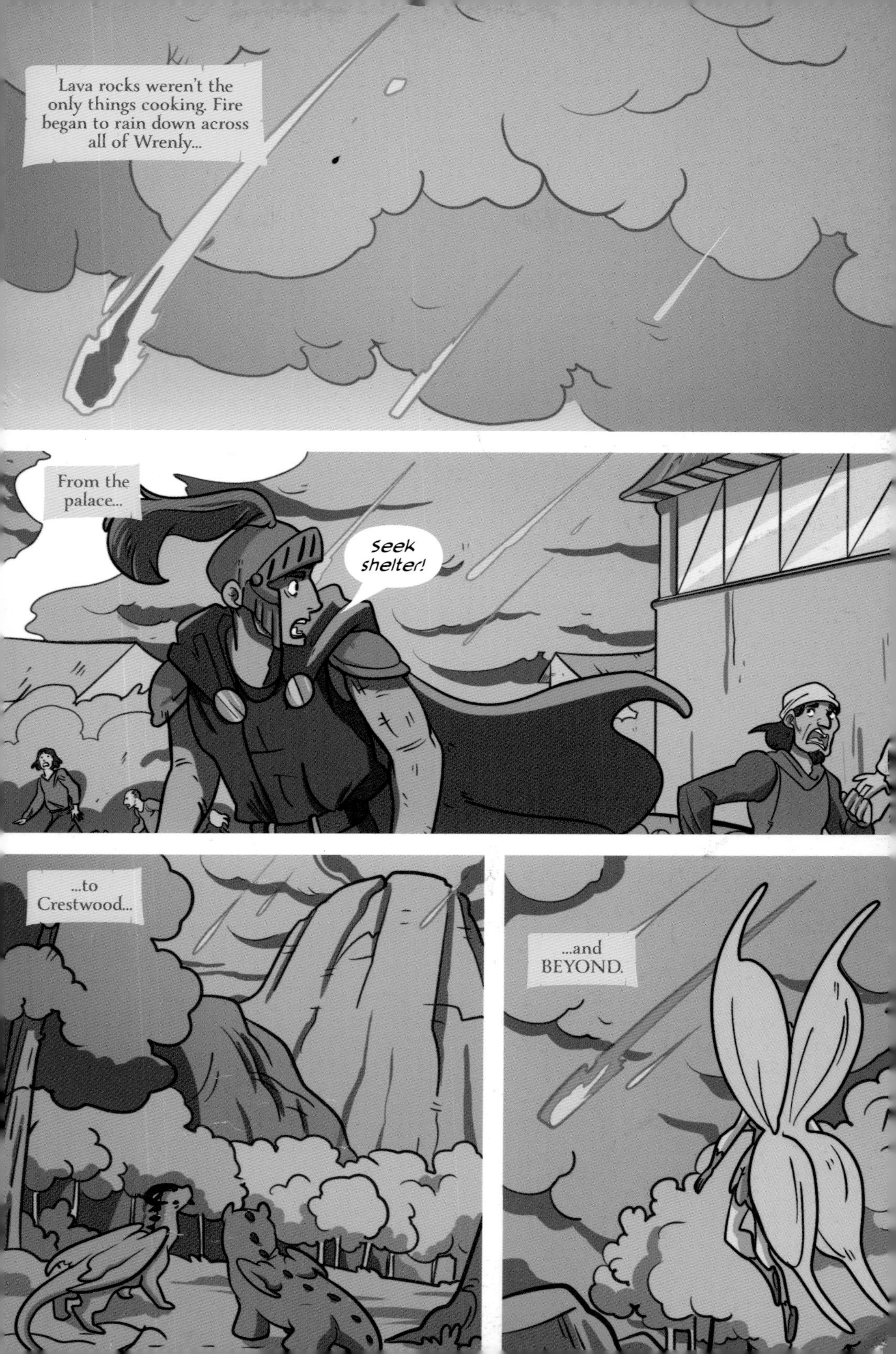
Lava rocks weren't the only things cooking. Fire began to rain down across all of Wrenly...
From the palace...
Seek shelter!
...to Crestwood...
...and BEYOND.

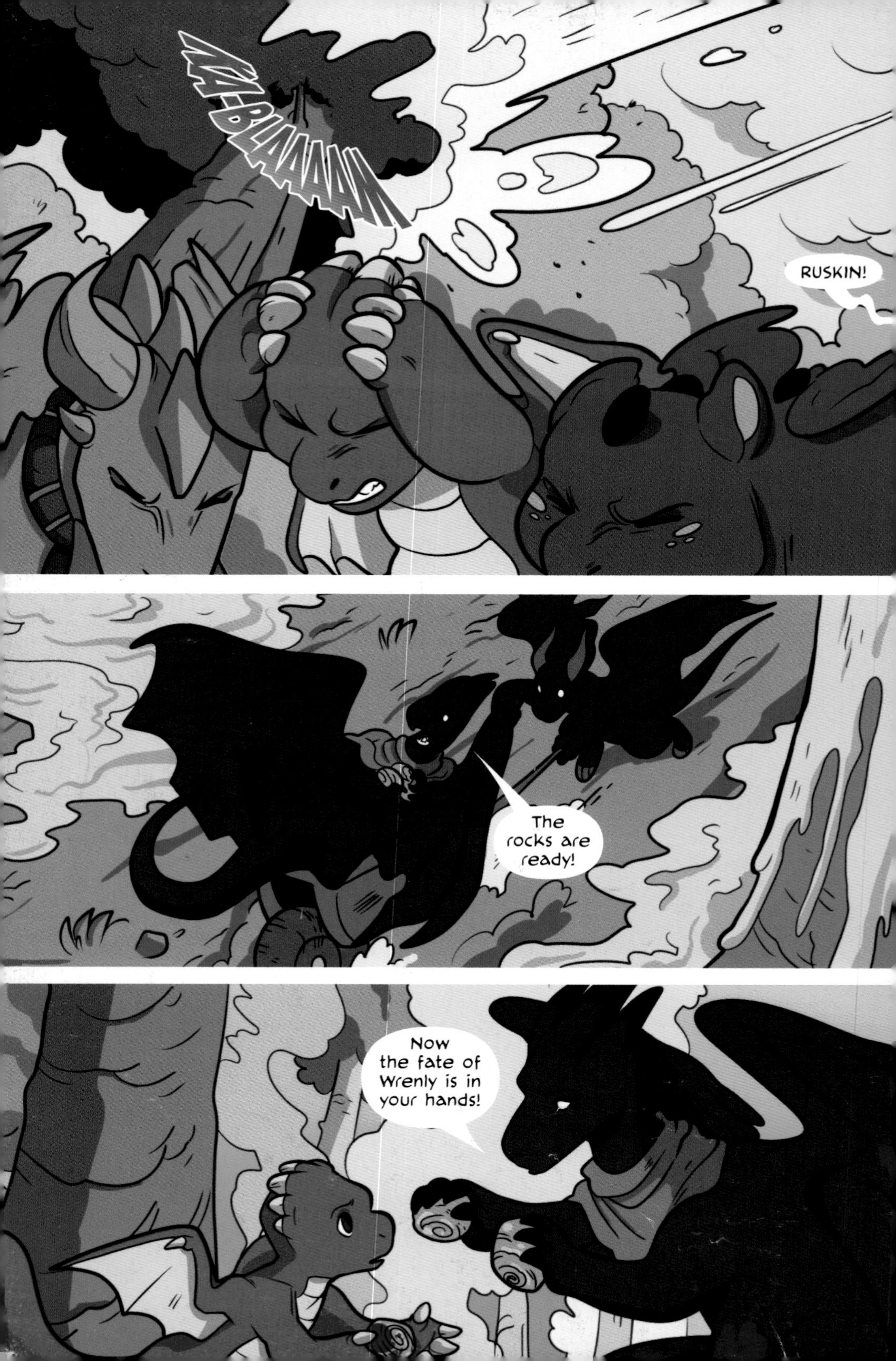

KA-BLAAAAAM
RUSKIN!
The rocks are ready!
Now the fate of Wrenly is in your hands!

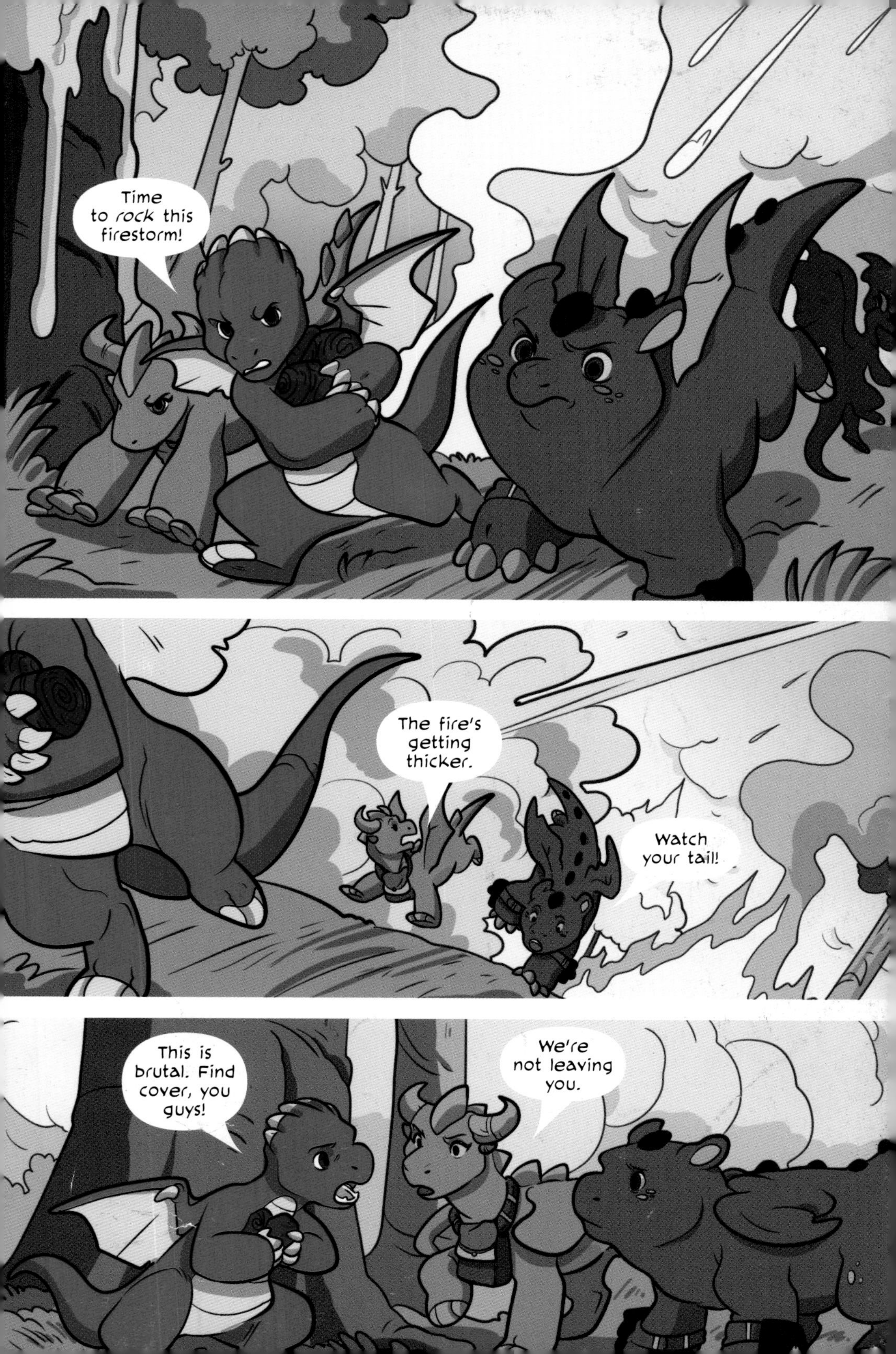
Time to *rock* this firestorm!
The fire's getting thicker.
Watch your tail!
This is brutal. Find cover, you guys!
We're not leaving you.

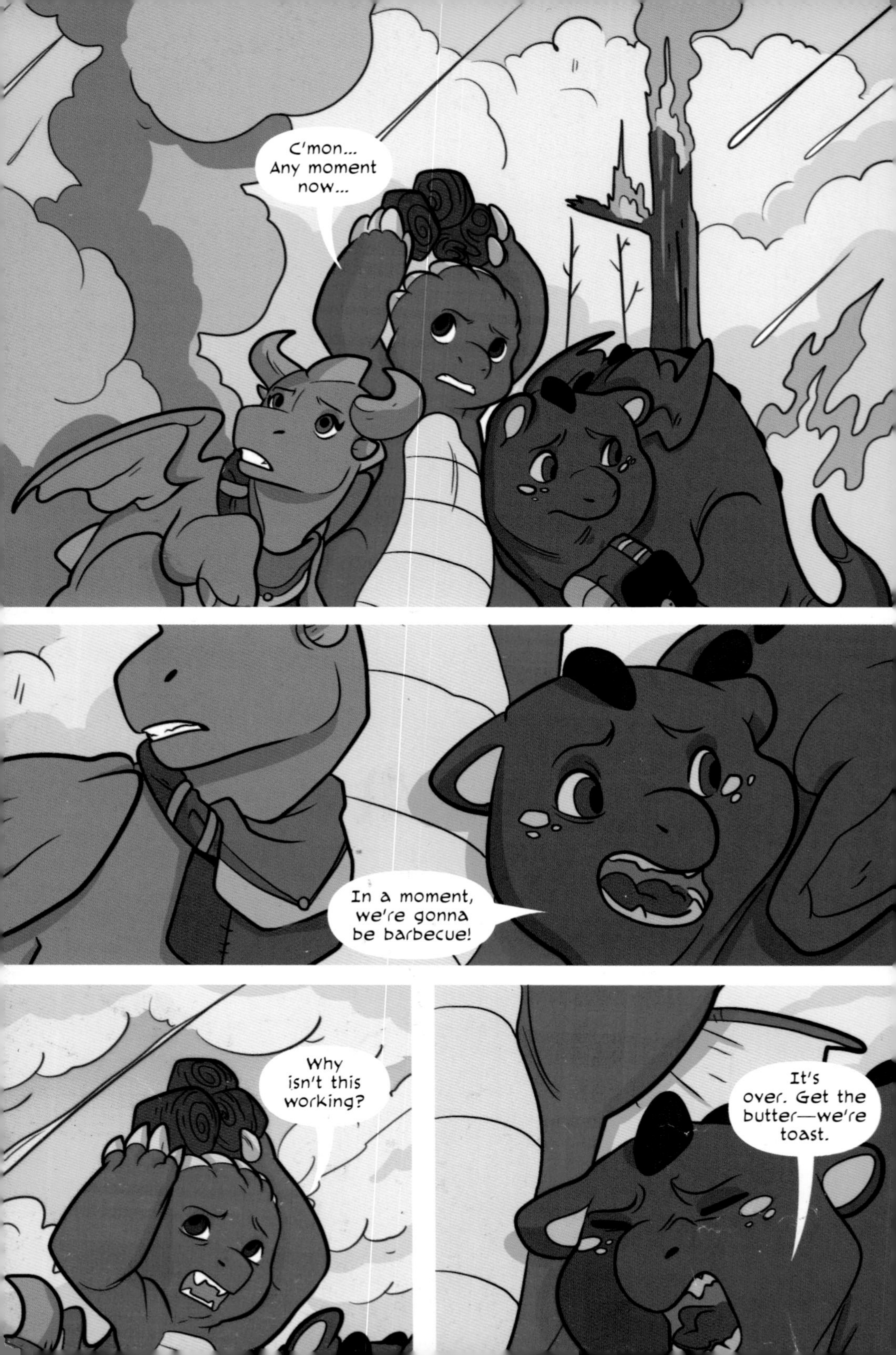
C'mon...
Any moment
now...
In a moment,
we're gonna
be barbecue!
Why
isn't this
working?
It's
over. Get the
butter—we're
toast.

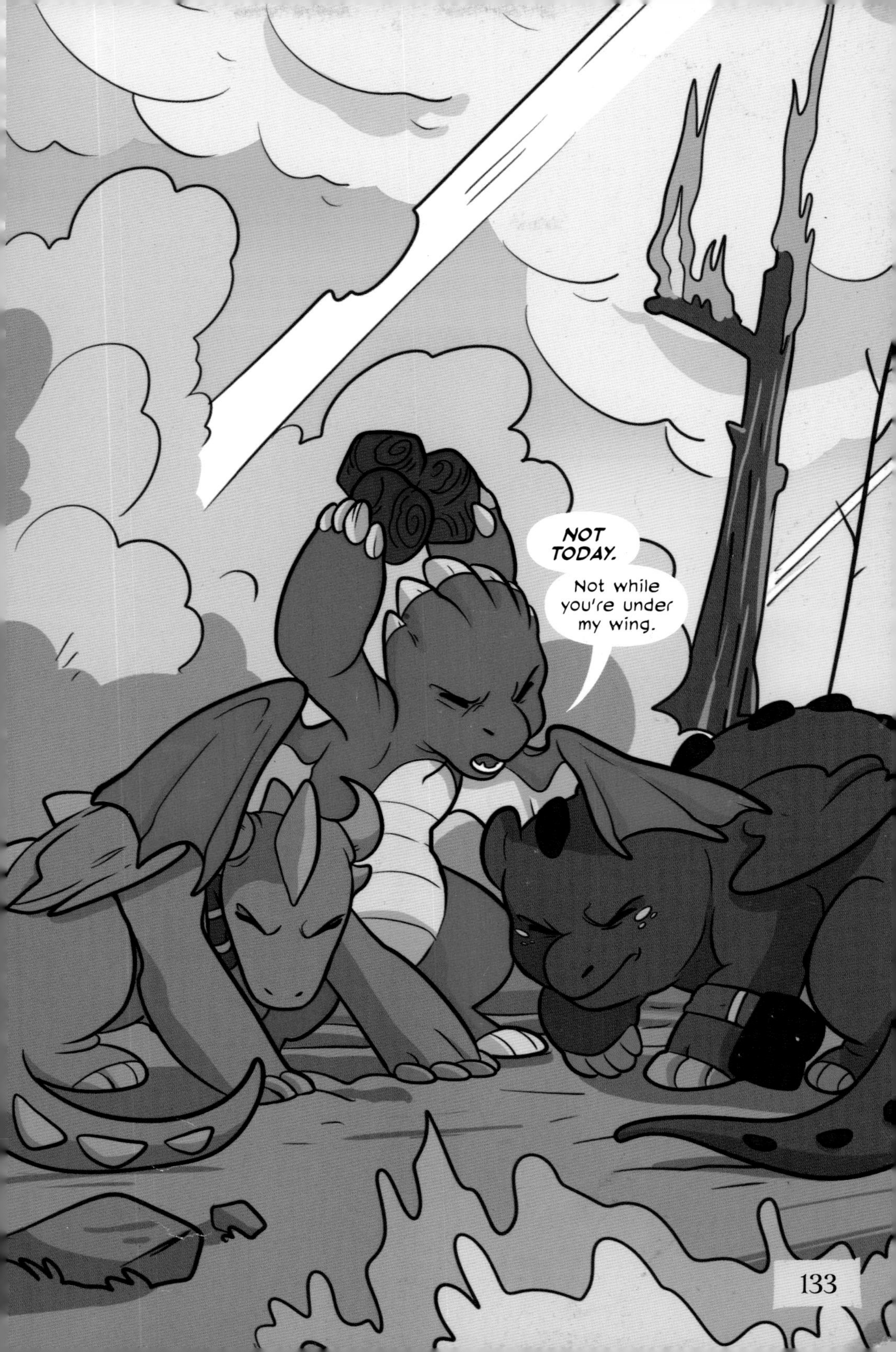
NOT TODAY.
Not while you're under my wing.

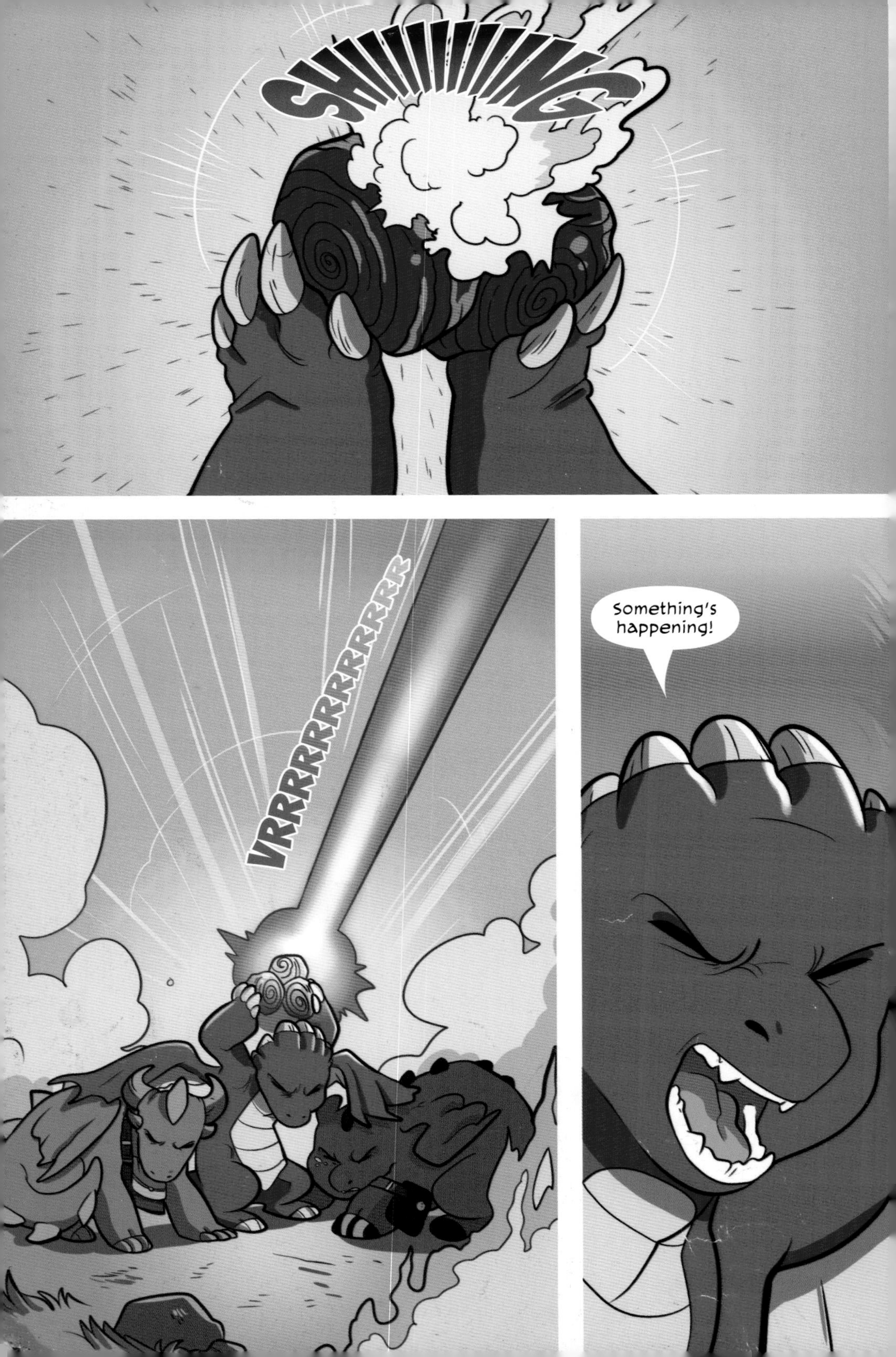
SHIIIIIING
VRRRRRRRRRRRRR
Something's happening!

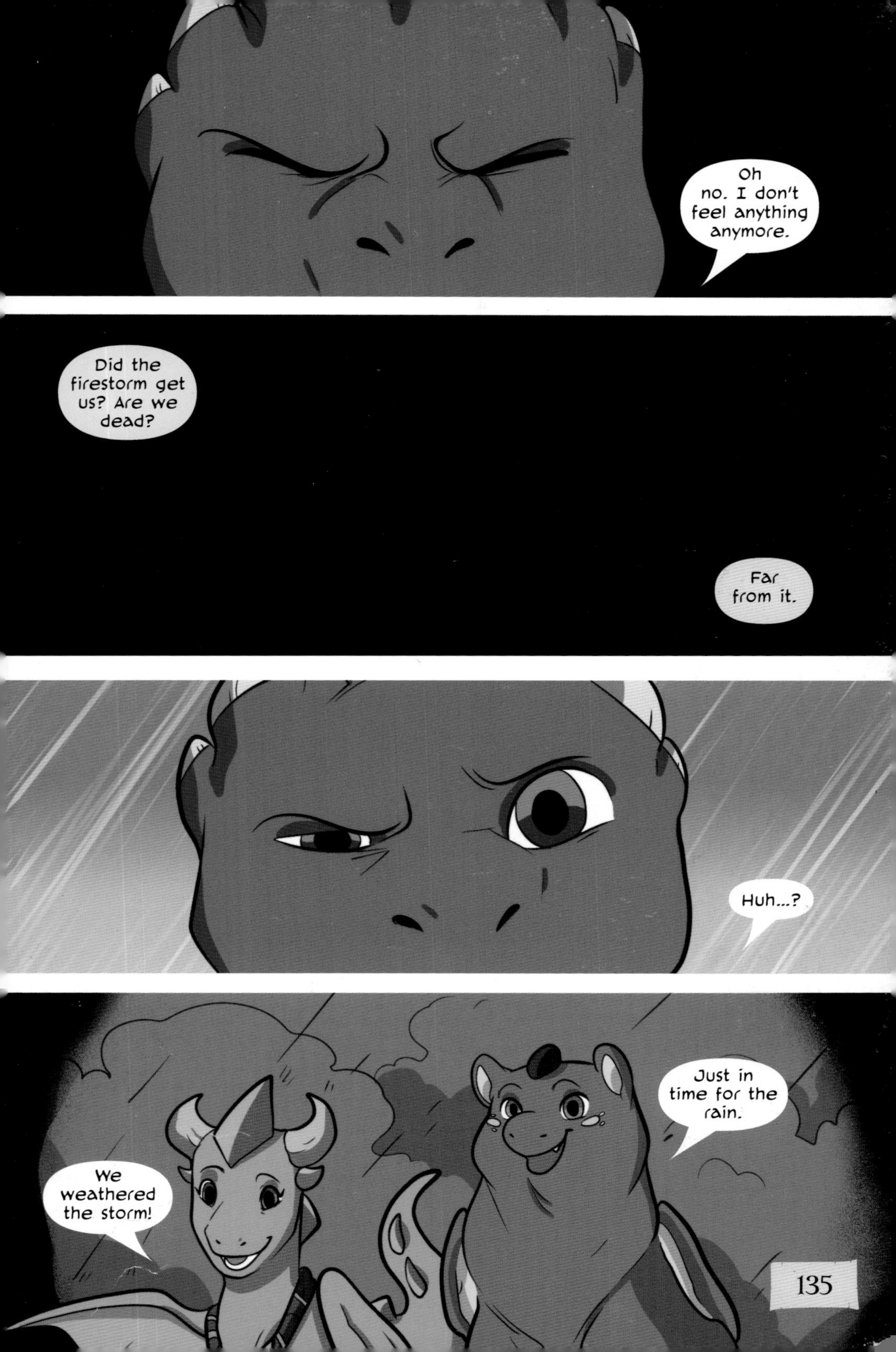
Oh no. I don't feel anything anymore.
Did the firestorm get us? Are we dead?
Far from it.
Huh...?
Just in time for the rain.
We weathered the storm!

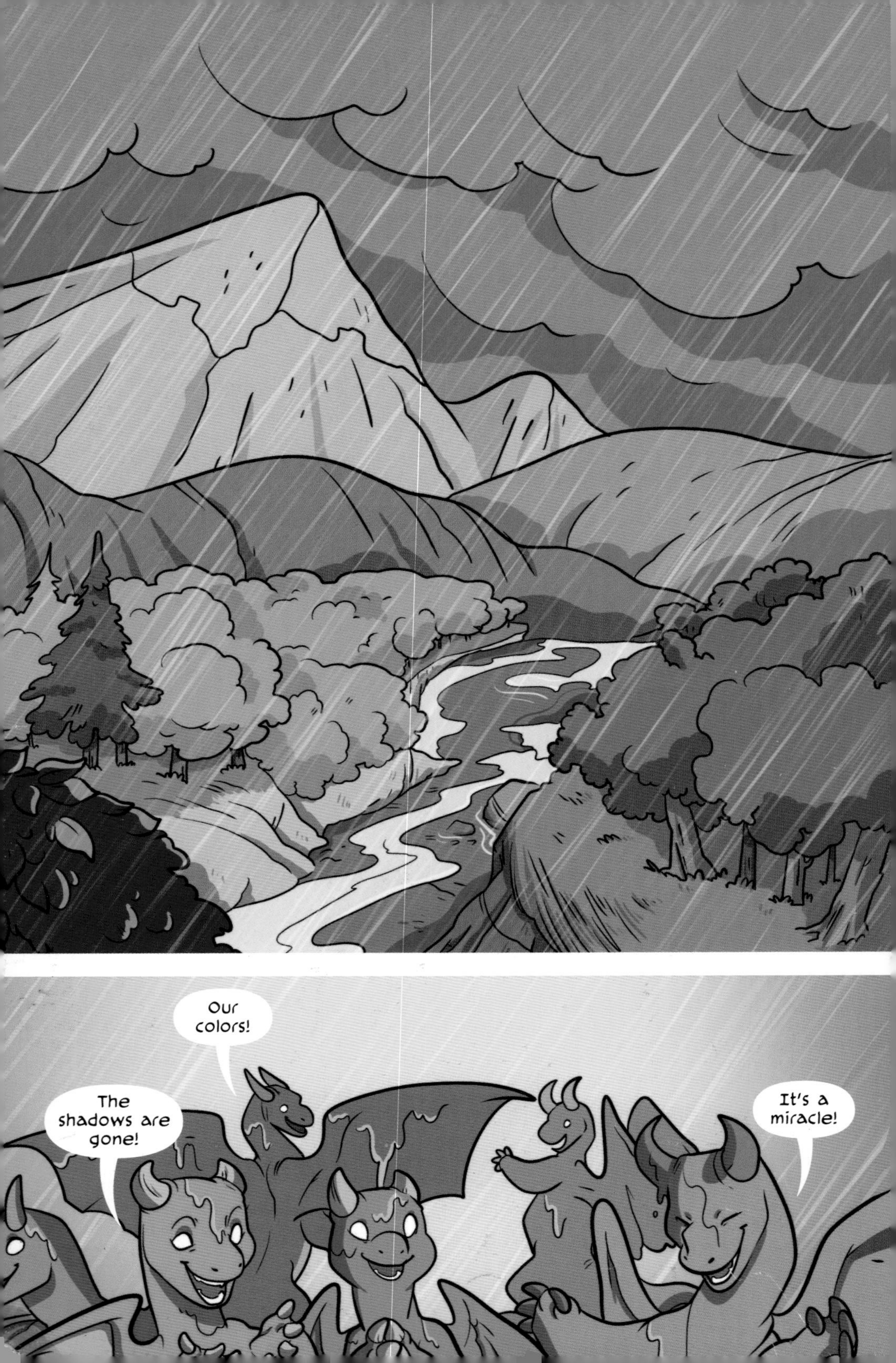
Our colors!
The shadows are gone!
It's a miracle!

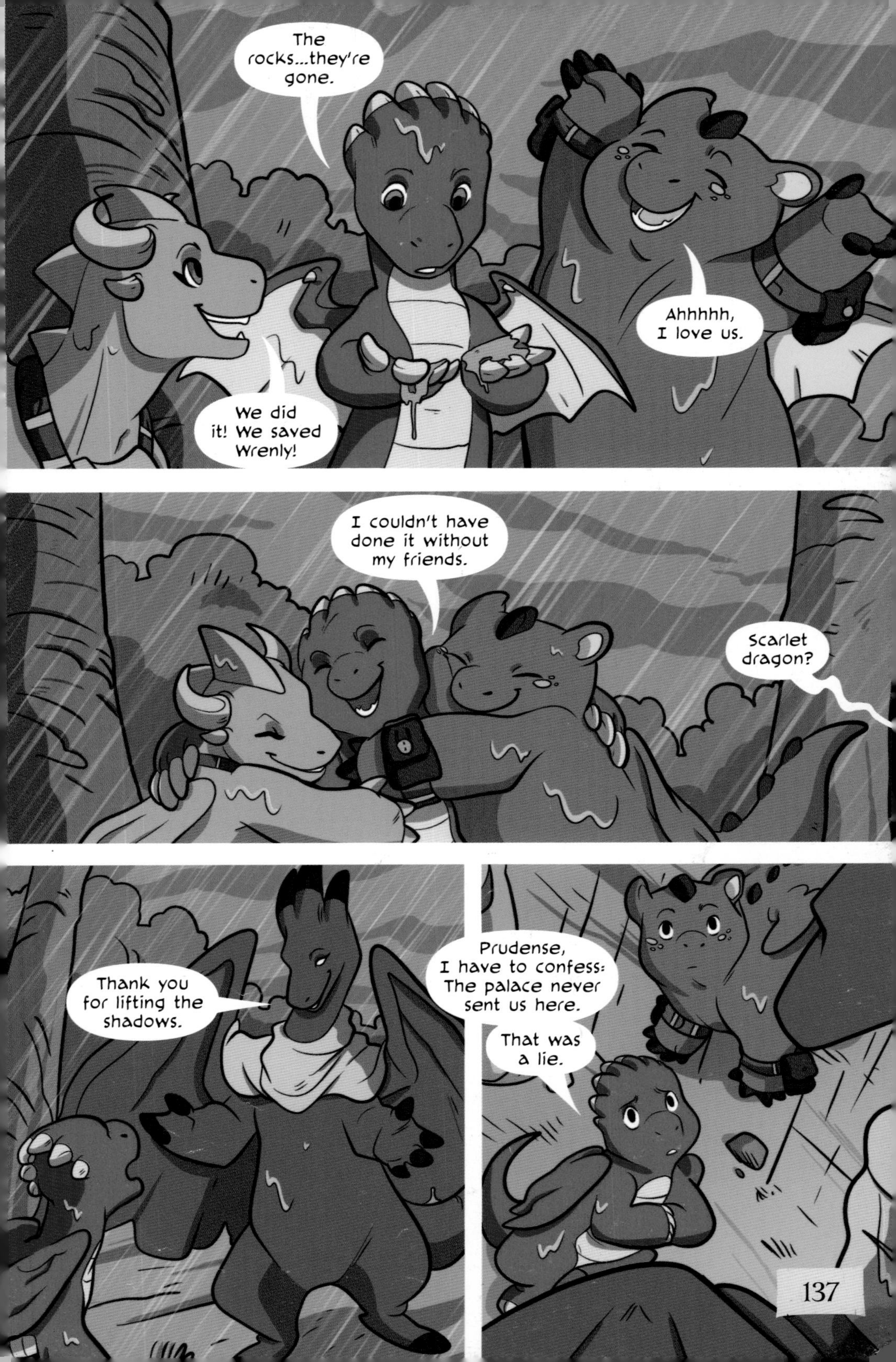
The rocks...they're gone.
We did it! We saved Wrenly!
Ahhhhh, I love us.
I couldn't have done it without my friends.
Scarlet dragon?
Thank you for lifting the shadows.
Prudense, I have to confess: The palace never sent us here.
That was a lie.

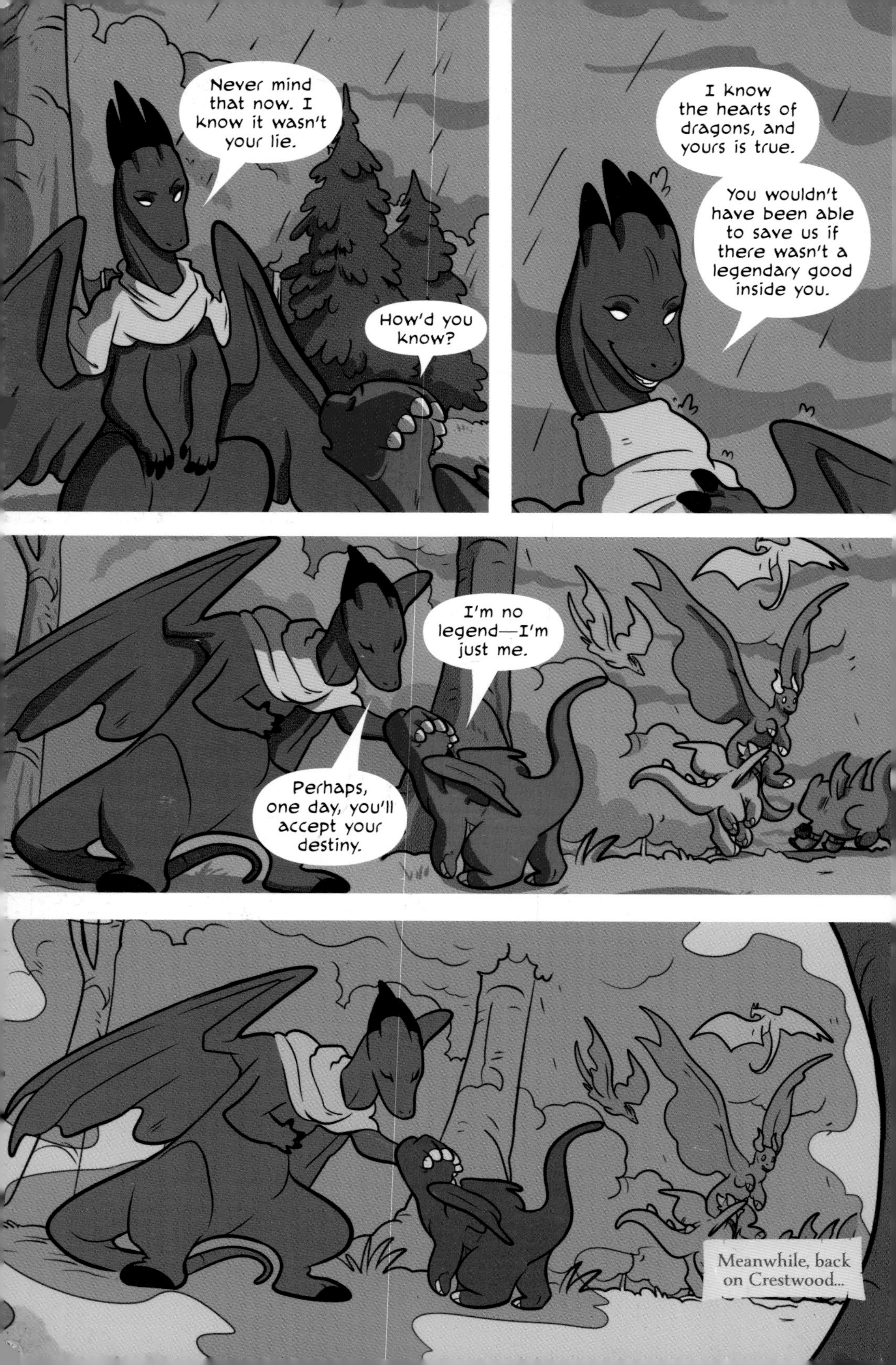

Never mind that now. I know it wasn't your lie.
How'd you know?
I know the hearts of dragons, and yours is true.
You wouldn't have been able to save us if there wasn't a legendary good inside you.
I'm no legend—I'm just me.
Perhaps, one day, you'll accept your destiny.
Meanwhile, back on Crestwood...

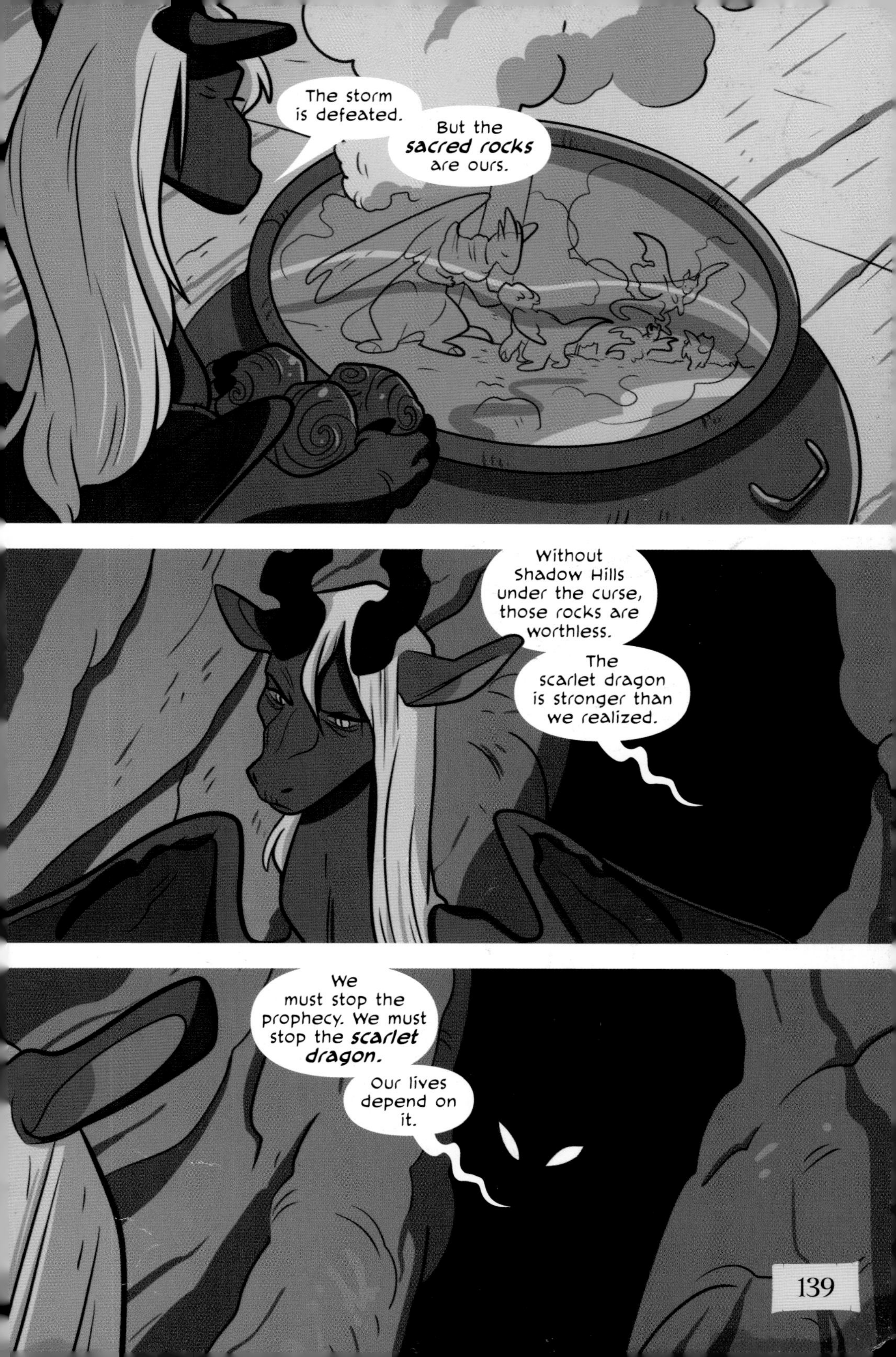
The storm is defeated.
But the *sacred rocks* are ours.
Without Shadow Hills under the curse, those rocks are worthless.
The scarlet dragon is stronger than we realized.
We must stop the prophecy. We must stop the *scarlet dragon.*
Our lives depend on it.

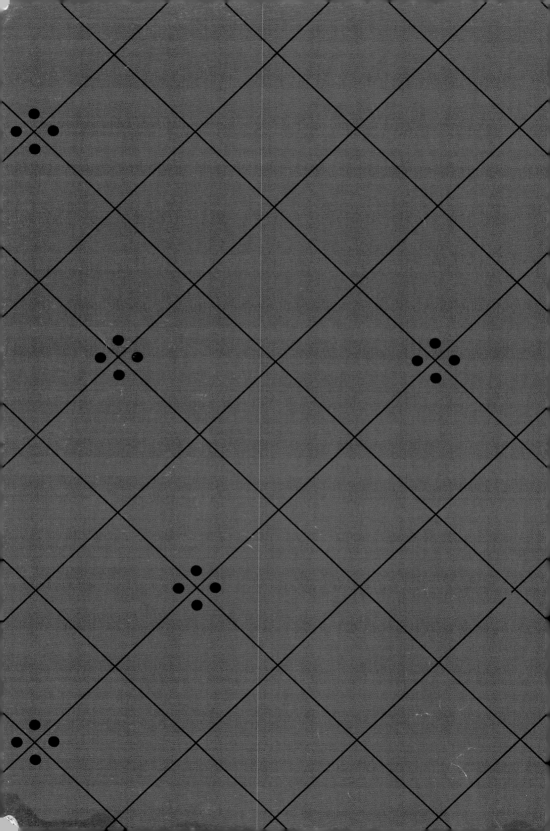

What's in store for Ruskin and his friends next? Find out in . . .

Graphic Novel
DRAGON KINGDOM
of Wrenly
NIGHT HUNT

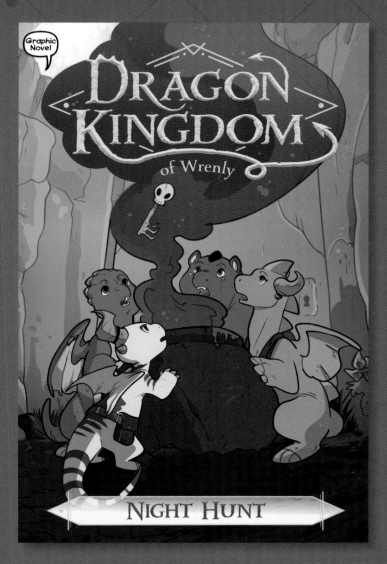

Turn the page for a sneak peek . . .

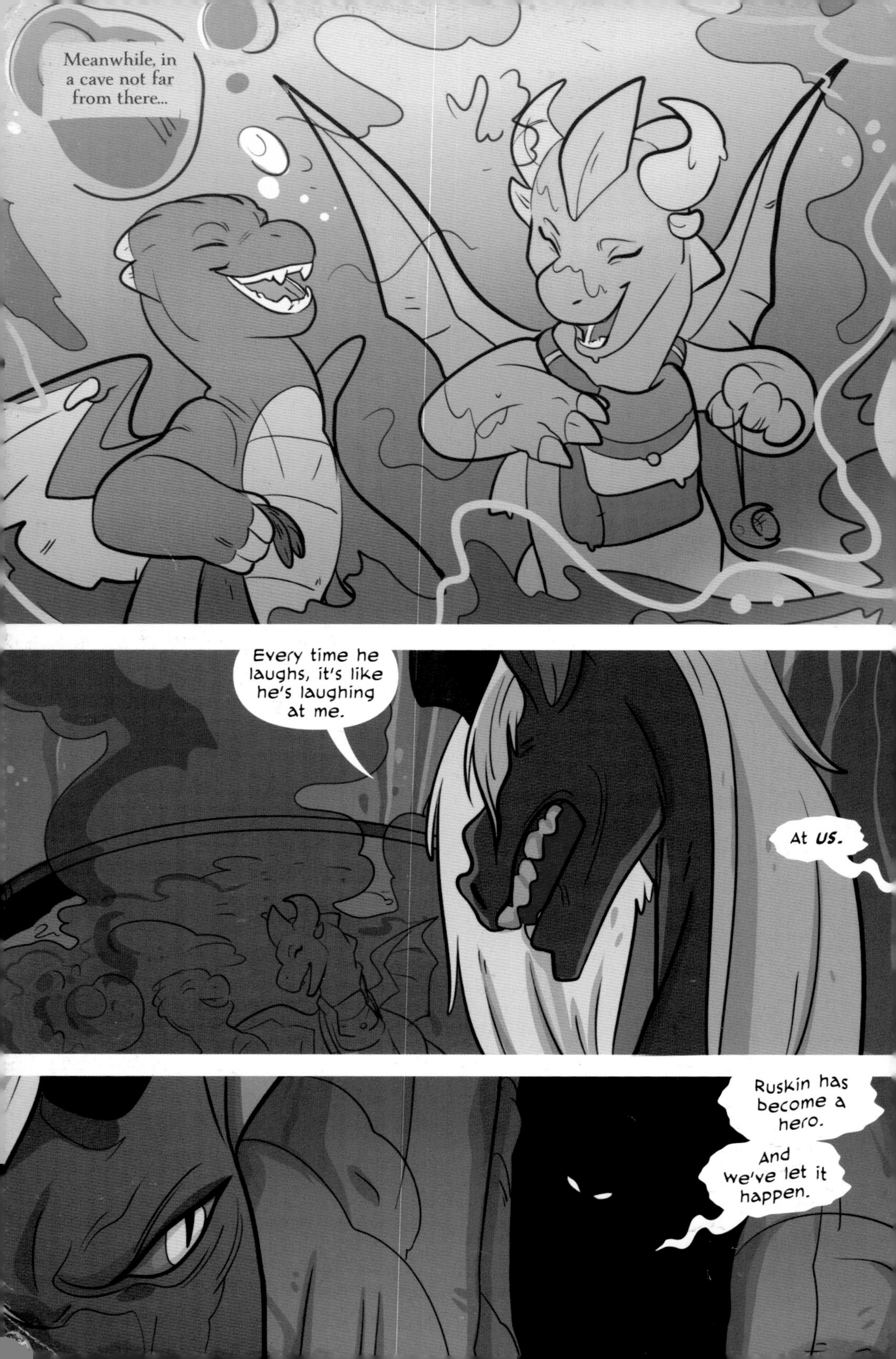

Meanwhile, in a cave not far from there...
Every time he laughs, it's like he's laughing at me.
At US.
Ruskin has become a hero.
And we've let it happen.

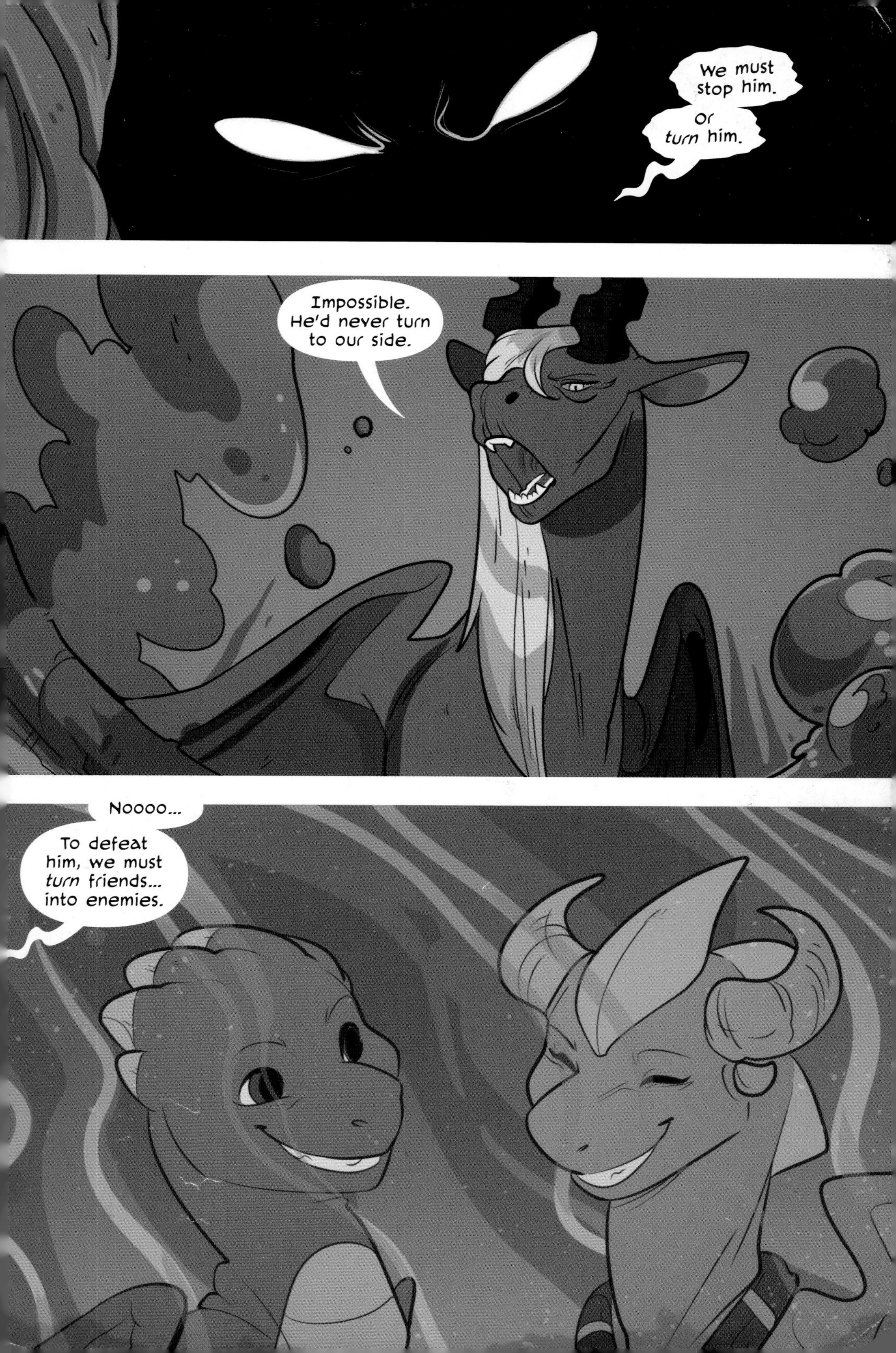
We must stop him.
Or *turn* him.
Impossible. He'd never turn to our side.
Noooo...
To defeat him, we must *turn* friends... into enemies.